A WORLD OF ALDERIA NOVEL

SHADOWS
OF THE
SUNDERED
LANDS

CORBIN ROOK

SVETLING
PRESS

Contents

Emily,

You believed in me and this book before I did. I'll never forget when you found all my worldbuilding notes and outlines so many years ago. I asked you to throw them away and said that I'd given up on ever writing my story.

I'm so glad you kept them.

This book is for you.

"The world breaks everyone, and afterward, some are strong at the broken places." — Ernest Hemingway

"Fall seven times, stand up eight." – Japanese Proverb

Prologue

The air in the Vorunis Citadel was thick with apprehension. The room, dimly lit by a few flickering torches, was silent except for the soft rustle of robes and the occasional creak of wooden benches.

The chamber was vast, yet the Elmias clustered together as if seeking comfort from proximity. Their usual composure, built over centuries of scholarly pursuit, was nowhere to be found. Instead, they exchanged uneasy glances, their eyes dark with sorrow and fear.

Luik couldn't sit still, pacing the circular chamber in an endless loop. As he walked, the floor-to-ceiling mural surrounded him, a sweeping chronicle of the Elmias' history. The images told a vibrant story of a people who once dominated their world before slowly dwindling into decline. The paint was still drying on the final image: a depiction of Queen Uriel signing the treaty that would bind them to an eternity of servitude.

And today was the day that the treaty would be signed.

He flexed his tired hands. The light from the flickering torches reflected quietly off his metallic blue-and-purple flesh. His heart pounded in his chest, a steady rhythm of dread that he could not dispel, no matter how hard he tried to focus.

Today, they would lose more than just their autonomy. The Treaty of the Tethering would bind their kind to the humans, shackling them in servitude for generations to come.

It was a harsh reality, but the threat of extinction can motivate people to make desperate decisions.

Luik couldn't stop his analytical mind from churning, dissecting every possible outcome, but each path led to the same bleak conclusion. They had no choice. There would be no more debates, no more councils to decide their fate. The decision had been made.

A sudden crash echoed through the hall, startling Luik from his thoughts. The doors burst open, and Gaalron stepped into the room like a storm.

Like all Elmias, his appearance was markedly distinct from that of humans. Though humanoid in form, his skin gleamed with a reflective metallic sheen. His body was a deep, lustrous black, marbled with streaks of vivid blue that traced up his neck and across his face.

A face twisted in rage.

"This cannot happen!" he bellowed, fracturing the fragile silence with a voice raw with emotion. "We cannot sign away our lives, our autonomy!"

Several Elmias moved to restrain him, their hands gripping his arms as he struggled against them.

"Gaalron, please," one of them pleaded, "it's already done. The humans—"

But Gaalron would not be silenced. He wrenched free, his eyes blazing with defiance.

"What the humans have offered us is worse than slavery! I would rather die than surrender to a lifetime of being Tethered!"

The struggle intensified, Gaalron's fury a desperate force that seemed to burn through the room. Luik watched, a hollow feeling in his chest. He understood Gaalron's rage, even shared some of it, but he knew it was futile.

The treaty was the only way.

Before Gaalron could break free again, the doors swung open once more, and the room fell deathly quiet. Uriel, queen of the Elmias, stepped inside, her presence commanding immediate attention. The red glow of the torches amplified the fiery hues of her red-and-yellow skin, making her seem ablaze.

Though her regal bearing remained, the defeat in her eyes was unmistakable, and her shoulders sagged.

"It is done," she said softly, her voice carrying the finality of a death knell. "The treaty has been signed."

The room seemed to exhale in unison, a collective release of breath they hadn't realized they had been holding. Gaalron sagged in the grip of those who restrained him, the fire in his eyes dimming as reality set in. The Elmias, all of them, were now bound to the fate they had so desperately tried to avoid.

"I will find a way," Gaalron whispered. His voice was so quiet that Luik wondered if he had spoken at all. The doubt went away as Gaalron spoke again, his voice louder and clearer. "I will find a way!" He looked up, eyes defiant, staring into the solid yellow eyes of his queen. "History will remember how you failed your people today. But I will find a way."

"Be silent," Luik hissed, glaring at Gaalron. "Show more respect for our queen."

Gaalron gave Luik a strange look, shaking his head in disappointment. "She's not our queen. Not after what she just signed." Shaking off the Elmias holding his arms, he turned and stormed out of the room.

Turning back to Uriel, Luik said, "When are we to meet our Tethers?"

"They're on their way right now."

Luik lowered his head, his heart heavy with the burden of a future now out of their control. The treaty was more than a loss of autonomy; it was the end of an era, the extinguishing of a flame that had burned bright for centuries.

And all they could do was bear witness to its final flicker.

Part One

187 Years Later

*I*t is with no small measure of humility that I set pen to page in pursuit of truth regarding the Elmias. Though my own encounters grant me the rare vantage of a firsthand witness, I do not presume that proximity alone conveys accuracy. Wherever possible, I have cross-referenced my accounts with the writings of others, weighing oral traditions against archival records and subjecting both to the scrutiny of reason.

My hope is that this journal may serve not as an immutable authority, but as a foundation upon which future scholars may build, correcting my errors where they find them and deepening our understanding where I have only scratched the surface.

Chapter 1

Cam didn't find sunsets beautiful. Where some gazed in admiration, he turned away, an anxious knot forming in his stomach.

The hues were too much of a reminder of how dangerous life was in the Sundered Lands.

As the sky turned to a cacophony of red overhead, he kept his eyes fixed on the ground, pushing his anxiousness aside, leading his exhausted horse up the dirt path towards Kevilton.

It was never enough, but it was all he could do.

Kevilton, nestled at the edge of the protective Aurora Shroud, exuded an air of quaint charm. Stone cottages with thatched roofs lined the narrow pathways, their windows adorned with vibrant curtains that billowed gently in the evening breeze. Blooming flowers cascaded from window boxes, adding splashes of color to the otherwise muted surroundings.

The market square showcased stalls brimming with fresh produce and handmade wares. Merchants with weathered faces called out to potential customers, their voices blending into a lively symphony. The smell of freshly baked bread wafted through the air, intertwining with the earthy scent of the grassy fields that surrounded the town.

It didn't take long for people to notice him.

"A Vanguard Courier!" several shouted as they ran up to him.

As Cam made his way into the village, the children playing in the grass paused to watch him, their eyes wide with a mix of curiosity and admiration. Kevilton, like many villages within an Aurora Shroud, had forged a symbiotic relationship with the Vanguard, which served as their only link to the outside world.

An elderly man wrapped his arm around Cam, offering him a cup of water. He eagerly accepted and poured it on his hand, washing the dark green and black scales that had appeared earlier in the day.

That was faster than normal, he thought to himself. Out loud, he said, "Thank you, sir."

The old man broke into a grin that wrinkled his entire face and revealed a few missing teeth.

"Eh, I only wish I could do more to help the Vanguard. When I was younger, I wanted to be a Courier myself. But, they said I just didn't have the physical fortitude. Couldn't handle the Sundered Lands." He playfully poked Cam on the arm. "But you...you have the physical fortitude of a mountain. I'd be surprised if they didn't let you in after just looking at you."

Cam shook his head.

"No, I had to do the same tests as everyone else."

"And it's no surprise at that!" the old man rattled on. "Seeing that if you transformed, you wouldn't be just an ordinary ol' scaletaint. You'd probably be a right full dragon!"

"No. I'd be turned into a scaletaint," Cam responded, a hint of annoyance entering his voice. The old man threw his hands up.

"No need to be offended. Only makin' a joke."

Cam smiled apologetically.

"It's...no. You're fine."

It had been a long day, the kind that set Cam on edge and made him want to drown out his nerves. He sighed, running a hand through his hair. Truth be told, that was just life as a Vanguard Courier. Constant danger, endless travel, and no guarantees.

After seeing Cam's size, the Vanguard had initially pegged him as a perfect fit for the Rangers—highly trained specialists who worked in teams to clear dangerous obstacles, restore Safe Paths, and eliminate threats in the Sundered Lands. They'd even begun putting him through the years of rigorous training needed to hone the skills required for such a perilous role.

But everything changed after he failed Silva.

Cam shook his head sharply, trying to dislodge the name that haunted him. His heart pounded erratically, each beat echoing like a drum in his chest. The cool air felt suffocating, pressing in on him as his breath quickened. He twitched his fingers at his sides.

The old man seemed to notice and gave him a concerned look.

"Boy, I won't pretend to know what it's like to travel the Sundered Lands. But I can tell by looking at ya that ya could use a drink. Now, I'll tell ya that Ol' Rhine charges less on a pint for the Vanguard." He held out a small silver coin and placed it in Cam's hand. "Buy one on me. And then go get some sleep."

Cam nodded gratefully, gently pocketing the coin in his black cloak.

"That's very kind of you," he said, offering a curt nod. The old man shrugged.

"We folk stick together. It's the only way we can survive, after the Sundering."

Cam closed his eyes.

The Sundering.

Almost one hundred fifty years later, and what caused it was still a mystery.

Growing up, Cam had heard stories about the day where the sky itself turned a hateful shade of red as the corruption spread across Avoni Overnight, Avoni went from being the most prosperous nation in the world to a realm of nightmares.

In that moment of horror, the Aurora Shrouds mysteriously appeared, enveloping and protecting a few of the settlements across the country. Just as no one knew what caused the Sundering, nobody knew where the Aurora Shrouds came from or why only certain communities were protected.

The survivors learned quickly that it was dangerous to leave the Shrouds. Not only were the Sundered Lands full of dangerous creatures, but the longer someone was outside of the protection of a Shroud, the more the corruption influenced them. Some people were simply killed by the oppressive environment. Others transformed, becoming monsters themselves.

The Aurora Shrouds saved some people, but they also trapped them. Many communities lacked the resources to continue thriving. Some didn't have the ability to grow large amounts of food, while others needed essential medicine or other supplies.

This led to a proposal: people who had proven to be more durable against the corruption would serve as messengers, bringing letters, news, and essential supplies to the isolated settlements by riding so quickly across the Sundered Lands that they could reach the next location without falling to the corruption.

Thus, the Vanguard was created.

Cam glanced down at his hand again. His right hand was still covered in scales, but now that he was under the safety of the Aurora Shroud, pink flesh was starting to reappear.

Almost in a Crimson Limbo state. Another day or so, and I might have become a scaletaint.

What a horrible thought.

"How long were you out there?" the old man said, pointing at Cam's hand. Cam sighed and rolled back his shoulders for a moment before answering.

"Almost two days." The old man's eyes widened, flickering down to Cam's hand where some persistent scales clung. "I'll be fine," Cam added. "Just gotta rest up here for a bit before I head back home."

The old man nodded, his silence pregnant with concern.

Cam settled onto a weathered oak bench, a solitary figure amidst the activity of the village square. As he gingerly flexed his stinging hand, the villagers sifted through the array of letters and documents he had painstakingly transported.

His gaze wandered, momentarily fixating on the rustic charm of the village where time seemed to linger in the ivy-clad facades and sloping rooftops. The soft murmur of conversation and the occasional creak of a cart wheel added a rhythmic undertone to the stillness, punctuating the interlude.

He sighed deeply. Any amount of time spent outside an Aurora Shroud was uncomfortable at best, mentally and physically. It was nice to be safe again.

Feeling like he had rested enough, Cam stood to examine his horse. An empathetic pang struck him for the weary creature, its flanks heaving with exhaustion. Cam had pushed the horse to its limits, and the toll on the beast was evident.

He squinted, walking around the horse carefully and looking for any signs of corruption or injury. To his relief, he couldn't find anything.

A young man—no older than seventeen—came running up to Cam. The patch on his jacket indicated that he was part of the Vanguard, the brown coloring denoting his position: Warden.

"So sorry I'm late," he said, chest heaving. "I only just now heard you were here." Reaching up, the young man grabbed the reins and led the horse away.

Cam turned back to the old man.

"That drink you mentioned sounds good."

The old man broke into another wide grin.

"I knew I liked ya. I think I'll join." Turning, the man motioned towards a nearby building. "Call me Sek."

Cam followed him.

"Sek?"

"Ya. Sek. It's short for Sekorlash. And yer name is?"

"Cam."

"Now, there's a good name. Short. Easy to say." He tapped the side of his head. "And easy for the aged to remember."

Sek led him up a set of wooden stairs into the small tavern. The steps creaked slightly under Cam's feet. Warm, flickering light spilled out as Sek pushed open the heavy wooden door. Inside, the tavern was cozy and well-worn, with rough-hewn tables and benches scattered across the stone floor. A fire crackled in the hearth, casting dancing shadows on the walls.

"Back again, Cam?" the barkeep inquired, a hint of familiarity in his gruff voice.

"Yes, just need a room for the night, Rhine," Cam replied, returning the nod. He then placed Sek's coin on the counter. "And something strong to drink."

Rhine nodded, stepping away for a moment. Once he was out of earshot, Sek spoke again.

"Hmmm...seein' that I gave you my last coin, I s'pose I'll just sit with you. Don't have enough for a drink." He then gave Cam a pleading look. Rolling his eyes, Cam placed a second coin on the counter, calling after Rhine.

"And something for my friend, too."

"Ah, why thank you, friend!" Sek said, thumping him on the back. "Mighty generous of you. Mighty generous."

Rhine returned with two thick, slightly chipped glasses filled with a deep amber liquid.

"He does this, you know," Rhine whispered, nodding towards Sek. "Gets the Courier to buy a discounted drink using his money, then has them buy him another one at full price."

"It's fine," Cam said, glad to finally have the drink in front of him.

He picked up his glass and raised it to his lips. The drink was sharp and earthy, with a bitter aftertaste that lingered longer than he liked. It wasn't unpleasant, but it lacked the smoothness of finer brews.

Cam was fine with that. He didn't need it to taste good for it to quiet his nerves.

The two drank in silence for a moment, with Cam quickly downing his drink. He set the empty glass on the counter with a thud, the sound sharp against the background murmur of the tavern. He slid a coin across the worn wood.

"I'll have another, please."

Rhine nodded, his gaze lingering on Cam for a moment before fetching another glass. Cam took it, barely pausing before drinking it in one long swallow. The burn in his throat was a welcome distraction, a fleeting numbness that almost felt like relief. He slammed the glass down again, the impact harder this time, and pushed another coin forward.

"Another," he said, his voice flat.

Rhine hesitated, a furrow creasing his brow as he looked at Cam.

"You just got here, right? Don't you have to report to the Vanguard tomorrow?"

"Please. Just do it," Cam said.

The barkeep gave him a strange look but didn't argue. He poured another glass, setting it in front of Cam with a bit more care this time, as if handling something fragile. Cam was just about to drink it when he heard a slight commotion behind him.

"Hmmm...looks like trouble's coming," Sek said, pointing a finger, a wry grin on his face.

Cam turned in the direction Sek pointed. Standing in the doorway was a young woman, petite and lithe, with long black hair cascading down her back. Her face was heart-shaped, framed by that dark curtain of hair, and her bright eyes scanned the room with quiet confidence. She wore a dark green cloak that draped elegantly over her shoulders, its long sleeves covering her arms down to the gloves on her hands. A green patch on her shoulder marked her as a Vanguard Healer.

A tall, broad-shouldered man blocked her path into the tavern.

"Come on, I'm just trying to be friendly, Illyria," he jeered.

Illyria didn't respond, her gaze steady as she tried to push past him again. But he reached out, grabbing her arm with a roughness that made Cam's blood boil.

Illyria tried to tug her arm away, but the man's grip was firm.

"Let's just talk somewhere private," he said.

"Let go. I need to get inside," she protested, her voice firm and frustrated.

"Come on, I just think—"

"She said let go," Cam growled, loud enough for the entire bar to hear him.

The young man turned and stared at Cam. For a moment, the two locked eyes, sizing each other up.

"I'm not scared of a Courier," he sneered, words dripping with disdain. "Come back with a Ranger, and maybe I'll care."

Cam didn't bother with a reply. Instead, he simply pushed his chair back and stood up, his movement deliberate and unhurried. The tavern seemed to shrink around him as he rose to his full height, the muscles beneath his cloak shifting like coiled steel. He was tall, broad-shouldered, and built in a way that commanded attention.

Built in a way that made men think twice before starting problems with him.

The man let go of Illyria's arm and left in a huff.

Illyria looked up at Cam and smiled.

"Thank you. You saved me the time of having to deal with him myself."

Sek raised an inquisitive eyebrow.

"And how do ya figure you'da managed that?"

She reached into one of her cloak's pockets and pulled out a small vial filled to the brim with a blue powder.

"Domps Powder," Illyria said, as if reciting from a book. "Administer to subjects pre-surgery. The subject will be unconscious within moments and will remain so for an hour. Most awaken with temporary paralysis lasting a few minutes."

Cam let out a quiet whistle. "I'm glad you didn't have to use that."

"Me too. It can make for a terrible mess sometimes." She stepped up to the table with Cam and Sek and gave Cam a judgmental look. "Of course, a lady like myself wouldn't have come to the tavern at all if the Courier had followed Vanguard protocol and checked in today."

Sek took a big swig of his drink before saying, "Eh...I think it's time for me to leave." He nodded to Cam. "Thank ya for the drinks, friend." Before Cam could respond, he scurried away.

Cam looked back at Illyria, her face disdainful.

"Sorry. It's...I mean, I feel fine," he lied, taking another gulp of his drink. Illyria eyed the two empty glasses on the counter and raised an eyebrow at him. Cam let out a deep sigh. "You know how it is. I just...I needed help calming down."

Her expression softened.

"Let me see it, Cam."

"See what?"

"Cam!"

"Fine." Cam groaned, lifting his right arm and setting it on the table. Though most of the scales had turned back into flesh, a few still clung tightly to the skin.

Illyria gasped. "Aurora's Name! That happened far too quickly." Then, she gave Cam a mock glare, deftly taking away his glass from him. "Nope. You're done with this." He reached for the glass, and she gave his hand a light slap. "None of that. The Healer is in charge right now."

Reaching into a different pocket, she pulled out a few clips of Aetherfern leaves and a small bottle of water. She mixed the leaves into the water and stirred it gently. Then, she handed it to Cam. "Drink up," she said, and he obeyed.

After finishing the drink, Cam decided to speak.

"Any other Couriers passing through recently?"

Illyria turned, a slight smile on her face, and shook her head.

"You're the first in several months. It's been quiet lately."

Cam nodded. Kevilton was a fairly small town and received few communications from the other settlements. As a result, it tended to have fewer Vanguard Couriers stopping in.

"I suppose that's good news for the village. No urgent messages or news from the outside world."

"Who's to say if it is good, when you're not receiving any news?" she responded curtly. "How long will you be in Kevilton?"

Cam pondered the question before saying, "This is my final stop before I can journey home. I plan on leaving after a few days."

If he were being candid, he'd admit that waiting at least a week before venturing out again might be wise, given the condition of his hand. The scales would likely reappear not long after entering the Sundered Lands.

A brief silence followed, during which Cam half expected Illyria to gently reprimand him for his planned swift departure. Surprisingly, the chastisement never came. Instead, she shifted the conversation.

"I do have some news for you. The Vanguard here has been working on ways to slow down the corruptive effects of the Sundered Lands. And guess who figured it out?" She beamed with pride as she spoke.

Cam pretended not to pick up the hint.

"Hmmm...one of the other Couriers? Maybe a Route Coordinator?"

She gave him a light punch on his arm. "And he's full of jokes too."

Cam smiled back at her. "So, what's the secret? How did you figure it out?"

"It's…complicated. Hard to explain. Basically, it's a special concoction that has to be prepared each night and given directly to the individual in the Sundered Lands."

"And it works well?"

"Quite well." She grinned again. "The Researchers say that they didn't see corruptive effects for a full four days!"

"Wow. Did the Vanguard let you go with them?" Cam asked.

Illyria's face looked flushed for a moment, and a look of annoyance appeared in her eyes. She gave a quick shake of her head as she simply said, "No. They said that they preferred someone who could better defend themselves."

He hated to admit it, but that's what he would have preferred too.

Especially after Silva.

While she wasn't looking, Cam snatched his cup. He took another swig of his drink and started to reach into his pocket for a coin to order another. Illyria rolled her eyes, getting up from her seat.

"Just remember to rest, Cam. The corruption from the Sundered Lands seems like it's impacting Couriers badly lately." She glanced toward Rhine and waved to get his attention. "This one," she said, pointing at Cam, "does not need another drink." She then lowered her attention and stared Cam directly in his eyes. "Rest. You need rest. Now, say it with me. I need…"

"Rest."

Illyria's lips turned up in a smile. "Excellent. I'll come check on you tomorrow." She turned and left the tavern.

As the door swung shut behind her, Cam became very aware of the nerves still gnawing at him. It was like a piece of him was still in the Sundered Lands. He let out a deep, shuddering sigh, his shoulders slumping as he sank back into his chair. The warmth of the drink had faded, leaving a cold knot of anxiety coiling in his stomach. His fingers drummed restlessly on the table, his gaze fixed on the empty glass before him.

Conversation in the tavern continued, the patrons indifferent to his internal struggle. Cam took another deep breath, attempting to calm the whirlwind within.

His eyes shifted to the stairway leading to the inn above the tavern, where he planned to rest for the night.

Maybe Illyria was right. Maybe rest was what he truly needed.

Cam shook his head.

For now, he'd see if Rhine would ignore Illyria and get him another drink.

There weren't many things that quieted the anxiety inside of him.

Chapter 2

Some people joked that cats had nine lives. If that were true, Chek could only hope she had inherited a bit of that feline luck.

She'd already burned through three of her own.

The first was spent on being born a twin. Rath, one of the few Avonian communities shielded by an Aurora Shroud, had always boasted a massive population. Now, after nearly one hundred and fifty years, that population was straining the city's resources to the absolute limits. To keep the population under control, the city leadership had issued a brutal edict: no family could have more than three living members—two parents and a child. Because she was born a twin, Chek's family was forced to make a choice. Her father, rather than sacrificing his daughter, chose to sacrifice himself.

The second was being born a girl. In a society where families could only have one child, boys were preferred. They had a better chance of thriving in Rath and were seen as more capable of supporting their parents in old age. Many parents, faced with the prospect of a daughter, quietly abandoned their child, hoping someone else would take on the burden of care.

The third was being born with...her condition. Throughout her entire life, her body had been plagued by involuntary muscle contractions, which made her right side stiff and uncoordinated. The spasticity affected her ability to walk smoothly; she often had to brace her leg and relied on a cane or crutch to help her move with any semblance of stability. People like her didn't live long in Rath, but she'd learned to survive.

Chek's life had never been easy, but then again, few in Rath's Eastern District knew anything but hardship. From a young age, she became intimately acquainted with hunger, learning to stretch meager rations far beyond their limits. Countless times, she had waited in line for hours, only to find the food had run out before she reached the front. Her slow, uneven gait meant others often pushed ahead, leaving her to return home empty-handed.

She had heard stories of the opulent Northern District, where food was more abundant, but living there required wealth far beyond her reach. There was only one path that might lead her to the promise of a better life: becoming a Vanguard Courier. Yet, that dream was dashed before it could take flight. The Vanguard refused her application, citing her muscle spasticity as a liability. Worse still, she failed her environmental test, meaning that her body reacted particularly poorly to the Sundered Lands.

Still, she was nothing if not determined. She applied again to the Vanguard. Her organizational skill and familiarity with maps led them to hire her as a Route Coordinator.

It wasn't the escape she had hoped for, but it was a start. It wasn't enough to lift her out of the Eastern District, but it was a foothold in a world she had always longed to be part of.

And in Chek's mind, a foothold was all she needed to climb.

"There's evidence of a scaletaint hive along the River Pass, just south of the bluffs," Rokesh said, scratching at his neck.

"Evidence? What kind of evidence?" Chek asked, her dark eyes focused on her writing as she carefully made notations in a small book.

"Uh, claw marks. Lots of loose scales. Bones everywhere."

Chek nodded.

"Sounds like a hive," she said, finishing her notes, sliding her notebook into her desk drawer. She raised a hand and brushed her tightly coiled hair out of her face. "I'll submit a report and request a team of Rangers go there to clear it out. Thank you for your report; that's all I need."

Rokesh shifted quietly. He had a nervous expression on his face.

Chek raised an inquisitive eyebrow.

"Unless that's not all you have to say?" The man's face looked conflicted, his eyes darting back and forth across the room. Chek let out a deep sigh, opening the drawer and pulling her notebook back out. "Come on. Out with it. I still need to catch the rations line."

The man groaned. Reaching up, he hooked a finger onto his shirt and tugged it down slightly, revealing the upper portion of his chest. Beneath the taut skin, something moved—a large, blue worm, pulsating just below the surface. The shape wriggled slowly, its shape grotesquely distorting his flesh with each subtle movement.

A Bluecoil.

Chek fought the urge to vomit.

"Did you not wear your mask?" she said, her voice aghast.

"Almost always," Rokesh protested. Chek stared wordlessly at him, and he added, "I mean, I took it off one night. Just to help me sleep."

"And how's your sleep been since...you breathed in a parasite?"

He glared at her. "Just...make sure the Rangers treat the area."

"And you make sure to wear your mask next time," she said. "What did the Healer have to say when she saw you?"

Rokesh shifted uncomfortably again, and Chek's eyes widened.

"You haven't seen the Healer yet? Aurora's Name, Rokesh. You'd think this was your first time out there!" She stood up, slowly stepping towards him, making a brushing motion with her left hand. "Go, go. Get over there."

He shook his head.

"There's one more thing. Something I wanted to get your thoughts on."

"Oh? Something more important than getting..." She pointed at the bulge on his chest, again fighting the urge to vomit. "...that taken care of?"

"It's quick...it's...have you noticed a lot of sickness going around?"

Chek snorted.

"Rokesh, this is Rath's Eastern District. There's always sickness going around."

"No, I mean...have the other Couriers mentioned anything about towns and cities dealing with sudden illnesses? Unusual illnesses? Boils, violent coughing. Things like that."

Chek cocked her head slightly, trying to act merely curious.

"I'd need to check my records. Why do you ask?"

He gave a weak shrug, wincing as the movement irritated his upper chest.

"Just wanted to ask. I feel like a lot of places have been dealing with it. I just came from Draymon. There was a lot of it going around. Just seems unusual."

"I'll make a note of it. Now go see a Healer, or I'll drag you there myself."

Rokesh's eyes darted down to Chek's leg. Now that she was standing, the brace around it was plainly visible. His eyes quickly came back to meet hers, but Chek cringed, knowing the thought that must have inevitably crossed his mind.

There was no way she'd be able to drag him anywhere.

He politely nodded his head and stepped out of her office. Once he was gone, Chek spun, stepping back to the map hanging on the wall. It was a map of all Avoni, with red lines outlining the established Safe Paths through the Sundered Lands.

Chek reached into her desk, pulled out her pen, and slowly circled Draymon. Then, she stepped back, looking at the multiple towns and cities circled.

"Another one..." she muttered.

"What's that?" a voice said. Glancing in the direction of the voice, Chek saw her brother Felix stepping out of the back room. He was pointing at the many circles on the map.

"Just...tracking reports from different Couriers," she said nonchalantly.

"Reports of...something all over Avoni? That doesn't make sense."

Blunt and direct. That was Felix.

Chek let out a deep sigh. "There's been reports of some strange illnesses. I figured I'd track it, in case the Vanguard needs the information."

Felix stood back, staring at the map. He gave a slight squint, his eyes narrowing behind his glasses. After a few seconds, he said, "Seems like a lot of it is going around." With that, he turned around and walked away.

Chek glanced up at the map.

Felix was right. A lot of strange illness was getting around.

"Patterns mean something," she muttered.

A few hours later, the rough cobblestones pressed against Chek's uneven gait, each step a delicate negotiation with the ground. She clenched her jaw, willing her right leg to move more fluidly, but it remained stubborn, dragging slightly behind the other. The cool morning air cut through the tattered fabric of her coat as she joined the line, already winding far down the narrow alley.

Ahead of her, the queue seemed to stretch endlessly, bodies huddled together for warmth, faces pale and gaunt. The stench of unwashed skin mixed with the damp scent of the streets, an odor she had long since stopped noticing. To her left, a child coughed, a weak, rattling sound that seemed to echo off the crumbling brick walls towering over them.

Chek shifted uncomfortably as she got to the back of the line.

It was going to be another long day.

In the distance, Chek heard a low murmur. She glanced over and saw a man slumped against the stone wall, muttering to himself. His eyes were an unnerving shade of red, faintly glowing in the dim light, and his hair was a striking purple.

Despite herself, she felt a pang of pity for the man. He was clearly under the influence of Emberroot—a hallucinogenic mushroom found only in the Sundered Lands. Though illegal to obtain or sell, Emberroot fetched a high price on the black market, and a few members of the Vanguard had secretly made quite a fortune by selling it on the side.

Chek found that despicable.

A few hours later, she finally reached the front of the line. The ration officer, a burly woman with deep-set eyes, handed her a small bundle wrapped in rough cloth. Chek accepted it with both hands, her fingers trembling slightly from the cold and exhaustion. She carefully unwrapped the bundle, revealing a meager portion of dried bread, a thin slice of cheese, and a few withered vegetables. It wasn't much, but it was something.

She gave the officer an authentic smile of gratitude. In turn, the officer gave her a curt nod before turning to the next person in line.

Clutching her rations close, Chek stepped aside, making way for the others still waiting. She glanced back at the line, which was just as long as when she had joined it. A part of her ached for those at the end, uncertain if there would be enough food to go around.

But for now, she had what she needed, and that was enough.

As she rounded a corner, the crowd grew denser, the people around her slowing to a near stop. Chek frowned, craning her neck to see what had caused the sudden congestion. She pushed forward, her bad leg protesting with each step, until she emerged into a small square.

In the center, the corpses of four women hung from a wooden scaffold. A large, crude sign was nailed to the front of the structure, its message stark and unforgiving:

The Penalty of Prostitution is Death.

The sight had grown increasingly more common over the last few years, especially since Duke Lorian had tried to crack down on the overpopulation problems in the city.

Chek's breath caught in her throat as she saw the bodies swaying gently from the ropes. A cold sweat broke out along her brow, and her hands instinctively clenched into fists, nails digging into her palms. She forced herself to keep moving, her eyes fixed on the ground ahead, but the familiar creak of the ropes as they strained under the weight echoed in her ears.

She turned away quickly, but the sudden motion caused her to trip. She stumbled to the dirty stone ground in a huff, grunting in annoyance at herself. A man offered her his hand, which she accepted, and pulled her up to her feet.

"You hurt?" he asked.

Chek shook her head.

"Only my pride."

The man gave a knowing smile and motioned with his head towards the dangling corpses behind him. "There's no shame in falling after seeing something as ghastly as that."

She brushed the coiled hair from her face and nodded.

"It's brutal," the man continued. "Absolutely brutal. I understand why Duke Lorian did it, but..." He trailed off for a moment before saying, "You just wonder if there is a better way."

"People in the Northern District wouldn't stand for this," Chek said, giving her head a slight shake. "My mother always told me 'If you don't like it here, you've got to get yourself to Northern.'"

The man offered a faint smile. "Foolish mum," he said. Chek cast an irritated expression his way, and he raised his hands apologetically. "I'm sorry. I offended you, and...I'm sorry." He motioned back towards the corpses. "Sights like this turn me into a bitter man."

"It's fine. But I need to go. Have a good day." Chek turned to leave. As she stepped away, he called after her.

"The Northern District's only a few years away from having the same problems." Chek paused, turning her head back to the man. "Either that, or mandated executions of folks in the other districts. We all know it. Rath is running out of time."

"I seriously doubt it would ever come to that."

The man shook his head. "This is just a rumor, but I've heard that Duke Lorian is considering another edict. One that would result in the deaths of the elderly"—his eyes flickered to the brace on her leg—"and the disabled."

Chek flushed and stammered, "A cheery thought indeed."

"Only cheery if you know how to escape," the man added. Chek rolled her eyes.

"Well, the Vanguard Couriers won't take me. I'm as trapped—"

"I'm not talking about the Couriers," he said, his voice lowering slightly. Chek gave him a curious expression. He smiled and continued, "The Shadows of the Sundered Lands."

Chek let out a startled laugh, saying, "Really? The Shadows? They're not even real." The man stepped even closer to her, leaning in enough so that Chek could smell his breath.

"Oh, they're real. I've been in contact with them, and I believe I'll be joining them soon."

"They're a cult."

"Oh, so now you believe they're real?" he said, grinning like he had just won an argument.

She rolled her eyes. "Anyone who has reached out to you, trying to get you to join the Shadows, does not have your interests at heart. Our Aurora Shroud protects us. It's impossible to live outside of it. Anyone who has tried has either died or been transformed."

"Anyone except the Shadows of the Sundered Lands. If you like, I can say that you're interested."

Chek shook her head in irritation. "I appreciate you trying to help me, but my brother and I will manage just fine. I also don't think we are going to reach an agreement on this topic. I must bid you farewell and return to my home."

The man gave an apologetic nod. "I apologize if I have offended you. But you must forgive me for trying to find salvation from this place."

Casting a dismissive expression his way, Chek turned and continued home.

She reached her destination as the last light of the day faded, casting long shadows across the narrow street. The familiar sight of the cramped, weathered structure offered little comfort. The door creaked as she pushed it open, the sound echoing in the overcrowded space. Inside, the air was thick with the smell of too many bodies and not enough ventilation.

Twelve people shared this tiny home, and each one's presence was keenly felt.

Wordlessly, Chek climbed onto her cot in the far corner of the room. She pulled out her small bag of rations and began to eat. But while she ate, all she could think about was her conversation.

In spite of what she had told the man, she found herself clinging to the desperate hope that he might be right.

But in a city like Rath, hope was a luxury few could afford. And as the night wore on, Chek feared that even this small glimmer of it might soon be extinguished.

Chapter 3

The next morning, Cam stirred from a restless sleep, blinking against the soft light filtering through the thin curtains of his room. He groaned quietly, pressing his fingers to his temples as a dull ache throbbed in his head.

Too much to drink last night, he thought, angry at last night's version of himself.

He swung his legs over the side of the bed, the cool wooden floor sending a shiver up his spine. Stretching out the stiffness in his muscles, he stood and moved to the small table where his clothes were laid out. The brown tunic felt rough in his hands as he slipped it over his head, the familiar weight of it comforting against his skin. Next, he pulled on his trousers, tucking them into the tops of his well-worn leather boots.

Finally, Cam reached for his black cloak, feeling the sturdy fabric between his fingers before fastening it around his shoulders. He briefly traced the outline of the red patch indicating his rank as Vanguard Courier. Then, with a deep breath, he rolled his shoulders back, letting the weight of the cloak settle comfortably against his frame.

After eating a quick meal, he walked across Kevilton to report to the Vanguard. The town's homes, shops, and school were set up on a short, looping road. In the center of the loop was a larger building where the local Vanguard members met.

As he traversed the cobbled path, the first rays of dawn cast a gentle glow, illuminating the surroundings with a warm embrace. The scent of dew-kissed flowers and the distant murmur of early risers set the backdrop for the day's unfolding activities. The quaintness of Kevilton was a tapestry woven with the daily routines of its inhabitants.

In the distance stood the Vanguard headquarters, a tall, imposing structure of dark stone. It was built with sharp angles and spires rising into the dim sky. A weathered sign bearing the Vanguard's symbol hung just outside the doors.

Cam stepped through the heavy oak doors, their groaning hinges echoing through the cavernous hall. The dim light from overhead lanterns cast long shadows on the walls, and the air was thick with the scent of old parchment and ink. The space was bustling with activity, but Cam's focus was drawn to the two figures waiting for him near the central desk.

The first was Harold, Kevilton's local Route Coordinator. He was a tall man with a no-nonsense demeanor. He stood with his arms crossed and gaze fixed firmly on Cam. His eyes were sharp, as though he was already sizing him up, though his expression remained neutral. Beside him was Gideon, the Vanguard Captain. His face was a mask of frustration, his fists clenched tightly at his sides.

"Late," he growled. "Late by nearly an hour." The irritation in his voice made Cam's heart race.

"Apologies, Captain Gideon. I overslept."

Gideon's face softened slightly.

"Are you okay? Illyria said that she noticed some scales on your right hand last night."

Cam instinctively flexed his hand. The scales had disappeared, but there was still a dull ache where they had been the day before.

"I'm fine. I was just tired. You know how it is in the Sundered Lands."

Gideon nodded.

"I do know. Make sure you check in with Illyria later today. Now, what's your report?"

For the next hour, Cam shared what he knew about the outside world. He was detailed and thorough, providing updates on recent elections in certain cities, as well as possible resource shortages. He also described the condition of the Safe Paths he had traveled to reach Kevilton, providing recommendations on where Rangers may need to be deployed.

Unfortunately, there was a growing number of communities that were at risk of running out of resources and raw materials. As he finished that section of the update, Gideon huffed.

"There's never enough of anything," he muttered to himself.

Cam ignored the comment and continued with his update.

"Reports from Runara suggest that the scaletaints have migrated south, closer to Rath. More Couriers go in and out of there, making it a more plentiful food source for them."

"Has Rath made any resource requests?"

"Nothing that I am aware of, outside of their standard food request."

Like many overpopulated urban areas, Rath depended on outside food sources to sustain its large population. Farming communities like Kevilton played a crucial role in keeping cities alive.

"Do they have an excess of any materials?"

"I don't think it's fair to say that anyone has excess," Cam responded dryly. "They have barely enough to take care of their people."

Gideon leaned forward, the intensity returning to his eyes.

"Nevertheless, we have a request to make of Rath. We've supplied them with food for decades, and it's time they paid back the favor. We need medicine."

Cam raised a curious eyebrow. "Medicine, sir?"

Gideon stood and began pacing the room. He placed his arms behind his back as he did so.

"Yes. Medicine. There's some kind of sickness that's broken out among the people here."

"What kind of sickness?"

"A strange kind. Painful boils. Fevers. Violent fits of coughing. Excessive vomiting." He shook his head. "It's a mess."

Cam recognized the symptoms.

It was what happened to most people after being exposed to the Sundered Lands.

"And your Healers—"

"Aren't able to stop it. Not permanently, at least. Illyria seems to have figured out a way to slow its progression, but it's not enough."

"How many people have gotten sick?" Cam asked.

"Roughly a tenth of the people here. And it's spreading. I won't lie to you, Cam. This one worries me. Kevilton is critical to food supply in Avoni. If too many of our people get sick..."

He trailed off, but Cam understood the implication.

"You need a Courier to go to Rath, request the medicine and have them sent back as soon as possible."

Gideon nodded and motioned to the Route Coordinator. The man stepped over to a map on the wall with red lines indicating established Safe Paths. He pointed to one of the routes leaving Kevilton.

"There's a problem on the existing Safe Path between Kevilton and Rath." Cam raised an eyebrow at this, but Harold simply shook his head. "Nothing major. Just reports that it's overgrown, and we haven't received confirmation that the Rangers have culled the plant life. Anyway, you'll need to go East first, following this Safe Path, through Runara. Rest there and then make straight for Rath, following this path." He continued tracing the line using his finger. "If there's another Courier in Runara who can leave sooner, have them deliver the message, with you traveling behind them as backup."

Cam nodded.

"That is all. You may leave now."

Illyria leaned casually against the stone wall across the street from the local Vanguard headquarters, her green cloak blending with the shadows cast by the tall buildings. Her eyes, sharp and calculating, tracked Cam's every movement as he emerged from the building and headed towards the Quartermaster, likely to receive new supplies for his journey.

Once Cam was out of sight, Illyria pushed herself off the wall and smoothly crossed the cobblestone street. Her cloak fluttered lightly behind her as she made her way to the entrance of the Vanguard building. With a practiced hand, she grasped the brass ring on the heavy oak door, giving it a firm pull. The door creaked open, and Illyria stepped inside.

Hearing her footsteps, Gideon turned around.

"Ah, Illyria. What brings you here?"

Illyria offered a slight smile that didn't quite reach her eyes.

"I saw Cam leave a moment ago. I assume you told him about the sickness?"

Gideon nodded.

"I did. He'll be leaving for Rath in a few days. With any luck, we should have medicine within the month."

Illyria tilted her head thoughtfully, her voice measured and calm.

"I thought I might accompany him."

Gideon's eyes narrowed.

"No. Absolutely not. We need you here. Why would you even suggest that?"

Illyria swallowed hard before speaking.

"I checked Cam last night. There were several scales on his right arm. He had at most a few more hours before becoming Crimson Limbo. This was after only two days in the Sundered Lands."

Her words hung in the air like a storm cloud, heavy with implication. She watched as Gideon's face hardened with worry, his eyes flicking towards Harold, whose head had jerked up.

"Only two days? Why, the journey from Runara to Rath is three days. And that's under ideal conditions." He jumped back over to his map. "No, no, no, no. This isn't good."

"Are there other routes, Harold?" Gideon asked. Harold shook his head.

"Nothing. This is the fastest route, while maintaining his safety as well."

Illyria could sense the tension mounting, feel the indecision brewing in Gideon's mind. This was the moment she had been waiting for. Without hesitation, she interjected, her voice smooth and assured.

"I can help him. I did, after all, come up with the method for forestalling corruption in the Sundered Lands."

She allowed a brief pause, letting the significance of her words sink in. Gideon's brow furrowed as he weighed her suggestion, his eyes darting between her and the maps.

"I don't like sending one of our Healers away, but I don't see a better option. I think you're right. Illyria, you accompany Cam on his journey. Your task is to make sure that our request gets safely to Rath."

Illyria bowed her head.

"You have my word. Thank you, Captain Gideon."

Then, she turned and left the building before Gideon could change his mind.

She gave a playful smile as she stepped into the sunlight.

That had worked out quite nicely.

Chapter 4

Over the next few days, Cam found himself with very little to do. A Courier's job primarily involved traversing the Sundered Lands. Once that was complete, it tended to leave a void.

The stillness that followed was something many Couriers cherished. It was a rare chance to rest before their next perilous journey. For Cam, it was anything but refreshing. The quiet moments left him alone with his thoughts, and his thoughts could be unforgiving.

Cam felt adrift, like a leaf tossed by the wind. His thoughts became a relentless tide, pulling him deeper into a sea of doubt and self-recrimination.

After a week of this, he found himself almost glad to be returning to the Sundered Lands.

Almost.

It was still the Sundered Lands.

Sitting in the privacy of his room in Rhine's inn, he prepared the final things he would need to safely journey to Rath. He sharpened his twin daggers and placed a new string on his bow.

The final task was to prepare his Aetherfern.

For some reason, the properties of the plant helped to counteract the effects of corruption outside of the Aurora Shrouds. It also was the only living thing that could not be corrupted by the Sundered Lands.

It was a complete botanical enigma.

Nobody quite agreed on where the plant had come from. Some believed it to be a gift from the ancient guardians of Avoni, a token of protection against the encroaching corruption. Others claimed that the tears the goddess Aurora cried on the day of the Sundering resulted in the Aetherfern.

Cam didn't care where the plant came from. All that mattered to him was that survival was impossible without it.

He meticulously clipped leaves from the Aetherfern and placed them in a stone bowl. When he was satisfied that he had enough clippings, he began grinding them up into smaller bits. Some of the clippings were placed in his water pouch, while the others were stored separately.

With all preparations completed, Cam stepped outside, trying to enjoy his final night in the protective embrace of the Aurora Shroud.

He sat on the edge of a low stone wall just outside the village, his gaze fixed on the ground, averting his eyes from the cacophony of scarlet above him. For most, the vibrant colors of the sunset that washed over the landscape were warm, comforting hues.

For Cam, the beauty of the scene only deepened the unease gnawing at his stomach.

He took a deep breath, trying to steady the anxiety that had been building within him all day. The air was cool, carrying the faint scent of pine and the earthy aroma of the forest. It was peaceful in Kevilton. The village was quiet, with only the occasional sound of distant laughter or the rustling of leaves in the breeze.

But the tranquility of the evening did little to soothe Cam's troubled mind.

The Sundered Lands had a way of sinking into a person, burrowing deep into their soul until the darkness became a part of them.

As the sun began to fall, turning the sky a deep shade of red, he glanced again down at his hand and worry began to course through him.

My hand was covered in scales by the time I reached Kevilton.

The transformation process had been painful. He first noticed the discomfort in his hand just a few hours into his trip. Eventually, his hand tormented him, making it difficult to even hold the reins. By the beginning of his second day in the Sundered Lands, scales had already started to appear.

He looked down at his hands, flexing his fingers as if to reassure himself they were still his. The memory of the transformation was still fresh in his mind. The pain, the scales spreading across his skin, the terror of not knowing if he would ever be whole again.

It was all too vivid.

Why am I doing this? Why am I going back? He'd struggled with these questions for years and still didn't have a good answer. He came to the same conclusion he often came to.

It was time to get a drink.

Cam stepped across the street back towards the tavern. However, his walk was abruptly halted by the arrival of Gideon. The Vanguard Captain closed the distance with purposeful strides, fixing a penetrating stare upon Cam as he approached.

Cam nodded respectfully as he walked up.

"Captain, it is good to see you again, before I leave in the morning."

Never one for politeness, Gideon said, "I have one more demand of you."

Cam looked on curiously. It was uncommon, although not unheard of, for local leadership to place additional tasks on an outgoing Vanguard Courier.

"You are to bring Illyria with you."

For a moment, the world seemed to tilt. Cam blinked, his mind struggling to process the words.

"Ill-Illyria?" he stammered.

The astonishment must have registered on Cam's face, as Gideon hastily raised his hand in a placating gesture.

"I know this is unusual. But, given the importance of this message, we want to ensure its safe delivery." As he said this, Gideon glanced ever so briefly at Cam's hand.

For a moment, he could only think about the last time he'd traveled with someone.

Silva.

He swallowed hard, his throat tightening; his hands slowly curled into fists. A cold sweat broke out along his spine, the chill seeping into his bones despite the warmth of the evening. His breath caught, a shallow hitch that he tried to disguise as a cough.

Flushing, Cam said, "With respect, sir, the best way to ensure delivery of your request is for me to travel as quickly as possible. Traveling in pairs is slower."

Gideon shook his head in disagreement.

"No, Cam. The best way to ensure that Rath receives our request for medicine is for you to not transform into a scaletaint in the middle of your journey. She's going with you."

Cam could feel his stomach turning. He took several deep breaths, trying to calm his nerves. He didn't like the idea, but how could he argue with the man?

Don't think. Just do what he says, Cam reminded himself.

After a moment of contemplative silence, Gideon spoke with a measured tone.

"We all understand the risk, but we all agree that the greater risk is letting you travel alone. We've already spoken to Illyria, and she is in agreement. She's going with you. The Healers have come up with interesting ways to help people survive longer in the Sundered Lands. Illyria has studied these techniques and is well prepared to support you."

Cam sighed in resignation. "Tell her that I'm leaving at first light."

Gideon's serious face nodded. Turning to leave, he said, "She'll be ready."

As Gideon walked away, Cam tried to focus on something—anything—other than the mounting pressure in his chest, but his thoughts raced too quickly to latch onto any one thing. His hands were restless, fingers tapping nervously against his thigh, a rhythmic, unconscious motion that he couldn't stop.

His heart pounded in his chest, a relentless hammering that echoed in his ears. He could feel sweat beading on his forehead, trickling down the back of his neck despite the coolness of the evening. His mouth was dry, the taste of fear bitter on his tongue.

Get a grip. Get a grip. He balled his fists so tightly that his fingernails began to draw blood.

His body didn't listen. The knot in his chest pulled tighter and tighter until it felt like he couldn't breathe at all.

You've done this before. You can do this.

Finally, the moment passed and Cam was able to take a deep breath. He sighed and leaned back, letting his head tilt toward the sky. The first stars were beginning to appear, looking like tiny pinpricks of light in the deepening twilight.

There was a time when he'd dreamed of traveling beyond the Aurora Shroud, but now he knew the horror that awaited him, all he could feel was fear.

The next morning, as light trickled in through the room's window, Cam woke with a start, his body jolting upright before his mind could catch up. The thin light of early morning filtered through the window, casting a pale glow over the room.

He rubbed his gritty eyes as he slowly got out of bed to get dressed. He wore simple brown trousers with leather boots and a dark brown tunic that clung to his large frame. Finally, he draped a black cloak over his shoulders and pulled the hood up, the fabric falling into familiar folds around his face.

But it wasn't until he reached for the mask that he felt the full weight of the role he was about to step into.

The mask was a tight-fitting wrap of cloth, drawn snug over his mouth and nose to filter the air and protect his body from airborne parasites, like the Bluecoils. With his hood up, only his eyes were left uncovered.

As Cam stepped into the waking village, the young Vanguard Warden was waiting for him with a new, saddled brown horse.

He was disappointed to find Illyria already awake, standing next to a black horse for herself. Her dark green cloak draped elegantly over her slender frame, its long sleeves falling just past her gloved hands. Beneath the cloak, she wore a fitted brown shirt tucked neatly into sturdy trousers. Her black hair had been pulled back into a tight braid.

Cam shook his head when he saw her.

"You're up early," he muttered, his voice muffled by the mask. He couldn't keep the irritation from seeping into his tone.

Illyria turned to him with a bright, almost mischievous smile. "Couldn't sleep. Too excited about our little adventure," she replied, her eyes sparkling with a playful challenge.

"Have you ever been outside the Aurora Shroud?" Cam said, trying to keep his voice friendly. In spite of his best efforts, there was a hint of frustration beneath his words.

Illyria's brow furrowed for a moment at the question.

"I know you don't want me here, but this is what's right. Your transformations are happening more quickly, so whether or not you want to admit it, you need me."

Cam shook his head, pulling the reins of his horse a little too tightly. "You don't understand what's out there, Illyria."

She stepped closer, her playful demeanor softening slightly. "I may not have been out there like you have, but I'm not helpless, Cam. I can handle myself."

He met her gaze, the tension between them palpable. "Just...stay close. And don't do anything reckless."

Illyria's smile returned, a sparkle in her eyes. "No promises." She mounted her horse with a graceful leap, settling into the saddle as if she had been born to it. "But I'll try to keep up with you, old man."

Cam climbed up on his mount in silence. For a moment, he gazed at her, her face a blend of resolute confidence and defiance.

She has no idea what this is going to feel like.

Finally, as he turned his horse, he broke the silence, his voice carrying the weight of experience.

"Let's go. Before we cross the barrier, make sure to put your mask on. It's a dangerous road. We need to ride quick." He shrugged. "With any luck, we should be in Runara in two days."

With a swift nod, Illyria pulled out a leather mask, similar to Cam's, and placed it over her head. The horses stirred beneath them, sensing the gravity of the journey ahead. As Cam urged his steed forward, Illyria fell into step beside him, the rhythmic beat of hooves against the earth setting the cadence for their shared venture into the unknown dangers of the Sundered Lands.

Chapter 5

Chek tightened the threadbare scarf around her neck as she and Felix made their way through the winding alleys of Rath. The morning chill clung to the air, cutting through the layers of their worn clothing. Felix walked beside her, his hands shoved deep into the pockets of his coat, a scowl on his face.

"I don't see why you insist on dragging me out here every time," Felix muttered, his breath misting in the cold air.

Chek shot him a sideways glance, a smirk tugging at the corners of her lips. "Because if I didn't, you'd stay holed up in that dusty bookstore of ours all day, and then I'd have to listen to you drag on and on about Elmias."

Felix rolled his eyes. "You make it sound like I'm obsessed."

Chek scoffed. "You ARE obsessed! That's all you ever want to talk about."

"It's not my fault that it's so interesting. Besides, at least it's warm in the bookstore. I don't have to stand out in the cold waiting to get a few scraps of food," Felix muttered.

As they turned the corner, the rations line came into view, snaking its way through the narrow alley and around the next block. Chek let out a small sigh. "Looks like we're in for another long wait today."

Felix grumbled something under his breath, but fell into step behind her as they joined the back of the line. The crowd was already restless, a low murmur of discontent rippling through the air. People huddled together, their faces drawn and pale, eyes darting anxiously toward the front of the line.

"Any bets on what we'll get today?" Felix asked, trying to lighten the mood. "I'm thinking half a loaf of stale bread and maybe, just maybe, a few wilted vegetables if we're lucky."

"Why are you always such a downer?"

"Only trying to manage expectations." Under his breath, he muttered, "And I'm only a downer when people take me away from my books."

Chek ignored him, craning her neck to try to count how many people were in front of them.

As the minutes dragged into hours, the murmurs around them grew louder, more agitated. Chek could feel the tension in the air, a simmering unease that was slowly building to a boil. She glanced toward the front of the line, but couldn't see much beyond the sea of bodies pressed together.

"I don't like this," Felix said quietly.

Before Chek could respond, a voice rang out over the crowd, sharp and authoritative. "Attention! There is no more food to hand out today. The rations have run out. Please come back tomorrow."

The effect was immediate. A collective gasp rippled through the crowd, followed by a surge of anger and frustration. Voices rose in protest, some shouting in disbelief, others demanding answers. Chek felt Felix tense beside her, his hand instinctively moving toward her arm as if to shield her from the growing chaos.

"This isn't right!" someone yelled. "We've been waiting for hours!"

"What are we supposed to do now?" another voice cried out.

"I thought Duke Lorian's Rooftop Farming initiative was supposed to keep this from happening!"

The crowd began to press forward, pushing against the invisible barrier between order and chaos. Chek could see the ration officers at the front, their expressions hardening as they realized they were losing control of the situation. Within moments, soldiers appeared, emerging from the shadows like specters.

"Chek, I think we need to leave," Felix whispered, grabbing her arm.

They turned away from the line, moving quickly through the side streets. The sounds of shouting and the clattering of boots against stone echoed behind them, a reminder of how close things had come to breaking. Chek's heart pounded in her chest, but she forced herself to stay calm, guiding Felix through the maze of alleys until they reached the relative safety of Felix's bookstore, which doubled as Chek's office.

The small shop was a familiar refuge, its shelves lined with books that Felix had painstakingly collected over the years. The air inside was musty, filled with the comforting scent of old paper and ink. Chek leaned against the door, catching her breath as she looked around at the worn furniture and cluttered desks.

Felix grinned as they stepped inside.

"If I'm going to be hungry, I might as well be hungry with a book."

As they settled into the shop, Felix grabbed a book and flipped it open. As he did so, a large piece of paper came fluttering out of it. Chek raised a curious eyebrow.

"What's that?" she said, pointing at the paper.

"*Elmias: A Scholarly Perspective into Myth and Reality*," Felix replied without looking up.

"No, I mean the paper that was in there."

He gave her an irritated expression before glancing at the ground where she was pointing.

"Ah. That's the census papers for this year. Just got it yesterday."

"And you're using it to mark your pages? What's wrong with you? What if we had lost it?"

"We didn't lose it. Anyway, it's just the same basic questions they ask every year," he said, before turning his attention back to his book.

She took a step forward, her movement deliberate as she shifted her weight carefully to compensate for her uneven gait. Bending down, she reached out and picked up the paper, feeling its rough texture between her fingers. She unfolded it, her eyes scanning the familiar lines of questions—names, ages, occupations—the usual details the city required.

Chek was just about to set the paper down when something caught her attention at the bottom of the page. Her brow furrowed, and she tilted the paper closer to her face, reading the last question carefully. It was a simple query, written in the same neat, official script as the rest of the document, but its implications made her stomach drop.

"*Are you or anyone in your household considered to be elderly or disabled?*"

"Felix," Chek said, her voice hollow. "Come look at this?" She held the paper out towards him, tapping the final question on the census. His brow furrowed.

"Huh. I didn't notice that before. Why do you think they'd ask that?"

Chek's hands began to tremble, and her eyes began to feel hot. Before Felix could see her, she turned sharply and rushed out of the room into the back closet.

Only once she was in the privacy of the closet did she begin to weep.

Chapter 6

As they reached the edge of the Aurora Shroud, Cam and Illyria shifted their horses into a canter and then into a gallop, racing towards it.

Describing the sensation of leaving the Shroud and stepping into the Sundered Lands was nearly impossible. Cam had tried before, but his words always seemed to fall short. The best way he could explain it was like walking out of a warm, firelit room into the heart of a brutal winter. The change was instant and merciless, the air filling your lungs suddenly strangely painful, and it's quickly understood that extended exposure to the environment will result in death.

As they crossed through the barrier, the sky above them shifted from a serene blue to a hateful, oppressive crimson, casting a sinister pallor over the land. The air suddenly became painful to breathe, as if Cam were breathing tiny needles into his lungs.

Cam's horse, sensing the change, snorted uneasily before him. However, he had been trained well and maintained his gallop.

"Illyria, welcome to the Sundered Lands," Cam said, his voice dry and serious.

Glancing over at his companion, he felt his heart sadden. The distress in her eyes was evident and mirrored the shock he had experienced on his first journey beyond the Aurora Shroud.

"It'll get easier," Cam lied. "Just make sure to keep your face covered. You don't want to accidentally breathe in a Bluecoil."

Illyria nodded in silent agreement.

The Safe Path stretched out before them, a band of stone cutting through the scorched earth, untouched by the wild and hostile land around it. On either side of the path, the ground lay blackened and barren, deliberately burned by the Rangers, ensuring no plant life could grow too close. Beyond the blackened perimeter, twisted trees loomed, their gnarled branches like skeletal hands stretching out, as if ready to snatch unsuspecting prey.

Cam's gloved hand tightened on the reins as they pressed forward, his eyes scanning the horizon for any signs of movement.

"Tell me if you see anything strange!" Cam called out. "There shouldn't be many scaletaints out here, but if something is off, I need to know."

Illyria shook her head.

"This whole place is strange!" she said, her voice sounding hoarse.

The rhythmic beat of their horses' hooves against the corrupted ground echoed like a dirge, marking their passage through a realm where time seemed suspended, and the very essence of life struggled against the transformative darkness.

Two days until Runara, Cam reminded himself. *Just two days.*

They rode in silence for a little over an hour, before signs of fatigue began showing on their horses. Slowing to a stop, Cam signaled that it was time for a rest. Sliding off his horse, he removed his mask and took a quick swig of his Aetherfern-infused water. Illyria followed suit.

Cam turned and looked at her. Her expression was strained and distant. In spite of his irritation with her being there, he found himself feeling a pang of empathy.

At least he couldn't spot any boils on her.

"How are you feeling?" he asked.

Illyria took a moment to put her mask back on. "It is as oppressive out here as Couriers suggest. I'm grateful to have spent my days behind an Aurora Shroud," she admitted, her voice muffled.

"You can always go back," Cam said.

"Oh, please." She shot him a sideways glance, her eyes flashing with defiance. "As if I was going to let you ride off into this nightmare alone. I've had worse days than this."

"Have you?" Cam asked, his tone skeptical, though there was a hint of amusement in his voice. She gave a quick nod.

"Absolutely. One time, I gave myself a concussion by walking into a doorframe right after diagnosing a patient with one."

"Wait, are you serious?" Cam snorted.

"Absolutely. Talk about awkward. Anyway, I'd rather be out here"—she gestured to the world around her—"enjoying the scenery. I'm one of the only people in Avoni who get to experience the beauty of the Sundered Lands up close."

Cam shot her a look, a mixture of disbelief and amusement dancing in his eyes. "Beauty? In this desolation? You have an interesting definition of beauty."

She chuckled. "You just need to appreciate it for what it is. There's a certain twisted charm to it, don't you think? Like nature decided to put on its most dramatic play just for us."

Shaking his head, a faint smile on his lips, Cam said, "You are peculiar."

As they rested, the silence of the Sundered Lands settled around them, broken only by occasional, distant howls.

"Do you ever get used to this?" she asked, her voice a mixture of awe and trepidation.

Cam's gaze fixed on the desolate landscape, a contemplative silence preceding his response. In truth, he was used to the danger, but the anxiety never went away, even under the protective embrace of the Aurora Shrouds.

After a moment of thinking, he simply said, "Yes and no."

Illyria nodded in understanding and said, "It's all wrong. It...it hurts to be out here. It's like...we're not supposed to be here."

Cam nodded in agreement.

"Not as we are, at least. This place...it changes you. Your physical self is being broken down and slowly replaced with a scaletaint. That's what you're feeling."

Her eyes widened with a momentary flicker of fear. For a moment, Cam wondered if she would ask if they could turn around and return to Kevilton. Then, as quickly as the fear had surfaced, it dissipated. Illyria's gaze returned to Cam, and in her eyes gleamed a newfound resolution.

"Then we best move quickly."

She took one final drink of the Aetherfern-infused water before climbing back onto her black horse. Glancing back to Cam, she said, "Are you ready, Courier?"

Cam nodded, mounted his horse, and began to ride.

The journey continued like this for several hours. Cam and Illyria would push their horses to run as fast as possible before stopping for a short rest.

Although they didn't see any scaletaints, they did see a few transformed creatures. One appeared as a deformed deer, its body a grotesque amalgamation of scales, visible bones and fur. It had huffed loudly at them as they passed, lowering its antlers in preparation to charge. The charge never came, however. A quick shot from Cam's bow caused an arrow to sink deeply into the creature's leg. It howled and ran away.

As they rode, Cam stole a glance at Illyria. In spite of this being her first time outside of her Aurora Shroud, she rode with remarkable tenacity, her gaze transfixed on the horizon. The unfamiliar landscape, with its harsh and unyielding terrain, had not dimmed her spirit. Instead, it seemed to ignite a fierce drive to tackle whatever lay ahead.

Cam couldn't help but feel admiration whenever looking in her direction.

Finally, after pushing themselves and their horses to the point of exhaustion, they decided to make camp for the evening. After quickly pitching separate canopy tents for himself and Illyria, Cam made two small fires in each of them, placing large Aetherfern leaves on top of the flames. He also made a third larger fire, again with Aetherfern placed on top.

Illyria watched him in amusement and curiosity and said, "If Gideon were here, he'd be upset that you're burning so much Aetherfern!"

"If Gideon were here," retorted Cam, "I'd tell him that this would help keep him alive tonight."

"It wards off creatures too?" Illyria asked, her eyes glinting in interest.

Cam nodded. "It helps. The aroma of the leaves keeps the creatures away. I can't rest too easily, though. The aroma dissipates very quickly, so I'll have to get up through the night to keep it going."

"It's no wonder you look so haggard whenever you arrive at Kevilton."

"Better haggard than dead."

"Or a scaletaint," Illyria added. "Speaking of which, I need to show you something."

From the folds of her cloak, Illyria produced two small vials, glistening with the ethereal glow of Aetherfern leaves suspended in water. She delicately mixed a powder into each vial, her fingers moving with practiced grace. Finally, she extended one vial to Cam.

"Drink it," she said, an enthusiastic smile on her face.

"What is it?" Cam asked.

She rolled her eyes in mock disdain for the question.

"You'd think a Courier would have a better memory! Remember how I told you that the Healers had figured out a way to slow down the transformation process for people? This is it. There's not much, so we can only use it once a day. Go ahead, try it."

Curious, Cam took the vial. It was quite small, and its glass sides reflected the angry red skies above. The powder had dissolved completely, leaving only the Aetherfern leaves floating gently in the water.

Cam drank it and recoiled. It was almost undrinkable. Aetherfern already had a particularly bitter taste, but whatever powder Illyria had mixed in tasted especially strong. Cam's initial reflex was to spit it out; however, he managed to force it down. Illyria grinned at his facial expression.

"Not quite as good as the mead at Rhine's inn," she said, laughing as she winked at him.

He was about to make a sarcastic response, when her face twisted in pain, a stream of violent coughing erupting out of her. In just a few seconds, she was gagging, her expression panicked as she clawed at her throat.

Cam acted quickly, pulling out a glass of water.

"Try to drink this," he said, a hint of urgency in his voice.

She managed to down a few drops, which slowed her coughing a bit. Chest heaving, she gasped and said, "Aurora's Name...what was that?"

Empathy in his voice, Cam explained, "It's a normal response. This is your first time in the Sundered Lands. Your lungs aren't used to breathing the air here."

Clearing her throat, she took another quick sip of the water, her hand clutching at her neck.

"It was like I couldn't even breathe. Does it happen to you?"

Cam shook his head.

"Not anymore. When I first started as a Courier, it happened a lot. After a few days of being out here, though, it stopped. Your lungs adjust."

Illyria nodded, lifting her hand to brush her hair back into place.

"Anything else I should be aware of?"

Cam frowned.

"Hard so say. It's really harsh out here. People react in different ways." He gave an exaggerated shrug. "The good news is that we'll be at Runara tomorrow."

Illyria nodded again and offered a fake-looking smile.

"I'll never take an Aurora Shroud for granted again," she said, the raspiness starting to disappear from her voice. She paused for a moment before saying, "I've heard stories about Runara. I never imagined I'd set foot there. What's it like?"

"Runara is different than Kevilton. It's crowded, but not quite as bad as places like Rath. The people there are pretty different too. Very artistic."

"It makes me grateful," Illyria whispered. "Before the Sundering, people might have looked down on people from Kevilton. But now, we are one of the few communities to never struggle with food."

The fire crackled softly in the cool evening air, casting flickering shadows that danced on the rocky ground of the Sundered Lands. Cam sat across from Illyria. His gaze lingered on her as she sat at the edge of the firelight, her face illuminated in soft, amber hues. The way the flames caught the strands of her dark hair, turning them to burnished copper, made it difficult for him to look away.

In spite of his previous reservations, he had to admit that it was nice to not be alone.

"What's that?" Illyria said, her brow furrowed in confusion as she pointed at something behind him. Cam turned his head to look.

In the distance was the shimmering, translucent form of an unmoving man. Judging by his clothing, he was a Vanguard Courier. He lay on the ground, clutching a wound in his chest, his silent face twisted in a grimace of agony.

"An Eternal Echo," Cam said, his voice grim. "You'll see a lot of those out here."

Illyria's face paled. "I don't understand."

Cam ran a hand through his brown hair before explaining. "The Researchers aren't quite sure what it is, but they have a theory. They think that when someone dies in the Sundered Lands, their soul doesn't move on. It gets...trapped here. Forever. They're stuck in the moment of their death."

She looked down at the figure, her face twisting in empathy. "So, this...this poor man is just reliving the end?"

Cam nodded. "For the rest of time."

"And if we die out here..." Her voice trailed off, but Cam understood what she was asking.

"We'd become Eternal Echoes too."

Illyria shivered. "I...I'm sorry. This place is a nightmare...I...I'm going to bed." She reached up to pull her face mask off, but Cam grabbed her hand.

"Gotta keep it on at night too. The Bluecoils don't care if you're sleeping."

Her eyes widened, but she gave a silent nod before stepping towards her tent.

The second day continued at the same relentless pace as the first. Illyria felt the exhaustion seeping into her bones. Her body wasn't used to riding this hard and ached from her efforts the previous day. Beneath the weariness, a thrill coursed through her veins, an exhilarating sense of freedom at finally venturing beyond the confines of Kevilton.

In spite of this, a sense of deep guilt gnawed at her.

I should tell him the truth, she thought to herself. *Not just use him as an escort. Maybe someday. But not yet.*

Raising a hand to her mouth, she faked another coughing fit. Cam heard her, quickly bringing his horse over towards hers. Before he got close, she drank some of the Aetherfern water, feigned a struggle to swallow, and flashed a smile in his direction.

"It's not as bad as it sounds," she said.

If only he knew how true that statement was.

Though she couldn't see his entire face, Illyria could tell from his eyes that Cam was smiling at her.

"It's just a little further. We're almost there." His voice was full of empathy, as if it pained him to see her in distress.

The guilt welled up in her again.

It wasn't easy being dishonest with Cam. He'd always been kind to her. She knew he deserved the truth, yet she couldn't bring herself to confess her secret. She wondered if someday she would find the courage to tell him, to unburden herself of the weight that lay heavy on her heart. But for now, she buried her guilt deep within, and continued her act.

She couldn't let him know that this was not her first trip into the Sundered Lands.

Chapter 7

Felix sat cross-legged by the fire, staring at the flickering flames. Chek sat beside him, her eyes hollow and distant.

It was the kind of quiet that made Felix's skin itch. Not because he didn't like the quiet—he did— but because there was something wrong about this quiet. It felt heavy, pressing on him like a weight he couldn't shake. Chek hadn't spoken in hours, and that wasn't like her. She usually filled the silence with idle chatter or a soft hum, something that gave Felix a rhythm to follow.

But tonight, there was none of that.

His fingers tapped a steady, repetitive beat on his knee. He stared at Chek, at the way her lips were pressed tight, her brow furrowed. Felix tried to name the expression on her face. He wasn't always good at reading them, but he knew this one. It was the look she got when she was upset. But why?

He thought of the rations, or rather, the lack of them. His stomach clenched in response, the gnawing hunger biting at him. Chek's must be worse. She needed food.

Of course. That had to be it. She was hungry.

Felix stood up abruptly.

"I'll be back," he said as he walked towards the door. She gave him a weak nod. Moments later, Felix was walking down the street.

Whenever rations had gotten thin in the past, Felix had gone to a friend to barter for more food. Well, to call him a friend was a bit of a stretch. In truth, there were very few people that Felix felt were his friends, but this man was nice enough.

At least, as long as you paid him what you owed.

Felix's feet moved quickly across the uneven cobblestones. The blackness of night had settled in on Rath, but the dark didn't bother him. It never had. The shadows weren't unpredictable, not like people could be.

He approached the house. It was small, squat, wedged between two crumbling buildings like it had been squeezed into the space. The door was closed, the shutters drawn. The place was unusually quiet.

Felix paused on the stoop, his fingers twitching at his sides. The air here was different, too. It was heavier and damp. He knocked once, his knuckles rapping against the weathered wood. Then, he waited for the door to open.

Nothing.

He frowned, stepping forward and knocking a second time, this time louder. Still nothing.

Felix's brow furrowed, his fingers now drumming rapidly on his thigh as he glanced up and down the empty street. It was strange. His acquaintance never took long to answer the door, even when he was in a foul mood.

He knocked again, the sound sharper, almost impatient. He craned his neck to peer through one of the narrow windows. The curtains inside were pulled tightly shut, allowing no glimpse of what lay inside.

The itch that had started earlier by the fire was back, crawling up Felix's spine, prickling at his skin. Something felt wrong.

He hesitated only a moment longer before pushing at the door. It gave way with a soft creak, opening into a darkness that felt thicker than the night outside. Felix paused in the doorway, his breath held in his chest. The smell hit him immediately. A sour staleness, like old sweat mixed with something...worse.

Far worse.

A sense of unease gnawed at the back of his mind. He stepped inside.

The house was perfectly still. The only sound was the faint scuffing of Felix's boots as he walked on the uneven floor.

The smell grew stronger. He couldn't quite place it. There was a hint of rot, but it wasn't overpowering yet. Felix moved cautiously, his hands trailing along the walls to anchor himself. His eyes darted across the dim shapes of the furniture, barely visible in the faint light. Everything was in its place, and yet, something was off.

"Reed?" he called out. "Reed, are you home?"

Silence.

He turned into the main room, where he'd been before on several occasions. The old wooden table was still there, cluttered with the usual mess of half-empty bottles, coins, and scraps of paper. But no sign of anyone.

Felix frowned as he crossed the room towards a closed door on the far side. The stillness around the house gnawed at him, making the space between his shoulders tighten. His hand hovered over the door, the urge to leave pulling at him. He turned the handle, opening the door with a creak.

The inside was dim, the faint glow of moonlight leaking through the cracks in the shutters. Dust hung in the air like a fine mist, and as Felix stepped over the threshold, he wrinkled his nose and recoiled. The source of the smell was definitely here.

That's when he saw the corpse.

The man's skin was a sickly, waxen gray, stretched too tight over brittle bones. Dark, mottled patches marred the bloated and discolored corpse, the flesh swollen and cracked. Beneath the broken skin, thin, pale green larvae squirmed in rotten cavities, their movements grotesque against the necrotic flesh.

Felix's eyes widened in shock; he knew what he was looking at.

This was the work of a Necrothorn Beetle—parasites that paralyzed their victims before laying eggs inside. They were said to thrive only in the Sundered Lands.

He stared at the corpse, dread settling in his gut like a lead weight.

Somehow, that thing had made it past the Aurora Shroud.

Felix didn't think. He turned and ran, his footsteps pounding in rhythm with the frantic beat of his heart.

Chapter 8

Nothing unusual occurred on their second day. Illyria fell into a few more coughing fits, but these were easily remedied by drinking the Aetherfern water.

A few hours after midday, the edge of Runara's Aurora Shroud was visible in the distance. It looked like a translucent yellow dome surrounding massive, spiraling buildings.

Illyria sighed with relief.

"That's Runara? It's so big!" she shouted.

Cam grinned and shouted back, "Just wait until you see Rath! Runara is nothing compared to it."

As they drew nearer, the buildings became clearer. The city was made of several towers, each twisting high into the sky like symbols of beauty and defiance against the Sundered Lands.

It wasn't long before they reached Runara's Aurora Shroud. As they breached the boundary, a gasp escaped Illyria's lips, a visceral reaction to the abrupt transformation in the atmosphere.

"The air! The...the air!" she exclaimed in astonishment. "It's...it's so much easier to breathe."

Cam smiled. Crossing back under an Aurora Shroud was always a shockingly refreshing moment. The air around them was no longer painful to breathe, and even the tension in their muscles evaporated.

The architecture of Runara sprawled before them, a mesmerizing blend of towering white spires and sprawling structures. Buildings adorned with intricate carvings and vibrant banners lined the streets, each structure seemingly competing for attention in a city that thrived on grandiosity. The bustling activity of the city enveloped them, a symphony of footsteps, distant conversations, and the occasional clamor of merchants haggling in the marketplaces.

And then, the two of them crossed through the city gates.

People hurried about their business, their attire reflecting the diverse cultures that converged in Runara. Merchants with vibrant wares displayed their goods in open markets, their colorful stalls inviting curious onlookers to peruse the array of trinkets, fabrics, and spices.

As they entered the city, people called out to them in greeting. Illyria cocked her head in surprise as they spoke. Cam gave a wry smile and pulled his horse up next to hers.

"You weren't expecting them to have accents?" he said.

She shook her head.

"I don't know why I wasn't. Obviously, there's nothing wrong with that. It just surprised me for a moment."

"It surprised me too. It's a strange side effect of all the cities living in isolation from each other. They're all starting to form their own dialects."

"But I never noticed an accent on you before."

"Couriers learn to fake it well," he said, perfectly mimicking the accent of the Runaran people. "It also helps that my natural accent is very similar to yours." He winked.

Cam guided his horse through the lively thoroughfare, his eyes darting between the streets and the faces of the bustling crowd. Illyria, her gaze wide with wonder, absorbed the sights and sounds around her. The fierce love of life pulsed through the very heart of Runara.

The road widened as they approached the city's central square, where a grand fountain sprayed crystalline water into the air. The sunlight caught the droplets, creating a dazzling display of rainbows that danced in the open space.

Cam pointed out a building to Illyria, its facade adorned with ornate carvings and a sign swinging gently in the breeze.

"We'll check in here," he said, pointing to the building.

As they approached, a Vanguard Warden ran up to meet them. He took their horses, and they stepped inside.

A voice rang out from a back room.

"Hold on, be right there."

A man emerged. He was a short man with a clean-shaven face and bald head. His nose seemed to stretch just a bit too far, and a few white hairs stuck conspicuously from his nostrils. The patch on his sleeve indicated he was a Vanguard Captain.

He snorted when he saw Cam.

"And you said you'd only spend a day or two in Kevilton. Ha! Looks like someone enjoys farm life!"

"Better than life in the Sundered Lands, Bryn."

Bryn gave an approving grunt, saying, "No doubt, my friend. No doubt." Turning and winking at Illyria, he added, "And are you a new Courier he is training? If I know one thing about him it's how much he eats. Don't let him near your food bag. You could starve out there!"

Ignoring the tease, Cam said, "Good to see you again too. This is Illyria."

Illyria offered a warm smile and nodded in greeting. Pulling her hood down, she said, "No, I am not a Courier, but I am part of the Vanguard. I'm a Healer from Kevilton."

Bryn's eyes widened in curiosity, his elongated nose twitching slightly. "A Healer, eh? I've heard stories of Healers traveling with Couriers, but none have traveled here."

"It might become more common," Illyria responded. "We've learned of ways to help slow down scaletaint transformation, but it requires us to travel with the Courier."

Bryn took in the information thoughtfully. After a moment, he declared, "You're welcome to stay here too. As long as you don't eat as much as your companion! Every time he shows up, my wife says that we should send him to other villages so that we don't face a city-wide food shortage!"

Illyria snickered slightly. Winking at Cam, she said, "Tell your wife to lock the pantry then."

Ignoring both of them, Cam set his bag on the counter. "Here are the missives from Kevilton. Can your team get these organized?"

Bryn opened the bag and took a quick look at the letters inside. "Aye. Happy to. And where will you be heading from here?"

"That depends. Kevilton has an urgent request for Rath, so that is our planned destination. We'll need to rest here for a few days, so if there is another Courier here that can leave sooner, I'll ask them to take the message instead."

He nodded in understanding. Taking Cam's bag from the table, he turned to leave. As he stepped into the backroom, he shouted to them, "Go take a seat at a dining table. I'll have some food out for you soon." Then, even louder, he said, "Sepherina! The massive Courier is back, and he's brought a friend. She told us to lock the pantry!"

Turning to Cam, a slight smile on her lips, Illyria said, "Poor Rhine is going to be so hurt when he finds out you prefer the food here."

Unsure of how to respond, Cam motioned to a door on his left.

"The dining hall is in there. Let's go get something to eat."

Her eyes twinkled in amusement for a moment. "Oh my, you really are all about the food here, aren't you?"

Acknowledging the joking slight with a snort, Cam opened the doorway and stepped through.

The dining hall was surprisingly lively for such a late hour. A half-dozen tables were scattered throughout the room, filled with locals enjoying their meals. The clink of cutlery and the low hum of conversation filled the air, and the scent of something rich and savory hung in the warmth of the space.

Illyria glanced around, her gaze lingering on the gathered crowd. "Are all these people Vanguard?" she asked curiously, taking in the scene.

Cam shook his head, leading her toward an empty table near the corner. "No. Most of them are locals. The Vanguard doesn't need this many people, and Bryn's more interested in running the restaurant than anything else." He shot her a sideways look. "If I didn't know better, I'd say he's more passionate about cooking than commanding."

Illyria stifled a laugh. "A Vanguard Captain who moonlights as a chef? That's...unexpected."

"Wait until you taste his food," Cam replied, his tone conspiratorial. "It'll make you forget he even has a badge."

As they settled into the rustic chairs, Bryn emerged from the backroom, balancing a tray laden with food. The tantalizing scent of roasted fish, fresh bread, and savory herbs filled the air.

"Here we go!" Bryn announced, placing plates before them. "A little taste of Runara's finest for our esteemed guests. Enjoy!"

The food smelled delicious. Although he was famished, after so many jokes about his appetite, Cam forced himself to eat slowly. Illyria took instant notice of this.

"Don't worry," she quipped, a mischievous smile playing on her lips. "I won't judge you for enjoying a good meal."

Cam smiled and joked back, "I'm hoping that if I eat slowly, they won't lock the pantry. I plan on raiding it later."

Illyria snickered and took a bite of her fish, savoring the rich flavor. After a few moments, she set her fork down, her expression thoughtful.

"I've been wondering," she began. "With a population as large as Runara's, have there been any problems with feeding everyone?

Cam paused mid-bite, glancing at her before swallowing. "Surprisingly, no. Runara's always had an easy way of handling it," he said, leaning back slightly in his chair. "It has lots of lakes and rivers, so fishing's a big part of life here. There's always fish, and plenty of it. They've never run out."

She tilted her head, intrigued. "No shortages? No lean seasons?"

He shrugged. "Obviously, there are times where things are leaner. But, the people here are really lucky. If you like fish, you'll never be that hungry here."

Illyria smiled, taking another bite of her meal. "Well, I certainly can't complain about that," she said, the warmth of the roasted fish lingering on her tongue. "It's delicious."

"Told you." Cam chuckled. "Bryn might as well hang up his Vanguard badge and just run a restaurant."

"It seems like he already has."

Nodding toward Bryn, who was now in the corner, chatting animatedly with another guest, Cam continued. "He'll never admit it, but this place? It's more a tavern than a Vanguard outpost at times."

She looked at Cam, her eyes bright with amusement. "I can see why you keep coming back."

Smirking, Cam popped a piece of bread into his mouth. "Like I said—great food, no shortage, and the best part? No one's counting how many helpings you take."

As she finished her meal, Illyria let out a contented sigh, leaning back in her chair.

Cam grinned, an idea coming to his mind.

"Stay here. I'll be right back."

She gave him a curious look, a smirk forming on her lips as he stepped away.

A few minutes later, he returned, plopping down a bowl in front of her.

"For you," he said, gesturing to the bowl. "To celebrate your first trip through the Sundered Lands."

Normally, he'd have purchased some sort of spirit, something to calm his nerves and help him sleep. However, his nerves didn't seem to be bothering him as much today, so he decided to get something sweeter.

Illyria glanced in the bowl, her face playfully suspicious.

"What is it?"

"It's called ice cream," Cam explained. "Runara's the only city that's figured out how to make it. Try it. It's the best thing you'll ever taste."

Illyria looked at the cup with open curiosity and poked at the cold, creamy surface with her finger. "It looks like snow."

"You're supposed to eat it, not poke it!" Cam teased as he handed her a wooden spoon.

Illyria frowned at the spoon, then tentatively dipped it into the ice cream. "Ice...cream," she echoed slowly. "This...this is food?"

"Just take a bite. Trust me."

Still suspicious, Illyria brought the spoon to her lips, her eyes widening the moment the sweet, cold treat hit her tongue. Her mouth opened in shock, and she quickly covered it with her hand. "It's cold!" she exclaimed, her voice muffled.

"That's kind of the point." Cam chuckled. "I mean, the word 'ice' is in the name."

Illyria's eyes darted to his. "Why would anyone eat something so cold?" She took another tiny bite, her expression softening as the flavor unfolded. "It's strange...but it tastes like...like flowers. No, better than flowers."

"I told you it was good."

She stared at the cup as if it held some kind of magic. "How did they do this?" she whispered, poking at the ice cream again, her fingers nearly numb from the chill. "It melts like snow, but it's sweet like honey."

"I guess it's a mystery. So, you like it?"

Illyria took another bite, larger this time, clearly enjoying herself. "I like this mystery," she declared, a smile tugging at her lips. "Though I still don't understand why it's so cold."

Cam smirked and leaned closer, his voice low as if sharing a secret. "The cold makes it better. You'll see."

Illyria paused, considering, then nodded seriously. "I will trust you," she said, lifting her spoon for another bite. "But only because you gave me this...'ice cream' thing."

She took another bite, closing her eyes as she savored the taste.

"I'm glad you like it. I guess you'd have to be in the Cult of Sundered Shadows to not appreciate it," Cam said.

Raising an eyebrow, Illyria asked, "The Cult of Sundered Shadows?"

"You haven't heard of them?"

Illyria shook her head.

"Just a legend," Cam explained. "Really, more of a joke between Couriers if anything. The stories about them change, depending on which city I'm in. In Rath, they're called the Shadows of the Sundered Lands, I think. Anyway, they usually involve a group of people trying to convince others to live in the Sundered Lands."

Illyria's brow furrowed in confusion.

"How would that even work?"

Cam shrugged.

"It wouldn't. Like I said, it's just a legend. It's not real."

"Could there be any truth to it?"

Cam shook his head.

"We've had to live under Aurora Shrouds for over a century," he said. "There have been many attempts to figure out ways to live in the Sundered Lands. Unfortunately, none of them work. It's just not possible to survive out there for more than a few days."

Their conversation was interrupted by the arrival of Bryn carrying a plate piled high with even more food. The aroma enveloped them, and Cam couldn't help but take a deep breath, savoring the fragrant steam rising from the bowl.

Bryn set the steaming dish in front of them with a grin. Looking at Cam, he said, "Some more food for my large friend"—then, he turned to Illyria—"and my pretty friend! It's fresh from the kitchen."

Illyria thanked Bryn before taking a quick drink of water. She cleared her throat slightly, pushing back a few strands of disheveled hair.

"So, what do we do next?" she said, a note of seriousness touching her voice. "What's the plan?"

"We'll need to wait in Runara for a few days. It's dangerous to go into the Sundered Lands without an extended respite. We'll make more Aetherfern water and pick up any letters that are being sent to Rath. If we're lucky, another Courier will be here that can leave sooner than us. I'll also need to meet with local leadership, to see if they have news they want me to share with other settlements. For tonight, though, we can rest."

Illyria nodded, her eyes betraying the fatigue that had settled in. A soft yawn escaped her as she said, "I like the resting part."

Cam gave a slight smile, his eyes reflecting a shared weariness, and replied, "Me too. Even a short trip is exhausting."

"Why do you do it?" Illyria asked.

The question was innocent, but it struck a chord in Cam. He stiffened slightly in his chair.

"Why do I do what?"

"Travel through the Sundered Lands."

"You want to know why I'm a Vanguard Courier?"

Illyria nodded.

Cam sat in silence for a moment, allowing his gaze to drift away from Illyria. Finally, he answered honestly.

"My uncle told me to."

Illyria's face twisted, as if she couldn't tell if he were telling a joke.

"You joined the Vanguard because your uncle told you to? What about your parents?"

"My mom died during my birth. My father...I'm not sure what happened to him. We think he became a scaletaint."

Illyria's eyes widened. "Cam...I'm so sorry. I didn't know."

Cam gave a shrug, not looking her in the eyes. She watched him for a few moments, but when he didn't speak, she changed the subject.

"I'm exhausted. I need to sleep."

"Bryn should have a room ready for you. You go ahead and get some rest. I'll catch up with you in the morning," Cam said, grateful for the change in subject.

Getting up and stepping out to leave, she said, "Great. Rest well, Courier."

Cam watched as Illyria left the room, her footsteps soft against the worn floorboards. The door clicked shut behind her, leaving him alone in dimly lit dining hall. The sounds of laughter and chatter from the other tables drifted in the background, faint but soothing, like distant waves on a calm shore.

When he had finally eaten his fill, he sat back and stretched his arms.

I should probably go get some rest, too.

He then blinked in surprise.

Wow. I'm relaxed.

When was the last time he had felt like that after a trip through the Sundered Lands?

A small smile tugged at the corners of his lips as he glanced towards the empty chair at his table. He could feel the tension in his shoulders loosen, as if the weight of his duties had momentarily lifted.

He stood up to leave but was interrupted again by Bryn.

"Cam! Luck is on your side today. I found another Courier to help you."

Cam perked up slightly, turning to listen to the short man.

"Really? Can I talk to him?"

Nodding enthusiastically, Bryn responded, "Absolutely. As a matter of fact, he said he wants to talk to you."

Footsteps sounded behind Bryn as a man dressed in traditional Courier garb walked through the open door.

No. Not him, Cam thought, his heart sinking.

"Cam," the man said in solemn greeting, his face serious.

"Hello, Soren."

Chapter 9

The morning sun filtered weakly through the dusty windows of Felix's bookstore, casting long, muted shadows across rows of mismatched shelves. A thick tension hung in the air, even heavier than the scent of old parchment and ink that usually gave the place its charm. Felix stood behind the counter, absentmindedly rearranging the same stack of books, his thoughts elsewhere. The bookstore was quiet today.

That suited Felix just fine. It was easier to read that way.

Chek entered, her expression grim, boots leaving faint traces of street grime on the floor. Her long coat was still damp from the night's cold mist, and her dark eyes scanned the room before settling on Felix.

"Any news?" he asked without glancing up from his book.

"The Eastern District's a mess," she said. "People are terrified that a Necrothorn Beetle is actually somewhere in the city."

Felix slammed his book shut.

"It IS in the city!" he said, his tone frustrated. "I know what I saw."

"Felix, I'm not doubting you," Chek replied, her tone calm, "but you have to understand why city leadership isn't convinced."

"They're not even looking for it, Chek. A Necrothorn Beetle is in the Eastern District! If this were the Northern District, they'd have found it already."

Chek's lips pressed into a thin line.

"I've been thinking about that myself. You're absolutely right." Her words were slow and measured. "We have to get out of here."

He raised a nervous eyebrow.

"Out of the bookstore? You think it may be inside here?"

Chek shook her head.

"No. I mean...out of the Eastern District." She hesitated before adding, "Maybe even out of Rath."

Despite himself, Felix burst out laughing.

"Out of Rath? You do realize that Necrothorn Beetles live all over the place in the Sundered Lands, right? Not to mention that you failed your environmental tests when you tried to become a Courier."

Chek visibly cringed. "I'm just trying to think about what's best for us," she said, her voice tight with concern.

Felix nervously rubbed the bridge of his nose. "I just don't see how running fixes anything."

Her face hardened, but not in anger. She crossed her arms as she spoke.

"I'm not talking about running. I'm talking about surviving."

"We're surviving fine now."

"But for how much longer?" Chek said, the emotion in her words startling Felix. She blinked for a moment, her eyes turning glassy with tears. "You were there yesterday, Felix. The city can't feed all of us anymore."

"Shortages have happened before. We'll be fi—"

"Why do you think they're trying to track down the elderly and the disabled?" Chek said. "Why do you think they're suddenly asking that on the census?"

Felix shrugged. "I just assumed they were wondering who might need some extra help."

Now it was Chek's turn to laugh. It was a sad laugh, the kind wrought from hopelessness.

"Felix, I love you, but sometimes you are just so clueless. They're not trying to figure out who to give extra help to. There's no extra help to give! They're trying to find who might be taking resources away from the more...productive citizens of Rath."

"Why would they do that?"

"Why do you think?"

Felix nodded, slowly realizing what she was trying to say.

"I don't think they'd ever do anything to hurt you," he whispered, but Chek didn't look encouraged.

"I've been doing some thinking," she said, her voice turning more analytical. "We have short-term and long-term problems. In the short term, we have to figure out a way out of the Eastern District. I'd love to be in Northern, but honestly, any of the others will be better than here. Long term, we need to find a way out of Rath. Maybe we can pay a Courier to escort us somewhere else."

"And how do we get out of the Eastern District?"

"We need more money. Look, I've got my job as a Route Coordinator, but I'm going to help you with your bookstore. We don't need to raise much money. Just enough so that we can live for a year in the Northern District."

"I don't know, Chek. The Eastern District is my home. I don't know if I could live somewhere else."

Chek shook her head in frustration. "Felix, you hate it here. What are you talking about?"

He shrugged, absentmindedly sliding his thumb against his forefinger. "I don't know. I just...I don't know."

The two of them stared at each other for a few seconds. Chek's face was pleading. She looked so sad and desperate. Finally, she said, "I'm not going to say you have to come. Aurora knows I couldn't force you to do something. But Felix, I also have to think about myself. So, if you want to stay in the Eastern District, that's fine. But I've got to figure out a way out of here for me."

Felix let out a deep sigh.

"So, what's your plan? Help me in the bookstore so that you can get enough money to move to the Northern District?"

"That's the start," Chek said. "But, I also need to be doing some research of my own. It's time I started learning."

"Learning about what?"

She gave a wry smile. "The Cult of Sundered Shadows."

He rolled his eyes, picking his book back up again.

"Now I know you're crazy."

She turned to leave, her boots scuffing the floor as she walked to the door. But just before she stepped out, she paused, glancing back at him with a hint of mischief in her eyes. "And don't roll your eyes too hard about the Sundered Shadows. We may need them before this is over."

Felix gave a tired smile, though his heart wasn't in it. "Yeah, sure. Whatever you say, Chek."

The door creaked shut behind her, leaving Felix alone in the quiet, dusty shop. He stared down at the book in his hands, but the words no longer held his attention.

What if she's right?

Chapter 10

Cam and Soren stood eyeing each other for a few long moments. The flickering light from the hearth cast their shadows across the floor. Cam's jaw tightened ever so slightly, while Soren's eyes smoldered.

Soren broke the silence, his voice deep and gravelly. "Bryn told me another Courier had a favor to ask of me."

Cam shook his head, casting an irritated look at Bryn. "I'll find someone else."

"There is no one else. We're the only two right now."

"I said I'll find someone else."

Bryn grumbled something under his breath about this not being worth his time. Turning, he disappeared back into the kitchen.

Soren scoffed. He rolled his eyes and, with a deliberate slowness that seemed designed to irritate, pulled back his dark green hood. His long black hair tumbled over his muscled shoulders. "Just tell me what you need," he said, his voice flat and disdainful.

Cam noticed that Soren's balled fists were turning his knuckles white.

Letting out a deep sigh, Cam said, "When are you leaving Runara?"

Soren shrugged and responded, "That depends. Why do you ask?"

"I just came from Kevilton. There is a strange illness there, and they're requesting medicinal support from Rath. I just arrived in Runara and didn't know if another Courier could leave for Rath sooner than me. They're pretty desperate to get medicine as quickly as possible."

Soren raised a curious eyebrow.

"Strange illness?"

Cam nodded. "Boils. Coughing fits. Vomiting."

Soren stroked his chin. "Lots of that happening recently. Interesting."

"What do you mean?" Cam asked, a note of alarm creeping into his voice. "Other settlements are dealing with that too?"

"It's happening all over. Lots of towns starting to develop those symptoms," Soren explained. "I'm surprised you didn't know that."

Cam flushed slightly and said, "Does anyone know what's causing it?"

Soren shook his head. "No idea."

"Regardless," Cam said, "the message still needs to be delivered. Will you take the message to Rath?"

Soren's response, when it came, bore the weight of reluctant acceptance. Giving a subtle nod,

he said in a voice laced with resignation, "Yes. I'll take the message to Rath."

At that moment, the door to the dining hall opened, and Illyria stepped inside. She had washed up, her face now clean and glowing in the firelight. The soft rustle of her Healer's cloak followed her, the fabric flowing with her movements. In her gloved hand, she held a small vial.

"Cam, I almost forgot, you should drink this before you go to bed." Turning, she noticed Soren and beamed. "Sor! It's so good to see you! It feels like ages since you've been in Kevilton."

Cam felt his jaw stiffen as Illyria walked past him, grinning at Soren.

Soren looked confused. "Illyria?" he asked, clearly flustered. "What...what are you doing here?"

"The Vanguard asked me to go with Cam to Rath," she said energetically.

Soren cocked an eyebrow and glanced back at Cam. "What, they're afraid he'd transform before he got there?" he said, a hint of amusement in his voice.

Illyria nodded and continued, "Yes. So, I finally got to leave Kevilton, just like we talked about. It's thrilling! I consider myself lucky."

Flashing a smile, Soren said, "Well, it looks like your trip may be cut a bit short. Cam asked me to take the message to Rath for him."

Illyria frowned. "So what does Cam do then?"

Cam opened his mouth to speak, but before he could respond, Soren spoke for him.

"He'll need to come to Rath too. Just in case something happens to me along the way."

"That makes sense. So, what happens with me?" Illyria asked. Her tone was friendly, but Cam noticed a tightness in her jaw as she spoke. "I'm supposed to make sure the message gets to Rath."

"Sure. Just come with me then," Soren suggested. "We can leave in a few days. Once we leave, it should only take three or four days to get there."

"Perfect!"

Cam gave Soren a quick glare.

"So, your first time in the Sundered Lands…" Soren's voice was a mixture of warmth, curiosity and empathy. "How did it go? How do you feel?"

Illyria smiled. "Pretty unpleasant. I don't think it's possible to prepare for how uncomfortable you feel while you're out there. I feel fine now, though."

"Good," Soren said. "Since you've only had limited exposure, we can leave fairly quickly. Let's leave the day after tomorrow. Will that be sufficient rest for you?"

"Only a Courier would know that," Illyria replied curtly. "Remember, this is my first time beyond Kevilton. But if you think it will be safe, I trust you."

Cam felt his chest tighten.

Soren nodded, before giving Cam a commanding look. "And you'll follow us a week later. Assuming all goes well, we should both be in Rath not long after you leave."

Cam's eyes bored into Soren's, his expression hard, unyielding. "Fine," he bit out.

Soren shrugged, turning his attention to Illyria.

"I'm going to get some rest. Tomorrow, we can plan more of the specifics. There's a really great restaurant I want to show you. You'll love it. Talk there?"

Illyria grinned.

"Talk there."

The next morning unfolded in a quiet routine, and Cam distracted himself in the familiar tasks of the day. Runara always impressed him, its streets a rich blend of history and art. Each cobblestone seemed to carry a story, every square filled with statues that watched over the bustling crowds. Galleries brimmed with paintings, showcasing the creativity and history of its people.

It wasn't just a city; it was art come to life.

In the early afternoon, Cam paused before a large mural of the Vorunis Citadel, depicting it in all its pre-Sundering glory. The brushstrokes brought the fortress to life, the banners fluttering in imagined wind, a reminder of a world long gone.

As he admired the intricate detail in the parapets, a sudden scream pierced the air behind him.

He turned, spotting a small crowd forming, their faces a mix of fear and confusion. Some gasped, others murmured in disbelief.

"What does this mean?" a voice shouted out to no one in particular.

Cam pushed his way through the gathering, his size making it easier to navigate the pressing bodies. As he reached the front, his breath caught.

Lying on the cobblestones was a creature unlike anything the people of Runara had ever seen. It was a bird, nearly the size of a grown man, and it was covered in a grotesque mixture of scales and feathers.

It lay lifeless on the ground.

Cam's eyes widened in shock.

"I thought the Aurora Shroud was supposed to keep them out?" another cried out, his voice a mixture of panic and desperation.

He wasn't wrong.

Since the Sundering, two forces had defined the world: the horrors of the Sundered Lands and the protective Aurora Shrouds. These mystical barriers had shielded cities like Runara from the monsters that roamed beyond.

But now, on the cobblestones, lay a creature that should never have crossed that boundary.

Cam's heart skipped a beat as he realized what was happening across Avoni.

By Aurora's Name...the Shrouds are falling apart.

Chapter 11

Nobody tells you that the worst part about having glasses is how they constantly slide down your nose when you read, Felix thought as he pushed his glasses back up and turned the page of his book. The page made a slight scraping sound as he did so.

Felix savored the solitude of his favorite nook in his bookstore. Nestled by the window, the cozy corner was bathed in a soft, golden glow from a lamppost near the shop. The shelves that surrounded him were a treasure trove to him.

The book in Felix's hands looked like an antique. Its leather-bound cover was weathered and cracked with age, bearing the faded remnants of intricate gilt lettering. The pages, yellowed with time, crinkled softly as he turned them. The text was a labyrinth of archaic script, its meaning obscured to modern readers.

At least, most modern readers.

Felix was so engrossed in its contents he didn't hear the footsteps approaching.

"Ha! Caught you reading again!" Startled, Felix jerked slightly and then relaxed. It was only Chek.

"I'm almost done," he said, pushing his glasses back up. "Just a few more pages."

Chek crossed her arms, unimpressed. "You said that yesterday. Time to close up."

Felix gave an exasperated sigh, loud enough for Chek to hear, and rose to his feet, pulling the book under his arm.

"Fine, but I'm bringing this home."

"What's this one called?" Chek asked. Felix held up the book with pride.

"*The Taxonomy of Elmias, Fourth Edition.*" Felix beamed.

"Sounds thrilling," Chek said, rolling her eyes.

"No less exciting for me than your old maps are for you!"

Chek opened her mouth to retort, but a sudden cry from the street cut her off. They both turned toward the window, peering through the glass. Outside, a small crowd was gathering, though most people were running away while city guards rushed toward something with their weapons drawn.

"Stay inside," Felix said, suddenly serious. Gingerly setting down his aged book, he ran towards the front door of the bookstore. He paused for a moment as his hand grabbed the doorknob.

I should probably have something to defend myself with.

Glancing around, he grabbed a large magnifying glass, then stepped into the street.

"Felix! Bring that back!" his sister shouted behind him. Ignoring her, Felix crept along the stone street towards the commotion. There were still a few people running away, most going into nearby buildings. An elderly woman grabbed his arm.

"Get inside, young man!" she said, her eyes and voice crazed.

Startled, Felix said, "What's happening?" A loud crash from behind caught his attention. Turning, he saw that the city guards had shoved a man into a pile of wooden boxes and were approaching him with weapons drawn.

Suddenly, the man growled, leaping to his feet, and Felix gasped.

The man's arm was covered in dark scales, the fingers elongated and twisted into a reptilian claw. Scales dotted his neck as well, creeping up toward his jawline.

Felix was too curious to be afraid, so he kept watching, even as the elderly woman tugged at his arm, trying to drag him into the bookstore.

Why are they attacking that Crimson Limbo Courier?

The Courier let out a feral hiss, slashing at one of the guards with his clawed hand. Blood sprayed across the cobblestones, and the wounded guard staggered back, clutching his face.

The sight of the blood snapped Felix from his daze. His stomach churned with a sickening mix of fear and shock. The elderly woman tugged harder, and this time, Felix let her pull him back into the bookstore.

Once inside, he shut the heavy door and bolted it.

"What's happening?" Chek asked.

"A Crimson Limbo Courier..." was all the stunned Felix could mutter. His knees felt weak, and his hands shook slightly.

The woman who was with him shook her head, eyeing Chek.

"I've never seen a Courier snap like that. He attacked civilians. It was like his mind had transformed before his body."

"Is that possible?" Chek asked in shock.

"I've never heard of it happening before, here in Rath," she said.

Felix and Chek locked eyes, and a moment of understanding passed between them. They had to escape the city.

Chapter 12

The discovery of the transformed bird's corpse immediately disrupted life in Runara. Most people went back to their homes, to seek the comfort of their family. Others stayed outdoors, peering anxiously into the sky, seeking reassurance in the strength of the Aurora Shroud.

Everyone was afraid.

That the bird had indeed somehow come from the Sundered Lands confirmed Illyria's worst fears. The implications were terrifying.

I was right, she thought. *By Aurora's Name...I was right.*

She wished she could be wrong, but she couldn't ignore the evidence in front of her. The sicknesses, the rapid transformations of the Couriers. And now this.

We need to find the Scepter of Alderia.

To do that, she'd need to move faster. Cam had gotten her this far. She'd have to trust Soren to help her take the next step.

In light of the sudden appearance of the bird, Runara's leadership scheduled a city-wide meeting that evening. As part of the Vanguard, Illyria felt like she should be present, in case any of the citizens had specific questions that she could answer.

As she walked to Runara's city hall, she found the streets much less crowded than normal. Only a few young men and women walked the cobbled streets towards the large central building. Apparently, most families had chosen to send representatives to the meeting rather than risking being outside their homes, should another creature cross the barrier.

Illyria shook her head at the thought.

The creatures of the Sundered Lands should be the least of your worries right now.

Ascending the grand stone steps, Illyria melded into the throng converging toward the imposing, pillared facade of Runara's central hall. The dual wooden doors stood ajar, allowing people to go inside where rows of wooden chairs awaited.

As she stepped in, Illyria saw Cam standing with his back to her. She reached out, lightly tapping him on his shoulder. Reacting to her touch, he turned around and gave a welcoming smile.

"It's your first trip to Runara, and problems have already started."

Illyria laughed and said, "I was hoping for a bit of a warmer welcome. But don't worry. I'm not blaming you yet."

"Yet? So, I'm only temporarily off the hook?" he said with a forced chuckle as he nervously rubbed at the back of his neck.

She shrugged playfully. "Well, you did bring me to a city that's suddenly under threat from the Sundered Lands. If I knew you were this much trouble, I might have stayed in Kevilton."

"Trouble? I don't know about that."

"I'll tell you that you're not entirely unbearable." She gave his arm a light poke.

"High praise indeed," he said, his tone distracted.

Illyria gave him a closer look, her smile fading slightly as she noticed the tension in his posture. His shoulders were a little too rigid, his smile not quite reaching his eyes. She'd seen it before in other Couriers. They spent so much of their lives in danger that they forgot how not to feel fear, even when they were supposedly safe.

Unfortunately, it was all too common amongst the Vanguard.

They were interrupted as Soren joined them.

"No weapons, Cam?" Soren huffed in disapproval. He patted the hilt of the broadsword strapped to his back.

Cam shook his head.

"No. Weapons make people feel uncomfortable. These people are frightened enough as is."

"I disagree," Soren said. "Our weapons remind them that they will be protected by us."

"We can't protect anyone if that Shroud comes down," Cam said just a bit too loudly. The room filled with silence as people craned their necks to listen. Cam flushed slightly, realizing how many people heard him.

Soren rolled his eyes. "Why don't you speak up a bit more next time?"

Cam opened his mouth but was interrupted by the man on the stage.

"I think it's time we begin," the man croaked.

"Let's grab a seat, shall we?" Illyria suggested, motioning to the open chairs nearby.

As they sat down, the elderly man spoke, his voice slow and deliberate.

"People of Runara," he began, his eyes scanning the worried faces below. "I understand the fear that has taken root in your hearts today. The Aurora Shroud has been an unwavering guardian, an impenetrable shield that has kept you safe. What we witnessed with the bird was an anomaly, a quirk of fate. The Shroud remains strong."

A ripple of uncertain glances passed through the crowd. Some faces softened with relief, while others retained a lingering skepticism.

"Evacuation plans have been set in motion, not out of fear, but as a precaution. Horses are stationed in every district, ready to carry you swiftly to neighboring villages. Runara's central location ensures that most settlements are within a few days' journey. This is a contingency, a safety net we hope never to use."

He glanced around slowly, locking eyes with several people in the room.

"Now, let us not succumb to fear but stand united," he declared, his voice echoing with a conviction that sought to pierce through the lingering doubts. "We face uncertainties, but together, as a community, we shall endure."

"But what if it happens again?" a man shouted from somewhere in the room. Several voices grunted in agreement.

The old man on stage shook his head in disapproval.

"If it happens again, we'll just have to clean up another dead bird."

"What if it's not dead next time?" a different voice shouted.

A look of irritation flashed through the aging man's eyes, as if he was offended that people were even asking questions. Speaking in a slow manner, as if talking to a child, he replied, "Our soldiers are more than capable of handling one of these creatures. It's important to note that while these Shrouds have been up for our entire lives, they actually haven't been up very long in terms of Avonian history. It's very possible that anomalies like this will appear normal, given enough time."

Another voice rose from the crowd.

"How can we trust these assurances when something breached the Shroud today? What guarantee do we have that it won't happen again?"

"The Shroud has served us faithfully, undisturbed for the span of our lives. What transpired today is an anomaly, an aberration that eludes easy explanation. We remain vigilant, ready to address any such incidents swiftly. Trust, my fellow citizens, is our strongest ally."

A woman in the audience voiced a sentiment shared by many.

"But why did this happen? Why now?"

The elderly man sighed, his expression a mix of understanding and frustration.

"The mysteries of the Shroud are beyond our comprehension. It has safeguarded us for generations, and we believe it will continue to do so. Today's events are a reminder of our vulnerability, but we shall not succumb to fear. Together, we endure."

The remainder of the meeting unfolded in a repetitive pattern. Audience members would continue asking questions, seeking reassurance in the face of the unknown. The elderly city leader, while well-intentioned, lacked charisma. Despite his best efforts, the room remained a tempest of apprehension, the murmurs of the crowd swirling with an undercurrent of fear.

After the city leader had had enough, he called an end to the meeting. A few people cried out in frustration, but most people stood up, quietly resigning themselves to whatever fate was in store for them.

As people began leaving the building, Soren turned to Illyria and said, "If we leave in the early morning, we should be able to make it to Rath in three days. Could be as many as four, depending on scaletaint activity." A quick spike of fear ran through Illyria at the mention of scaletaints. Soren must have noticed, because he quickly added, "Don't worry. They tend to prefer aquatic environments. We'd just need to stay away from rivers and lakes. We'll be safe."

Illyria nodded, uncertain. She turned to Cam and said, "And you'll be following us a week from now?"

Soren answered for him. "At least a week. He may need to stay longer, seeing that his body isn't handling the corruption very well."

Cam frowned and added, "I'll leave when it's safe and will come straight to Rath. I'll meet you there."

She couldn't help but notice that he didn't say "meet you both."

Soren simply rolled his eyes. "I'll see you in the morning, Illyria."

As he walked off, Illyria turned her eyes to Cam.

"Why don't you like him?" she said, her voice a mix of curiosity and judgment. Cam offered a curt shrug.

"Why doesn't he like me?" he said in a flat tone, causing Illyria to shake her head.

"That's not an answer. That's a question. What happened? Every time he's shown up in Kevilton, he's seemed perfectly friendly."

"We have...we have a bit of a history," he said, his hand beginning to tremble.

Illyria wanted Cam to elaborate, but he remained silent. She waited a few moments for him to speak and furrowed her brow when he didn't say anything. Finally, she changed the subject.

"What is Rath like?"

Relief flickered across his eyes at the change in topic. "It's huge."

"Like Runara?"

"No. Even bigger."

Illyria's eyes widened in a mixture of surprise and anticipation.

"Bigger than Runara?"

Cam chuckled as he responded.

"Well, yes and no. Yes, in that its population is much larger than Runara. Runara has almost five hundred thousand people living in it, but Rath has almost two million. And no in that the buildings are not larger. It's actually fairly flat, but covers a very wide area. It's pretty crowded, which can be uncomfortable."

Illyria nodded, her gaze drifting toward a paned window. Night had descended, and the faint edge of the Aurora Shroud painted an ethereal border, concealing the stars beyond.

"I don't want to go back out there," she said, her voice sounding quiet and hollow. "We don't belong out there."

Beside her, Cam sighed deeply, his own gaze distant.

"It's always a struggle to leave an Aurora Shroud," he acknowledged.

Illyria turned to look at him, studying his face. His expression was guarded, but there was something in his eyes that she couldn't quite read.

"Why do you do it?" she asked again, her tone serious.

Cam looked at her, blinking as though the question had startled him. "Someone has to be a Courier," he said, but she wasn't satisfied with the surface answer.

"There are other Couriers," she pressed. "Why you?"

She watched as Cam hesitated, his usual confidence faltering. For a moment, it seemed like her question had taken him somewhere deep inside himself, someplace he didn't visit often. His gaze fell to the flickering lanterns, and Illyria could almost see the uncertainty in the way his fingers fidgeted at his side.

"I don't know," he finally admitted, his voice low, almost lost in the quiet hum of the night beyond the window. "Like I told you, I started because my uncle pushed me into it. I'm not sure why I've stayed this long."

Illyria stepped closer. The warm light from the lanterns bathed her in a gentle glow, and for a moment, the heaviness between them seemed to lift.

"I want you to think about your reason why," she said, her voice tender but insistent. "When you get to Rath, will you tell me?"

Cam nodded, though his expression remained uncertain. Illyria smiled at him, hoping she could ease some of the tension he carried.

"I should go," she said, the lightness returning to her voice. "I need to prepare more Aetherfern for tomorrow's journey."

Cam's face softened at the mention of her healing work, and he shifted slightly toward her. "That healing water you made in the Sundered Lands...it worked wonders. Is there any way I can take some for my trip to Rath?"

Illyria frowned, the apology already forming on her lips. "No, unfortunately. It's a complicated process. If I gave it to you now, it would be useless by tomorrow. It has to be prepared right before it's used. I'm so sorry."

Cam nodded, though a flicker of disappointment passed over his face. "Then you'll have to teach me how to make it."

A playful gleam sparked in her eyes, and she couldn't resist teasing him. "Or maybe I'll teach Soren and let him teach you. That'd be much more fun to watch."

Cam snorted, shaking his head. "Forget I even asked."

Illyria's smile widened. "Let's make a deal. You tell me why you choose to stay a Courier, and I'll teach you how to prepare the Aetherfern."

He met her gaze, and for the first time since their conversation started, a glimmer of something more settled in his eyes.

"Deal," he said, his voice firmer now.

Satisfied, Illyria turned toward the inn, the breeze catching the edges of her Healer's cloak and making it ripple behind her. She glanced back at him one last time and winked at him.

"I'll see you in Rath, Courier," she called out, a playful smile on her lips.

As soon as Illyria turned her back, the smile slipped, her shoulders sagging as she discarded the mask of playful ease. Her brow furrowed as she felt the familiar twinge of guilt.

A part of her screamed tell Cam what was happening.

To tell him what was about to happen.

It's too late now, she told herself. *And there's nothing he can do anyway. All I can hope for is that I find the Scepter before any of this gets worse.*

Chapter 13

After waiting a lonely week in Runara, Cam was ready to make the journey to Rath.

He bounced with anxious energy as he saddled the horse assigned to him. The Vanguard Wardens hadn't told him the horse's name, so he chose to call it "Scoop" after the strange scooping motion it made with its hooves as it waited for him.

Time to go.

As he rode into the Sundered Lands, the familiar oppressive nature of the environment settled upon him, causing him to wince. Each breath was a painful struggle, with the acrid air biting at his mouth and lungs.

"Alright, Scoop, let's make this fast," he croaked, kicking the horse into a gallop.

The road stretched endlessly before Cam, his horse's steady hoofbeats the only sound cutting through the stillness, marking the slow passage of time. It was a three-day ride to Rath, yet with each mile, the weight of solitude pressed heavier on him. The journey felt achingly empty, the vast stretch of desolate land offering no reprieve from the isolation.

On the morning of the third day of his journey, he tried talking to Scoop.

"I guess it's just you and me out here, huh?"

Scoop continued its gallop in silence.

"You could at least pretend to be listening to me. Horses have that—" Cam stopped speaking and let out a quick gasp of pain.

His right hand felt as if it had been stabbed by a long, large needle. Glancing down, he grimaced. Just at the base of his thumb was a solitary scale.

The transformation was already beginning.

In another day or two, he'd be a fully transformed scaletaint.

Cam's eyes widened in shock. For a fleeting moment, he considered turning back to Runara, but at this stage, it'd be faster to get to Rath.

"Scoop, I need you to go very fast."

As the day wore on, the transformation continued, marked by a series of sharp stabbing pains, followed by the appearance of new scales, weaving a grotesque tapestry across his hand and up his arm.

To save time, he strayed from the Safe Path, taking shortcuts. It was a risk, but one he knew he had to take. Rath was still a day away, but he only had hours left.

He slowed his horse when he reached a river. It was narrow, but the current was flowing violently, its waters agitated and wild as they thundered downstream. Ahead stood a simple, weathered stone bridge, arching gracefully over the raging current.

He paused, tension rippling in the air. His eyes scanned the surroundings, checking for any signs of scaletaints. He didn't see any, but he wasn't convinced.

"Chances are that scaletaints live under that bridge, Scoop. I'd prefer looking for a different route to Rath," Cam said, "but that will take too long. We have to risk this." He then kicked his horse into a gallop onto the bridge.

And learned that his instincts were correct.

A sudden splash of water sounded, followed by an animalian shriek. Before he could react, a blur of motion on his left knocked him out of his saddle.

He landed on the unforgiving stone bridge with a pained grunt, opening his eyes to see Scoop galloping away. Instincts kicked in, and he jumped to his feet.

Before him, hissing and croaking, stood a scaletaint. Cam was tall, but this beast towered over him, its black scales subtly reflecting the angry red sky above. Its lizard-like head remained fixated on him, its mouth agape, revealing a set of sharp, menacing teeth.

As predator and prey eyed each other, the scaletaint began hopping back and forth, trying to confuse him. Cam had only fought a few scaletaints, but he was familiar with this pattern. Unfazed, he drew his twin daggers with a practiced grace, assuming a defensive stance. He patiently awaited the scaletaint's move. After a few more side-to-side hops, the creature lunged forward, soaring above Cam.

He dove to the side, coming up in a roll. His dagger flashed in the red-tinged light as it sliced through the air, leaving a deep gash in the scaletaint's left arm. The creature gave a short howl before swiping its muscular tail at him.

This move caught Cam off guard, and as the tail smacked into his chest, he was lifted from the ground and thrown forcefully against the railing of the stone bridge, causing him to drop both daggers. The scaletaint raced towards Cam, its hungry jaw open and ready to deliver a killing bite.

Cam desperately reached into the quiver on his back, fingers closing around an arrow. As the scaletaint closed in, he thrust the arrow into the creature's left eye. It let out a shriek of agony and crumpled to the ground, writhing in pain.

Cam was reaching for his fallen daggers when a second splash of water echoed from behind him. Whirling around, he saw a second scaletaint mid-leap, poised for a deadly descent. Cam jumped backward, out of its path.

The new scaletaint landed in a crouch before swiftly rising onto its hind legs. With a wide-open maw, it projected a long, sinuous tongue towards Cam, wrapping it several times around his right arm.

Scaletaints were strong, but so was Cam. He twisted his hand to grip the creature's tongue before giving a strong yank. Pulled towards him, the scaletaint fell onto the ground, its face just in front of Cam. He stomped on the creature's head. There was a slight cracking sound, and the scaletaint lay still, its tongue relaxing around his arm.

Before he could pull his arm free, something slammed into his back, throwing him several feet forward onto his face. He quickly rolled over to see the first scaletaint was standing again, an arrow still protruding from its eye.

He jumped to his feet, gripping his daggers with determination. Cam executed a feint to the left before delivering a slashing strike to the scaletaint's face. The creature shrieked, toppling backward, badly wounded but still alive.

Advancing with measured intent, Cam pulled his arm back for a killing blow.

An overwhelming surge of searing pain erupted in his right hand. Gasping, he dropped his dagger, the metallic clang echoing across the stone bridge as he sank to his knees.

He looked at his burning hand and immediately felt horror. Black, iridescent scales were rapidly manifesting, popping up like sinister blooms across his skin. His fingers elongated, contorting into razor-sharp claws. He could feel the change from his fingertips all the way to his elbow.

Crimson Limbo. Only hours away from complete scaletaint transformation.

Amidst the relentless agony, Cam scarcely registered the muffled thud of a third scaletaint landing behind him. Cradling his transformed hand, he twisted his head and saw it running at him on all fours.

The scaletaint surged forward, a blur of motion, clamping its jaws onto Cam's right arm. A sharp scream escaped Cam's lips, but the intensity of the pain honed his focus. Grabbing his dagger, he drove it into the creature's chest.

The scaletaint recoiled, injured but far from dead. Cam gritted his teeth as he slowly stood up. He locked eyes with the creature, a silent challenge passing between them.

Without hesitation, the scaletaint lashed out, its massive tail sweeping towards Cam. The force of the blow launched Cam into the air, sending him over the bridge's railing and plummeting towards the churning waters below. The raging currents immediately claimed him, dragging him into their inky depths and propelling him downstream.

Hundreds of tiny spots of sharp pain popped up across his body as the corrupted fish swarmed him with a predatory fervor, their small teeth sinking into his flesh. Instinctively, Cam tried to kick his legs and flail his arms as the water became a realm of pain.

I have to get out of here.

Ignoring the onslaught of biting fish, Cam feverishly kicked his legs, desperation propelling him in an attempt to reach the water's surface. His lungs burned as he swam.

Cam gasped as his head broke through the water. He frantically searched the surroundings, seeking any way out of the rapids as the fish continued to bite at him.

Suddenly, a faint glow caught his eye. On the edge of the river sat a bizarre Aetherfern plant. It was massive, easily mistakable for a small tree. It was also giving off a faint glow, luminescent leaves casting a soft blue light across the ground. One of its branches was just within Cam's reach.

Without pausing to think, he extended his scale-covered right hand, his reptilian claw coiling around the sturdy branch. With a grunt, he pulled himself closer to the shore. After a few laborious moments, he was back on dry land.

He lay down on his back, chest heaving, feeling the hundreds of tiny cuts on his body. Bathed in the blue glow emanating from the Aetherfern, he allowed himself the luxury of catching his breath.

He glanced around. The scaletaints hadn't followed him through the water. He breathed out a sigh of relief.

Rolling onto his feet, he examined the glowing plant.

What type of Aetherfern is this? Cam wondered if Illyria would know.

Running his fingers through the foliage, he decided to collect some of the leaves. He plucked several gently from the branch. As he did so, Cam sensed a powerful energy emanating from the plant flowing seamlessly into his very soul. At the same time, a tattoo of an Aetherfern plant snaked up his fingertips and along his arm.

And then he heard a voice.

What is going on?

The abrupt question echoed in Cam's mind. It wasn't his own thought, yet it resonated within him as clearly as if he had spoken it himself.

How long has it been? What year is it? Again, they were not Cam's words.

A wave of fear gripped Cam, his senses heightened. These thoughts were foreign, intruding upon his mind with an unsettling force.

A sudden dizziness overwhelmed him, and he crumpled to the side of the riverbank, the world spinning around him. Darkness encroached on the edges of his vision. In the haze of fading consciousness, he heard an enigmatic question.

Who are you?

Part Two
Tethered

*T*he Elmias are astral beings—entities of pure spirit—incapable of inhabiting the material world without a vessel steeped in astral energy. This process, known as Tethering, is as much a survival mechanism as it is a binding contract between worlds.

Shadow One

Duke Lorian

Lorian, the Duke of Rath, stood at the head of the war table, his eyes scanning the room as his officers took their places. The candles flickered in the dim light, casting long shadows over the scattered maps and reports. His fingers drummed rhythmically on the edge of the table, but his face was like ice.

"Report," Lorian ordered, his voice cutting like a blade.

Captain Holt stepped forward. His face was etched with fatigue, his tone tight with urgency. "The creatures hit us hard, Your Grace. Half the Northern District's granaries were destroyed in the attack. We've lost nearly a third of our supplies. Even with the food we redirected from the Eastern District, it won't be enough."

It had only been a few days since the attack. Two nightmares born of the Sundered Lands had crossed the Shroud, leaving death in their wake. The Vanguard had never encountered anything like this creature before.

They simply called them "the Reapers."

Out of fear of a city-wide panic, they'd done their best to suppress news of the event. So far, it appeared that only people in the Northern District knew what happened.

Lorian's jaw tightened imperceptibly, though he kept his voice measured. "How many dead?"

"Hundreds. Even more wounded."

A ripple of tension passed through the room. Lorian's eyes narrowed slightly, but he didn't speak.

"Your Grace, the Eastern District has already sent what it can spare," said another soldier, Lieutenant Harrow. "They're facing severe shortages themselves. People there are growing restless. Some are asking why their children should go hungry for the sake of the North."

"And what would you have me do, Lieutenant?" Lorian's voice was steady, though the weight of the question hung in the air. "Let the North starve after they've faced the Reaper?"

Harrow glanced down at the floor, his voice quiet but firm. "No, Your Grace. But if we take any more from the East, there will be riots. We barely have enough to hold the districts together as it is. If the Easterners feel abandoned—"

"There are not enough rations to feed every mouth. Some people are simply going to be abandoned," Lorian said through gritted teeth. "This is not up for debate. Send more of the Eastern District's rations to the North."

"Yes sir," Captain Holt said, turning to leave the room.

"I did not dismiss you, Captain," Lorian said. Captain Holt nodded apologetically and turned back around.

"Apologies, my lord."

"What of the Necrothorn Beetle? Has it been found?"

The captain fidgeted nervously.

"No, my lord. We also can't be sure that it's only one beetle. There could be others."

"Have other corpses been found?"

Captain Holt shook his head.

"No. At least, not yet. But it's a large city."

"Find it," Lorian bit out. "And find it quickly. If it manages to lay eggs in another person, and those eggs turn into full-grown beetles, the resulting infestation could kill us all."

A few murmurs rippled through the ranks, but no one spoke against him.

"Let us return to our topic of the Reapers," Lorian continued. "Do we know where they came from yet?"

"We've sent Vanguard Scouts into the Sundered Lands tracking them. Best we can tell is that they come from somewhere to the northwest of Rath, possibly from the Jaram Mountains."

Duke Lorian nodded contemplatively. He drummed his fingers on the oak table in front of him as he thought. Finally, he said, "We have to assume more Reapers are out there."

Captain Holt nodded in agreement. "The Vanguard Rangers have already built a protective wall around Rath."

"Are soldiers protecting the wall?" Lorian replied.

The question seemed to shock Holt.

"Soldiers? Sir, the wall is in the Sundered Lands."

"Yes. It is," he said, his voice calculating. "And are soldiers manning the wall?"

"No sir. A few Vanguard Scouts, but no—"

"Put troops on the walls. If a Reaper comes, I want it killed before it can get into Rath. You are dismissed, Captain Holt."

Captain Holt nodded, abruptly turning and leaving the room.

The doors to the room creaked open, and a young soldier stepped in, his expression tense.

"Duke Lorian," the soldier announced, "a Vanguard Courier has arrived and seeks an audience."

Lorian straightened, his brow furrowing slightly, but he motioned for the soldier to let him in.

"Grant him access."

A moment later, a man with long black hair stepped into the room, his dark cloak dirty from travel. His eyes were sharp, though there was a subtle weariness in his face.

Lorian recognized this man.

Soren.

"Your Grace." Soren bowed deeply, but his tone was clipped, urgent. "I bring a message from Kevilton."

Lorian raised an eyebrow.

Please don't say that Kevilton can't make its next food shipment.

"Kevilton? Well, speak up, boy."

Soren met his gaze, his voice dropping to a grave tone. "The people there are sick. An illness has spread through the district, and it's getting worse. Boils, coughing, fever. Their Healers can't treat it. They are requesting medicine from Rath."

The Duke glowered at Soren.

"My own people are fighting the same illness. I cannot help them."

Soren held his ground, though his expression tightened. "Your Grace, Kevilton has always been loyal—"

"Loyalty doesn't shield us from reality," Lorian snapped, his frustration finally breaking through. "Do you think Rath's stores are endless? That we can simply divert what little we have to every corner of Avoni?"

The room fell silent again. The officers exchanged uneasy glances, none daring to speak.

"Everyone leave," Lorian said suddenly, his voice sharp as steel. "Except for you," he added, pointing at Soren.

The command was clear, and the soldiers didn't hesitate. Soon, only Lorian and Soren remained in the dimly lit war room. The heavy doors closed behind the last officer with a resounding thud.

Soren stood still, his face calm, but Lorian's keen eyes didn't miss the tension in his posture.

For a moment, the Duke said nothing, pacing slowly around the table, his gaze fixed on the maps. When he finally spoke, his voice was low but carried an unmistakable edge.

"You're the one who is smuggling people out of Rath."

Soren's expression didn't falter, though his eyes narrowed ever so slightly. "I don't know what you mean, Duke Lorian."

Lorian chuckled, though there was no humor in it. He turned to face the Courier, his eyes cold and calculating. "Spare me the theatrics, Soren."

Soren didn't immediately respond, but the slight clench of his jaw betrayed him. He met Lorian's gaze, the mask of feigned innocence beginning to slip. "I've done what I can to help those who were desperate. But that's not—"

"You think I don't know what's happening in my own city!" Lorian roared. "I know what it is you serve."

Soren's calm facade finally cracked. His brow furrowed, and the glint of defiance in his eyes grew sharper. "Do you blame me?" His voice was bitter, his words tinged with frustration.

"Blame you? Why would I blame you? Rath is overpopulated as is. I should thank you. I need you to continue doing it."

Soren shook his head.

"I'd have nowhere to send them, sir. I only serve the Vanguard now."

Lorian's fingers drummed once more on the edge of the war table. His anger simmered just below the surface, but he reined it in, forcing his voice to remain even. "You had better hope the Vanguard is enough. The storm that's coming..." He paused, his gaze locking with Soren's. "It will sweep away those who stand alone."

Soren met his eyes, the defiance slowly fading, replaced by a kind of grim acceptance. "I'm not standing alone, Your Grace. The Vanguard is stronger than you think."

For a moment, Soren stood in the candlelight, his face hard, unreadable. Then, without another word, he bowed slightly and turned on his heel, his footsteps echoing through the empty hall as he left.

Lorian closed his eyes, letting the silence settle around him like a shroud. The shadows danced on the walls, but there was no comfort in the flicker of the flames.

A soft knock came from the door, but Lorian didn't respond.

If his fears were true, there was no chance that Avoni could survive what was coming.

Chapter 14

C am's eyes slowly opened. He blinked, adjusting to the light around him. Overhead, he could see the hateful red sky of the Sundered Lands between the leaves of the giant Aetherfern.

He took a second to breathe, absorbing the strangely serene atmosphere under the plant's embrace. For just a moment, he felt calm and relaxed.

Cam pulled himself up to his feet before gasping in surprise.

His left arm looked like it had been tattooed, the image of an Aetherfern snaking up his fingers, wrist and arm. His right hand was monstrous, covered in scales just like a scaletaint. Bewildered, Cam stood, staring at his hands.

How long was I out? he wondered.

Not long. Only a few minutes, responded a male voice, inexplicably clear in Cam's mind yet devoid of a source.

Cam jumped backward, scanning his surroundings.

Calm down. It's just us, and I can't hurt you, the voice repeated.

"Where are you?" Cam shouted.

Quiet! the voice in his mind hissed. *There are more of those creatures still out there.*

Still looking around warily, Cam took a deep breath that turned into a surprised gasp. He hadn't noticed it at first, but the air of the Sundered Lands no longer hurt to breathe. In fact, the oppressive feeling was completely gone. If Cam hadn't seen the scarlet skies above, he would have thought he was back under the safety of an Aurora Shroud.

"What's going on? Show yourself," Cam whispered, his tone calm and cautious.

I'm afraid I can't do that, came the response. *I'm in your mind.*

What is he talking about? Cam thought. *In my mind?*

Yes, I am in your mind. I wanted to let you know that up front. It's impolite to not declare yourself after Tethering, if the Tethering was an accident.

Cam's eyes widened in confusion, his gaze darting around the landscape as he continued to search for the source of the mysterious voice. Seeing nothing, he spun backwards, looking at the raging river. He then jerked his head back to the Aetherfern.

He couldn't see anyone.

Would you quit moving around so quickly? it said again. *I haven't been Tethered to a human in over a century, and this is making me quite dizzy.*

"Show yourself!" Cam shouted.

Something strange happened inside of him. He could feel a mixture of annoyance and anger, yet he knew they were not his own emotions. Rather, he was attuned to the unique feelings of another entity.

I must insist that you calm yourself, sir. I told you to keep your voice down. There are more of those creatures out here, the voice said, a hint of irritation in its tone.

What is going on? Cam wondered in bewilderment.

I know this must be very disconcerting to you. Tethering is an unusual process, even when one does it on purpose, the voice said. *Please try to stay calm. I will explain everything.*

Nodding slowly, Cam took a deep breath, his mind racing to understand the situation he found himself in.

You can...you can hear my thoughts? Cam thought. He felt the entity's approval at this question.

Feeling the emotions of another seemed so wrong to him, as if he had purposely committed a vile intrusion on someone's privacy. The other being didn't seem to mind, though.

Yes. I can hear your thoughts. Just as you can hear mine. Like I said, I'm in your mind. Actually, that's not an accurate description. More truthfully, I am in your soul.

What are you? Cam wondered.

I am an Elmia, and my name is Luik. I'd like to say that it's a pleasure to meet you, but the more truthful statement would be to say that it's been a frustration to meet you. Out of respect for you, I must also tell you this: you will find that it is best for us to speak the truth with each other, as we can feel when the other is lying.

Cam's mind swirled with a tempest of emotions, confusion and fear intertwining like vines of uncertainty. Part of him wondered if he were dreaming.

Get out, Cam thought. *Get out!* He tried to make the thought sound as loud as possible, while also wondering if a thought could be loud.

I apologize, but just as I am stuck with you, you are stuck with me. I could leave you, but based on the environment you are in, I have a feeling that both of us would transform if we broke our Tethering. For now, I believe we are to remain with each other.

Luik resonated within him, a presence both alien and intimately connected to his thoughts. Cam grappled with the sheer impossibility of the situation. He felt like a puppet entangled in a cosmic play, the boundaries between reality and delusion blurring with each passing moment.

I'm trapped, Cam thought.

Actually, I'm the one who is trapped, Luik corrected. *You are simply Tethered. You're free to go wherever you like, while I am an unwitting passenger. Unfortunately for me, the Elmia is always the one who is trapped. Such has been my life since the Treaty of the Tethering.*

An Elmia. Cam repeated the words in his mind, as if the act of vocalizing them would bring clarity. Instead, the more he tried to comprehend, the deeper he sank into the quicksand of uncertainty.

Was this some manifestation of the scaletaint transformation, a descent into madness, or a strange reality woven by the corrupted threads of the Sundered Lands?

"I must be losing my mind," he mumbled to himself, the words barely audible over the rush of the river.

No, you are still sane, and you are in no danger from me, Luik said in a commanding voice. *Also, please understand that this is disconcerting for me as well. Spending over one hundred years within that plant has not been an easy endeavor.*

Within him, Cam felt the distinct rise of two emotions—his own anxiety, and the growing undercurrent of Luik's frustration with him.

It was confusing, frustrating.

Violating.

Luik, Cam thought, choosing to trust that his senses were not betraying him, *please tell me what's going on.*

Luik hesitated before responding. His silence, however, was not a refusal to respond to Cam. Rather, Cam could sense that Luik himself was not sure of the best way to explain the situation the two of them had gotten themselves into.

Finally, Luik spoke. *What do you know of the Elmias?*

The truth was that Cam knew very little. As a child, he had heard stories of magical creatures called Elmias that could manipulate certain elements throughout the world. He'd also heard that they served the royal family before the Sundering.

None of the stories, however, involved speaking with an Elmia inside one's own head.

Very little. Everything I know is likely not true, he admitted, feeling another flash of irritation from Luik as he did so. Strangely, Cam was able to sense that Luik's irritation was directed at the situation, not at Cam's confusion itself.

I'm afraid there's a lot to explain, then, Luik said. *There are two types of energies in the world: physical and astral. These exist at the same time, but cannot take up the same place, like water and air. You are a human, and that means you can only survive in a physical environment. Elmias can only survive in the astral. Just like a fish cannot survive out of water, an Elmia cannot survive out of a place of strong astral energy. The same is true of humans in the physical world.*

So, how are we talking now? Cam asked.

Our Tethering. An Elmia can Tether itself to a physical being, allowing it to survive in any environment. That same benefit is also passed onto the host that the Elmia Tethers to.

And you chose to...Tether with me? Cam thought.

Not with you. I chose to Tether with the Aetherfern plant. When you tore the leaves off, I was pulled into a Tethering with you.

Cam stood stunned for a moment.

Why did you choose the Aetherfern? he thought.

A moment of desperation, I'm afraid, Luik responded. *I would've preferred a human Tether, but there were none available at the time.*

And you aren't able to get out of my head? Why not?

I apologize, but I won't sever our Tethering. If I were to do so, I would die. An Elmia cannot exist in physical reality. An Elmia can only manifest and survive as an autonomous being in an astral Nexus Point. I suppose I could survive here if I Tethered again with the Aetherfern, but I refuse to spend another moment trapped in that prison.

Cam's anxiety began to recede, replaced by an ascending tide of anger. The amalgamation of his own emotions and Luik's growing frustration morphed within him, forging something completely new.

What do we do now?

That is for you to decide, Luik answered. *Per the Treaty of the Tethering, my purpose is to serve humans. I may be an unwelcome guest to you, but that purpose is unchanged.*

Tell me where you came from, Cam thought, trying to place an angry edge into the words. As he did so, he sensed Luik's emotions lighten a bit, as if he were humored by the attempt at intimidation.

You cannot frighten me, Luik said to him. *And I cannot hurt you; however, I can sense your unease. Please tell me, what is your name?*

Cam hesitated. Having a being hear his thoughts and feel his emotions was so violating that he wanted to hide any part of him that he could, even his name.

Luik must have sensed his unease. *Apologies. This must be overwhelming for you, and it's been so long since I've had to do this. I fear I am not doing an adequate job. Please, allow me to try again. I am your servant. What can I do to make you feel more comfortable?*

You can leave, Cam thought venomously.

Alas, I cannot. I can only—

Only survive in an astral Nexus Point. I understand. Where is the closest one?

I do not know, Luik admitted. *Before I Tethered with the Aetherfern, I was only aware of two remaining points: the Vorunis Citadel and the Elmia Temple. Unfortunately, the former has vanished and the location of the latter is a mystery. Per the arrangement in the treaty, I was forbidden to know its location.*

I don't understand what is happening. What are you? Though the words were only thought by Cam, he felt as if he had shouted them to Luik.

I see you are very confused. I'll explain from the beginning. Please accept my apologies if, for the sake of thoroughness, I tell you something you already know. I am an Elmia. Elmias are astral beings. Many generations ago, Avoni was our kingdom. It was completely blanketed in astral energy. Now, it belongs to the humans.

As Cam heard the words, he could sense Luik's emotions shift, a mixture of anger, sadness, and fear.

The creature was feeling grief.

What happened? Cam asked.

The astral tides began to recede, Luik continued, his voice tight with sadness. *At first, it was subtle, like a flicker in the stars. But over the centuries, we felt it more and more. The astral energy that sustained us was fading, vanishing from Avoni's soil. We tried everything to find out why. None of our scholars could explain it.*

Cam could sense Luik's anger rising as he spoke.

We were being...confined. By who or what method, I do not know. Slowly, we were pushed back, unable to leave the Vorunis Citadel, the last bastion of astral energy. Our forms weakened. Our essence drained. We were prisoners in the land we once ruled.

That's when the humans came to us. They saw the void left by our fading power, saw the lands ripe for the taking. And we—weak, desperate—had no choice but to make a deal with them. The Treaty of the Tethering.

Humans offered us survival, a chance to stay Tethered to this world. But the price was our servitude. The treaty bound us to them. Each of us Tethered to a human, our very existence reliant on the astral link we shared with them. And in return for our survival, we were to serve their royal family.

So, Cam started thinking, *you can't manifest in an autonomous body? You're always trapped?*

That is correct. We sacrificed our autonomy for life...if you can even call this life. It is my dream that someday we may be able to leave this bondage and be our own people again.

And you served the Avonian king before the Sundering? Cam thought.

The Sundering? Luik responded. *Is that what you call the corruptive force that covers Avoni?*

No. The Sundering was the event that brought about the corruption. How do you not know this?

I merged with the Aetherfern plant to save myself just before this Sundering took place, Luik responded.

You knew it was coming? Cam asked.

Yes. In fact, I was one of the Elmias who tried to stop it, Luik replied. As the words appeared in Cam's head, he could sense a deep conflict and guilt inside of Luik. *Unfortunately for both of our kind, we failed, though your presence here suggests part of our plan worked.*

A sudden revelation pierced through the fog of Cam's thoughts.

Did you create the Aurora Shrouds? He could sense the words brought confusion to Luik.

The Aurora Shrouds?

The protective barriers around the different settlements in Avoni. Without them, we would be doomed.

Ah, I understand now. It pleases me to know that that part of our plan succeeded. We wanted to keep population centers safe. We saved as many as we could, Luik responded. *But we didn't create anything. We just established a boundary to keep out the effects of the Scepter of Alderia.*

Cam furrowed his brow.

The Scepter of Alderia? he wondered.

It is an Elmia artifact. It's a tool designed by our engineers to invert physical and astral energies. It also helps to amplify the natural abilities of an Elmia. Our engineers had hoped the Scepter could be used to create more astral Nexus Points for my people.

Cam nodded, taking in this new information. Luik continued.

Another Elmia, and his disciples, used the Scepter in an attempt to return Avoni to its previous state where it was full of astral energy and Elmias had their own autonomy, not having to rely on being Tethered to a human. Unfortunately, he only succeeded in creating a chaotic reality where both astral and physical energies were combined. It is an abomination that would transform all living creatures into monsters.

Well, Luik, that's exactly what happened. Why did the other Elmia do this?

His name is Gaalron, Luik said, his voice growing serious. *He swore to not rest until the Elmias were free of the humans and could exist as our own people again.*

This Gaalron...he tried to kill us all? Cam thought.

Absolutely not. By seeking to transform Avoni, he wasn't trying to harm humans. He thought he could rewrite reality so that Elmias could survive independent of humans. Unfortunately, he would not listen to our scholars who insisted that mixing astral and physical energies would create this oppressive and corruptive environment.

So, you can't survive in the Sundered Lands? Cam asked.

Not for long, Luik answered firmly. *An astral being would be transformed into something monstrous.*

Like a scaletaint?

Is that what you call those creatures? Those are transformed humans. No, we would transform into something different.

As Luik spoke, Cam raised his right hand to his eyes. The reptilian claw he saw was alien to him. It was hard to believe that it was his own hand.

Oh my! Luik exclaimed when he saw it. *It appears we found each other at the perfect time. You were about to become one of them.*

Luik, I need to get out of here, before I transform completely. I need to get to an Aurora Shroud.

Luik's response was calm and clear.

No, you are safe. We have merged, and you are now a being that walks in two planes: physical and astral. This world, outside of your Aurora Shrouds, cannot transform you.

Understanding dawned on Cam.

That explains why the air doesn't hurt to breathe, he thought.

A strange sense of peace enveloped him. Throughout his entire life, the Sundered Lands had been a menacing threat. However, as he stood in the midst of this transformed landscape, he felt an unexpected liberation. The once-dreaded lands seemed to have lost their grip on him.

In a symbolic gesture of defiance and celebration, Cam took a deep, invigorating breath of air.

No, the Sundered Lands were no longer his enemy.

Cam, he thought. *My name is Cam.* He could feel Luik's satisfaction in the demonstration of trust.

Thank you, Cam. Tell me, what is your business out here in such a dangerous place?

Choosing to extend his trust, Cam began to unravel the tapestry of his world for the Elmia dwelling within him. He delved into the intricacies of the Vanguard, explaining the significance of their role in Avonian society.

He only spared one detail.

He refused to tell him what happened to Silva.

So, you are traveling to Rath as a backup, in case the others cannot make it?

Yes. We're only a few hours away by horseback, although I'm not sure where my horse ran off to, Cam responded. *I'll need to make my way on foot.*

It will be dangerous, Luik interjected. *Do you have any weapons with you?*

Suddenly, Cam remembered. He'd dropped his daggers on the bridge. The peace he had been feeling suddenly descended into panic. The thought of being alone in the Sundered Lands without a weapon turned his stomach into knots.

He turned and started walking towards the bridge in the distance and felt Luik's anxiety flare.

Cam, didn't you say that you were attacked crossing the river? And now you want to go up unarmed? Those scaletaints are still out there.

Cam ignored him. Without his weapons, he felt completely exposed and at risk.

Please stop, Luik commanded. *If you die, I die as well. There must be a safer way to do this.*

This is the Sundered Lands, Cam retorted. *I'm safest if I'm armed.*

In the recesses of their mental connection, he sensed a subtle inner conflict within Luik. The Elmia grappled with indecision, wavering between the choice to withhold information and the inclination to share it. After a moment of hesitation, Luik opted to break his silence.

Please, don't do this. Not yet. Let me teach you something.

Chapter 15

As Cam stepped towards the bridge, a cold sweat slicked his palms, and he wiped them hastily on his pants, but it didn't help. His heart pounded so loud he was certain Luik could hear it. His breath hitched, each inhale shallower than the last.

Cam, are you alright? Luik asked.

I need my weapons. I have to—Aurora's Name. It's happening again.

What's happening?

The fear was beginning to take hold.

A sharp pang of self-loathing stabbed through him. His hands balled into fists at his sides, nails digging into his palms hard enough to hurt. Shoving his emotions down, he crouched and took another step towards the bridge.

Crouching in this manner is not likely to mask your approach. You're just too big. It's like trying to sneak a horse into a church by placing it in priest's robes, Luik said.

Cam ignored him.

As he crept closer, he could see some of his belongings. There were a few arrows that had fallen out of his quiver and now lay scattered on the ground. There was also an arrow sticking out of the eye of a now-deceased scaletaint. In the middle of the bridge's arch, by the stone railing, was his dagger.

Just wait one moment, sir. Give me a chance to—

Cam ignored Luik's plea, dashing forward.

He knew that once his hands gripped his twin daggers, he would feel in control of himself again.

He decided to ignore the arrows scattered on the ground. He'd lost his bow when he fell in the river, so they'd be of little use to him now. Rather, he sprinted directly at his dagger, its blade reflecting the swirling red sky above.

After only a few steps, a scaletaint lunged from the side, muscles coiling and releasing in a single violent motion, its claws outstretched and jaws snapping for him. Cam twisted away at the last instant, but the creature landed in a low crouch between him and his dagger, cutting off his path.

It bared its teeth and hissed before charging at the weaponless Cam.

Just before it reached him, Cam's vision narrowed. His hand shot out, but not toward the dagger lying just out of reach. It was a blind, desperate gesture, as if his body was acting on instinct, driven by something deeper than conscious thought.

And then something strange happened.

Time seemed to slow, the noise around him fading until all he could hear was the beat of his own heart. A cold pulse surged from deep within his chest, rushing down his arm. His fingers curled, as if reaching for something already there.

Darkness gathered in his hand. A blade took shape, weightless and cold, its edge flickering like smoke. It felt less like a weapon and more like a part of him.

His heart pounded harder.

Without hesitation, he thrust the blade forward, driving it into the scaletaint's open mouth. The creature's hiss caught in its throat, eyes wide with shock as it fell.

The blade vanished. A chill snapped back up his arm, leaving Cam shaking in its wake.

Darkness crept into the edges of his vision as an unexpected weakness seized him. Cam, grappling with the sudden onset, managed to take only a few unsteady steps forward before succumbing to the overwhelming force within him. He fell quickly, collapsing to his knees as the world mercilessly spun around him.

I warned you, Cam, Luik's voice chided him in his mind.

Closing his eyes, Cam took several deep breaths, each inhalation a deliberate effort to anchor himself. A moment later, the weakness began to subside.

Luik, what was that? Inside him, he could feel Luik taking a slight, judgmental pleasure in Cam's suffering. They could feel the other's emotions, but apparently, Luik was not impacted by the physical weakness Cam felt.

Before the Sundering, we called it Soul-Forging.

What? Cam thought, blinking weary eyes. He gritted his teeth, trying to remain conscious.

It's part of an art we call Tethering, Luik said, his voice curling through Cam's mind. *Through it, we Elmias can shape the astral world and bring fragments of it into yours. What just happened—that was Soul-Forging. I used your spirit as a conduit and forged a weapon from it. A blade formed from your very essence.*

Cam's stomach turned. *Is that...is that why I feel this way now?*

Yes. Again, please accept my apologies. I did try to warn you, though.

Slowly rising to his feet, Cam emitted a soft groan. He shook his head as if dispelling lingering traces of fatigue. Feeling his strength being restored, he took purposeful steps toward his dagger, the metallic glint of its blade catching the ambient light.

As he walked past the dead scaletaint, Cam could feel Luik's emotions lurch, clearly disgusted by the display.

You have a weak stomach, don't you? thought Cam.

Sir, in my Tethered state, I have no stomach.

Cam shook his head. *I mean, what just happened to this scaletaint. You found that disturbing.*

Elmias are a scholarly people. We believe all violence is disturbing and unnatural.

True, but better unnatural than us dead, Cam thought wryly. *Speaking of which, is there anything else I should know about our Tethering? I'd hate to accidentally hurt myself.*

Many things, Luik's voice echoed in Cam's mind.

Cam bent down and picked up his dagger. The brass handle felt cold in his hand.

Care to explain them, so I don't get caught off guard again?

It's better for me to explain where the power comes from, Luik responded. *It is all part of the art of Tethering. When I Tether to you, I can reach through the Astral Plane and touch aspects of the physical world.*

Cam frowned. *I'm...I'm not sure I understand.*

You humans are so frustrating! You never change, Luik chastised. He was silent for a few moments before he spoke again. *Perhaps it is easier to show you. Do you remember the Aetherfern plant I was trapped in?*

Yes.

Suddenly, the world morphed around Cam. Everything spun with dizzying speed, a kaleidoscope of shifting shapes and colors distorting his vision. The familiar stone bridge and the roaring river vanished, replaced by the towering presence of the Aetherfern plant.

He abruptly found himself standing amidst its colossal leaves and branches. A grunt escaped him as he stumbled forward, grappling with the sudden and bewildering change in his surroundings.

Verdalink, explained Luik. *The Elmia using this ability finds an object high in astral energy—such as an Aetherfern—and uses it as an anchor. This transforms it into a temporary doorway. Upon entering the plant, your consciousness travels along the Astral Plane, bypassing physical obstacles, and emerges from another suitable plant at the chosen destination.*

And...does it always make people so dizzy? Cam asked.

Unfortunately, yes, Luik answered. *The farther you travel, the more disoriented you'll become. Traverse more than a few miles, and you could lose all sense of direction and spatial awareness. You could even pass out.*

Cam gave a slight nod, suddenly feeling a strange dizziness settling within him.

Also, while the Aetherfern plant is a superior anchor, it's possible to use other objects as anchors, provided they're high in astral energy.

What makes Aetherfern different? Why is it a superior anchor? Cam thought.

Aetherfern has a particularly strong connection to the astral world, Luik explained. As he did so, Cam could feel Luik's sense of pride rising. *When I served in the Vorunis Citadel, my project was to establish this particular connection in plants. This is how the Aetherfern was first cultivated.*

Cam stepped back, stunned.

You created the Aetherfern?

"Created" is the wrong word. I simply strengthened its astral connection.

Cam got the sense that the Elmia was choosing to be very humble. In his heart, he could feel the pride and accomplishment welling up inside him. It brought a smile to Cam's face.

How did you do that?

It was incredibly complicated and involved me mixing bits of my blood with the seeds of the plant. It took me decades to determine the correct mixture. Decades more for the plant to truly flourish and spread across Avoni.

Decades upon decades. Cam raised a curious eyebrow, wondering just how ancient this Elmia was.

How old are you? Cam asked.

Ancient. I am old enough to remember when all of Avoni was covered in astral energy, and the Elmias were able to survive autonomously.

And you don't know why all the astral energy went away?

Elmia scholars have spent centuries seeking the answer to that question. It is still a mystery.

Although Luik's voice was calm and even, Cam could sense a pained longing emanating from the Elmia. Deciding not to press the matter further, he changed the subject.

What else can you do? he thought, feeling both cautious and curious. *What other powers can you access?*

I will not answer that question just yet, responded Luik in a dry tone. *I do not know if I trust you. I've only told you enough to escape from danger.*

For reasons unclear to him, Cam found a strange mix of frustration and satisfaction in Luik's response. It was as if the Elmia's cryptic explanation, while not entirely enlightening, held a certain reassurance that intrigued and, in an odd way, comforted him.

That's fine, Luik. I suppose you've essentially saved my life today. You're entitled to keep a few secrets.

I was actually using you to save my life, Luik said.

Regardless, Cam continued, *I need to get to Rath. That's where I was going when I was attacked. I intend to go there, but...* He trailed off for a moment, unsure of how to describe what he was feeling.

You feel as if you are taking me against my will, Luik said.

The degree to which Luik could sense Cam's emotions was more than unsettling.

I apologize for any discomfort you feel regarding our connection, Luik said.

"Stop doing that," Cam said, speaking out loud. "My feelings are my own."

Unfortunately, I cannot stop. We are Tethered, and I cannot break the Tether without being in an astral Nexus Point. Also, you don't need to speak out loud. I am able to hear your thoughts just fine.

"That's exactly why I'm speaking out loud," Cam muttered. "I should be the only one able to hear my thoughts."

If it's any consolation, our arrangement makes me uncomfortable as well.

The thought brought little comfort.

Turning away, he directed his steps toward the nearby dirt road. The path stretched ahead of him, a narrow strip of trodden earth flanked by overgrown grass and scattered rocks.

"I'm going to travel to Rath," he said. "If there are any Nexus Points around, let me know. At least you can have the option of coming with me then."

There are none, but I appreciate your sentiment.

Cam turned and began trekking down the path towards Rath. Above him, the sky brooded in angry hues, casting an ominous glow upon the desolate expanse. As he walked, he felt Luik observing the world around him. They journeyed in silence for a while before Luik spoke again.

Avoni has changed significantly.

"What were things like before all this?" Cam said.

Before the Sundering?

"No. What was it like before you needed humans to survive?"

It was beautiful. Avoni was such a powerful nation. There was such prosperity and peace. As Luik spoke, Cam could sense the Elmia's yearning and nostalgia.

"You must miss it."

I miss simple things, like the feeling of the wind. Feeling the warmth of the sun on my face. Knowing that my thoughts and emotions are private, known only to myself.

Cam nodded silently. After a moment, he glanced down at his left hand, curious as to why the image of an Aetherfern had been imprinted there.

Luik must have felt Cam's curiosity, for he answered the question before it was asked.

That is the symbol of our Tether. Any human Tethered to an Elmia will receive a similar mark.

"Are there other Elmias in Avoni?" Cam asked. A sense of guilt and shame welled up inside of Luik.

Perhaps, but I doubt it. To be honest, I would prefer we discuss other things.

He is strange, thought Cam.

I can hear you, Luik responded, causing Cam to flush.

This was going to take some getting used to.

Chapter 16

Chek slipped through the narrow alley, her right foot making a slight scraping sound as it dragged on the damp, uneven cobblestones. The stench of rot and mildew clung to the air, mingling with the faint, sickly-sweet scent of Emberroot smoke. Somewhere deeper in the alley, she spotted a man slumped against the wall, his eyes half-lidded from the drug. His fingers twitched erratically, tracing invisible patterns in the air.

She didn't slow her pace. Emberroot users weren't her problem.

Not tonight.

The man she was here to meet was waiting further in, where the alley narrowed and the shadows grew thicker. A faint orange glow from a nearby lantern barely reached him, casting his form in sharp relief against the brick wall.

Chek's stomach knotted as she approached. She hated needing help, but she didn't know where else to turn.

"You're late," the Vanguard Courier muttered, not turning his head as she stepped closer.

Chek crossed her arms, her voice flat. "I'm here, aren't I?"

The Courier finally looked at her, his face partially hidden by a hood, eyes gleaming with a cold edge. He gave her a quick once-over, unimpressed. "This better be good. I don't make a habit of doing business in alleyways."

Chek smirked slightly. "Funny. You seem right at home."

The Courier grunted, his expression unchanging. "What do you want?"

Chek glanced over her shoulder once, checking to make sure no one was watching. The Emberroot addict in the corner hadn't moved, his vacant stare still locked on nothing in particular. Satisfied, she took a deep breath and turned back to the Courier.

"Help getting out of Rath. I need an escort across the Sundered Lands," she said, her voice low but direct.

For the first time, the Courier's expression shifted. His eyes widened in disbelief, a bitter laugh escaping his lips.

"You're joking," he said, shaking his head. "That's illegal. You know that, right? No one's allowed to take anyone without clearance through the Sundered Lands." His eyes flitted down to her right leg. "Let alone someone like you."

"I know it's illegal," Chek replied, trying to keep her voice steady. "But I know that many Couriers do it anyway. For the right price."

The Courier scoffed. "You think you can just flash a few coins and I'll risk my life, my job, everything, to haul you through there? No way." He pushed himself off the wall, about to leave.

Chek moved quickly, reaching into her jacket and pulling out a small, tightly wrapped pouch. She held it out to him, her hand unwavering. "This is all I have, but I think it should cover it."

The Courier eyed the pouch, then sneered, his lips curling in disdain. He snatched it from her hand, weighing it in his palm before unwrapping it. His fingers brushed over the coins, his mouth twisting into a humorless grin.

"This?" he said, chuckling darkly. "This is nothing. You think this'll be enough to get me to drag you across the deadliest stretch of land in existence?"

Chek's jaw tightened. "Please. I...I have to get out of Rath."

He tossed the pouch back at her, the coins rattling as they hit the ground at her feet. "Not enough. Not even close."

She bent down, gathering the coins, her fingers trembling as she tucked them back into her jacket.

The Courier's gaze hardened as he stepped closer, his voice dropping to an angry growl. "Let me guess. You think because you've got a bit of fight in you, you're tough enough to survive out there? Stupid girl. I've seen people ten times stronger than you get ripped apart, torn to shreds by things you couldn't even imagine. You? You'd be dead within an hour."

Chek straightened, forcing herself to meet his stare. "I've survived this long. I'd manage."

He barked a laugh, shaking his head. "Sure, you might've scraped by here, but the Sundered Lands?" He leaned in closer, his breath hot on her face. "You think you'd survive with that limp of yours? You'd probably need me to carry you before we even left the Shroud. You'd just be a corpse waiting to happen."

Chek clenched her fists at her sides, her nails biting into her palms.

The Courier glared at her. "And who's this for, huh? You? Or someone else? Because trust me, if you think you're going to play protector out there, you're delusional."

Chek's voice came out colder than she intended. "I don't need you to believe in me. I just need you to get me through. I'd go on my own, but I—"

"Need protection?" She froze, and a satisfied smile came to his lips. "That's what I thought." His eyes flicked toward the entrance of the alley, as if considering walking away right then and there. "And what happens when that limp of yours turns you into dead weight? When you're *responsible* for someone else getting killed?"

Her patience frayed. "Felix and I will handle ourselves."

The Courier raised an eyebrow, his smirk deepening. "Felix? Is that who you're dragging through the Shroud with you? Some poor fool with no idea what he's in for?"

Chek didn't answer. She wouldn't give him the satisfaction. Her eyes stayed locked on his, cold and unflinching.

The Courier shook his head slowly. "Everyone thinks they can handle the Sundered Lands. And then they go out there. There's a reason so few people ever try to escape."

"What about the Sundered Shadows?" Chek asked, desperate. "Can you just take me to them?"

He looked surprised, as if he didn't expect the question.

"You...you want me to take you to the Cult of Sundered Shadows?"

Chek nodded. "I have to get out of Rath."

He chuckled.

"I admit it. You've either got lots of guts or your judgment's impaired, because there's no way I'd want to be anywhere near those crazies."

"I don't think it's crazy to want to live outside of the Aurora Shrouds."

"It is crazy, because it's impossible," he growled. "They don't exist. And even if they did, I'd want nothing to do with them."

He began to turn away, as if he'd had enough of the conversation, but Chek stepped forward, her voice cutting through the alley. "Name your price. I'll pay it."

The Courier stopped, glancing back at her with an amused expression. "Price? I told you, there's no price you can pay that would convince any Courier to help guide a cripple through the Sundered Lands."

"Then tell me what *is* enough," Chek said, her voice hard. "Because I'm not walking away."

For a moment, the Courier didn't respond. He studied her with a mixture of curiosity and contempt, as if weighing whether or not he believed her. Finally, he said, "Well that's a good thing. Because you're awfully bad at it." Turning, he left.

Chek stood there, her fists clenched and her breath coming in sharp, uneven bursts.

"I'll find a way," she whispered.

She always did.

Chapter 17

The remainder of the trip to Rath took longer than what Cam was used to. What should have been a day's journey on horseback turned into an arduous four-day trek through the wilderness. He had ventured far off the established Safe Paths, and the roads he traveled on hadn't been maintained in over a century, so there were many places where it was completely overgrown with plant life.

In spite of his initial discomfort with Luik, Cam found himself grateful for the Elmia's presence. Through their strange Tethering, the constant pain of the Sundered Lands was completely gone, its harsh grip loosening on Cam for the first time in his life.

The air no longer clawed at his lungs, burning with every breath. Gone were the sudden fevers, the boils that erupted on his skin, and most importantly, the terrifying, creeping signs of scaletaint transformation.

Luik might be an unwelcome guest, but he was also a shield.

Throughout the journey, Luik remained mostly quiet. If it weren't for the visible tattoo on his left arm, Cam would have forgotten that he was even there. Occasionally, Luik would speak up, making an observation about the environment or asking questions about the state of the world.

So, Avoni has no formal leader? he asked at one point in wonder. *Who takes care of the people?*

"Each settlement has its own leadership. Some are run by a council of elders, while others elect individual leaders. They coordinate across settlements through the Vanguard."

It's like each settlement is its own small nation, Luik had mused thoughtfully in response.

"That sounds accurate to me, but Avoni hasn't had interactions with other nations since the Sundering occurred. No one here understands international politics anymore."

That makes sense. How do you organize against the scaletaints?

"Scaletaints tend to operate in hordes. If a Vanguard Courier or Scout sees evidence of scaletaint activity, they have a Route Coordinator dispatch the Rangers to deal with them."

Are there other creatures in addition to these scaletaints? Luik asked.

Cam nodded.

"In the early years after the Sundering, there were all kinds of monsters roaming the Sundered Lands. Most of them died out, though. Every now and then, an animal escapes an Aurora Shroud and transforms, but that's about it. It's mostly just scaletaints and transformed birds out here. Lots of bugs too. The Necrothorn Beetles are a nightmare."

Do the scaletaints not die out? How are there so many still out here?

Cam shrugged.

"I assume they die, but humans seem to be the one creature that consistently leaves the safety of the Shroud."

Cam could sense Luik's confusion.

Why do people try to escape the Shrouds?

"You try being trapped in one place for your entire life. It's awful."

Luik's anger flared up in a wave that startled Cam.

Much of my life has been spent trapped, Luik said, his tone bitter. *Before the Treaty of the Tethering, I was trapped in the Vorunis Citadel. After the treaty, I was trapped inside the body of my Tether. Since the Sundering, I have been trapped in a plant. I haven't felt the ground beneath my feet or the sun on my face in almost two centuries. Humans know nothing of what it means to be trapped.*

Cam stood stunned for a moment.

"I...I'm sorry. It—"

Luik was silent for a few breaths, his presence simmering with restrained frustration. Cam could feel him wrestling with the weight of his own words before a long sigh slipped through their connection.

No, please accept my apologies, Luik said. Cam could feel his regret at the sudden outburst. *I will speak more respectfully of your kind in the future. It...it has been difficult for the Elmias for many, many years. I only yearn for the day that I can operate as my autonomous self again.*

Though the Elmia's tone was respectful, Cam could feel the undercurrent of conflicting emotions in him.

"I have no idea what that must be like. I'm so sorry," Cam said, a pang of empathy running through him.

It is not the fault of the humans that I am in this predicament, Luik whispered. As he spoke, his feelings hardened into bitterness. *It is the fault of Gaalron and the Elmias who were unable to stop him.*

"What happened to you all?"

Let us speak of this another time.

Cam could sense twinges of guilt and regret in the Elmia. He decided not to press the issue. "Anyway, yeah. That's the story of the scaletaints and why there are so many still out here."

It is fascinating that they still prefer the company of other scaletaints, Luik said, his mood perking up. *Perhaps it is because they have a soul, while the corrupted animals do not. This would make for an excellent opportunity for scholarship, if we have the time.*

"I doubt we'll have the time to study the social habits of scaletaints. I'm not even sure how we'd do that."

Oh, but I do! We'd need to collect several of them. We'd need some to be in a control group—perhaps we could build a large fence to contain them, while others would be given different tests. Given enough time, I—

"That's not happening," Cam said, feeling Luik's dejection as he did so.

In spite of the many obstacles that had marked his arduous journey, Cam finally reached the outskirts of Rath. He could see the edge of the Aurora Shroud and the tops of the city's many buildings.

The heart of the community lay within the network of mines that riddled the earth beneath the surface. Industrial chimneys punctuated the skyline, exhaling plumes of smoke that mingled with the ever-present red haze of the Sundered Lands.

Ah. The grand city of Rath. I've visited a few times.

"Only a few?"

This city is not an astral Nexus Point. For me to come here, I would need a human Tether. As my assignment was the study of plants, my Tether and I spent most of our time in more agrarian communities.

"Who were you Tethered to?" Cam asked, curiosity piqued.

I do not wish to speak of this, Luik said, his tone flat.

"Fine, suit yourself. In a few minutes, we'll—"

"Halt! Stop right where you are!" a harsh voice called out.

Alarmed, Cam did as commanded, his eyes darting around the rocky landscape to see who had shouted at him. A group of twelve men stood up from small holes dug into the rocky terrain, and their armor was a perfect mimic of the surrounding landscape.

Three of the men pulled out swords and approached him, while the others nocked arrows and pointed them at Cam. Their leader stepped forward, a middle-aged man with short hair where gray mingled with brown. His eyes bore an intense and mistrustful gaze, assessing Cam with a sharp scrutiny. As he advanced, the distinctive clink of armor echoed through the air.

Is it typical for a city to place soldiers in the Sundered Lands? Luik asked.

No. This is different, Cam thought, shocked.

He instinctively raised his hands to show he meant no harm. This ended up being a mistake. The leader's eyes darted straight to Cam's transformed right hand, the scaly claw reflecting the light in the sky above.

"Crimson Limbo!" the leader shouted. "Crimson Limbo Courier!"

Soldiers rushed forward. Two held a large net, while others leveled spears at him. Cam's eyes darted around in bewilderment.

"Is this how you treat the Vanguard?" Cam asserted. "I'm not here to hurt anyone. I've come bearing a message from Kevilton."

The leader eyed Cam suspiciously and nodded to one of the spear-wielding soldiers. The soldier put away his weapon and walked up to Cam.

"Keep your hands raised," he huffed as he circled Cam. He took his daggers away and then patted him down to make sure he had no other weapons. After he was satisfied that Cam was unarmed, he stepped back and nodded to his leader.

The leader strode forward. He took a few moments to look over Cam, who still had his hands raised, as if he were unsure of what to do with the man in front of him. Finally, he said, "What Courier travels the Sundered Lands with only daggers?"

"One who lost many of his belongings in a scaletaint attack," Cam answered back.

Is this a typical greeting for Vanguard Couriers? Luik inquired inside his mind.

No, Cam answered back. *Something is very wrong about all of this.*

"How long have you been in the Sundered Lands?" the leader asked again.

I believe it is prudent to err on the side of secrecy here, Luik suggested. Cam agreed.

"I left Runara almost three days ago," Cam lied. Feigning weakness, he added, "Please. I must enter the city."

The leader's face softened slightly, an expression of conflicted empathy crossing his weathered expression. After a moment, he said, "My name is Holt. I am a captain here at Rath. I'm afraid you won't find the city to be the sanctuary it used to be."

A frown creased Cam's brow. "What happened here?"

Holt, with a solemn shake of his head, gestured to his men. One among them retrieved a rope and expertly bound Cam's hands behind his back.

"Come with me," Holt said. As he did so, most of the archers put their arrows back in their quivers, although a few kept one ready to be shot. The soldiers kept their spears out, as well.

In a matter of minutes, they ascended the rugged terrain. As they trekked, Cam noticed that there was a large stone wall surrounding the city.

A wall in the Sundered Lands. What do you think happened here? Luik said, his voice speculative.

No clue. This is strange, Cam thought back.

A few minutes later, they crossed the Aurora Shroud and entered the Eastern Gate.

Cam had been to Rath many times, but never to the Eastern District. His routes had always taken him through the other parts of the city, places that, while worn and weary, still clung to some sense of normalcy.

He'd heard the rumors. None of it had prepared him for the reality.

As Cam moved through the narrow streets, the air felt thick with unease. People huddled in small groups, their eyes darting nervously, hollow cheeks and gaunt faces betraying their hunger. Others sat slumped in corners, their twitching fingers and purple hair revealing signs of heavy Emberroot usage.

A few of the citizens scratched at angry red boils on their mottled skin. Cam raised an eyebrow.

"Rath's people are getting the sickness too?"

"It's the Eastern District," Holt grunted. "The people are always sick."

The soldiers led Cam down the street and turned into a small, dimly lit structure, the flickering lamps casting long, wavering shadows across the bare walls. The room was mostly bare. A lone desk sat pushed into the corner, cluttered with papers and empty bottles, while in the center of the room stood a cage, its iron bars dark and foreboding.

I guess that cage is for me? thought Cam.

For us, corrected Luik. A moment later, Cam thought he heard Luik chuckling.

What's so funny?

I am trapped in our Tethering, caged, and in a locked building. In other words, I am in a cage within a cage within a cage. That's funny!

You have a strange sense of humor.

Apologies if my perspective on life seems strange. I was trapped by myself in an Aetherfern plant for over a century.

The soldiers guided Cam into the cage, their grip firm on his arms. As they moved to untie the ropes binding his wrists, Cam rolled his shoulders and gave them a sideways glance. Before their hands could even reach the knot, he flexed his arms with a sharp, practiced motion, and the rope snapped with a satisfying crack. He smirked as the frayed strands fell to the floor, the guards pausing mid-reach, caught between surprise and frustration.

"Don't worry," Cam muttered, rubbing his wrists. "I've got it."

"Didn't know we'd be rounding up giants. Maybe we could sell tickets," a guard said with a scoff. This earned a stern look from Holt.

The soldiers retreated, leaving him isolated within the confines of the cage. The door slammed shut with a resounding clang that echoed through the small space. The lock clicked into place, sealing Cam in with an audible finality that reverberated in the stillness of the chamber.

As the soldiers made their exit, Holt approached Cam with measured steps. Although his words carried the weight of command and determination, a subtle conflict played out in his eyes, revealing an inner turmoil at the necessity of treating Cam in such a manner.

"We need to ensure that your mind hasn't been impacted by the transformation," he explained. Despite the authority in his voice, there was a palpable lack of satisfaction, an unspoken reluctance that lingered beneath the surface of his firm demeanor.

"Another Courier should have arrived before me," Cam replied. "His name is Soren, and he was traveling with a Healer named Illyria. Are they here?"

Holt shrugged in indifference.

"It's possible, but I haven't heard of him. I wouldn't know, though. If they are here, they didn't come through my outpost. I'll let my superiors know that you've asked about them." With that, he turned and left the building.

Perhaps all humans should be forced to spend some time in a cage. It would give them a unique perspective into what life is like for the Elmias. Luik's voice, although lighthearted, had a slight edge to it.

I have a feeling that your suggestion wouldn't be well received, Cam thought.

One would think this to be the case, yet you let yourself be caged quite willingly.

They'll let me out as soon as they realize I'm not dangerous.

Glancing up at the three guards in the room, Cam said, "I'm very hungry. I've been traveling through the Sundered Lands. I lost my horse and had to finish the journey on foot. Please, is there anything I can eat?"

The guards nodded to each other, and one grabbed a bag and opened it. Inside was a loaf of bread. He cut off a section and then brought it over to the cage.

"Stand on the far side."

Cam obeyed, and the guard tossed the bread through the bars to him. Cam moved quickly, catching the loaf so that it would not hit the dusty ground.

"We'll get you something more substantial soon," the soldier added, a touch of empathy in his voice. "We just need to make sure you're safe."

His mouth full of bread, Cam said, "What happened here? No Courier has ever received this treatment in Rath or any other settlement."

A dark expression crossed the guard's face. He turned and walked back over to the large desk in the corner. In a quiet voice, he muttered, "Death came here. The end is coming."

Part Three
A Hastening Decay

The Elmias are people in every sense that word can bear—capable of joy and sorrow, loyalty and treachery, vision and folly.

The earliest credible records, if one can call them such, reach back over ten millennia. These fragments are maddeningly incomplete, and no serious academic can claim to verify them beyond reasonable doubt.

Shadow Two

Lucian

L ucian closed his eyes and drew in a deep breath of the Sundered Lands' air. The corruption no longer burned his lungs. It hadn't in decades. A faint smile tugged at his lips. In that time, he had begun to build something that would change all of Alderia.

He opened his eyes. Standing just a few feet in front of him was Rath's Aurora Shroud. From where he was standing, the city on the other side looked fuzzy and yellow, the slight blur the result of a faint visual distortion from the Shroud. The hour was late, so he couldn't see any people in Rath.

It had been roughly forty years since he'd first seen what an Aurora Shroud looked like from the outside. Desperate to escape a lifetime of being trapped in one place, Lucian had volunteered for the Vanguard as soon as he could. His first trip through the Sundered Lands had been painful, but the pain paled in comparison to the freedom that he felt being able to finally journey beyond the Shroud.

Contrary to the rules of the Vanguard, he'd begun exploring the Sundered Lands on his own, venturing far off the established Safe Paths. As the years went by, he went further and further, learning what he could from the corrupted lands. Mastering them. Learning their secrets.

It was then that he'd found the Grove.

More accurately, it was then that he had found someone.

Lucian glanced down at his left hand. There, starting at the tips of his fingers and circling up his arm, was a tattoo of a vibrant green Aetherfern. In the decades since he'd encountered the Elmia, he'd completely abandoned the Vanguard. For all they knew, he had died somewhere in the Sundered Lands.

He closed his eyes again, willing the Elmia he had Tethered to seek out his acolytes. All of his followers wore specially designed armor that helped to resist the effects of the Sundered Lands. The armor was extremely high in astral energy, thereby making it easier for his Elmia to find them.

Sensing his will, the Elmia reached out through the Astral Plane, locating his followers. Because of the strength of their bond, Lucian was able to discern their locations as well. Most were still in the cave. Only a trusted few were ever allowed to leave.

He gave a slow nod, satisfied that none of his followers were attempting escape, and continued waiting.

Several minutes later, motion on the Rath side of the Aurora Shroud caught his eye. He focused as several figures emerged in the Sundered Lands. A few were clad in the black armor of his followers. As they stepped beyond the protection of the Shroud, a grim smile crept up his face.

It was always obvious who had never been in the Sundered Lands before.

Some of the people twinged in discomfort as they crossed the barrier, but showed no other signs of distress. They had likely snuck past the Shroud on their own in the past.

Others had a more dramatic reaction. Their eyes widened in distress as the painful air stung their lungs. One even fell into a coughing and gagging fit.

"Welcome," he said, his voice clear and powerful, "to the Sundered Shadows."

The group of newcomers shifted uncomfortably, nodding at him. The one who had been coughing tried to speak but stopped after falling into another violent fit.

"From this moment forward," Lucian continued, "you obey me. Completely. I am more than your leader." He held his hand out to the side, palm open. The Elmia Tethered to him sensed his intent, forming a Soul-Forged blade in his hand. The Rathian newcomers gasped as the blade appeared from thin air. "I am the Sundered God."

Uncertainty flickered across their faces. A few cast nervous glances towards Lucian's armored followers. After a few moments, the Rathians began to fall on their knees in front of him.

You may dismiss the blade, Lucian thought to his Elmia. The next moment, the blade vanished, smoking away in the air. Gritting his teeth to combat the corresponding dizziness, Lucian stepped forward, holding out his arms towards the group.

"You are all mine. Mine to use as I wish. Fear not, however. The Sundered God rewards loyal followers."

He then approached them, kissing each one of them on the very top of their head. When he had finished, he addressed them again.

"You are all merely Shadows. Shadows cast by my light. And yet, I will use you all to change the world."

"Hail the Sundered God!" one of Lucian's followers shouted.

"Hail the Sundered God!" the Rathians repeated.

Lucian grinned in satisfaction. "Go. I will meet you all at the Jaram Mountains in a few days."

The followers slowly rose to their feet. Without a word, the Rathians followed the men in black armor, heading toward the distant mountains.

Lucian waited.

Only when he was certain they were out of sight did he move forward, stopping mere inches from the edge of the Aurora Shroud. He extended his hand and placed it flat against the barrier.

The moment his skin met the surface, sensation bloomed. The Shroud's energy throbbed beneath his palm, slow and hot, like fire pressing against the sky. And beneath that pulse, he felt something else. Something more subtle.

The tremor of decay. The slow unraveling.

Let's speed this up, shall we? Lucian's Elmia said in his mind.

In the decades he had traveled with the Elmia, they had crossed many lands together. Not only through the Sundered regions, but beyond, past the borders of corruption, into the fractured nations that lay scattered across Alderia.

What they found there was chaos. Division. Weakness.

It was then that Lucian understood what the world truly needed.

Leadership.

And who better to lead than the Sundered God?

But uniting Alderia would not begin with thrones or treaties. It would begin with power. With people. With loyalty. To raise an army, he would need followers. And to gather followers, the Aurora Shrouds would have to fall.

The Shrouds were failing on their own, but Lucian could accelerate things a bit. His Elmia called it Lucian's "Complex"—an astral ability, which Lucian could control, that was the result of their unique pairing.

Lucian called it "Energy Inversion." It was a delicate process, like flipping the weight of reality itself. Lucian could convert astral energy into physical force, or reverse the flow, transforming physical energy into its unseen astral form. He often likened it to a cup of water. Empty it, and air rushed in. Fill it again, and the air was forced out. One form always displaced the other.

There were limits, of course, otherwise all of the Aurora Shrouds would have been destroyed. He had to siphon off the energy into actual objects, and he was always limited by what those objects could contain.

He pulled out several Elmia artifacts, carefully laying them down on the ground in front of him. He'd found each of them in his journeys through the Sundered Lands. All of them were glowing with astral energy.

With one hand, he lifted the nearest artifact. With the other, he touched the Shroud. A current flowed.

He felt it, subtle but powerful as the barrier's strength flowed into the artifact like breath filling lungs. As the Shroud's energy entered, the artifact's own glow began to dim.

When the exchange was complete, the object was hollow.

He repeated the process. Again. Then again.

Each time, Rath's Aurora Shroud weakened. Each time, another relic went dim.

It is a shame that so many Elmia artifacts must be destroyed in order to rectify this world, Lucian's Elmia said in his head.

We will make new ones, Lucian promised. *Together.*

Through their bond, Lucian could sense the Elmia's conflicted emotions. He could feel the twinges of guilt tugging at the creature, knowing that saving many would mean dooming a few.

Don't worry, Lucian thought, trying to comfort the Elmia. *Once we have the Scepter of Alderia, all will be made right.*

The Elmia scoffed at this. *Once we have the Scepter, we will have no more need for each other.*

True, Lucian agreed. *And yet, I believe our partnership will be a lasting one.*

He stepped back from the dying barrier, eyes on the distant horizon. The gods had abandoned this world long ago. It was time someone took their place.

Chapter 18

Illyria had always found it astounding that Kevilton did not teach Avonian history to its children. Up until recently, she had assumed that her village was unique, but she was quickly learning that the isolation created by the Sundering had done more than just separate settlements. It instilled strong regional biases in which people were largely uneducated in the broader history of their nation, instead being primarily educated about the history of their respective cities.

It was maddening.

"I'm just trying to learn what I can about Avoni before the Sundering," she said, her tone exasperated. She stood in a small bookstore that she had found in Rath's Eastern District. The locals had told her that this was her best chance to learn about Avoni's history. She'd searched through several piles of books, but after a few fruitless minutes, she'd decided to speak to one of the owners.

He was not very helpful.

"Elmia theory is essential to understanding pre-Sundered Avoni!" the young man, who had introduced himself as Felix, said. His dark, bespectacled face was shining with passion as he held out a book titled *The Cultural Anthropology of Elmias, Version 6.*

"There's nothing more I wish to learn of this subject," she insisted. "What I want is to learn about old Avonian culture. Religion, landmarks, holy sites. That sort of thing." She paused for a moment before adding, "Especially holy sites."

Felix nodded insistently.

"That's what I'm saying. Pre-Sundered Avonian culture was tied to the Elmias. You can't study one without studying the other."

Frustrated, Illyria shook her head again.

"That won't be helpful for me. Please, is there anything else here that can help me?"

Felix's shoulders sagged in disappointment. Deflated, he turned and said, "Chek, can I get your help?"

In response, a woman's face poked around the corner. She had dark brown eyes and rich ebony skin, with her brown hair parted in the middle, cascading just past the edges of her face in tight curls. There was an intensity in her expression that was almost unsettling to Illyria, but when she spoke, her tone was friendly.

"Don't let Felix bother you. What do you need?"

"She wants to learn about Avonian holy sites from before the Sundering," Felix said, his tone dour.

Chek nodded, motioning for Illyria to join her before disappearing behind a bookshelf.

Illyria rounded the corner and saw Chek sitting on the ground, surrounded by books, scrolls, and weathered maps strewn haphazardly about on the floor. Despite herself, Illyria chuckled. Apparently, Felix was the organized sibling.

"So," Chek said as she searched through her maps. "You're interested in ancient holy sites?"

"Yes. I just want to learn what I can about our culture before the Sundering."

Chek nodded, still searching through her pile of maps. As she worked, Illyria noticed the patch on her sleeve.

"You're a Vanguard Route Coordinator?"

"That's right," she said without looking up.

"What's a Route Coordinator doing working in a bookstore?"

Chek glanced up briefly, a faint smile playing on her lips. "Space is tight in Rath, so the bookstore doubles as my office. Plus, people around here tend to need help with research more than directions these days." She returned to the many maps and scrolls on the ground. "I end up assisting with scholarly work just as much as routing the Vanguard."

A few moments later, she let out an exasperated sigh before moving to a different pile.

"I really was more curious if you had any books," Illyria said hesitantly. Chek held up a quieting finger as she continued rifling through her disorganized stack. Finally, she found what she was looking for, pulling a map from the pile with a flourish before spreading it on the floor.

"So, Avonian holy sites," she said, her voice calm and direct. "That depends on what period in Avonian history you're interested in."

"What do you mean?" Illyria asked.

"Depending on how far back you go, there could be lots of holy sites. From what I've studied, though, there were only two in Avoni during the time just before the Sundering."

That's what I need.

"And those are?"

Chek raised an eyebrow and held out her hand.

"Not free. I'll need to research this one on my own and pull together a portfolio for you."

Sighing in frustration, Illyria reached a gloved hand into her satchel and pulled out a coin.

Chek shook her head, her expression serious. "That's not enough."

Illyria frowned and pulled out a few more coins. "This should cover it."

The dark-skinned woman glanced at the coins, then back at Illyria with a grim smile. "Prices in Rath have gone up...a lot. Supplies are spread thin, so things are expensive. You'll need to pay four times that if you want anything of value here."

Illyria's eyes widened. "Four times?"

She shrugged, her tone matter-of-fact. "That's the reality we're living in. I'm surprised the Vanguard didn't tell you that. Are you a new Courier?"

"No, I'm a Healer. It's...it's a long story. Anyway, I can't give you what you're asking for. Can you accept half of that?" After she asked the question, Illyria could have sworn that she heard Felix whisper, "I'd research Elmias for free."

After thinking for a moment, Chek said, "Sure. It'll take some time for me to pull everything together, though."

Nodding, Illyria dropped her coins into Chek's outstretched hand.

"Thank you very much!" Chek said before motioning to the map. "Like I said, there were two locations considered holy in the time just before the Sundering. One was the Vorunis Citadel. The other"—she slid her finger across the map—"was located in the Jaram Mountains."

That's what she was looking for.

"Where in the Jaram Mountains?" Illyria said.

"Like I said, I'll need to do some research on that and pull together a portfolio for you to look through. It's possible that we have it in a book. I may need to piece together parts of multiple books, though. Hard to say. Write down where you're staying, and Felix or I will bring it by when it's ready."

Illyria thanked them and left the store.

The streets were crowded, filled with weary faces and bodies pressed too close together, every inch of space claimed by someone or something. People moved quickly, heads down, tension rippling through the crowd like a current, as if a single spark could ignite the unrest simmering beneath the surface.

The buildings rose tall and imposing, their rectangular forms devoid of ornate detail. Soren had once explained that Rath's mining heritage prioritized functionality over aesthetics, resulting in a cityscape characterized by practicality rather than artistry.

Practicality over artistry. Why not just call it ugly? Illyria thought.

As she walked through the city streets, she heard the impassioned shouts of a young newsboy.

"Captain Holt just detained another Crimson Limbo Vanguard Courier!" he shouted repeatedly as he ran.

Illyria's eyes widened with anxiety.

Could it be Cam?

Cam paced the cramped cage, his eyes darting to the door as it creaked open. Holt strode in, carrying a small tin plate that rattled with every step.

All that was on the tray was a hunk of bread and a few dried strips of meat.

Holt approached the cage, his expression revealing a trace of sympathy. He set the plate down on a ledge near the bars, allowing the aromatic steam to rise and mingle with the still air of the enclosure.

"It's not much, but it's best eaten while it's warm," Holt said, his voice carrying genuine concern. "We're not monsters here. Just need to be sure your mind is still your own."

"This is it?" Cam said, staring at the plate. Holt nodded.

"Times are tough in Rath. Tougher than normal."

Cam wanted to ask Holt more questions, but his appetite got the better of him. He reached out and began eating. It wasn't good, but he was so hungry that he didn't mind.

Moments later, the door swung open with a sudden force. In the doorway, silhouetted against the evening sky, stood a mysterious figure draped in a hooded cloak. After surveying the room, the cloaked figure spoke in a delicate yet playful voice.

"Even when caged, Cam still figures out how to get a meal. What is your secret, Courier?"

It was Illyria.

Cam, in the midst of swallowing a mouthful of food, couldn't help but break into a broad smile. Despite the embarrassment of being found in a cage, the joy of seeing a familiar face in the unexpected setting outweighed any sense of vulnerability.

"It's good to see you," he said, rising to his feet and walking to the edge of the cage.

She stepped towards him, attracting the attention of one of the guards.

"Best not do that, lass," he huffed. "We need to make sure he's not going to hurt anyone."

Illyria ignored the guard, walking straight up to the cage. Her movements, measured and deliberate, exuded an air of quiet confidence.

"You shouldn't do that," the guard warned more insistently.

"Can't you see that he's clearly not lost his mind?" Illyria said in exasperation.

"Lady," the guard replied, his tone growing more authoritative. "Look at his right hand."

Up until that point, Cam had kept his hands behind his back. However, after the guard's comment, Illyria looked Cam in the eye and raised an inquisitive eyebrow. With a sigh, he moved his arm, revealing his hand.

Illyria gasped.

"Has a Healer come here to see him?" she asked, a hint of urgency in her voice. The guard shook his head.

"No, he can't see anyone until we know he's safe. It's possible that—"

"Oh for goodness' sake!" Illyria opened a pouch and pulled out a small vial of Aetherfern water. She shook it before offering it to Cam.

"Pour a bit of this on your hand and drink the rest."

He did so. Nothing changed.

Illyria frowned.

"You need more. It'll take me time to prepare." She turned towards the guard, her brow furrowed in anger. "Why didn't you call for a Healer the moment you saw him?"

I could be wrong, but due to our Tethering, and your body existing on both the physical and Astral Plane, it's likely your hand won't return to normal, Luik said.

The guard was about to say something, but Cam cut him off.

"No, Illyria. I'm going to be okay."

Illyria did not seem convinced and responded in a hushed tone, "Your body isn't weathering the corruption very well. Your hand should have transformed back by now, but it is still..." Her voice trailed off as she stared wide-eyed at the monstrous reptilian claw.

"I can't explain right now," Cam said, also in a whisper. "But something happened out there. I...I won't be affected by the corruption."

"What are you talking about? Just look at you. You're Crimson L—"

"I know. And I don't think that's going to change. It's...I don't know how to explain it right now."

Suspicious and confused, Illyria raised an eyebrow at him. She hesitated for a moment before glancing at his left arm.

"You also got a tattoo?" she said incredulously. Cam shook his head.

"No...I...it's a long story. I'll tell you when I get out of here."

"They're not going to let you out with your right hand transformed like that."

"It'll work out," Cam insisted. Illyria looked unconvinced. Before she could ask more questions, he quickly added, "What do you think of Rath?"

She gave a wry grin and shrugged her shoulders.

"You know me. Farm girl at heart. It also looks like I got here at the wrong time. They've declared martial law." She leaned closer to the cage and whispered, "Cam, something is very wrong here."

"You think?" Cam said, nodding his head at the cage bars.

"You need lots of rest. Let's see what we can do to get you out of here, so you can recover somewhere proper."

"I don't know. I feel like this spot is kind of cozy," he said with a bit of a wry smile. Illyria frowned, clearly not appreciating the joke.

She opened her mouth to speak but was interrupted when a new figure stepped in the room.

The man entered with a commanding presence, his frame cutting an imposing figure even in his advanced years. His hair, stark white and neatly combed, framed a stern face etched with deep lines of authority and a lifetime of hard decisions. His eyes were sharp and calculating as they glanced around the room.

Cam knew this man well.

"Hello, Duke Lorian."

"You can call me General Lorian now," the man responded, his voice stern and authoritative. Cam thought he saw Illyria roll her eyes as he spoke.

"General?" Cam asked. "Avoni hasn't had true generals since before the Sundering."

"Avoni hasn't needed generals," Lorian retorted, "because the Sundered Lands kept enemy nations away. However, we stand on the brink of a new kind of war, and the need for true military leadership has returned."

Cam frowned. "Lorian, what—"

"General Lorian," he corrected. Cam narrowed his eyes and began again.

"General Lorian, tell me what happened here. What happened to Rath for it to have set up defenses in the Sundered Lands? What happened that a Vanguard Courier is placed in a cage?"

"What happened? Quite possibly the end of our world."

Lorian turned up his nose and shook his head. He walked towards the desk on the far side of the room. Once there, he picked up a large sheet of paper. He brought it over towards Cam and, using his knife, hung it onto the wall.

It was a map of Avoni. Several of the cities had circles drawn around them, including Rath. Lorian pointed at the map emphatically before speaking.

"I tell you this in confidence. The Aurora Shrouds are beginning to fail. While they still are strong enough to sustain life, there are reports of creatures breaching the barriers. At first, these creatures would die upon arrival. However, things changed."

Cam raised an eyebrow in curiosity. Lorian continued.

"A month ago, a group of scaletaints broke through, infiltrating our water supply. Town guards were able to destroy them, but not before they killed several people. Then, a few days ago, a Courier in Crimson Limbo—such as yourself—arrived. He snapped not long after entering the town, killing even more."

He placed an aged finger on the map, pointing at the circle drawn around Rath.

"And it's not just us. Through the Vanguard, we've learned that this has been happening to settlements all across Avoni."

Cam shook his head slightly and said, "Something similar happened in Runara while I was there. We found a dead bird from the Sundered Lands."

Lorian nodded and pointed at the dot that represented Runara on the map. "So I heard. Local Vanguard has instructed your colleague Soren to travel back to Runara as quickly as possible to warn them of what might come next."

"What comes next? General, what are you talking about? Runara can handle a few scaletaints," Cam said.

As he spoke, Lorian's face darkened. The older man turned, his hand resting on the pommel of his sword. In that fleeting moment, the aura of a battle-hardened general gave way to a man wearied by the weight of despair, resigned to the inevitability of impending doom. He took a deep breath and began speaking again.

"But it won't be just a few scaletaints. Vanguard Scouts are reporting evidence of thousands starting to gather. It's like they can sense that the Shrouds are weakening. But, even if they repel scaletaints, they won't be ready for the Reapers."

Cam furrowed his brow in confusion. The mere mention of these Reapers seemed to drain the hope out of the room. Even the guards standing watch by the cell lowered their eyes as an expression of worry crossed their faces.

Lorian continued. "We weren't ready for the Reapers. Even with all our resources, all our soldiers. We...we just weren't ready. And the people of Rath are still paying the price."

"I don't understand," Cam said. "What are the Reapers?" The question caused Lorian to shake his head.

"I don't know what they were before the Sundered Lands corrupted them. All I know is that they're not like any creature Rath has ever come across." He looked at Cam, ice in his eyes, before continuing. "They're powerful and brutal. Two of them killed over four hundred people in the Northern District before our soldiers finally brought them down."

Cam found his eyes widening in shock. A chill went down his spine.

"Two killed over four hundred? How...how is that even possible?"

"I'll tell you how it's possible," Lorian said, rage simmering as he spoke. "We were unprepared for the most powerful creature the Sundered Lands has ever thrown at us. We simply were not ready. But no more. I placed this city under martial law until I am confident that my people are safe again."

Up until this moment, Illyria had remained quiet. However, as Lorian finished speaking, her eyes flared with anger. Walking up to Cam, she said, "And that's why he's denying Kevilton's request for medicine."

The comment earned a glare from Lorian, who eyed Illyria with disdain.

"General Lorian, without Kevilton, Rath would be at risk of starvation. The city can't produce enough of its own food to support its population," Cam said.

"Our people won't be worrying about food if they're killed in a scaletaint attack," Lorian retorted. "Or worse, another Reaper attack. Two Reapers killed hundreds of our people. What would happen if dozens of them came here? What about hundreds? Not to mention that people across Avoni are struggling with the same illness. This isn't a plague that can be cured with medicine. It's the first symptom that the Shrouds are failing."

He stopped speaking again, staring at the map for a moment. His eyes darted across the parchment. "I can't help but wonder if the Reapers are somehow related to the Shrouds failing. We've sent out Scouts, but haven't learned much in the last month. They were able to track the Reaper activity back to here." He pointed a finger at the Jaram Mountains, near the very top of the map. "Unfortunately, the Scouts were unable to uncover anything helpful. They had to return home or risk scaletaint transformation."

With our Tethering, you are immune to transformation, Luik interjected. *You could find the answer.*

Cam nodded in agreement with the Elmia. He stepped forward, gripping the bars of his cage, and addressed Lorian.

"I can help you. I know the Sundered Lands. Let me out of this cage, and I will help you."

The general turned to leave but paused for a moment in the doorway. Without turning around, he said in a voice full of ice and bitterness, "Not while your hand still looks like that. You'll stay in that cage until I am convinced you are not a threat to my people. Welcome to war-time Rath, Courier."

Chapter 19

L uik simmered with frustration.

The small window in the corner let in just a bit of light, but was large enough for Cam to see through. Today's sunset was particularly beautiful, fiery hues spreading across the sky, but Cam refused to look at it. Every time it came into view, Luik could feel Cam's heart rate and breathing quicken.

How could anyone not love a sunset? It was one of the parts of being Tethered that Luik genuinely enjoyed.

He knew that Cam would be able to feel this, and wished he could hide it from the man. Unfortunately for both of them, that's just not how a Tethering worked.

On a much deeper level, he was disturbed by the evidenced breakdown of the Aurora Shrouds. That mysterious failure cut deep. He and the others had poured everything they had—some even their lives—into creating those barriers. Now, just over a century later, they were already unraveling.

They hadn't miscalculated. They couldn't have.

Had they?

The second day in the cage proceeded similarly to the first in that it had been incredibly boring, with both Cam and Luik growing in agitation. The silence and boredom was only interrupted by the guards occasionally stepping into the room to bring Cam something to eat, which he would quickly devour.

Out of all the people Luik had been Tethered to, nobody seemed to appreciate eating quite like Cam.

Illyria had visited again. She didn't stay long though, which Luik could sense disappointed Cam. Apparently, she was expecting some bookstore to deliver her research materials. When Cam asked her what she was researching, Illyria said something about regional healing differences for Rath.

As the sun arced across the sky, its rays cast fleeting patterns of light and shadow upon the cold, unforgiving metal bars. Luik's world had been reduced to the rhythmic echoes of Cam's footsteps against the cage floor and the subdued hum of distant activity beyond the confines of the prison.

The light in the window outside shifted and darkened. It was a slow process, but Luik's years trapped in the Aetherfern had changed his perception of time. A few hours of stillness passed in what felt like a blink for him. Not long after that, a few stars appeared in the sky, obscured slightly by the blur of the Aurora Shroud. Even blurred, it made for a beautiful sight.

Finally, as night settled in, the dim room grew colder, shadows stretching long and deep between the bars of Cam's cage. Luik drifted restlessly within his Tether.

Then, just as the first faint shimmer of moonlight peeked through the small window, Luik felt a subtle shift. It felt like a ripple in the fabric of his own consciousness, and it tugged at him, foreign and familiar all at once.

Someone was reaching through the Astral Plane trying to find him.

For a fleeting moment, hope sparked in Luik's heart. There was a possibility that he was not the last of his kind, that perhaps another Elmia had survived the cataclysm that had decimated their race.

But that hope was short-lived, extinguished the instant he recognized the voice that reached him.

Luik.

The voice was sharp, confident, and brimming with that insufferable calm that had always grated on Luik's nerves.

It was Gaalron.

The conversation took place in the Astral Plane, away from Cam's awareness. Luik could have allowed Cam to listen in, but he chose to shield the words from the man's ears. This was not a conversation for any human to hear.

Not yet, at least.

Gaalron, Luik responded, his tone dripping with bitterness. *Traitor to your queen. Traitor to your own kind.*

Ironic, isn't it, Luik? You accuse me of betrayal, yet you're the one who helped cause the genocide that almost ended our race, Gaalron's voice returned.

How did you survive? Luik asked.

The same way you did. Gaalron's tone was smooth, unwavering. *By knowing when to leave. By escaping the death that you set in motion. The two of us, Luik, are among the last of the Elmias. The ones who endured your so-called sacrifice.*

Luik's frustration boiled over, and he lashed back. *The Elmias gave their lives willingly to stop the ruin you unleashed. They stood against your madness, your thirst for power. Don't you dare twist it into something else.*

Always the martyr, Luik, Gaalron replied. *But we need to put the past behind us. That chapter is over, and there's no going back. I didn't reach out to reminisce. I need your help.*

Why would I ever help you? Luik demanded.

The Shrouds are failing. You can feel it, can't you? They are unraveling all across Avoni. It won't be long before they're all gone.

Luik's anger sharpened. *Isn't that what you wanted?*

No, Gaalron said, his voice earnest. *Not like this. The decay is too slow, too random. If the Shrouds fall piece by piece, it will lead to uncontrolled destruction. There will be panic, bloodshed. More than we can handle. We need them to vanish all at once, on our terms. It's the only way to create a world where humans and Elmias can live side by side.*

Luik felt a sharp sting of anger. *Let them fall? You think dismantling the Shrouds will save lives? It's a death sentence for everyone. Humans, Elmias, everything we've tried to protect. The second those barriers come down, the Sundered Lands will consume everything.*

You're wrong, Gaalron said. *My engineers and I did extensive experiments. Our models indicated that both Elmias and humans would thrive, side by side. Our people would finally be free. We could negotiate a new treaty. One that doesn't require our servitude.*

No, Luik bit back. *And we've talked this to death already. Your models were incomplete. There's so much they didn't account for. We'd only doom both races.*

There was a chilling pause before Gaalron responded, his voice dropping to a near whisper, dark and threatening. *I'm going to bring down the Shrouds, try as you might to stop me, old friend. I'd prefer to save as many human lives as possible, but I won't hesitate to spill blood if it means freedom for the Elmias. This world will be ours again.*

You're a murderer. And I will stop you, no matter what it takes.

No. I am a liberator. And I will free our people with or without your help. And when I do, I truthfully hope you're still alive to see it. Too many Elmias have died to protect the humans. I'd hate to lose you too.

Just like that, Gaalron's presence vanished.

Luik's insides twisted. He wanted to tell Cam everything Gaalron had said, but now wasn't the time. Cam was on edge, pacing like a caged animal, and Luik could feel his rising anxiety rippling through their Tether.

Luik knew they needed to focus on one thing first: escape.

Cam, I need you to listen to me. We need to talk about a way to get you out of here.

Cam jumped slightly, startled by Luik's voice. The moment of fear was followed by one of annoyance.

Can you warn me before you do that? he asked.

Warn you before I speak? How would I even do that? I'd have to speak to warn you.

Luik felt Cam shrug.

I don't know. It's just...it's been so quiet. I forgot you were there. How long did it take for your last Tether to get used to it?

Luik hesitated a moment before answering, feeling embarrassment at the question. He didn't want to discuss his previous Tether, but he could sense Cam's curiosity rising as he struggled.

The lack of emotional privacy in a Tethering was quite difficult sometimes.

I don't think my last Tether ever got used to it, seeing that I was commanded to leave. If you get used to me being here, perhaps that indicates we're a superior pairing.

As he spoke, Luik could feel Cam's emotions stirring.

Don't give me your pity, Luik said, his voice more demanding than he intended. *There are not many things that I can call my own in this world. I don't have freedom, autonomy or a family. I may not even have a people to call my own. I intend to hold onto my pride. It is the one thing I can truly call my own.*

Cam accepted this and was silent for a moment. He glanced out the window at the stars before shifting his head back towards the wall. A moment later, he said, *I don't think they're going to let me out of here anytime soon.*

I agree. Not while your hand remains transformed. Assuming all things remain the same, we should begin considering an escape plan.

Cam shook his head.

No, I don't know if I can do that. They'll let me out eventually.

You perplex me, Cam, Luik said in a flat voice.

Turning towards the guard, Cam said, "It's obvious that I'm not going to hurt anyone. How much longer are you going to keep me here?"

This guard was new. He was a portly man with short black hair and an unkempt beard. His armor didn't fit him quite right, and he sat down with his feet kicked up on the desk. He appeared annoyed when Cam spoke to him.

"That's not my choice," he said in response. "I'm just supposed to make sure you don't leave."

"You really think if my mind had snapped I'd still be here?"

The guard sighed, pointing a fat finger at Cam's arm.

"That hand of yours isn't transforming back. I've never seen that from someone in Crimson Limbo. Now, maybe you are harmless. But maybe you are only pretending so that you can hurt people as soon as we let you out."

"May I speak with General Lorian?" Cam asked, causing the guard to raise an eyebrow.

"The general? No. He's very busy. Besides, I'm not of high enough rank to even request he meet with you."

Luik felt a flare of anxiety constrict Cam's chest as a disgruntled grunt escaped the man's lips. Turning, he began to pace again, each step echoing against the cold, metallic bars.

Luik could feel him simmering, a restless energy that throbbed through the Tether binding him to Cam's soul. It started as a faint prickling at the edges of his consciousness, like an itch he couldn't quite reach, but quickly intensified. It was sharp, jagged, and impossible to ignore. Cam's pacing set the rhythm like a drumbeat in Luik's mind, his anxiety bleeding through the bond.

As Cam paced, he heard a sudden, peculiar sound in the distance. It sounded like a group of people singing. It was far away, but it slowly grew louder, emerging like a cascade of crystal-clear notes weaving together. Men, women, and children seemed to converge in a celestial choir, their voices rising and falling in beautiful harmony.

The enchanting sound stirred an inexplicable sense of longing within Cam.

"Who are they?" he asked, causing the guard to look up.

"Who? The singers? They're the Devoted," he said in a slightly wistful tone.

"Their singing is beautiful," Cam remarked.

"Yes, it is beautiful. I was supposed to be with them tonight, but I owed someone a favor and got stuck with you."

Stuck with us, Luik corrected, knowing only Cam could hear him.

"What are they singing for?"

The guard reclined in his chair, a creak echoing through the room as he leaned back. His eyes, once guarded and vigilant, now reflected the echo of a yearning soul.

"We sing because we have faith," he said, his tone earnest. "Our praise gives strength to the Aurora Shrouds, and in turn, the Aurora Shroud protects us."

Cam frowned. "You're praising the Aurora Shrouds?"

"In a way. The Devoted believe that the Shroud weakened as a result of our weaker faith. Ever since the Reaper attack, we have been singing our songs together, showing our renewed faith. The Shroud will respond with greater strength."

Luik chuckled for a moment.

Apparently, this type of religion was not uncommon across cities in Avoni. During their journey to Rath, Cam spoke of the myriad of similar belief systems. Unfortunately, their show of faith was fruitless.

What good did faith provide if the object of the faith was misplaced?

The Aurora Shrouds didn't create themselves. Their strength or failure has nothing to do with people's faith.

Ignoring Luik, Cam simply said, "I hope you are right."

"Would it bother you if I opened the door?" the guard asked. Cam shook his head.

The guard walked over to the door, its metallic hinges creaking as he swung it open. With the door ajar, the enchanting melody of voices, now unobstructed, flooded the confined space. The guard even joined the chorus with a fervor that transcended his off-key notes.

A moment later, the song ended. The guard gave a smile, turning and stepping back to his desk.

"I hope you didn't mind my own voice back there. I've always said that I enjoy music far too much to have been given such a bad singing voice. It's a travesty!"

The true travesty, Cam, is that I am not able to plug your ears to silence that man, Luik said.

This comment caused Cam to chuckle for a moment, and the guard raised his eyebrows.

"Oh, you thought that was funny, did you? I'll have you know—"

The guard stopped, his eyes widening as he clutched at his wrist.

Then, he let out a scream, causing Cam to jump. The guard collapsed to the ground, grabbing at his hand and howling. Cam moved to the side of the cage closest to him.

"What happened? Are you hurt?" Cam called out.

The guard's breathing quickened, each breath shallow and hurried. He stared at his arm for a moment, his eyes wide and mouth agape.

"It doesn't make sense. It doesn't make sense," he panted.

He held up his arm for Cam to see.

It was covered in scales.

They are most certainly not letting you out, Luik said.

Illyria sat in her room, reading by the light of several candles. The room was small and smelled musty. There was barely enough room for her bed and the few bags she had brought with her. Nevertheless, she sat on the edge of her bed, completely focused on the papers scattered around her.

Although the organization of the materials was chaotic, Chek had been quite thorough in preparing information on locations considered holy in the days just before the Sundering. She had included several maps from that period, all of which indicated different locations for a temple in the Jaram Mountains. To help explain the discrepancies, Chek had scrawled annotations in the margins.

Overall, Illyria was impressed.

In addition to the maps, Chek had also found several books that touched on the subject. When she'd given them all to Illyria, she said, "I hate to say this, but I think Felix might have the right idea. Sounds like the scholarly perspectives on these holy sites are heavily influenced by Elmia theory. You should come by the store tomorrow and get his thoughts."

Illyria could only assume how thrilled the young man must have been to realize his knowledge might be useful. The problem was that there were very few primary sources in Rath that gave concrete evidence or theories as to the exact location of the holy site in the Jaram Mountains.

Sounds like there are two options then. Either I go to a different settlement and hope they have better resources, or I go to the Jaram Mountains myself, she thought.

A week ago, deciding to get more information from somewhere else would be easy. Now, having seen the beginning of the breakdown of the Aurora Shrouds, Illyria's mind warred with itself. She needed to find the Scepter very quickly, but without an idea of the exact location of the holy site, going to the Jaram Mountains would be incredibly dangerous.

She still needed a guide through the Sundered Lands.

I know what I need to do, she thought to herself.

A sudden knock interrupted her thinking. Illyria took a quick moment to brush her hair out of her face before stepping over to the door and opening it. Soren greeted her on the other side.

"Oh, good evening, Sor," she said cheerfully, before quickly adding, "Is there something you need?"

Soren gave a weak smile in response, his eyes nervously darting towards the floor.

"I was wondering if we could talk. Do you have a moment?"

She nodded. "Sure. Give me just a minute." Illyria quickly shut the door, leaving Soren waiting in the hallway. Stepping over towards her bed, she gathered up the loose papers, books, maps, and her notes and hid them under her blanket. When she was confident that they were hidden well enough, she stepped back to the door and opened it.

"Okay, I'm ready."

Soren gave a wry smile, motioning towards her room.

"You writing a book?"

Illyria's face flushed.

"Oh, you saw that? No, I'm not writing a book. Just doing some research."

"Research that...includes multiple maps of Avoni?" he asked incredulously.

"I am being quite thorough," she said, as if that settled the matter.

Soren either was not very interested in her research, or he accepted her lack of an explanation. He gave a quick shrug before scratching the back of his head. "Okay then. Are you too busy right now? Because if so, we can talk at another time?"

Illyria shook her head and stepped out the door. "Oh no, I needed to take a break anyway. Let's go for a walk."

The two of them walked through the long hallway of the inn. It was illuminated by flickering lanterns, and its carpeted floor led to a second-story balcony.

Soren led her towards this balcony, opening a heavy wooden door for her. Illyria looked out over the sleeping city. The buildings in Rath were not beautiful to look at, but the serene stars in the sky made up for the lack of decoration.

Illyria turned around, facing Soren.

"So, what did you want to talk about?"

He gave a sheepish smile, walking past her and looking out over the city. As he did this, his fingers twitched with a nervous energy. Finally, he began to speak.

"I've been thinking about things. I was thinking about moving to Kevilton."

The statement did not surprise Illyria. Everyone in Avoni was trapped in whatever settlement they were born into. The Vanguard Couriers were the only ones who could leave. While some chose to move to one of the larger cities, most preferred the safety of agrarian communities.

"Really? Has Rath spoiled city life so much for you? I hear it's wonderful here when they're not caging Couriers."

Soren shook his head.

"Now that doesn't bother me so much. Actually, I kind of appreciate that Lorian did that."

This made Illyria frown.

"Soren, shame on you! Even a casual outsider would realize you two don't like each other, but Cam doesn't deserve that. Imagine if it were you in the cage."

"If it were, Cam would say the same thing."

"What's the matter? Did something happen between the two of you?"

Soren averted his eyes from Illyria's. "We have a bit of a history." Illyria gave an exaggerated eye roll, which Soren must have not noticed, because he continued speaking. "Anyway, that's not what I wanted to talk about. The...moving to Kevilton."

"To be closer to the farms?"

"Well, not really. In reality, I want to be closer to you," he said, turning to stare directly into her eyes. The statement caught Illyria by surprise, and she stammered for a moment before regaining her composure.

"You...you...want to be closer to me?"

Soren nodded, stepping towards her. "Kevilton has been my favorite place to visit, because of you. I love our conversations, our jokes. I love how kind you are to everyone. I...I miss you when I'm anywhere else. Seeing your strength in the Sundered Lands has just been a reminder of that. I want you to be part of my life."

"Aurora's Name, Soren, are you asking me to marry you?" Illyria said, shocked. Soren shook his head.

"No, no. Not that. I mean, not yet. But maybe someday. Not without getting to know each other better first. Anyway, I didn't want to move without talking to you..." He trailed off, looking hopefully at her face.

Illyria let out a deep sigh.

"Soren, I can't think about this right now." His face fell instantly, so she quickly added, "There's something I need to do first. Once it's done, I promise to give you an answer."

He smiled. "I understand. Whatever you need. Is there a way I can help?"

She thought for a moment, wondering if she could trust him. She didn't want people to know what she was doing, but she also knew that it would be dangerous to go alone through the Sundered Lands. Finally, she said, "I need to go to the Jaram Mountains." She hesitated, taking a deep breath before saying, "Would you go with me?"

He frowned in confusion. "The Jaram Mountains? There's nothing up there. Not even an Aurora Shroud. Why do you want to go there?"

"You're wrong. Something is there. And I need to get there soon."

He scratched his head and said, "Lorian—General Lorian, that is—wants me to go back to Runara. Would you be able to wait until then?"

Illyria hesitated before shaking her head.

"I need to go as soon as possible. And I'll go with or without you."

Soren opened his mouth to speak but was interrupted by the sounds of a man screaming. Both of them turned their eyes towards the sound and saw a soldier running down the street.

"I need a Healer!" he screamed, his eyes desperate. "The Crimson Limbo Courier is contagious!"

The man's hand was covered in scales.

Chapter 20

Heart racing, Cam paced in his cage, rubbing his fingers together as he did so.

The hour was late, but the guard's cries were waking the sleeping city. It hadn't taken long for a small crowd to gather, angrily demanding answers. A small contingent of soldiers stood between them and the building, leaving Cam by himself.

The tension in the city had already been high. Now it was boiling over. Biting his lip in frustration, Cam breathed out a quick curse.

I should probably inform you that I view cursing as a particularly offensive form of communication.

Not the time for this, Luik.

Apologies. As you appear to be a kind person, I mistakenly assumed you'd take into account my preferences, especially as I have no autonomy of my own.

Cam ignored him, turning his attention to the people gathered outside the building. From within the confines of the cage, he could hear the outrage of the growing crowd. His heart raced.

"Send him back out!" a man screamed.

"No, that would only risk exposing more of us! He needs to be isolated here."

"We can't just let him stay here! He'll infect us all!"

"This is all Lorian's plan! He wants us dead so he can feed the Northern!"

Through the narrow window, Cam watched as the crowd swelled, bodies packed tightly together, their movements growing more aggressive with every passing second. Faces twisted in fear and anger, fists raised and shaking, the throng inched closer to the small cluster of soldiers who stood rigid and tense, hands hovering near the hilts of their swords.

Someone in the crowd threw a heavy stone that knocked a soldier to the ground.

We need to escape, Luik said.

I agree. Cam struggled to focus. *I need to think.*

He paced the cell some more as the voices grew more intense outside. It was becoming difficult to understand what the people were saying, as they all struggled to shout over each other. One thing was clear, though.

"This entire city isn't safe for me," Cam said, thinking out loud. "I...I need to get back to the Sundered Lands."

The irony of the Sundered Lands becoming his place of safety was not lost on him.

So what's the plan? Luik asked.

I'm not sure. What should I do? Cam thought in sudden bewilderment.

His pacing quickened, his steps erratic and uneven as he moved back and forth. His breath came shorter, shallower, catching in his throat with every sharp turn as his heart pounded like a drum.

He rubbed his hands together, trying to ground himself, but they were clammy and unsteady, refusing to obey. His gaze snapped back to the window, to the chaos unfolding beyond, and a surge of restless energy spiked through him, setting every nerve on edge.

His anxiety pulled vivid memories to the surface: a young boy under his uncle's care, enduring a brutal beating for the simple mistake of burning a dinner he had hoped would be a surprise. The haunting image of his father, walking away from Perth and vanishing into the Sundered Lands without a word or explanation.

Silva's death.

Fear began to take hold of Cam. Fortunately, he still had Luik.

Cam, you can't control those people outside, but you can control what you do next.

The words calmed Cam, even as outside the building, a voice began screaming, "Burn it down! Don't let it infect us!"

He steeled his jaw in resolution.

I—we're going to the Jaram Mountains, Cam thought, feeling Luik's approval inside of him. *It's too slow to go on foot. I'll need to steal a horse and go to Perth first. There's a stable in the Eastern District. I can get the horse there.*

Good, Luik said. *And how do you plan on getting there?*

Cam thought for a moment.

You can still use Verdalink even when I'm not looking at the object, right?

Yes. But remember, the farther you travel, the more disoriented you'll be.

The crowd continued getting larger and louder outside the building.

I'm not sure I have much time to worry about that, Cam thought, closing his eyes and trying to focus. *Right, so here's the plan: First, use Verdalink to escape this cage. Second, steal a horse. Third, escape into the Sundered Lands and head towards the Jaram Mountains to find out where these Reapers came from and what they are.*

I prefer a few more...details to be included in plans, but under the circumstances, I assume this is the best one we'll come up with.

Cam felt Luik steady himself as he tapped into his powers and looked for an astral anchor. As he did so, the acrid stench of smoke hit Cam's nostrils.

They're trying to burn this place, he said.

Yeah, I picked up on that, Luik thought back. *Let me focus.*

You'll need to find an anchor quickly.

I'm working on... There!

Through their bond, Cam could sense what Luik had found: a full-grown Aetherfern plant somewhere on the far side of the city.

Time to go, Luik said, reaching through the Astral Plane to touch the plant. Instantly, the world transformed around them, spinning and folding in on itself. The shifting kaleidoscope changed a moment later, filled with stained-glass windows and brick.

Finally out of his cage, Cam took a step forward and immediately fell to his knees, his vision swimming wildly around him. He tried climbing back to his feet, but the dizziness was overwhelming.

Remember, there's always a cost, Luik's voice reminded him.

Luik, he thought. *How far did we travel?*

Judging by your reaction, I'd say almost two miles. Possibly further.

Cam rubbed his head, struggling to rise to his feet again. He failed. *I think I'm going to need a minute.*

Take your time. They'll only burn us to death if they find us, Luik said. In spite of the remark, Cam could sense that Luik found some sort of twisted joy in the disorientation.

You're enjoying this? he thought.

I apologize, sir, but I do find it a bit humorous. You're like a big, muscular baby trying to learn to walk.

Shaking his head, Cam felt his sense of orientation returning to him. He rose to his feet, dusting himself off as he did so.

At least one of us is in a good mood.

Quite right. And I'll be even happier once we're safe.

Sounds good to me.

Cam glanced around. The room was dark, lit only by the flickering street lamps outside shining through large stained-glass windows, casting shifting images on the wooden floor. In front of him were several rows of wooden benches.

Unsure if he was alone in the building, Cam crept silently towards a large steel door at the far end of the room, cringing at the creaks and groans of the floorboards below.

I just thought of something, Cam thought to Luik. *Before using Verdalink, it would probably have been a good idea to find a backup anchor. Just in case there were problems here.*

That's...actually a really good point, Luik answered. *Next time a mob is trying to burn down the building I'm in, I'll keep that in mind.*

Next time? You think this happens a lot to me? Cam asked.

Only a joke, my friend. Well, a partial joke. There is a part of me that wonders if this is a normal occurrence for you. It's not like we've known each other for long.

Rolling his eyes, Cam reached the doorway. He reached out with his right hand to grip the doorknob, but struggled to grasp it with his elongated, transformed fingers. Grunting, he used his left hand to open the door instead.

The streets around him were quiet, without a soul in sight. In the distance, he could vaguely hear the shouts from the mob.

Okay, we escaped the cage. Next step is to steal the horse.

Steal a horse! Steal a horse! Steal a horse! Luik chanted.

That part was going to be difficult. In the city of Rath, only soldiers had access to horses. With the city under martial law, they would be heavily guarded. Sneaking in would be next to impossible.

That was assuming he'd be able to even reach the stables. With the mob forming just a few miles away, the city guard was likely to be highly active, and the streets would be very busy with curious citizens who would surely notice a rogue Vanguard Courier in a state of Crimson Limbo.

He needed something else.

You said that there's more abilities than just astral power and Verdalink. Any other tricks that could help me right now?

There is one, Luik mused. *It's...it'll require a bit more cooperation, though. I can teach you.*

Fair enough, Cam thought back. *Teach me something new, Elmia.*

Well, now I will teach you two things. The first is this: in Elmia culture, it is considered rude to refer to someone by their race, rather than their name. I must insist that you call me Luik and not simply "Elmia." I would never refer to you as simply "Human," for you are more than your race.

Fine. Teach me something new, Luik, Cam thought, knowing that Luik could feel his irritation.

Luik, ignoring Cam's obvious frustration, appeared satisfied with their arrangement. In fact, if he were visible in the room, Cam felt that Luik would likely be smiling that very moment.

Thank you, Cam. Now, let us begin.

Luik called the new skill "Shadowmelding." According to the Elmia, it was a branch of Tethering that allowed a Tethered pair to sink into the astral veil where it touched the physical world. In practice, it let Cam blend with shadows so completely that light itself seemed to pass over him. To an outside observer, he became invisible, present only as a faint distortion or flicker if they looked too closely.

In the height of Avonian power, many of the king's spies used this ability to great effect, Luik had explained. *Avoni's military was strong, but even they could be rendered useless by warriors literally hiding in the shadows.*

According to Luik, Shadowmelding was most powerful under the cloak of night, where the world itself became a sprawling canvas of shadows. While still possible during daylight hours, the risk inherent in its use escalated, for as soon as a light shone that removed the shadow, the user was forcibly and painfully brought out of the Shadowmeld.

Remember, as with all things, there is always a cost. The same is true of Shadowmelding. Emerging from the shadows into the stark illumination of light can momentarily blind you. The art of Shadowmelding demands not only mastery but an intimate understanding of the delicate equilibrium between the realms it straddles.

Cam stood in a dimly lit alley, the soft glow of distant lanterns casting elongated shadows across the cobblestone pathway. His surroundings, a labyrinth of buildings and obscured corners, provided the perfect canvas for the two of them.

Alright, I guess we're doing this.

Through their bond, Cam could feel Luik's power shifting as he embraced the shadows, allowing them to enfold Cam like a protective cloak. The transition was ethereal, a merging of his form with the inky darkness that surrounded him. The world outside the shadowy embrace seemed to blur and distort, as if reality itself had granted him passage into an unseen realm.

Cam, now concealed, moved silently through the alley. The experience was bizarre, more akin to swimming than walking. It was an uncanny sensation, the feeling of being both present and absent, a ghostly observer navigating the realms between light and shadow.

Time to steal a horse.

Steal a horse! Steal a horse! Steal a horse! Luik chanted again.

The screams of the guard woke people from their slumber. While some watched quietly from the balconies, others streamed into the streets. Decades of fears and superstitions surrounding the Sundered Lands were taking effect as the people began panicking.

Illyria stared as the crowd swelled with fervor. Soldiers arrived on horseback, brandishing staffs, attempting to corral the people back into nearby buildings. In a moment of defiance, a cobblestone flew from the crowd, striking a soldier and sending him tumbling from his mount. Chaos erupted as the soldiers' attempts to assist their fallen comrade resulted in one of their own horses trampling a citizen.

"The soldiers of Rath attack their own people!" a voice cried.

A full-on riot ensued.

Having grown up in the peaceful confines of Kevilton, Illyria had no context for this level of chaos and confusion. For a moment, she stood frozen in shock and horror as looting started. Rioters took advantage of the chaos, knocking down the doors of buildings and taking what they could.

We need to get to the Jaram Mountains.

Right, the mountains.

Illyria took a few deep breaths, settling her nerves. Then, she narrowed her eyes in determination.

Time to get to work, she thought.

Turning to her left, she took hold of Soren's arm. His eyes widened for a moment at her touch, and he turned to look towards her. She feigned a fearful expression and said, "Soren, look at all this. We need to go."

The man frowned. "Go?"

She nodded.

"We need to go to the mountains." Moving her other hand, she gestured towards the growing riot. "This isn't safe. I'll be safer in the Sundered Lands...safe with you." The last part of that sentence made her cringe, and she was surprised at the guilt she felt at the words.

Careful. You'll break someone's heart this way.

She'd deal with broken hearts later. Right now, all she knew was that she had to get to the Jaram Mountains, and she needed to get there quickly. What was happening in Rath was likely a precursor of what was to come for all the settlements in Avoni very soon.

She looked into Soren's eyes with a pleading expression.

He stood still, giving Illyria a conflicted look.

He's going to say no, she thought.

Ignoring the guilt that flared up in her, Illyria slid her hand down the man's arm, grabbing his hand and giving it a squeeze.

"Please," she said.

That did the trick.

After whispering a quick curse, Soren smiled.

"Fine. I'll do it. And you're sure you want to go now?"

Part of her heart sank as he said this. She almost winced at the realization that she'd have to continue leading Soren on.

Maybe it will turn into something real, she thought, trying to ease her conscience.

"Yes, let's not waste any time."

Soren nodded, turning back towards the inn.

"We need to move quickly. Grab only what you need. Perth is located right at the base of the mountains. We can resupply there."

As they stepped back into the inn's second-floor hallway, Soren was still holding her hand.

Chapter 21

Cane in one hand, bag of daily rations in the other, Chek walked down the dark streets of Rath. The flickering lights of the lampposts created dancing shadows on the rocky walls around her. Behind her, Felix was snacking on a carrot, his chewing loud and harsh as they walked.

"Felix, please. Chew with your mouth closed," Chek said.

"Sorry. I'm just distracted."

Glancing back, Chek noticed her brother was eating while reading a book. His dark, bespectacled eyes were hungrily devouring the words of whatever he was reading.

Chek reached out and snatched the book from him.

"Hey!" he protested.

"Look where you're walking! You're going to run into things…" She hesitated before adding, "Again."

He glowered at her, using a finger to push his glasses back up the bridge of his nose.

"That was one time. One time and—"

A sound rang in the distance. Chek stopped walking and strained to listen. The noise grew louder, rising from somewhere deeper in the city, a chaotic blend of angry voices and the unmistakable clash of metal.

Chek frowned.

"What do you think that is?" she asked.

"Another rations run? Maybe they ran out again?" As Felix spoke, a group of mounted soldiers rode past them.

"Return to your dwelling!" one of them yelled. "Return immediately!"

Felix rolled his eyes.

"Something bad happening in Rath? Different night, but same story."

Chek cast an anxious glance at him. "What if it's another attack?"

She had heard the whispers circulating through the crowded streets about a mysterious creature that attacked one of the other districts. The details were conflicting, but the creature's name remained the same: the Reaper. The city's officials were doing everything they could to suppress the rumors, trying to keep the panic at bay, but the more they tried to silence it, the faster word spread.

"Maybe we should head back to the store. It's closer than home," Felix said.

"We'll be fine. Let's just go quickly," Chek replied.

They picked up their pace, navigating the darkened streets of Rath as best they could. Chek could feel the nervous energy in the air, prickling at the back of her neck. Felix clutched the bag with their meager rations close to his chest, his eyes darting around as if expecting someone to lunge out from the darkness at any moment.

The distant clamor of voices grew steadily louder, swelling like a tide that had been waiting to break. Chek glanced over her shoulder, her unease growing with every passing second.

A bottle shattered somewhere in the distance, followed by a chorus of angry shouts. Chek's grip tightened on her cane, her heart beating faster. Felix threw her a worried glance, his brow furrowed.

"We have to keep moving," he urged, his voice edged with anxiety. "It's getting closer."

Chek nodded, swallowing her frustration as she pushed onward. The noise of the crowd grew, shouts and chaos drawing nearer with every second. Chek pushed herself as hard as she could, her uneven steps echoing off the cobblestones, one foot dragging behind the other, her movements jerky and strained.

And then, a mob spilled onto their street, like the crashing of angry waves.

Felix grabbed Chek's arm, his eyes wide with urgency. "We can't stay here," he said, his voice barely audible over the noise. "Come on! We're going back to the store."

She nodded, fear clawing at her as the crowd pressed in. They turned to flee, but the streets quickly became a tangle of bodies and violence. Soldiers shoved through the mob, swinging clubs to keep the rioters at bay, while people fought back with whatever they could find—rocks, broken glass, anything that could be used to strike out.

Chek struggled to move forward through the crowd, her legs protesting with every unsteady step as she was jostled from all sides. Felix pulled her forward, guiding her through the chaos, but it was impossible to avoid the crush of bodies. Someone crashed into her from behind, sending her sprawling to the ground.

She hit the pavement hard, pain shooting through her palms and knees as she tried to push herself up. Around her, the riot raged on, the sound of clashing metal and angry voices melding into a deafening roar. Felix was there in an instant, dragging her upright before the stampede could overtake her. He braced her with one arm, shielding her as they stumbled toward the nearest alley.

"Come on!" Felix urged, half carrying her as they pushed through the last of the crowd. They ducked into the narrow side street, the noise dimming slightly behind them as they made their way toward the bookstore.

The familiar door was just ahead. Felix fumbled with the key, his hands shaking as he shoved it into the lock. The door swung open and they tumbled inside, slamming it shut and throwing the bolt across with a resounding click.

Panting, Felix pressed his back against the door. "Are you alright?"

Chek nodded, though her entire body ached, and she could still feel the echo of the crowd's panic thrumming in her veins. She slumped against the wall, sliding down to sit on the floor, her legs too weak to hold her up any longer. "I'm fine," she said, her voice trembling slightly. "But we can't go back out there. Let's just stay here tonight."

As they sat in silence, the sharp sound of a knock reverberated through the small bookstore. Felix shot to his feet. Chek tensed, heart pounding in her chest.

"City guard. Open up!" a muffled voice called from beyond the door.

Felix unbolted it cautiously, revealing a soldier, faceless behind the grime-streaked visor of his helmet. The guard's armor was scratched and battered, evidence of the escalating chaos outside. He spoke quickly, glancing over his shoulder as if expecting more trouble at any moment.

"Lock your doors and stay off the streets. Some Crimson Limbo Courier started a riot. If you see him, stay away from him and report it to the guard."

Chek leaned forward, her exhaustion momentarily forgotten. "What does he look like?"

"Right arm is transformed completely and hasn't transformed back. His left arm is marked. Some kind of plant tattoo."

Felix perked up the instant he heard the description, his eyes sharpening with sudden interest. Chek noticed, her gaze narrowing at him as the guard hurried off to warn the next building.

"What do you know?" she whispered.

Chapter 22

Grateful for the abundance of shadows provided by the night, Cam swam through the darkened streets of Rath.

Moving while Shadowmelding was a bizarre experience. Were he in a less tense situation, Cam might have enjoyed the invisible journey.

He was not far from the Eastern District stable, but he had to make several measured detours for the sake of safety, as people continued to throng the streets. It sounded like a full-on riot was forming, and the flicker of carried torches could easily dispel the shadows, revealing him.

Luik had promised that such a revelation would be quite painful and end the Shadowmeld.

The Shadowmeld is quite fragile, I'm afraid, he had said.

After a few hours of travel through the darkness, Cam finally arrived. Fortunately for him, the chaos in Rath appeared to have not yet reached this section of the city.

Unfortunately for him, the sun was rising, dispelling the many shadows he was using to hide.

I recommend we exit the shadows now, before anyone can see you, Luik advised.

Cam propelled himself out of the shadows, reemerging into the glaring morning light. The abrupt shift from darkness to light elicited a groan, and he instinctively raised his right arm to shield his eyes from the searing brightness.

I would advise against revealing that arm of yours, Luik said. *It will give you away.*

Blinking as his eyes adjusted to the light, Cam nodded and pulled his long sleeves down and his cloak around his arm. The temporary blindness lifted, and he continued walking towards the stables.

As he walked, he kept his head down. In spite of himself, he rubbed his fingers together nervously and bit his lip.

My cloak won't fool anyone for long. I better get moving.

Cam walked more quickly, feigning confidence, as if he had nothing to hide.

As he stepped out of the alley onto the white stone street, the sound of marching caught his attention. Turning his head, he saw a group of twenty Rath soldiers all armed with spears and large riot shields. One of the soldiers suddenly turned his head and locked eyes with Cam.

Quickly averting his gaze, Cam pivoted and walked away from the stable, towards a bookstore. As he did, he listened intently to the soldiers. So far, they hadn't seemed to realize who he was.

What are you doing? Luik hissed. *You're supposed to go to the stables!*

Sorry. I panicked for a second, and it'd be suspicious now to change directions again.

Cam could feel Luik fuming, but there was no turning around now.

"I'm a Vanguard Courier; I'm supposed to have access to the stables." Soren's voice was insistent and frustrated. He'd been arguing with the soldiers for the last several minutes.

Supposedly, the riots in the Eastern District were beginning to dissipate, but the soldier guarding the stable wasn't listening.

"Get back to the inn," the soldier hissed, "or I'll take you to a cell."

"I need to speak to your captain," Soren said.

"He's indisposed." As the guard spoke, Illyria saw his hand grip his spear a bit tighter. "Now, what's it gonna be? Your inn or a cell?" The two locked eyes in a tense staredown.

Reaching out, Illyria touched Soren lightly on his shoulder.

"It's okay. We can go," she said, trying to make her voice sound defeated. Soren gave her a quick bewildered expression and opened his mouth to speak. Before he could say anything, Illyria turned towards the guard.

"Is this because of the riots last night?" As she spoke, she opened her eyes wide, trying to exude innocence and naivety. "It started near the inn. It...I was so scared."

The soldier nodded his head slightly. He still looked suspicious but appeared more trusting of Illyria. She flashed an appreciative smile at the soldier.

"Thank you for keeping us safe." Grabbing Soren's hand, she then turned to leave.

Once they were out of earshot, Soren whispered, "What are you doing? I thought you wanted to get out of the city?"

"We're not getting out if they put you in a cell. At least now we can go somewhere private and make a plan."

"You have a place in mind?"

"As a matter of fact, I do. It's a bookstore close. Just a few minutes away."

"A bookstore?"

"Yes. A bookstore." Then, in a playful tone, she added, "Can't a lady enjoy the ambiance of books while she plots her first heist?"

Cam stepped up to the bookstore, paying careful attention to keep his right arm hidden. He turned the handle of the door, but it was locked. He tried again, but it didn't budge. Frustrated, he rapped his knuckles against the wood.

The door swung open with a light creak.

A dark-skinned man looked at Cam as he walked in.

"I wondered if the riot would keep people away, and yet, here you are. Greetings to you! Welcome to Avoni's foremost hub of knowledge—scientific, historical, and mystical!" As he spoke, the woman next to him continued her work tracing her fingers along a map.

"Thank you. I'll only be here for a few moments," Cam said. The man jumped up enthusiastically, taking large, purposeful strides over to him.

"Stay as long as you want! What is your area of interest?"

Unsure of what to say, Cam said the first thing that came to his mind.

"Elmias."

The man's bespectacled face shone with delight.

"Splendid! Another fellow student of the mystical world. Exciting!" He paused for a moment, raising a suspicious eyebrow at Cam. "You're not a member of the Cult of Sundered Shadows, are you?" Before Cam could respond, the man started laughing. "Of course not. You're not one of those lunatics."

This last statement caused the woman to lift her head from her map.

"They're not lunatics, Felix."

Felix gave a quick, polite smile at Cam before turning to the woman. "Chek, we've talked about this. I don't want people to think you sympathize with them."

Chek shook her head. "I do sympathize with them. How can you not sympathize with people seeking freedom from the Aurora Shrouds?"

"Because they'll just turn themselves into scaletaints!" Felix yelled before turning back to Cam. "Please excuse my sister. She likes to be difficult." This earned him a glare from Chek. "What is your specific interest in Elmias? We have it all—legends, history, the science of Tethering."

"I'm not really sure," Cam said, stepping away slowly. "I'll just find something on my own."

Felix, however, was determined to assist.

"Ah, perhaps you're seeking something a bit more basic and general then. I have just the thing." He turned around, stepping over to a nearby bookshelf. He eyed the books very quickly before smiling and selecting one.

"This one is perfect. I read this almost fifteen years ago and have become increasingly fascinated by the Elmia legends. I promise you, once you're done reading this, you won't be able to stop studying, either. That's what happened to me. I consider myself a student of Elmia lore. There's a lot I could teach you, if you're interested."

This one's annoying, Luik's voice said in Cam's mind.

"And I'm the crazy one for sympathizing with the Cult of Sundered Shadows?" Chek snorted.

"They literally have 'cult' in the name, Chek," Felix retorted.

"I doubt they call themselves that. I've heard they prefer 'The Shadows of the Sundered Lands,'" Chek responded flatly before going back to her map.

"Anyway, you will not regret reading this book. You'll learn so many fascinating things." He handed the book to Cam. Instinctively, Cam reached out with his left hand to take it. As he did so, his sleeve pulled back just slightly, revealing the beginning of the Aetherfern mark.

Felix's eyes widened in shock for a moment. He took a step back, his mouth agape.

"You're the one they're looking for," he whispered.

Time to go, Cam thought.

Agreed.

Without hesitating, Cam turned and began to rush towards the door.

"Leave, and I'll call the guards over," Felix said, his voice trembling.

Cam turned around. Both Felix and Chek were on their feet, backed into the corner of the room. Felix stood in front of Chek, shielding her from Cam. In his hand, he wielded a pen, held out as if it were a longsword.

"You'd rather me stay here with you?" Cam said. Felix nodded.

"You're going to stay here and answer my questions," he said, his voice still shaking. "And if you try to leave or hurt Chek, I'll call the guards."

Cam's eyes narrowed.

"You...want to ask me questions?"

Felix nodded, still holding the pen out towards Cam. Cam pointed at it.

"And if I don't answer your questions, you're going to stab me with that?"

"Yes."

Cam momentarily locked eyes with Chek, and she offered an apologetic shrug.

Any suggestions, Luik?

After a pause, Luik said, *Offer to buy him flowers.*

Cam blinked, frozen for a moment.

Wait, really?

I admit that it's a bad suggestion. I simply said the first thing that came to my mind. Actually, that isn't true. My first thought was to try to bite his fingers, but that would not be helpful.

Rolling his eyes, Cam said, "What do you want to know?"

"Are you Tethered to an Elmia? I saw the mark on your arm." In spite of the tension in the moment, there was a gleam of eagerness in Felix's eyes.

Cam hesitated for a moment, weighing whether or not he should admit the truth. After a moment, he simply nodded. This caused Felix to relax a bit.

"Well that perfectly explains the permanent Crimson Limbo. Your body is walking in both the physical and the astral world. Okay, next question. When did you get Tethered?" His voice had stopped shaking, and scholarly curiosity was beginning to creep into his speech.

"Not long ago. Just a few days."

"Can you fly?"

"What?" Cam asked, caught off guard.

"Can. You. Fly," Felix said, emphasizing each word.

Cam was about to respond, then hesitated.

Luik, can I fly?

This conversation is ridiculous. No, you cannot fly.

"He says that I can't."

Felix's eyes widened in surprise and joy. "He? Is he talking to you right now?"

Oh no, Cam and Luik thought in unison.

"Is pooping awkward? I feel like it would be awkward," Felix blurted out. Chek let out an exaggerated groan.

Cam felt his face turn red.

"I mean..." he stammered. "It's...it's for sure awkward. But, when you're already sharing thoughts and emotions, you're kinda used to awkward."

At that moment, the door to the bookstore swung open. Cam let out a grunt of frustration, glancing to see if there was anywhere he could hide.

"Cam?" a gruff male voice said.

Turning, Cam saw Soren and Illyria step into the room, packed bags in their hands. Both of them were dressed for a journey through the Sundered Lands.

"Get out!" Felix yelled, scrambling towards them. "This is important!" The shouting must have hurt his throat. He gave a few quick coughs and grunted, trying to clear his throat.

Illyria brushed past him, relief in her eyes.

"Cam! You're alright!"

"Wait, how did you get out of the cage?" Soren added.

Cam glared at Soren.

"It's a long story."

Actually, it's a bit of a short story, but a long explanation, Luik corrected, causing Cam's annoyance to flare.

Illyria looked worried. "How long have you been hiding here? The whole city was in an uproar last night."

"Illyria, I need to get out of here. But the soldiers are looking—"

"We know," interrupted Soren, who was beginning to breathe heavily. He cleared his throat before continuing. "And now people think you're contagious."

"That's absurd," Chek said. Up until now, she'd been quiet, but as she spoke, the group turned and looked at her. She lightly pushed Felix—who was still standing between her and Cam—out of the way as she stepped towards them. She gave a sudden cough before continuing.

"Scaletaint transformation isn't a disease. At least, not in the traditional sense. It's the result of your body reconciling existence on different planes of reality. At least, that's the belief held among most scholars alive today."

I like this one. She's clever, said Luik.

"Of course he's not contagious," Illyria said. "Who in their right mind would think that?"

"This IS Rath," Chek said. Soren looked concerned and turned to Cam.

"The guard who had scales appear... Is it possible that he had developed the scales during a trip to the Sundered Lands and was hiding them?" His breathing became more labored.

Cam shook his head.

"No, he didn't have them earlier. Besides, why would he hide them for part of the day, then go screaming through the streets about it?"

"So, if it's not contagious, and the guard wasn't hiding an earlier condition, then the most logical conclusion..." Illyria trailed off as the light entering the room changed. A few minutes before, it had shone through the window as a soft, bright yellow. However, in the few minutes they had been in the store, it had shifted to red.

Blood red.

In the distance, a few screams rang out.

Oh no.

Cam stepped towards the open window, jaw dropping as he looked up into the sky. It was a jagged patchwork of peaceful blue and angry, swirling red, as if parts of the Aurora Shroud had broken, allowing the Sundered Lands to begin to seep into Rath.

People stopped in the street, pointing up in horror.

Cam, it's time to leave. We can't stay here, Luik's voice insisted. In the corner of his vision, Cam saw Soren reach out and take Illyria's hand.

"Come on, we're taking that horse. We have to get under another Shroud," Soren said, his tone focused and urgent.

Cam followed them into the street. Chaos reigned as eyes turned skyward, catching sight of the fractures in the Aurora Shroud and the crimson hue beyond. Even the soldiers began deserting their posts in a frenzy. Amidst the turmoil, several individuals succumbed to violent fits of coughing.

Sharp fingernails bit into Cam's shoulders.

"Help! Please help!" a woman said in a desperate voice, her face and exposed arms covered in boils.

There's nothing you can do, Luik said. *You can't stop this.*

Heart wrenching in him, Cam turned away from the woman, chasing after Soren and Illyria. The two were running hand in hand towards the stable. Other people must have had the same idea, because a crowd was beginning to form as people attempted to force their way in to steal a horse and escape.

Soren tried to push his way through the crowd, but it was getting thicker by the moment. As panic began to settle in, the group turned violent; people shoved and threw punches, desperately trying to secure a horse. One of these punches connected with Soren's face, and he collapsed.

Cam charged forward, plowing through the crowd towards Soren. Illyria kneeled next to him, fingers touching his forehead. Moving quickly, Cam picked up the unconscious Courier.

"Illyria, follow me." He turned and rushed towards the city gates.

"What are you doing?" Illyria shouted, catching up to him.

"You two were never going to cut through that crowd. Our only chance is on foot. We'll head for Perth."

"We're coming too!" a voice shouted behind him.

Cam turned and saw Felix and Chek trailing them, Felix clutching a small bag of books close to his chest. Chek was beside him, her movements awkward and halting as she fought to keep up. Her foot twisted slightly with each step, dragging just enough to catch the uneven stones beneath her.

"No you're not! I'm going into the Sundered Lands."

"Can't be much worse than here!" Chek replied.

They're not wrong, Luik said.

Cam grunted in response as he passed through Rath's open gate back into the Sundered Lands.

Chapter 23

"I declare to the universe that the Sundered Lands are awful!" Felix cried out to nobody in particular. Outside of a few frowns, those around him didn't react to him. He'd been complaining for the better part of the day.

He'd heard stories about the Sundered Lands, mostly from the Vanguard or the idiots who left the Shroud on a dare. He had always assumed those stories were exaggerations. Now, he knew the truth.

If anything, the Sundered Lands were even worse than promised.

After only a few hours of exposure, boils had begun to appear on Felix's face and arms. They burned furiously, and he kept finding himself unconsciously scratching at them.

There was also the problem of the air. Every inhalation was a forced and laborious exertion; each breath hurt, like tiny stabs inside his lungs.

At least his hair was untouched.

Poor Chek. Her hair had fallen out in large clumps, and her scalp was now mostly flesh with a few stubborn patches of stringy hair. When it first started, Cam had seemed surprised. Apparently, it was an uncommon side effect of being in the Sundered Lands. Chek pretended that it wasn't bothering her, but Felix knew his sister, and in her eyes, he could see her deep sorrow.

"We're not supposed to be out here!" he cried out, absentmindedly scratching at the boils on his arms, his voice muffled by the makeshift face mask Cam had made for him.

At least, the rest of them weren't supposed to be out here.

Cam, on the other hand, made things look easy.

The massive man strode effortlessly along the barren, rocky terrain, breathing easily, as if the Sundered Lands were his natural environment. For the first few minutes, he'd even been carrying the body of another Courier—Soren—across his back.

An idea suddenly struck him.

"Cam, would it be possible to share your Elmia? Help give each of us a break?"

The Vanguard Courier paused a moment, his expression distant, before replying. Felix had quickly learned that this was a regular behavior for Cam as the man consulted with his Elmia. Finally, Cam said, "First off, his name is Luik, and he's not 'my Elmia.' He's not a pet and doesn't belong to me, any more than I belong to him. Secondly, I already spoke with Luik about this. He says that it wouldn't be worth it, and as soon as he removed himself from someone, they'd experience a compounded rate of corruption as their physical body adjusts."

Felix nodded in silence, discreetly pulling a notebook from his pocket and beginning to write.

Luik rejects possessive terms, viewing the Elmia–host bond as mutual. This challenges pre-Sundering assertions that Elmias are akin to domesticated companions.

That was helpful to confirm.

Satisfied, he tucked the notebook back into his pocket. He hadn't meant to insult Luik, but at least he'd learned something. Hopefully, he'd learn many things about Elmias over the coming days. There were very few primary source accounts regarding Elmias, so most of the books he had studied were full of conflicting information, such as whether or not Elmias could be considered pets.

In spite of his discomfort, he smiled in anticipation. He was going to write the first study of Elmias in over a century using a primary source.

Assuming they all survived, of course.

"What would happen if Luik manifested in the Sundered Lands?" Felix asked. "Is that even possible?"

"Luik says it's possible," Cam answered. "There's enough astral energy here. Though, I'm still in Crimson Limbo. It wouldn't take long for me to transform into a scaletaint. Plus, he'd also start transforming into something."

After making a quick note, Felix felt at his throat, where a dull pain was starting to emanate.

Is that from the air? Hopefully we get under a Shroud soon.

Cam was confident that they'd all be able to reach Perth by foot. Supposedly, it was the village in which he grew up. Before the Sundering, the citizens in the tiny village must have felt insignificant in the shadow of Rath.

Now, Perth represented salvation.

After what seemed like an eternity, Cam called out, "We need to make camp. Let's set up here."

Soren frowned and said, "There are hours of daylight ahead of us and a long journey tomorrow. Now is not the time to make camp."

"If it were just the two of us, I'd agree with you. But there are three others here with very limited experience in the Sundered Lands."

Illyria snorted.

"Oh, I'll be fine. Don't you two worry about me."

"Yeah, I'm pretty sure we can take care of ourselves," Chek added. Her voice was confident, but Felix could tell by the way she leaned on her cane, her right leg dragging behind her, that she was exhausted.

Shaking his head, Cam said, "I'm not doubting your competence, but a group this size is dangerous and could attract scaletaints. We're making camp early."

Soren slowly stepped over towards Cam, staring him directly in his eyes. Cam met the stare with an icy one of his own. For a few moments, neither spoke. Finally, Soren said, "And what are you going to do if I say we need to keep going?"

"Let you leave. But I'm staying here." He dropped his pack to the ground, punctuating his statement. "And for the rest of you, you can decide whether it's safer with Soren or with myself and Luik."

Well that's an easy choice, Felix thought, setting his book bag down. Illyria followed suit. Her mask obscured most of her face, but from the shape of her eyes, it looked like she was smiling.

Chek stepped over to Felix and said, "So, I know I acted all confident a minute ago, but I actually don't know what I'm doing out here. How does one 'make camp'?"

Felix shrugged. For a moment, he regretted studying Elmias so much at the expense of other important skills.

It was only a moment, though. Elmias were just so interesting.

Leaning in towards his sister, he whispered, "I guess we'll just have to ask Mr. Grumpy Muscles."

His sister chuckled and said, "Really? Mr. Grumpy Muscles? That's the best you can do?"

Before he could respond, that stupid air from the Sundered Lands sent him into a coughing fit. Once it had subsided, he said, "You think you can do better?"

"Sure can. Cam the Cantankerous Colossus."

Felix blinked. "Cantanker-what? You came up with that just now?"

"A girl's gotta be able to think on her feet." On instinct, she reached up to brush her hair out of her face. She cringed as her fingers touched her mostly bald scalp.

I know how to make her feel better.

Felix gave her an encouraging smile and said, "I have an idea. Insult contest. See who can come up with the best insult for Cam before we reach Perth."

Her expression brightened a bit, and she said, "Your turn then!"

"Chek and Felix! You planning on helping?" Cam shouted.

"Yes, sorry!" Felix said. Then, in a whisper that only Chek could hear, he added, "Lord Needsabath. Your turn now." She snickered.

It didn't take long at all for them to create a camp. They didn't have any tents or canopies with them, so the group used dead branches and stones and built a small protective barrier around them. Illyria then prepared some sort of concoction for them to drink to help stave off the corruptive transformation. It tasted awful, but it did help Felix to feel more refreshed.

Soren built a small fire, and Cam tossed some Aetherfern leaves into it. Shortly afterward, the air took on the earthy scent of the plant. The group sat around the fire.

Chek spoke first.

"So...what's the plan? I mean, with the mess that is Rath right now, Felix and I are pretty committed to going to Perth. But once we get there, is that it? We're just gonna stay there until the mess is over?" She paused for a moment before adding, "Assuming it does ever end."

Cam straightened his back and said, "I'll get both of you to Perth, but after that, I'd like to figure out what those Reapers are."

"How do you plan on doing that?" Felix said.

"The Reapers that attacked Rath supposedly came from the Jaram Mountains. I want to find out where they came from and if more exist. Maybe that will give us a clue as to why the Shrouds are starting to fail."

At the mention of the Jaram Mountains, Illyria perked up, her eyes darting from the ground over to Cam. Soren seemed to notice the subtle look, and his eyes narrowed for a moment.

Fascinating, Felix thought, pushing his glasses up his nose.

"Does Luik know where the Shrouds came from to begin with?" Felix asked, his hand sneaking into his pocket to grab his notebook.

"He said that he made them." Cam paused quickly, eyes going distant, likely listening to the Elmia's voice. "Sorry, Luik. I stand corrected. He says that he only helped make them, along with several other Elmias serving in the Vorunis Citadel."

Felix gave a gasp of joy, which quickly sent him into a violent coughing fit.

This cursed air! How are the others handling it so well?

Reaching out with a gloved hand, Illyria gave him a sip of her water, which Felix drank with gratitude. Once the coughing subsided, she asked, "You okay, Felix?"

"More than okay," Felix said, energy returning to his voice. "The Aurora Shrouds being a creation of the Elmias confirms the theories of Dr. Protti Mor. This is huge! I...I'm thrilled! Luik, can I ask you more questions?"

Cam listened to Luik before saying, "He says yes. He also thanks you for addressing him directly. I guess most people ignore the Tethered Elmia, instead acting as if the human is the only being that matters. He says it makes him feel appreciated." Cam was silent for a few moments before saying, "Don't repeat that last part. Luik didn't realize I was going to share it and is embarrassed now." Another pause. "Luik, I said I was sorry. No need to keep harping on about it."

Felix nodded, discreetly writing in his notebook.

Observation: Elmias possess emotional capacity similar to humans, including embarrassment, and respond positively to direct acknowledgment.

Chek leaned over to Felix and spoke in a hushed tone.

"Cam's voice is so annoying that even Luik plugs his ears when he speaks. Your turn."

Felix snickered and said, "Luik, how did you all make the Aurora Shrouds?"

For the next several minutes, Luik explained through Cam that the Shrouds were created by the Elmias of the Vorunis Citadel, one of the old astral Nexus Points. Apparently, they destroyed it by using its astral energy to create the Aurora Shrouds. There wasn't enough to save all of Avoni, so the Elmias had to be strategic about which spots they saved, such as cities with large populations or farming communities. They left border towns alone, as those people would have a chance to escape.

"And what happened to the other Elmias?" Chek asked.

"He's not sure," Cam said. "He says they likely died as soon as the Nexus Point collapsed. They didn't know if the plan would work, so they asked Luik to escape. He used Verdalink to Tether himself to an Aetherfern, where he remained trapped until I found him a few days ago."

Felix quickly scribbled Cam's words into his notebook. While he wrote, he spoke. "So, Luik sacrificed his own autonomy to save the lives of the humans, and then spent over a century and a half trapped in a plant just to make sure we were safe?"

Cam gave a slight nod.

"Well, he says there is another astral Nexus Point out there somewhere, so he didn't completely sacrifice his own autonomy. But the rest is true."

Luik demonstrated extraordinary selflessness, relinquishing his autonomy for over 150 years to protect humanity. Such prolonged sacrifice reflects remarkable resilience, loyalty, and moral conviction, Felix wrote in his notebook. He gritted his teeth before adding, *I should try to be more like him.*

"Does Luik have any idea why the Shrouds are starting to decay?" Illyria asked.

"He says that it's possible that the Shrouds are experiencing some sort of natural decay, but that it's also likely that there's an external force making it happen more quickly. Possibly an Elmia or group of Elmias." Cam sighed, running his transformed hand through his hair. He winced as one of the claws on his reptilian finger left a light cut just below his hairline. "It's possible other Elmias survived the destruction of the citadel. Even if they didn't, there were other Elmias out there who could still be alive now."

"Why would an Elmia want to destroy the Aurora Shrouds?" Felix asked.

"Most Elmias wouldn't. But Gaalron and his disciples would."

Cam went on to explain how the Elmia, Gaalron, feeling oppressed by the humans of Avoni, sought to eradicate their reliance on humans by turning Avoni into a nation where both species could thrive independent of each other.

"Gaalron wanted to create a land where Elmias and humans could live together in harmony," Cam continued. "He believed that could only happen if Avoni had the perfect balance between the astral and the physical. Tilt that balance too far in either direction, and you end up with..." He swept his arms toward the ruined landscape around them. "...all of this. If he's right, then the Shrouds should be destroyed."

"I've got to ask, then. Is there a chance that this 'Gaalron' is right?" Illyria asked. "I hate to suggest that the Shrouds should be destroyed, but would that get rid of the Sundered Lands?"

"I trust Luik," Cam said emphatically. "Gaalron was an Elmia leader but not a scholar. All the Elmia scholars, when presented with this plan, said that it would ultimately fail. Gaalron went ahead with it anyway."

Felix scribbled notes very quickly. It was hard to keep up with all of this.

There wasn't even enough time to think of good insults about Cam!

"So basically, what Luik is saying is that either Gaalron escaped and is working to destroy the Aurora Shrouds, or it's a random group of Elmias from a different astral Nexus Point?" Chek asked.

Cam's face went distant as he listened to Luik. Moments later, his eyes widened.

"Luik!" Cam complained. "Why didn't you tell me about that?"

"Tell you about what?" Illyria said, her voice curious.

Cam shook his head in frustration. "Supposedly, Gaalron talked to Luik."

Illyria's jaw dropped. "What! When did that happen?"

"Last night, before the riots. Well, I guess that confirms that suspicion."

"So, Gaalron has a human Tether?" Felix asked.

"Either that, or he found the other astral Nexus Point," Cam answered. "Unfortunately, Luik doesn't know where it is. Its location was kept secret from him, as part of the treaty they signed."

A silence fell on them for a few seconds. The only sound was the light crackling of wood from their fire.

"I...I think I know where it is," Illyria said, her voice a whisper. Everyone, except Soren, looked stunned. She gave an embarrassed shrug and continued. "Back in Kevilton, I noticed the sickness starting on the borders, closer to the edge of the Aurora Shroud. I started doing some research of my own, and with a little help"—she motioned towards Chek—"I think I figured it out. It's in the Jaram Mountains. There's supposed to be a holy site there."

Cam nodded, his hand scratching at his chin.

"The Jaram Mountains. Hmmm. The same place the Reapers supposedly came from."

The mountains. Holy sites. Elmias.

Felix dropped his charcoal and leapt to his feet as understanding dawned on him.

"The Elmia Temple?" he shouted. He cringed as the group cast annoyed glances his way. "Sorry for shouting. I got excited. I've researched Elmias a lot over the last several years. There's a lot of conflicting information, but many historians believe there was some sort of temple in the mountains. Supposedly, the temple stored and designed Elmia artifacts."

"Like the Scepter of Alderia," Cam said, his tone thoughtful. "Luik said the Scepter inverts physical and astral energies and can amplify an Elmia's abilities. It's what Gaalron used to create the Sundered Lands in the first place. Supposedly, after Gaalron used it, it would have returned to its place of creation."

That's interesting! Write that down! Felix thought.

"Wait, so let's regroup for a second," Chek interjected. "The Reapers came from the mountains. The temple is in the mountains. The Scepter is in the mountains."

Cam nodded and added, "And it's possible that Gaalron is also in the mountains. Either that, or he's heading there now. Either way, that's definitely where I need to go." He paused for a moment, letting a defeated sigh escape his lips. "Unfortunately, the mountain range is huge. I won't be sure where to look. It could take years."

"That's not true!" Chek exclaimed, reaching into her satchel. She pulled out several sheets of paper and rolled them open, careful not to tear them on the rocky ground.

They were maps, which made Felix chuckle.

Always the Vanguard Route Coordinator—it was just like Chek to have the clarity of thought to bring maps into the Sundered Lands.

"Some of these are from before the Sundering," she said, her voice growing hoarse from the air. "A few of them give indications of military settlements in the mountains. Wouldn't it make sense that the settlements would be near the temple?"

Cam nodded again.

"Then we know it's one of three locations!" Chek said, her voice breathless. "We just have to go to each of the three."

Cam raised an eyebrow.

"We?"

"Yes, we!" Felix exclaimed, throwing down his charcoal again as he rose to his feet. "Don't think that we're going to sit this one out. Nobody knows those old maps better than Chek, and Luik's already shown that he doesn't know much about the temple. You'll need me too."

He shook his head.

"And what happens if we run into a Reaper?"

"That's where you and Luik come in. You're the muscle. Chek and I will be the brain." He gave a wink to Chek, hoping she picked up on the subtle insult cast Cam's way.

Soren stood up in a huff.

"This is stupid," he said, bitterness in his voice. "This is...this is just so stupid. What in Aurora's Name are you thinking, Cam? There's too much area to explore. That's assuming you're even right about the possible locations. And it's too dangerous. We can't do this on our own."

Cam frowned.

"Soren, if you have a better suggestion, I'm open to hearing it. But I'm going into the mountains. You don't have to come with us."

Soren froze in frustrated indecision. Then, he frowned, glaring at Cam.

"Sorry, I can't do this," he said, turning to leave.

"Sor, stop! Where are you going?" Illyria called out.

Without turning around, he simply said, "To get you all some real help."

Chapter 24

Cam awoke with a start, his heart already pounding before his eyes even opened. The harsh red light from the sky bled over the jagged landscape, casting long, sinister shadows that stretched across the rocks. His muscles were tense, his chest tight, and his breaths came shallow. He shifted uncomfortably on the uneven stones he'd slept on, though he knew the sharp edges weren't what had kept him awake.

No matter how still the night had been, the presence of the others nearby gnawed at him.

As Cam adjusted the strap of his cloak, movement caught his eye. A Necrothorn Beetle, massive and armor-plated, was skittering towards him over the rocky ground. Its jagged legs clicked with every step. A spike of fear shot through his chest. Instinctively, he willed it to turn away. For a breathless moment, nothing happened. Then the creature paused, its antennae twitching, and veered off to the side, disappearing into a crevice in the stone.

Eyeing the spot where the beetle disappeared, Cam stood, brushing the pebbles from his cloak, his hands trembling despite his efforts to steady them. He clenched his jaw, forcing his gaze upward to the blood-red sky, its oppressive hue casting a suffocating weight over the landscape. Above, the black fog churned violently, swirling like a restless, furious soul trapped in an eternal dance of rage.

Good morning, Cam. It's so nice to see you wake up. Was last night restful for you?

How was Luik always so energetic?

Cam grunted in response, stretching his back. He winced, feeling the ache in his muscles.

I was afraid you might not have slept well. You seemed to startle with every sound.

Shaking his head, as it to cast off his grogginess, Cam thought back, *Luik, I'm curious about something. Do you sleep when Tethered?*

Elmias never sleep, he answered. *Even if I were in my own body right now, I wouldn't need to sleep.*

Are you still aware of the environment when I'm asleep?

Yes.

So, you're basically watching me while I sleep?

Cam felt Luik's emotions stir in slight embarrassment.

It's not that I'm watching you. Rather, it's more like I'm aware of you. Additionally, in the interest of full transparency, I must admit that I'm able to see some of your dreams. Tell me, who is Silva? Your thoughts kept going to her while you slept.

At the mention of her name, Cam felt his heart race, a familiar fear working its way into his stomach.

She's nobody, Cam thought, angry at Luik for bringing her up.

She's somebody, Luik corrected. *Who is she?*

Cam struggled for a moment, wondering if he should answer or not. After a moment of indecision, he responded by thinking, *She's dead. She's an Eternal Echo, forever trapped in the Sundered Lands*, and refused to elaborate.

Ah. Thank you for the explanation. Apologies if my intrusion into your dreams made you uncomfortable.

He shrugged his shoulders and rolled his eyes.

It did make him uncomfortable, but there was little he could do about it now.

I'm not thrilled about it, but we're already sharing thoughts. I guess this is just something I'll have to get used to, Cam thought, eager to change the subject to anything else. *So, you don't sleep. Does that mean you never get tired?*

Yes and no. It's a different kind of tired than what you are referring to. A more accurate statement would be to say that I grow weary. Weary of things, to be exact.

Such as? Cam asked, truly curious.

Such as always being Tethered. Luik paused for a moment, contemplating his words more carefully. *I am not suggesting that being Tethered to you specifically is unpleasant. Rather, all Tetherings grow unpleasant. After a period of time, one is simply weary of lacking an autonomous body, as I'm sure you can imagine.*

Cam nodded, trying his best to empathize. He'd lived most of his life trapped under an Aurora Shroud, but even then, he'd been able to make his own choices. What would it be like to have that freedom stripped away?

You said that an Elmia can manifest in the Sundered Lands, right? Would...would you want to stop being Tethered to me?

I appreciate the sentiment, but that's a bad idea, Cam, Luik replied, a note of melancholy in his voice. *As you told Felix last night, you're in Crimson Limbo. Separation for any length of time would risk your life.*

It doesn't have to be long. Maybe just a few minutes.

Through their bond, Cam could sense Luik's emotions churning.

No, the Elmia almost whispered after a few seconds of contemplation. *To taste freedom, just to have it taken away so quickly? It'd be torture.*

I'm sorry, Luik. I have no idea what it must be like.

But you do, don't you? Luik said. *You've lived most of your life in your own sort of Tethering. You're trapped by your own fear. You Tether yourself to others, allowing them to make choices for you, rather than making decisions for yourself.*

Scratching at the scales on his right arm, Cam shook his head.

Why would you say that?

Please, we haven't been Tethered but for a few days, yet I have learned this about you. You're afraid. Afraid of failure. It controls you. It's caused you to stop trusting yourself.

There's nothing wrong with being careful, Cam countered.

This is more than trying to be careful. You're trying to avoid being accountable, Luik corrected, his voice firm, yet gentle, like a parent teaching a child. *Sometimes, the most courageous thing someone can do is to make a choice and live with the consequences.*

Cam thought about this for a moment, fidgeting slightly in discomfort.

So, in creating the Sundered Lands, Gaalron was being brave? he thought, trying to deflect.

Yes. In spite of what others said, Gaalron sincerely believed he was making a choice that would better the lives of humans and Elmias. That took tremendous bravery, and in spite of the terrible consequences of his decision, I respect that bravery.

Cam's heart raced for a moment, and he could feel his face getting warmer. He knew that Luik would be able to sense that this struck a nerve with him.

You feel respect for the being that destroyed Avoni, ending and changing the lives of millions of people?

I can respect his conviction, even if I don't trust it. Additionally, I will say this. I trust you. And I believe it's time for you to start acting with conviction. Your fears have been your constant companion, and it's time for you to lead them, rather than letting them lead you.

Great. Just be more like Gaalron.

Ignoring the Elmia, Cam began to gather what few belongings he still had. His daggers had been taken by the Rathian soldiers, leaving him with only his bag of Courier maps and spare Aetherfern leaves. After last night's campfire, he had very little Aetherfern left.

To his left, Chek began to stir. Boils and scales were already starting to appear on her neck, twisting up onto her face. They likely extended all over her body.

Cam's face twisted in pity.

She sat up quickly, shaking her head. Instinctively, she reached up to brush hair out of her face, cringing visibly as she touched her bald scalp.

At least nobody has lost bone strength, Cam thought, remembering hearing a story of a Courier in training who had become crippled after only a day in the Sundered Lands as his bones wasted away. Even now, that man had trouble walking correctly.

Stepping over towards Chek, Cam said, "We'll be under an Aurora Shroud before the end of the day."

"Can't come soon enough for me," she said, her voice hoarse. "I have a new respect for the Couriers. This is all pretty awful."

Say something kind to her. She's likely struggling inside, Luik said.

Cam gave an empathetic smile, squatting next to her. In a low voice, he said, "You're right, it's harsh out here. Extremely harsh. There's a reason nobody ever leaves the Aurora Shrouds. You're showing a lot of strength; I truly admire that about you." Chek flushed for a moment, and Cam added, "You'd make an excellent Courier."

"I'm not sure my body handles the environment as well as a Courier's," she said, her tone mocking, but her eyes smiled in appreciation. "Not sure how I fooled you otherwise. It must be my forehead. You must have a thing for bald women."

He chuckled softly, leaning back on his heels. "Maybe it's the confidence. Bald or not, you're handling this better than most would. And, you know, foreheads are underrated."

Chek raised an eyebrow, smirking despite the weariness in her eyes. "Underrated, huh? That your professional opinion as a Courier?"

"Absolutely," he said with mock seriousness. "Big foreheads mean big brains. Or something like that. Anyway, you've got nothing to worry about."

Chek shook her head, but her smile lingered. "You're impossible."

As she rifled through her pack, Cam stood and glanced toward the horizon, where the faint, shimmering hues of an Aurora Shroud were just barely visible in the distance. "Let's get moving," he said, offering her a hand. "We've got a lot of awful to outrun before nightfall."

Chek took his hand, pulling herself to her feet. "Fine, but don't think this means I'm letting you off the hook about the forehead thing. You owe me some better compliments."

Cam grinned as he stepped away. "Deal."

As a follow-up on that conversation, do you have "a thing" for bald women? Because all Elmias are bald. If any of my friends survived, I could introduce you, Luik said.

Rising to his feet, Cam turned away from Chek.

Luik, I'm not sure how to answer that. How would I even be able to see an Elmia in person?

You'd have to be in an astral Nexus Point. However, your body can't survive long there, so you'd have to be Tethered to a separate Elmia in order to court her.

That sounds awkward.

That's what I've heard. I hear that it makes lovemaking a particularly unpleasant ordeal for all parties involved.

Cam shook his head, banishing those thoughts from his mind.

Luik, that's so gross. The Elmia seemed to chuckle in response.

Please accept my apologies for the crude comment. A disadvantage to being Tethered is that I get bored sometimes. I'll try to restrain myself in the future. Then, in a slightly mischievous voice, *Plus, we both know that another has your attention.*

Sparing a quick glance towards Illyria, Cam thought back to Luik, *I'm not sure what you're talking about.*

Oh please. You cannot lie to me. Remember, I can feel your emotions and hear your thoughts.

Yes, and I wish you'd stop that, Cam thought, irritated.

Turning, he stepped towards Illyria, who was studying some sort of book. Her dark hair had been pulled back into tight braids and was hidden by the hood of her green cloak.

"Sleep well?" he said. She jumped slightly as he spoke. "Sorry, I didn't mean to startle you."

"I slept fine, considering the environment. Not the softest bed I've ever used," she said. Then, with a smile, she added, "Rumor has it that there's a dangerous Crimson Limbo man out here just waiting to eat up all our food."

Cam grinned.

"Well, I've got bad news for you. I hear this man has a big appetite and is close by."

"Don't worry, Courier. I'll keep you safe," she said with a wink.

"Okay, Gloves," Cam said. She wrinkled her brow at this.

"Gloves?"

"Yeah. Gloves." He pointed a reptilian finger at her hands. "Because you're always wearing gloves."

She scrunched her nose in a cute expression that brought another smile to Cam's face.

"Many of the ingredients I use to make elixirs burn the skin." She waggled the fingers of her gloved hand at Cam. "Hence the gloves. Maybe Luik can think of a better name?"

Absolutely I can: Cam's Future Wife.

"He's got nothing," Cam said, wishing he could give the Elmia a glare. "Turns out that Elmias completely lack creativity."

That's actually true, Luik said.

Illyria snickered. "Well, Gloves it is then. At least until you or Luik can think of something better."

"Hey...uh...I made breakfast," Felix said sheepishly. In his hands were several sausages. "We didn't have any pans, so I kind of just threw them in the fire."

They all walked toward Felix and sat in a loose circle to eat. After finishing one, Cam grabbed another. And then another.

"Wow, someone's hungry," Felix said, a mixture of amusement and irritation in his voice. "Being Tethered to an Elmia, do you have twice the hunger?"

Cam shook his head as he finished eating the sausage.

"I'm a big guy. Big guys need more food," he said simply.

"Well, is the 'big guy' ready to leave?" Felix said as Chek stepped up next to him. "Because I'm very ready to be under an Aurora Shroud." He leaned over to Chek and whispered, "Anything to not have to smell Mr. Stench Tower anymore."

Cam shrugged, pretending to not hear the comment.

"You'll be there tonight. Assuming that it hasn't started fragmenting." Chek turned and whispered something to her brother who began snickering. Cam rolled his eyes and stepped away.

It didn't take long before they broke camp and began the remainder of the journey towards Perth. The progress was painful. Chek had to step carefully over the rocky terrain, her right leg stiff and dragging as she walked. The boils began to spread onto her hands and up her face.

Felix fared only slightly better than his sister. Some boils had begun to appear on his hands, and he appeared to have a difficult time breathing. A few hours into the day, a blue lump began to form on the side of his neck, indicating that he'd breathed in a Bluecoil at some point.

"Illyria, can you do anything about that?" Cam asked, tightening his own face mask.

"Not here. Not on the road," she said. "But I can surgically remove it once we get to Perth."

Cam nodded and continued forward, grateful for his Tethering with Luik.

The pain the others were experiencing served as another reminder that life was not supposed to exist in the Sundered Lands.

Cam tried to steady his nerves as they trudged forward, but his thoughts churned relentlessly. What if the citizens of Perth had all been transformed?

He shuddered, glancing at Chek and Felix. If the people of Perth were gone, if they arrived to find the Shroud broken, what then? What would he do with them? The thought of abandoning them to die in the Sundered Lands was unthinkable, but the alternatives weren't much better.

Just as the sun was beginning to set on the horizon, they finally began to approach the edge of Perth's Aurora Shroud. The town was located in a canyon at the edge of the Jaram Mountains. The canyon loomed ahead, its majestic form split down the middle as if cleaved by a giant's blade, creating two towering halves with steep walls.

A collective relaxation seemed to seize the group, knowing that rest was only a few minutes away.

Illyria stepped over towards Cam. Speaking in a voice slightly muffled due to her face mask, she said, "How's it feel to be coming home?"

Cam shrugged. "Honestly, after what happened in Rath, I just hope that it's still safe."

Illyria nodded in understanding. "At least there's no cracks in the Aurora Shroud. None that we can see, at least."

At last, they came up on the edge of the protective barrier. As they stepped through the Shroud, Felix and Chek audibly gasped in relief and began to laugh. Cam smiled, knowing that at least the three people traveling with him were safe from the Sundered Lands.

He also felt a great deal of relief knowing that the people of Perth were safe from corruption. A week ago, their safety would have been a foregone conclusion, but after the decay of Rath's Aurora Shroud, he had feared walking into a village full of recently transformed scaletaints.

Perth was a small village, and as such, it received few visits from the Vanguard Couriers. Because of this, they often had welcome crews located at the beginning of the canyon road to greet any newcomers.

There was no such greeting for Cam. Instead, there was only silence, interrupted only by the sound of their light footfalls.

Cam froze for a moment before setting off at a jog.

Something is wrong here, he thought, beginning to hurry down the road.

Wrong how? asked Luik.

I'm not sure. It's just too quiet.

A moment later, he reached the road's final bend. The path beneath his feet twisted sharply as the narrow canyon began to widen. Heart pounding in his chest, he turned and looked down into the valley of Perth.

All he could do was stand and stare in horror.

Illyria was the second to round the bend. As she reached Cam, she gasped, holding a hand to her mouth.

"Cam...what happened?"

He had no words. Instead, all he could do was stare at the carnage.

Bodies lay haphazardly in the streets, the ground beneath them dark from blood.

It was a massacre.

Chapter 25

Throughout his entire life, Luik had hated violence. No amount of military expeditions from the Avonian king could change the fact that he was more comfortable in his garden. Causing someone pain—even an enemy—felt so wrong to him.

Watching through Cam's eyes as the man scanned the macabre scene in Perth, Luik felt sick.

The once-vibrant lives of Perth's citizens were now frozen in haunting scenes of despair. The air hung heavy with the acrid scent of death, and scattered body parts served as grim reminders of the violence that had transpired.

Some figures were sprawled on the ground, their futile attempts to escape evident in their final, contorted poses. Others clutched makeshift weapons, their dead hands still gripping tools of defense against whatever creatures had slaughtered them.

For several minutes, the group stood without making a sound. The silence was broken when a mournful whimper escaped Chek's lips. Illyria, her eyes fixed on the lifeless forms surrounding them, enveloped Chek in a silent, comforting embrace.

"I'm going to throw up," Felix said, staring into the dead eyes of an elderly woman, her face still transfixed in a terrified expression.

Luik agreed with the young man, feeling his stomach turn. It was a strange feeling, likely his mind's response to the sight of death. Cam must have sensed Luik's discomfort, and he averted his gaze from the gruesome scene, sparing Luik the visual assault of the devastation.

Thank you, Luik said, feeling slightly embarrassed.

It's okay. I don't want to look either.

"I didn't know scaletaints could do this," Illyria said, her voice hollow. Cam shook his head.

"This wasn't scaletaints." He pointed at the body of a middle-aged man lying face down on the ground. "Look at the wounds. This man was gored and then left for dead. A scaletaint wouldn't do this. Scaletaints eat their prey."

"Reaper?" Illyria whispered, looking over towards Chek and Felix. The twins looked at each other before nodding.

"I didn't see any of the bodies," Chek said, her voice hushed, "but the descriptions of their corpses match these remains."

The bobbing of Luik's vision suggested Cam was nodding. The change in perspective forced Luik to briefly look at the corpses again, causing him to cringe. For a moment, he felt a sense of jealousy at Cam's ability to remain so calm.

No. Wait. Cam wasn't calm.

He feels numb, Luik realized.

What was that? Cam asked.

Apologies for my intrusive thought, Luik said, slightly flustered. *I merely came to a realization about your emotional state.*

Cam scratched at the back of his head for a moment.

I lived most of my life here. All these people...I knew them.

The emotions in Cam slowly began to stir. It was slight at first, like faint movements of individual blades of grass in the wind. However, upon closer inspection, Luik could sense the serpentine movements of guilt mixed with self-doubt.

None of this was your fault, Luik said, his voice firm.

Before Luik could hear Cam's response, a raucous laugh filled the air. It was harsh and grating, like stones being ground against each other. The sudden voice caused Cam's vision to jerk quickly towards the sound.

Approaching them on all fours was the figure of a man. He had unkempt, matted black hair falling around his weathered, wrinkled face. His ragged clothes hung in tatters, and though his laughter echoed through the air, his contorted expression revealed a hidden agony beneath the facade of mirth.

"Vaelin!" Cam said with a gasp, hurrying over towards the man. He crouched down next to him, offering him some water. Vaelin shook his head.

"She was right. She was right. She was right."

Cam gripped the wild man by the shoulders.

"Vaelin, tell me what happened. Are you hurt? Did anyone else survive?"

The harsh laughter grew louder. The man was wheezing now, struggling to catch his breath.

"She was right. She was right." Though he was continuing to laugh, his face took on a pained and pleading expression, as if he were silently begging Cam to help him.

"Vaelin, it's going to be okay. Breathe with me." Cam took slow, exaggerated breaths, raising and lowering his hands to help guide Vaelin. The wild man nodded slowly, trying to match his breathing with Cam's.

A moment later, Illyria was at Cam's side, her hands digging through her medicine pouch. Luik felt Cam's appreciation for the help.

"What's wrong with him?" she said, her voice calm and even.

"He was born this way. He has fits," Cam said, continuing to breathe in an exaggerated manner.

She nodded, reaching out and grabbing the man's arm. She pulled down his long sleeve and placed two fingers on his wrist to check his pulse.

"Vaelin, you're going to be just fine. Are you able to drink something?"

Vaelin nodded, and Illyria reached back into her pouch. She pulled out a small vial of purple powder and sprinkled it into a separate vial, shaking it to make sure it all dissolved. Then, she handed it to Vaelin.

"Drink this. It'll help you relax." The man obeyed. Another burst of laughter interrupted his first drink, laughter mixed with coughing as he choked on the liquid. However, he managed to swallow it the second time, and the elixir quickly took effect. After a few minutes, his breathing had settled, and the harsh laughter had ceased.

"I didn't know Aetherfern could do that," Cam whispered.

"Actually, that wasn't Aetherfern at all. That was Black Horn extract."

I'm impressed. That's a rare herb indeed, Luik said in approval.

"I've never even heard of that before," Cam whispered to Illyria.

"And that is why you're not a Healer, Courier," she teased, poking gently at his arm.

"Whatever you say, Gloves." Then, Cam turned towards Vaelin and spoke in a serious voice. "Can you tell me what happened here?"

"She was right," the man repeated, this time in a whisper. Cam frowned.

"I don't know what you're talking about. Who was right?"

"She...she was right," Vaelin said again, gripping Cam's arm as he did so. He looked intensely at Cam, as if he were begging the man to understand what he was saying.

Try a different tactic. Something he can answer in his current state, Luik suggested.

"Did anyone else survive?" Cam asked.

Vaelin groaned, frustration crossing his face, and he glanced towards the ground.

"She was right. She was right. She was right," he muttered. Cam grunted and rose to his feet.

"Look, Cam, I don't think we're going to learn anything. He's clearly lost it," Felix said.

Cam shook his head and replied, "No, he's just upset. It happens to him sometimes. Once he calms down enough, I think we can get him to talk to us."

Illyria stepped over towards a corpse. She knelt down, inspecting the body, her face remaining stoic. After a few moments, she spoke.

"Judging by the decay and condition of the corpses, I'd guess that they were killed recently. Possibly just a few days ago."

"We need to take care of the bodies," Cam said.

Perth had never faced the overpopulation issues that plagued the larger cities, but, like all settlements, space was an invaluable commodity. Burial wasn't an option. As was the custom, all who died were burned, their ashes scattered to the winds.

The scale of what awaited them was staggering. Burning all the citizens of Perth would take days. Cam pushed the thought aside and focused on what he could do. The weight of responsibility bore down on him, but he would do what was necessary.

As Illyria was preparing Felix for surgery to remove the Bluecoil, he suggested families be burned together in their own fire. Although it made the process much more inefficient, his idea felt like a better way to honor the dead.

Faces of friends and acquaintances, once vibrant and alive, haunted Cam's thoughts. Every street corner whispered memories of shared laughter and the camaraderie that once defined Perth. The very air seemed to resonate with the collective sorrow of a community torn asunder.

The guilt returned when Cam found the body of his uncle. In his mind, he could still hear the man's judgmental voice.

This is your fault. This happened because of you, the voice said. Cam's brain knew it was speaking lies, but his heart couldn't help but wonder at the possible truth in the statement.

As he surveyed the burning forms that once comprised the heartbeat of his hometown, the initial emotional numbness had gone away and grief, like an unrelenting tide, began to consume him.

He clenched his jaw, trying to ignore the pain.

I am sorry, Luik said. *No one should have to bury his entire village.*

I'm fine, Cam thought. *And they're not being buried. They're burning.*

Your emotions are understandable, Luik said, his voice calm and gentle. *Most would feel exactly as you do. If I may, please allow yourself to feel your pain. You don't need to suppress it.*

He rolled his eyes.

A lecture was the last thing that Cam wanted to hear.

I'm not suppressing them, Cam replied.

Cam, I can feel your emotions. More than that, I know what you are feeling, and what you are trying not to feel.

Then stop that, Cam thought bitterly. *My emotions are my own.*

I wish I could stop. I know this feels invasive, Luik said in a patient and empathetic tone. *I remember the first person I was Tethered to. The lack of privacy was very uncomfortable for both of us, but it ultimately led to us becoming very close.*

Then why did you leave him? Cam asked, a hint of anger leaking through.

Luik paused for a moment, conflicted, before answering.

Her. Luik's voice was weak in Cam's mind. *Her name was Nahliah. And I didn't leave her. She left me.*

The revelation hung in the air, leaving Cam momentarily stunned. The boundary between his emotions and Luik's blurred, and for a moment, they shared the weight of sadness, guilt, and anger in a tapestry of pain.

I'm sorry, Cam thought. *I didn't know.*

She agreed with Gaalron, Luik said, a deep bitterness entering his voice. *She wanted the Elmias to be free. She wanted...she wanted me to be free.*

Cam could feel Luik's emotions stirring. A tumultuous mixture of loathing, misery, and betrayal.

And something else beneath it all. Was it affection? No, that wasn't it.

Cam's eyes widened.

You loved her, he thought with sudden realization.

Yes, the Elmia admitted, his voice sad. *And she loved me back. When the Treaty of the Tethering was signed, I thought my life was over. Little did I know that it was just beginning. When you're literally Tethered to someone's soul, sharing thoughts and feelings...every secret made visible, every fear laid bare, and to still accept each other? I would have given up my autonomy just to stay by her side.*

Cam felt a rush of warmth and tenderness radiate from Luik, mingled with the weight of sorrow. *But she didn't want that, did she?*

She wanted me to be free, to live my own life. I understood her reasoning, but...the thought of losing her was unbearable. I thought we could make it work, but she didn't want me to be her prisoner.

What happened to her? Cam asked.

I do not know where she was on the day of the Sundering, yet it would have been quite difficult for her to reach an Aurora Shroud. I'm assuming she became a scaletaint. Even if she didn't, she would have died of old age by now.

Luik, I'm sorry to make you relive all this. I...I wish I hadn't said anything.

Please, do not apologize. Cam, for all your strengths, you have yet to learn that it is not your responsibility to keep others from feeling their own pain.

The thought felt alien to him.

What was Cam apart from his ability to carry out the wishes of others?

Then what is my responsibility? Cam thought back. *What am I supposed to do now?*

You can only do that which is right, Luik said.

He rolled his eyes in an exaggerated manner.

I wish it were that easy, Luik. Maybe it is for you, but it's not for me. What if I choose wrong?

You will often choose wrong. If the point of life was to avoid failure, nothing good could be accomplished. But you can own your failings. They belong to you. Use them. Let them shape you, sharpen you, and guide you toward something greater.

A hush fell over them as Cam absorbed Luik's words. On the surface, it resonated with perfect clarity. Yet, in his heart, doubt, the relentless beast that he'd been trapped with his entire life, gnawed at him.

Perhaps it was time to cage that beast.

Perhaps it was time to act.

So, what do I do?

Know you will fail. Act anyway, Luik said.

"Act anyway," Cam whispered.

Their conversation was interrupted by uneven footsteps. Cam turned his attention from the flames to see Chek stepping towards him. The boils and scales were beginning to recede from her face, but she was still swollen around her eyes.

She joined Cam, lowering herself to the rocky ground beside him. For a while, neither of them spoke. Words felt unnecessary. They simply sat staring at the dancing flames.

Finally, she spoke to Cam, her voice quiet in the night.

"I'm an orphan. My father died when I was born, due to Rath population control laws. My mother died when I was sixteen. Prostitution." She hesitated for a few moments before speaking again. "I know this hurts."

"I lost my parents at a young age, too," Cam replied. Chek looked him in the eyes with a disarming expression, so he continued. "My mother died during childbirth. She was sick, and the Vanguard wasn't able to get her medicine on time. My father died a few years later."

"How did he die?" Chek asked, her voice kind and delicate.

"I don't know for sure," Cam admitted, his voice hollow. "He just...he left Perth. Left the Aurora Shroud. I guess he couldn't handle the grief anymore. He probably became a scaletaint."

She nodded for a moment before saying, "So these people were your family."

Cam felt the truth of her words strike him deeply. His throat tightened, and he gave a brief nod, unable to fully voice the emotion swelling inside him.

He turned to look at her and froze when he saw that she was staring right back at him. In the quiet solemnity of that moment, he looked into her dark eyes and saw her soul. He saw her pain, her loss, and years of carrying burdens others wouldn't understand.

And even deeper, he realized something. In spite of her life, Chek radiated the quiet strength of someone who had made peace with the parts of herself that were broken.

There was no frailty in her, but a deep strength that he envied and admired.

She silently put her arm around Cam and gave him a tight, comforting squeeze. Her arm felt warm against him. They sat that way in silence.

After a few minutes, Cam said, "This is why we need to find the Scepter. So that this will never happen again."

Even as he spoke, the self-doubt gnawed at Cam, its relentless grip tightening with each passing moment. He tried to push it aside, to ignore the nagging voice in his mind that whispered of inadequacy. Was it even possible for him to find the Scepter?

What was it that Luik had said?

Know you will fail. Act anyway.

"I'll find it," Cam said in a hushed but firm voice. His heart didn't agree with the words leaving his mouth, but he could only hope that his emotions would follow his actions.

Perhaps he could be strong like Chek.

Soren grunted as he walked through the barren landscape. The corruption from the Sundering had destroyed much of the natural flora in Avoni, but here, it was a complete wasteland. Cleanly cut trunks of trees served as the only reminder that any life had ever appeared in this place.

With each stride, ash and gravel crunched beneath his boots, the ground bearing witness to the ruin that surrounded him. Above, the scarlet sky stretched endlessly. Swirling black clouds loomed overhead, their ceaseless movement mirroring the turmoil below.

He'd traveled all night, but he was close now.

The wind caused his tattered black cloak to billow as he trekked up the rocky terrain towards the mouth of the cave. It had been a few months since he had been here, and a nervous energy filled his stomach. His hand instinctively drifted towards the hilt of the broadsword strapped to his back.

"Captain Soren requesting a formal audience with the Sovereign," he cried out, his voice echoing across the rocky terrain. For a moment, the only response to his cry was the slight hiss coming out of the mouth of the cave.

He cringed, remembering the nightmarish screams of pain. He wasn't far enough into the cave to hear them now, but he knew that the screaming was still continuing unabated.

There was no mercy for those poor souls.

Finally, he heard the approach of footsteps. Two figures emerged, their bodies encased in formidable, yet surprisingly agile, bulky black armor. Tubes rose from the breastplates, connecting to their helmets, completely obscuring their faces. In their hands, they wielded broadswords with a menacing aura.

"What do you desire to discuss with the Sovereign?" the first guard said in a deep, growling tone.

Soren grinned in defiance.

"The location of the Scepter of Alderia."

Chapter 26

The following morning dawned with a heavy atmosphere lingering over Perth. The aftermath of the mass cremations cast a somber shadow across the town, a town whose once lively streets now bore the weight of profound grief, punctuated by the pyres scattered across its streets.

Cam hadn't slept well. Even in the comfort of his own bed, he found a disquiet in his soul and struggled to shake the pain he felt at the loss of life. The constant tossing and turning had led to a pain in his neck, causing him to wince slightly when turning his head.

By the looks on everyone's faces, it seemed like nobody else felt rested either.

At least there was food. Felix had gotten up first and raided the inn's kitchen, cooking a breakfast for the group.

For that, Cam was grateful.

They sat in dismal quiet, silently eating their meal until Felix spoke up.

"So...what's the plan? How are we going to find the temple?"

Time to lead, Luik's voice prodded.

Cam's heart began to race, and he nervously bounced his foot under the table. Narrowing his eyes, as if the focus would ward off his own anxiety, he took a deep breath and said, "Each of us brings something to the table." He pointed at each one of them. "Illyria is a Healer. Felix, you understand aspects of Elmia lore that even Luik was unaware of. And Chek, you've studied the topography of pre-Sundered Avoni." Lastly, he pointed at himself. "I know how to traverse the Sundered Lands."

"And fight scaletaints," Chek added. Cam nodded.

"Yes. And fight scaletaints."

Don't forget about me, Luik said.

"And none of this would be possible without Luik. His bad jokes and intrusive commentary will wear on us so much that we will be grateful for the end of the world."

That's hardly fair! Luik exclaimed, but Cam could sense that the Elmia appreciated the joke.

"Obviously, I'm coming," Illyria said, a smile on her face. "I'd go by myself if I had to."

"But what's the plan?" Felix said insistently.

Cam set his fork down, leaning forward as he braced his hands on the table.

"The plan is simple," he began, keeping his voice steady despite the nervous energy bubbling in his chest. "Chek has narrowed down a few potential locations using her maps. These places fit the profile of where the temple could be. We'll hit them one at a time, starting with the closest. It'll be dangerous, but if we move quickly and stick to the plan, we have a shot." He paused, glancing at each of them. "I'll bring Chek and Illyria with me the first few times. They're essential for this."

He took a deep breath, preparing for the reaction he knew was coming, then spoke again. "Felix, I want you to stay behind."

Felix's face fell, his expression twisting into disbelief. "What? Stay behind? But...but nobody knows Elmias like I do!"

"You're recovering from yesterday," Cam said firmly, pointing at the bandage on the side of his neck where Illyria had removed the Bluecoil. "You need to heal. If those stitches come out or you strain yourself, you could bleed out. Quickly."

He opened his mouth to argue, but Chek spoke up, her voice calm but supportive. "It'll be okay, Felix. You've already done so much. Let yourself rest, so when we need you, you'll be at your best."

His shoulders sagged, his frustration evident, but he didn't push further. He leaned back in his chair, crossing his arms. "Fine," he muttered, though his tone made it clear he wasn't happy about it.

Cam gave him a faint smile, trying to ease the tension. "I promise, you'll have your role in this. Just not yet."

Felix didn't respond, but he gave a reluctant nod.

"So, when do we leave?" Illyria asked.

"Soon."

After helping gather food for the group, Cam reached out to talk to Luik.

You said Elmias have other abilities. If we're going to the mountains, I need to know what they are. I don't want to be caught off guard by anything.

That's true, Luik's voice said. *It will be important for you to learn these things. Let's take a walk to the edge of town.*

At Luik's suggestion, Cam embarked on a solitary walk through the vacant streets of Perth. The emptiness that now pervaded the town echoed profound loss.

Luik, possibly to distract Cam from the pain of his own emotions, began speaking.

All Elmias have access to five standard abilities, Luik explained. *There is also a sixth ability called the Complex. We'll discuss it in a moment.*

And I know three of these. Soul-Forging, Verdalink, and Shadowmelding. As Cam thought these words, he felt the oddest sensation. It felt as if Luik were nodding his head. In the past, he could hear Luik and feel his emotions, but this was the first time he felt like he could sense physical movement from the Elmia.

Correct. Just as important, you know the cost of using these abilities. The fourth ability also has a cost.

Understood, Cam thought in response.

I know you understand. I can feel it, remember? Luik said, a touch of humor in his voice. It brought a smile to Cam's face.

The next ability you should understand is called Time Shifting, Luik said, his tone calm but focused. *It is a more advanced use of Tethering. By concentrating my astral energy on a target, I can create a temporal focal point, changing its flow through time.*

Cam's brow furrowed. *You're saying you can...stop time?*

Not quite. It is more like...slowing or accelerating time around a single object. Without a conduit like the Scepter, the effect is limited. I can only shift one thing at a time, and only if it is small.

Cam nodded. *And what's the cost?*

Your own body, he answered. *It ages you. Ages you very, very quickly.*

We'll have to be careful, then, Cam thought. *And you said that the Scepter impacts these abilities?*

That is correct. The Scepter is powerful enough to break the rules of astral powers. For instance, in my battle with Gaalron, he used the Scepter to Time Shift multiple objects at once.

Cam nodded, taking it all in. *And what is the fifth ability?*

Astral Echoes, Luik answered. *Although, many Elmias see this as an extension of Verdalink, rather than being its own ability.*

How does it work? Cam asked.

Rather than sending your entire body, it is possible to just send part of your consciousness. You will be physically in one place, but you'll also be present mentally somewhere else. Here, let me show you.

Cam felt Luik tapping into the astral powers inside of him, searching for an anchor. After a few seconds, he began to speak again.

I found one. I'm going to cast an Echo of myself now. Through our bond, you'll see what I am seeing.

To his shock, Cam suddenly felt himself in two places at once. He snapped his eyes open. He was on the edge of Perth, close to the inner edge of the Aurora Shroud, but he was also in the village.

Through the Astral Echo, he could clearly see Felix speaking to Illyria, who looked annoyed and had likely been distracted by the young man for a while.

The input of sensory information was a bit overwhelming. Cam shook his head, slightly disoriented, and Luik continued speaking.

Hypothetically, I can cast an infinite number of Echoes. However, your brain's ability to process the new stimuli does not increase with the Echoes. The more Echoes cast, the more split your mind will become.

How far away can you cast an Echo? Cam asked. *If I used Verdalink to travel very far, I'd lose sense of spatial orientation, right? Does that occur with an Echo?*

Cam could feel Luik shaking his head.

Distance is not a limiting factor when casting an Echo, Luik explained. *As you are not physically in a new location, your sense of orientation is not impacted.*

Fascinating, Cam thought. *What about the sixth ability? You said it's called the Complex?*

That's correct, Luik said. *And I do not have that ability. You do.*

Me? thought Cam, suddenly bewildered.

Yes, you. Though, to be frank, I don't know what your Complex is. It changes depending on human and Elmia pairings. The Complex is a result of mixing the unique characteristics of a Tethered pair. For instance, my previous Tether was able to control plant life. This was due to my inherent connection to plants, and her love and skill in gardening.

I'm no gardener. I doubt my connection will be to plants.

Perhaps, Luik said in response. *Or perhaps not. Only time will tell. Typically, the Tethered human discovers their Complex on their own and often quite by accident.*

Well, I hope it is something useful, Cam replied.

When the time is right, I have every expectation that it will be.

Chapter 27

Chek tightened the brace on her leg, wincing as she adjusted the straps, before picking up her bag. A heavy bag would just slow her down, so she had decided to pack light. A few pieces of dried meat to eat, some bandages, and her maps of the Jaram Mountains.

At first, she had felt conflicted about whether or not to venture back into the Sundered Lands. Her short trip to Perth had left her exhausted, pained, and sick. She also knew that she'd likely slow the group down.

But what had ultimately pushed her to go wasn't duty or obligation. It was the quiet conversation she'd had with Cam the night before, the way he stared into the fire, shoulders hunched under the weight of grief she knew all too well. It was a pain she recognized and understood. In that moment, something had stirred within her.

Because on a certain level, she wondered if he could understand her too.

Felix, of course, was less than thrilled with her decision.

"What are you thinking?" he blurted, his voice tinged with disbelief as he paced in front of her. "You saw how your body reacted last time. You were barely hanging on by the end of that trip."

She shouldered her pack and reached for her cane.

"You heard Cam. He needs help."

Felix rolled his eyes, but there was a tension beneath the sarcasm. "Yeah, lots of it. I heard he once outwitted a rock—barely." He grinned, but the joke fell flat between them. "Okay, your turn."

Chek shook her head. "I think he's better than that. Plus, he'll need me. You know how unreliable these maps are."

He stopped pacing and looked at her, his usual lighthearted demeanor dropping as concern etched deep lines into his face. "But, Chek...what if you get too sick? What if the corruption sets in again? What happens if you start transforming?"

"I'll figure it out," she said, her tone flat.

"Figure it out? That's your plan?" His face twisted in disbelief. "Chek, it's not just about you getting sick out there. You could—" His voice faltered, but then he pressed on, his fear spilling out. "You could kill someone."

She felt her face flush with anger, but she managed to keep her voice calm.

"Felix, what do you want me to do? Stay here, under the Aurora Shroud? How much longer is it going to last? We saw what happened to Rath. It's only a matter of time before that happens here."

He looked down, the weight of her words sinking in, but his expression remained conflicted. "But you're a Route Coordinator," he said quietly, desperation creeping into his voice. "You don't have to go out there. You could send word to another city, have the Rangers investigate. There's no reason for you to go."

Shaking her head, Chek's grip tightened on her cane. "It'd take too long. And I'd still have to go out into the Sundered Lands to reach them. If I'm going anyway, I might as well go with Cam and see this through myself. You know as well as I do that the Vanguard moves slow. We can't afford to wait."

Felix's eyes searched hers, a silent plea lingering in them, but she held his gaze with quiet determination. Finally, he sighed, the fight leaving his shoulders as he slumped slightly. "You're really going, aren't you?"

Chek nodded, her resolve unshaken. "My mind's made up. I'm sorry, but I'm going."

Her brother's expression fell, his dark eyes staring at the floorboards beneath his feet. Fingers twitching, he said, "Besides mom, you're the only one who's ever tried to understand me."

Her face softened, and she stepped towards her brother, wrapping her arms around him. She gave him a tight squeeze, whispering into his ear, "And I'll always try, even when I get back."

Felix nodded, pulling away from the hug. Physical affection made him feel awkward, even if it was obvious that he appreciated it.

"And, if you'd finally put those books down for a few minutes, I think you'd realize that there's a lot of other people out there who like you."

He frowned. "Well, in Perth, it'll be just me and Vaelin. That guy is...he's not all there. I just hope he doesn't try to eat me while you all are gone."

"Felix, don't say things like that. Try to be nice to him." She shrugged. "Who knows. Maybe you'll grow to understand him."

He glowered at the ground. "Unlikely," he muttered.

The sound of approaching footsteps caught their attention. Cam strode toward them, his expression steady, though there was a weariness in his eyes.

"Ready to go?" Cam asked. His eyes briefly met Chek's, and she gave a small nod, avoiding his gaze just as quickly as she felt a strange flutter in her chest.

"All set," she replied.

Then Illyria appeared beside him, her long sleeves and dark green Healer's cloak sweeping gracefully as she moved, the deep, rich color complementing her skin. Her black hair was pulled back into neat, tight braids, not a single strand out of place.

Chek shifted, feeling the ache in her leg and the weight of her own worn clothes. There was a sharp pang in her chest as she watched Illyria. So composed, so perfect.

Aurora's Name, how was she that beautiful?

"Courier, let's not keep the Sundered Lands waiting," she said, her voice light and melodic.

"Whatever you say, Gloves," he replied.

As they set off, Chek fell in step behind Cam and Illyria, the weight of her pack pressing down on her shoulders. She focused on the rhythm of her steps as she followed them back into the Sundered Lands.

Chapter 28

She'd done it. It had taken months, but she had finally reached the Jaram Mountains.

Illyria breathed heavily, stepping through the rocky landscape, nearly tripping as a rock shifted under her foot. Instinctively, she raised her hands to break a fall that never came.

"Watch your step," Cam said in front of her.

She forced a smile to her face—she'd been doing that too much lately—and said, "Cam, the master of the Sundered Lands, and the speaker of profound proverbs!" Her tone was playful, but her emotions were not aligned with the facade. As Cam turned around to reply to her, she averted her gaze, fearful that her eyes would betray her truth.

The truth that she was consumed by guilt.

In the past, she had justified her decisions by knowing that what she was doing was for the good of all. This proved to only temporarily bandage her emotions, however, and her shame was beginning to eat her alive.

As she journeyed through the desolate expanse of the Sundered Lands, she had ample opportunity for introspection. This period of self-reflection had not been gentle on her emotions. After a long hour of contemplation amidst the bleak terrain, she had reached an inescapable realization.

She couldn't keep lying, so she was going to tell Cam the truth.

"It's a bit of a stretch to call me 'Master of the Sundered Lands,' and an even bigger stretch to say that I speak proverbs, but I'll take it," Cam said back to her, his tone friendly as he flashed a rare smile.

Well, rare for everyone else at least. He always seemed a bit more disarmed around her.

There was that spike of guilt again.

I'm going to tell him, she thought to herself, trying to silence her emotions. *As soon as we settle into camp.*

As the scarlet sky began to darken above her, she knew that she wouldn't have to wait long.

They continued walking in silence for a while, the sound of boots crunching against stone the only noise that filled the heavy air, until Chek, who had been trailing behind, slowly made her way up to Illyria's side. She moved with a careful determination, her leg brace slowing her pace, but she kept going, her cane tapping lightly against the ground.

"You're doing better than me out here," Illyria said, turning to Chek with a smile, trying to push her inner turmoil aside for a moment. "I've nearly tripped a dozen times already."

Chek smiled back, the warmth in her expression genuine despite her obvious exhaustion. "It's not a race," she replied, her voice calm and resilient. "And if it were, I think we'd both lose to Cam."

Illyria laughed softly, grateful for the distraction. "True," she admitted. "He moves through this place like he was born in it. Meanwhile, I'm over here stumbling on every rock."

Illyria glanced over at her, watching how Chek navigated the terrain. Every step she took was precise, deliberate, as if she was constantly aware of her body's limitations but never letting them define her.

"How are you feeling?" Illyria asked, her voice softening. She knew the journey had been tough on all of them, but especially on Chek.

The woman exhaled, glancing down at her leg for a brief moment before meeting Illyria's eyes. "Tired," she admitted. "But...this is important. I know I'll slow you all down, but it's better than staying behind and doing nothing."

"You're not slowing us down. Do you know how many times we'd have gotten lost out here without you?"

Chek gave a half-hearted grin. "I am the one with the maps."

"And I don't know if I'd trust a Courier with directions."

In front of them, Cam turned and gave them a wry expression.

"I can hear you, Gloves."

"Just want to make sure you stay humble!" Illyria shouted back at him. For a moment, the guilt gnawing at her faded into the background, replaced by the warmth of connection.

But as the sky continued to darken and the night began to settle over them, Illyria knew the feeling wouldn't last. She glanced at Cam, watching the way he moved with that quiet, steady confidence, and her heart ached. Tonight, she would tell him. The truth had waited long enough.

For the first time, Cam was journeying through the Sundered Lands but not as a member of the Vanguard.

It was an odd feeling. Rather than galloping at a breakneck pace through the Sundered Lands, he was slowly trekking up a rocky mountain, seeking out an ancient artifact with the power to save Avoni.

The thought filled his stomach with a heavy dread.

How did he even get to this point? Surely, someone would show up, relieving him of duty and allowing him to return to his regular life.

But no one showed up, so Cam continued forward, suppressing his rising anxiety.

"Stop. We need to scale this cliff. The path that was here likely eroded," Chek said, interrupting his thoughts.

He smiled. At least he didn't have to worry about navigation.

Chek had emerged as an indispensable asset. Armed with a wealth of maps, she showcased an unparalleled ability to analyze the terrain and chart the safest routes. Her quick thinking and map-based solutions proved crucial when faced with dead ends or impassable areas.

As the journey progressed, Chek meticulously updated her maps, annotating details that would aid future travelers in navigating the intricate labyrinth of the Jaram Mountains.

Cam gave her an approving smile. She smiled back, though her body was clearly struggling with the oppressive environment. Her hair had completely fallen out, including her eyebrows, and boils and rashes had already appeared on her neck and arms.

Cam stepped back, examining the cliff she had indicated. Really, it was less of a cliff and more of a very steep hill. Likely, it had once had a smooth incline up, but time and erosion had shifted the landscape.

Nodding, he said, "Sounds good. Who's coming with me first?"

Moments later, Cam was scaling the rugged cliff face, Chek securely strapped to his back with makeshift harnesses they had fashioned from spare rope. Each foothold was precarious, the rocky surface crumbling slightly under the weight of his boots. The jagged edges bit into his palms as he gripped the rough stone, his muscles straining with the effort of supporting not just his own weight but Chek's as well.

Chek clung to him, her arms wrapped tightly around his shoulders, her breath warm against the back of his neck. Though she remained silent, Cam could feel the tension in her body. There was a slight tremor in her grip as she tried not to show her discomfort. He moved carefully, his every step deliberate, eyes focused on finding the next solid handhold. The wind whipped at them, cold and relentless, sending loose pebbles skittering down the rock face.

Then, he climbed back down and carried Illyria up.

Illyria had amazed him these last few days. Despite having only slightly more experience in the Sundered Lands than Chek, she stood as a beacon of resilience, navigating the environment with a seasoned ease.

She'd make an excellent Courier, he thought to himself.

Maybe, when all of this is done, the two of you could be Couriers together, Luik suggested.

Maybe. Cam grunted slightly as he climbed the cliff.

And then you could get married and have babies.

Luik... Cam thought warningly.

Then you'd have an entire family of Couriers. And you could put the infant Couriers in baby-sized uniforms. It would be equally adorable and effective.

I'll make you stop, Cam thought.

What are you going to do? How could you possibly threaten me?

Cam ignored him, continuing to scale the cliff.

"Will we be making camp soon?" Illyria asked. Her voice was friendly, but there seemed to be a thread of tension in her voice.

"Yes. Chek...setting...up...now," he said through heavy breaths. Fortunately, the climb did not take long. A few minutes later, Cam pulled himself and Illyria up onto a plateau.

Once she unstrapped herself from his back, he collapsed the ground, chest heaving. Moments later, he sat up, shaking his sore, calloused hands.

Chek had built a roaring fire, and the scent of burnt Aetherfern was thick in the air. Cam nodded in approval. The young woman was learning quickly.

Still breathing heavily, Cam stepped toward the fire and sat down again, the flames casting dancing shadows across the ground around him. He closed his eyes, feeling the heat on his skin as he tried to calm his racing thoughts.

Within him, Luik stirred.

Drawing upon the Astral Plane, Luik reached through their Tether and cast out four Echoes of Cam into the unseen dimensions. Each Echo was Tethered to a separate anchor, invisible threads stretching into space beyond ordinary perception.

The sudden surge of sensory input hit Cam like a wave. It was too much at once, too loud, too bright, too strange. A familiar headache bloomed behind his eyes, sharp and insistent.

"What are you doing?" Illyria's voice said. It made Cam feel dizzy as he continued dealing with the stimuli.

"We're scouting," he said, his voice giving off a distracted tone. "Trying to make sure this is a safe spot."

"Is it safe?"

"As far as I can tell, but I'm still looking," he responded, his eyes still closed. Something seemed off about one of the anchors. It almost felt like it was moving.

Luik, is that normal? Cam asked.

It's possible that you are experiencing disorientation from casting too many anchors. My recommendation is that you keep the Echoes active and see if it continues.

After a short pause, Illyria said, "Can we talk?"

"Sure," Cam said, still not opening his eyes.

Illyria fidgeted slightly, beginning to have second thoughts. Maybe she didn't have to tell him everything?

Why in Aurora's Name is this so hard?

"Can you open your eyes?" she asked. "This just feels weird."

A few moments later, Cam's eyes opened, although he still had a distracted expression on his face.

"I'm still receiving the input from the Astral Echoes," he explained. "I promise I'm listening. Just don't want to be caught off guard by anything out here."

She nodded.

"Cam, I'm afraid I have to tell you something. I haven't been entirely honest with you." This made him cock an eyebrow in curiosity.

"You mean to tell me that you're not a Healer, and you've been making stuff up for years?" he replied in a joking tone.

"Please, don't joke. I'm being serious," she said, her voice muffled behind her face mask. "I lied to you."

"About what?"

"Well, to start out, back in Kevilton, I told you that I'd never been to the Sundered Lands before. But that wasn't true."

"You left the Kevilton Aurora Shroud?" he asked, shocked.

"Yes. Many, many times," she stammered. "It was part of an experiment. I wanted to test different healing methods, and I used myself as the test subject."

"Illyria...that's... Well, that's illegal. But at this point, it's not something I think you need to apologize to me for."

"There's more," she continued, her eyes beginning to sting a little bit. "I started going deeper and deeper into the Sundered Lands. Often, I went off the established Safe Paths. Stupid, I know. Anyway, Cam...I found something while I was out there."

Cam didn't move for a moment. He had the same distracted look on his face.

This is hard enough as is. Please just listen to me, she thought, annoyance rising in her. She tried to drown the annoyance with her own shame.

How dare this bother you, after what you've held from him? she told herself.

"What did you find?" he asked, his voice quiet and eyes staring into the distance.

Illyria paused for a moment, frozen in her emotions.

"I found— Oh, would you please just pay attention to me?" she said, her anxiety getting the best of her as she stalled for more time.

"Sorry. Luik cast four separate Astral Echoes. That's too many. I'm having trouble keeping up with it all."

Illyria frowned.

"Can you stop the Echoes and scout later?"

"I could, but something's off right now. One of my anchor points is moving. I've never seen that before."

She felt her stomach drop.

"Moving? What do you mean?"

"I mean that it's moving. All the other Aetherfern plants are staying stationary. Why is this one moving?"

Because it's not a plant, Illyria realized.

Cam closed his eyes again, his brow furrowed in a perplexed expression, intensifying his concentration on the Echo. In the recesses of his mind, a vivid scene unfolded. He could see a dimly lit expanse beneath the agitated scarlet sky, damp soil underfoot, and the looming presence of tall trees, their skeletal branches reaching out like spectral appendages.

And several footprints.

The footprints sprawled across the terrain, grotesque imprints that defied the semblance of humanity. Distorted and unnaturally large, these tracks seemed to mock the conventional human stride. The toes, elongated like sinister fingers, stretched out eerily from the base of the foot.

Cam...I don't think you anchored to an Aetherfern. This...this is something else.

His eyes snapped open.

"We've got to go," he said, urgency in his voice. "We're not safe here."

Chek and Illyria both looked up, concern in their eyes.

"What's going on?" Chek asked, as Cam quickly began gathering his things.

"I'm not sure. But something is out there, and it's moving closer."

The tendrils of dread tightened their grip on Cam's stomach, a visceral response to whatever monster was out there. The air itself bore witness to an impending horror, as if the very fabric of reality were warping in response to an unseen, malefic presence.

"I don't understand, what did you see?" Chek asked, hurriedly scooping up her bags.

"I don't know. But it's alive, and it's nearby."

And I've never seen anything make footprints like that before, he thought. *Luik, why would this thing be so high in astral energy?*

I'm afraid to find out, came the response.

In the distance, Cam heard the sound of scraping rocks along with quick and heavy footfalls. Whatever was out there was coming towards them, and it was coming quickly.

"Drop everything. We've got to go," Cam said, his monstrous right arm instinctively reaching for the dagger at his hip.

It was in that moment that Chek collapsed, falling into a sudden coughing fit. This one was especially violent, her body convulsing in a harsh symphony of hacks and gags. Panic etched across Chek's face as she clutched desperately at her throat, eyes widening in distress, and she slumped to her knees.

Cam and Illyria both turned around and ran to her.

And then, the creature was upon them.

In his years traveling the Sundered Lands, Cam had never seen a monster that looked remotely similar to this one. It was huge, standing several feet taller than even Cam. Its body appeared to be made out of some strange red-and-black goo, and as it ran, its flesh pulsated, as if it were a beating heart.

Its legs were long and thin, propelling the creature forward with a startling grace. Its upper body was hunched over, its chest and back covered in grotesque, tumorous bulges, and thick vine-like protrusions emerged from its back. There were several bulbous eyes scattered in bizarre spots across its body. One on its nose, one on a shoulder, and one on the side of its neck.

Its mouth was open far too wide, like its jaw had been unhinged, revealing two sets of sharp, yellow teeth. Its arms were long, hanging down past the creature's knees. Each hand had four spindly fingers that looked like the legs of a spider. Bones protruded from the tips of these fingers, creating sharp claws.

As the creature careened towards them, a symphony of shrieks rent the air like a ghastly chorus of animalistic delight that echoed through the desolate expanse.

It was a nightmare given life.

Chek, through her fit of coughing, managed to choke out one word. "Reaper!"

Chapter 29

Cam sprang into action, sprinting past Chek and placing himself between her and the Reaper. The towering creature didn't even seem to register him as a threat. It swiped casually with a massive claw, the force of the blow sending Cam flying and slamming into the ground.

A few years ago, that impact would have left him broken. But the Sundered Lands had taught him to recover fast. He rolled to his feet, already searching for his next move.

Without warning, he felt the sharp pull in his chest, the telltale drain of a Soul-Forging. A short knife formed in his hand mid-motion, cold and weightless. Feeling a flash of irritation at Luik, he pulled his arm back and threw the knife at the Reaper. As the knife sank into its shoulder, it turned, twisting back towards him.

Try to warn me before you do that! Cam thought, as the corresponding feeling of weakness hit him.

Sorry. It's instinct.

As the knife smoked away, the Reaper spun, its bizarre out-of-place eyes staring at Cam. With a shriek that almost sounded joyful, it charged. Cam dove out of the way, rolling to the side and out of the creature's path.

For a fleeting moment, a strange courage and confidence surged through Cam. In that instant, his fears and insecurities were drowned out by a powerful wave of fear-driven rage.

He, not the Reaper, was Master of the Sundered Lands.

Cam stood tall, pulling out twin daggers he'd found in Perth.

"You will not touch them," he growled.

He then leapt towards the creature with an angry shout, swiping a dagger at the Reaper's front leg. The blow connected, but it wasn't a clean cut, the blade remaining awkwardly stuck. Not giving him a chance to recover it, the Reaper yanked its leg away, causing Cam to lose his grip.

He gave a quick curse, knuckles whitening around his second dagger. The Reaper swung at him, its spindly fingers outstretched like the hand of death. Cam ducked the blow and jumped forward, stabbing at the creature's stomach as he did so. The stab was true, and this time, Cam quickly pulled the blade free.

The Reaper roared at him before it leapt into the air high above Cam's head. As it came down towards him, each hand and foot were ready to deliver a killing blow.

Cam moved to strike again, but the Reaper twisted mid-lunge, collapsing toward him with all its weight.

Suddenly, the world lurched.

The creature's descent slowed, unnaturally so, its massive body dragging through the air as if caught in thick water. Cam's limbs felt lighter by contrast, but the shift was clumsy. His balance wobbled as his foot landed a half-step too early, and his reaction came just a beat too fast.

Luik, what are you doing?

Attempting to Time Shift you, came the strained reply, *but your movements are too irregular.*

Cam stumbled sideways, narrowly avoiding being crushed. He stepped out from under the creature as it hit the ground in slow motion, the impact sending up a spray of dirt and stone.

Still off balance, Cam slashed at its face, his blade cutting deep across one of its many eyes. The Time Shift faded just as the Reaper let out a shriek, and Cam could already feel the strain of it echoing through his body.

I told you to WARN ME before you do that!

I will need more warning next time you decide to move so unpredictably, Luik responded with forced composure.

Suddenly, the movements of the creature accelerated. Even with the power of the Time Shift on himself, the Reaper's pace quickened dramatically as it stood back on its two legs. To Cam, everything in the world was moving slowly, except the Reaper, which appeared to be moving at its normal pace.

Luik, what is that thing? Cam thought, panic beginning to set in.

It has access to astral powers, Luik said, his voice stunned. *Is...is that thing...that...was it once an Elmia?*

The Reaper opened its mouth and began speaking. Its voice was harsh and guttural, lacing the air with a chilling sound.

"Feast on your soul," it hissed through its teeth. "Your soul!" It reached towards Cam with startling quickness.

Cam gasped as the Reaper's elongated fingers wrapped around his chest, pinning his arms to his sides. The creature lifted him off the ground, its grip tightening around him like a vise. Cam gave a shout of agony as pain shot through his left arm. The snapping sound he heard meant it was likely broken. The creature squeezed again, and this time, Cam felt the same breakage in his ribs.

He couldn't breathe. He was in so much pain that he couldn't think.

Warning you! Shadowmelding! Luik spoke with expeditious calm, and Cam barely had time to register the message before they merged with a nearby shadow.

From his two-dimensional vantage point, he could see the creature look around sharply and in confusion. The eye on its neck suddenly seemed to snap towards Cam's position. With a quick movement, the Reaper stomped its foot on him.

The force of the blow ended the Shadowmeld, and Cam lay on the ground in a groaning heap. He looked up blearily, realizing that Illyria and Chek were no longer in the camp.

Good, he thought weakly. *I just need to keep the Reaper busy a bit longer. Maybe they'll escape.*

Cam rolled onto his stomach, his broken ribs screaming at him, and swiped his clawed right hand at the Reaper's foot. The claws sunk in deeply, and the Reaper shrieked.

As Cam tried to pick himself up, his mind clouded by agony, a strange sensation rippled through him. Something dark and cold, yet oddly familiar.

It was his fear, and it felt like it was flowing into the Reaper.

His heart pounded harder, not just from terror but from something deeper, more primal. As the Reaper loomed over him, its inhuman eyes glinting with malice, Cam felt the inexplicable flow.

For a brief moment, through the haze of agony, it felt like his fear had reached out, tangling with the creature's own essence, drawing its attention, almost bending it. The Reaper paused, its head tilting unnaturally, as if sensing something it didn't fully understand.

Then, just as quickly, the moment was gone, and the Reaper roared at him.

Luik! Cam shouted in his mind. *I need a weapon!*

He reached out instinctively, but the weapon didn't form in his hand right away. There was a flicker of hesitation, then with a sudden rush of cold through his palm, a small axe materialized, Soul-Forged by Luik.

He swung the axe hard. The blade sank deep into the creature's head with a sickening crunch before smoking away.

The Reaper seized for a moment, dropping to the ground, its skin continuing to pulsate. Cam fell to his knees, weakness overtaking him. He took a few deep breaths and then let out a scream as the creature jabbed the bone claws on the tips of its fingers deep into Cam's abdomen.

Slowly, the creature lifted itself—and Cam—off the ground. Cam groaned, darkness creeping in at the edges of his vision. The Reaper opened its mouth, moving its teeth towards him.

Using the last of his strength, Cam swiped his claw at the eye on the side of the Reaper's neck, goring its bizarre eye and watching it burst like a broken egg. The creature shrieked again, dropping Cam and clutching at the hole where its eye had once been.

Cam lay on the ground, bleeding from the wound in his chest and unable to rise.

Cam? Cam? Are you alright? Can you get up? Luik screamed.

At least Illyria and Chek got away, he thought weakly.

He gave a deep sigh and all went black.

Chapter 30

Felix had been bothered when Cam asked him to stay behind during the initial excursion into the Jaram Mountains. On the surface, he understood the request, as he was still recovering from the Bluecoil removal surgery. However, the thought of them discovering an ancient Elmia temple without him made his insides churn.

He found himself doing what he could to distract himself while they were gone. There wasn't much to distract himself with, but he was a fairly simple person. He didn't need many options and spent most of each day studying his books.

He had to admit that, in one sense, he liked the solitude. The stillness in the air made it easier to read his books without distraction. Unfortunately, he found himself reading far too quickly for his liking. He wished he'd brought more with him before leaving Rath, so that he didn't finish them all too soon.

And so, he distracted himself with his other hobby.

His secret hobby.

Using a long wooden spoon, he gently stirred the cast-iron pot hung over the small fire. The aroma of his stew gently wafted up to his nose, bringing an anticipatory smile to his face. This one might be his best stew ever.

Felix had known he was different from a very young age. Outside of Chek, he struggled to understand others and, frankly, often preferred his own company anyway. While other boys had taken up wrestling and fencing, he had buried himself in reading and cooking.

Cooking had always been a bit of a guilty pleasure for him. Back in Rath, he'd often found relaxation in the simple joy of cooking. He wasn't sure why he was compelled to keep this interest a secret, but the compulsion was there and it was strong. Because of this, he had followed one simple rule.

He would only cook when he was completely alone.

"She was right," Vaelin said to his left.

When I'm alone or with a crazy person, he thought to himself. Out loud, however, he said in a dismissive tone, "Yes, I'm sure she was."

Before he left, Cam had insisted that Vaelin would speak more as he calmed down. The Reaper attack had likely traumatized him, leaving him crawling on all fours and muttering the same repeated phrase.

At least Vaelin was walking on two legs now. The bestial crawling had been unsettling.

Almost just as unsettling was Vaelin's digging. It had just started over the last day. Every few hours, he'd go missing, and when Felix found him, he'd be in the bottom of some hole he was digging.

Felix suspected it had something to do with creating hiding spots. He'd seen Vaelin digging these holes everywhere—near their small camp, at the edges of the village, and even deep in the woods, dangerously close to the Shroud. He also suspected that Vaelin would hide in a well in the middle of the town.

Whatever made the man happy. At least it gave Felix some time to be alone.

"Stew's almost done. Are you hungry?"

"She was right," Vaelin replied, as Felix mouthed the words in sync.

The least Vaelin could do was vary his vocal tempo. Felix had, after all, made dinner for him.

Moments later, the two of them were sat at a long table in Perth's small inn. The table was worn and scraped, with the legs at slightly uneven heights causing an awkward rocking motion when one rested their arms on the surface.

In between small bites of stew, which was as delicious as Felix had hoped, he let his eyes dart around the room. It was a fairly cramped and dark space, lit only by the occasional dusty lantern. Despite its lack of ornamentation, Felix found himself studying the room intently to avoid locking eyes with Vaelin, who wouldn't stop staring at him.

After a few minutes, Felix pulled out a book and began reading. The book, titled *A Monograph on Elmia Lexicography*, would provide him some easy entertainment while also blocking the intense stare of the crazed man.

Unfortunately, this did not elicit the response that Felix was hoping for.

Vaelin lurched forward in a sudden movement, almost spilling his stew, leaning over the table. He raised a filthy hand and pointed towards the book.

"She was right!" he shouted.

"What?" Felix said, leaning back on his bench. He cringed at the thought of Vaelin's greasy hair brushing the pages of his book.

"She was right!" Vaelin repeated, stretching his arm so that his finger lightly brushed the cover of the book. As he spoke, some of his stew spilled out his lips, falling onto his matted beard.

"You want me to read to you?" Felix said, bewildered, as he stifled a retch at the sight of Vaelin's beard. Vaelin glowered at him, crossing his arms with a huff.

Clearly, reading was not what he had in mind.

Felix had had enough.

"I don't know what you want!" he shouted, rising to his feet and stepping away from the man. "I know you can't seem to say anything else, but how am I supposed to know what you want if you just keep repeating the same three words?"

Vaelin opened his mouth to speak, but Felix interrupted him.

"And don't even think about saying 'She was right.'"

In response, Vaelin took on a contemplative look, as if he were lost in thought. Moments later, he nodded, as if he had reached an agreement with himself. He rose to his feet and walked awkwardly towards Felix.

He held out his left arm and gently pulled back his sleeve.

Felix's eyes widened in disbelief.

Starting at Vaelin's fingertips and snaking up his arm in a spiraling pattern was the image of an Aetherfern plant.

It was identical to Cam's.

Vaelin pointed emphatically at the mark.

"SHE was right," he hissed.

By Aurora herself, Felix thought as realization dawned on him.

He pointed towards the mark, locking eyes with Vaelin.

"I know you can't talk much right now," he said, his words slow and measured, "but is 'she' trying to speak to me?"

"She was right!" Vaelin said, jumping up and down, his voice exuberant and full of energy.

I assume that's a yes, Felix thought, nodding to Vaelin.

"Okay...okay...well, I'd very much like to speak to her too," Felix said, his mind spinning. "Can she Tether with me, so I can talk directly to her?"

Vaelin hissed, yanking his marked arm away from Felix, cradling it close to his chest.

Well, this could be tricky.

"Okay, fine. We'll find another way," Felix said, gently setting his book on the weathered table. Reaching into his pocket, he pulled out his small notebook. He flipped until he reached a blank page, then he pulled out a pen.

You can do this, he thought to himself, heart beginning to race. *This is what you've studied all your life.*

Chapter 31

*A*urora's Name, where is he? What happened to him? Illyria silently prayed as she and Chek stumbled down the rocky path back towards Perth. Her mind kept recalling the horrifying image of the Reaper bearing down on them and Cam standing against it. She had doubted she would have been able to help much in the struggle. Cursing herself for leaving The Tool behind, she had chosen to help Chek get to safety.

At the time of the attack, they had fled, seeking refuge in a shallow cave which had thankfully been devoid of any creatures. Illyria left a trail of cloth shreds behind them, a guide for Cam should he come searching.

An anxious hour passed with no sign of him. Bracing themselves, they had cautiously returned to the scene of the confrontation. Blood stained the ground, but Cam's body was nowhere to be found.

Part of her assumed that he'd been killed by the Reaper, but the logical side of her mind could see that there wasn't much evidence of that. Yes, there was plenty of blood on the ground, but the lack of bones and gore suggested that Cam had somehow escaped. They searched for hours but could not find him.

As they searched, Chek's health continued to deteriorate. The young woman even began to limp on her right leg. It was a slight difference from the way she normally walked, but Illyria knew that it was likely the symptom of a much deeper problem that would worsen at a rapid pace.

Pained, Illyria decided that she had to get Chek back to Perth.

Best not lose two lives today.

Don't think that way, she reminded herself. *He may not be dead.*

Of course, if that were true, he'd likely die shortly from his wounds. She had seen enough before they fled. Illyria had to ignore that thought for now.

Searching for him won't guarantee his safety, but it will doom Chek. Save the one you can.

As they slowly made their way towards Perth, Illyria supported Chek as she struggled to walk. The young woman winced in pain whenever her left foot touched the ground. As they got closer to the Shroud, her slight limp worsened to the point that she couldn't put weight on that leg, confirming Illyria's fears.

Corruption-induced bone degeneration, Illyria thought, her brain instinctively snapping into a Healer's mindset. *She needs bed rest and a splint. If we get to Perth soon, she might be able to walk again.*

She gave a deep sigh, her heart breaking at the pained expression on Chek's boil- and scale-covered face. Chek was one of the rare individuals who the Sundered Lands would kill before scaletaint transformation was complete.

It was a reminder of the depth of their failure.

No. Not their failure.

Her failure.

You just might be the worst person in all Avoni. You have lied and manipulated to get here, and for what? All you have to show for it is a dead man and a dying woman, she told herself.

She gritted her teeth.

Dying, yes, but Chek can still be saved.

It was a cold morning when they finally walked into Perth. As they crossed under the Aurora Shroud, the skies above shifted from red to a cloudy gray, and light droplets of rain fell on them. The stone road beneath their feet became slick, making it a struggle to maintain footing.

Finally, they stepped into the village that had once been Cam's home. As they approached the building, Felix flung the library door open. His normally neat hair was messy, and his eyes betrayed a sense of exhaustion. He ran down the steps of the building towards Illyria and Chek. As he approached, a look of confusion flashed across his eyes.

"Where's Cam?" he asked, his tone filled mostly with curiosity, as if he expected Cam to be off somewhere else, doing something more important.

Chek shook her head, tears coming to her eyes. In a moment of vulnerability, she hopped on her good leg towards her brother, arms outstretched. He embraced her, a bewildered expression on his face. With a quiet whimper, Chek buried her face in his shoulder.

Felix held her close and cast a questioning glance at Illyria. Illyria simply looked down and continued walking.

"What happened?"

"It was my fault," Chek said, choking back tears. "It was my fault. We all could have gotten away, but I fell."

Felix held his sister close.

Shaking her head, Illyria walked past Felix towards the inn. Silently, she ascended the wooden steps towards the door.

Chek was wrong. Whatever happened to Cam was not her fault. After all, Chek hadn't been the one to leave him behind.

And while Chek had someone to hold her close, comforting her, there was no similar comfort for Illyria.

It's not your fault either. You didn't fail Cam. You saved Chek. The words rang hollow and empty in her mind, but she held onto them, as they were the only comfort she had.

The group had served its purpose, but no one else was going to get hurt because of her.

She stepped into the inn, its dark interior lit by a few hanging lamps and a roaring fire. As she walked, she raised a confused eyebrow. Crumpled paper and old books littered the floor. One of the walls was covered in letters, while another depicted very simple drawings of people and basic objects. Vaelin sat in one corner, his face covered in mud.

Illyria squinted.

No, it wasn't mud.

Was that chocolate?

The man saw her staring at him, and he leapt to his feet and hissed. With a dismissive shrug, she stepped down a short hallway, opening up the heavy wooden door on her right, its creaking hinges protesting as she did so.

The room on the other side was filled with what meager belongings she had been able to bring with her. The air inside was infused with the distinct scent of aged parchment, mingling with the faint aroma of herbal concoctions and remedies.

She stepped past the bottles towards her bed, gently pulling back the blanket. Concealed underneath was a small wooden box. Reaching out her gloved hand, she popped the lid open. Inside rested a simple dagger.

The Tool.

Why oh why did I leave you behind? she thought, furious with herself.

The answer was simple. She had left it behind because she didn't want to attract the Reapers, something she had been promised The Tool would do. In a cruel twist, a Reaper came anyway, and all she could do was run.

The pommel of The Tool was short and simple, lacking ornamentation except for a ruby at its base. Its blade was the appearance of fractured glass, reflecting the light in the room in dazzling patterns.

She frowned, looking at the dagger. It no longer spoke to her, but how many poisonous secrets had started the day she first heard its voice?

A part of her wanted to leave it behind, but keeping it locked away wouldn't bring back her past life of blissful ignorance.

Sometimes, the only way to go back is to go forward.

She paused for a moment to gently tug off her glove. Then, reaching out, she grasped the handle of the dagger, removing it from the box. The metal felt cold in her hand.

The dagger responded to her touch as if sensing its master had arrived and changed its appearance into its more familiar pattern. The blade lengthened by several feet, shifting from a harsh, straight line to one with a gentle curve, an intricate pattern dancing down the length of the blade.

In spite of herself, Illyria smiled.

If only all weapons could look this beautiful.

"I don't need a sword right now. Become a staff," she said. Instantly, The Tool obeyed, lengthening and locking into place. It changed form whenever her bare skin touched it, often without her meaning to, so the gloves were her safeguard. Supposedly, with time and practice, she'd learn to control the transformation. Until then, the gloves stayed on.

At least, that was what The Tool had told her.

And so far, it had been right about everything.

She shook her head, remembering the day she'd discovered The Tool hidden in an abandoned armory deep within the Sundered Lands. At the time, she had assumed its voice to be a figment of her own imagination. She first realized it was telling the truth when the sickness in Kevilton started. It was then that she believed its warning that the collapse and corruption of all life across Avoni was coming.

Since that day many months ago, she had obeyed the voice of The Tool, keeping its discovery a complete secret. If she told everyone what she knew, the best-case scenario was that they'd ignore her.

And the worst case? She struggled to imagine it.

How would anyone respond if they knew the Sundered Lands was coming for them all?

And so, she followed The Tool. Its command was simple and short.

"The Scepter of Alderia is the solution. You must find it and bring me to it."

It had taken some time to leave Kevilton. After all, she would need help to get through the Sundered Lands. Once a certain Courier had been tasked with delivering a message to Rath, Illyria had convinced the Vanguard that she should go with him.

To keep him safe.

She cringed.

Just go back out there. Find the temple. Maybe you'll find Cam too, she thought to herself. *And this time, bring it with you.*

Determined, she turned around and walked out of the room, closing the door softly behind her. As she did so, she heard soft footsteps in the hallway. Turning, Illyria saw Felix. His dark eyes looked particularly serious.

"What's wrong with Chek? Why can't she walk right?"

Illyria reached into her pack, pulling out a vial of Aetherfern-infused water. She gave it a quick shake before handing it to Felix.

"Bone degeneration. It's a rare effect of being exposed to the Sundered Lands."

The young man nodded, his brow furrowed in deep concern.

"But she'll recover, right?" His voice trembled as he spoke.

"I want to tell you that she will, but the truth is that she may not. It depends on the extent of the damage. We're lucky we got here as soon as we did. A few more hours, and she could have lost the other leg too. She might have even died."

Felix gave a solemn nod and glanced out a window. Outside, Chek could be seen sitting on the deck of the inn, her arms wrapped around her legs and a blank expression on her face.

"Why didn't you come back sooner?"

"I had no idea she was in so much pain," Illyria said honestly. "Your sister is very strong."

Felix paused before responding. When he spoke, his words were slow and measured.

"She can't go back out again, can she? Ever again."

Illyria shook her head.

"I'm afraid not. Nobody handles the effects of the Sundered Lands well, but some, like your sister, react worse than others."

"So, what do we do now?" Felix asked, a defeated tone in his voice. "No Cam, no Luik. Chek and I are stuck here too. Are we just going to wait things out until this Shroud collapses, and we all die?"

She took a deep breath.

Nobody else gets hurt because of me, she thought.

"I'm going back out," she said, her voice almost a whisper. "It's up to me now."

Felix frowned.

"Are you serious? You'd have to go by yourself. I'm not leaving Chek here."

"Nor should you," Illyria said. "Stay here with her. I'm going to find the temple on my own. And who knows, maybe I'll find Cam too."

Felix nodded awkwardly, his gaze shifting uncertainly around the room. He seemed to be weighing whether or not to share something with her. Finally, he spoke.

"Before you go, there's something you need to know. Vaelin's Tethered to an Elmia."

Illyria stood for a moment, totally stunned and trying to process what Felix had told her. She stammered, "Wait, are you joking? How do you even know that?"

"He's got the mark," Felix said, hopping over towards the man. Pulling up Vaelin's sleeve, he pointed at the distinct Aetherfern mark snaking up his arm.

Another one survived. Fascinating.

"Have you been able to communicate with it?"

"No, and I've been trying everything. Vaelin is...uncooperative."

Vaelin hissed again behind Felix.

"I said no more chocolate!" At the sound of Felix's reply, the crazed man let out a mournful whimper, lowering himself onto the floor. Turning back towards Illyria, Felix gave a quick shrug.

"I'll figure it out. Anyway, are you sure it's smart to leave now?"

"I wish I could rest, but I need to move quickly. And who knows, maybe Cam is still out there. We weren't that far from here when the Reaper attacked."

"No sign of his body, right? I guess it's possible he could've used Verdalink to escape somewhere."

The thought of Cam being alone and wounded in the Sundered Lands while a predatory Reaper hunted him made Illyria's stomach turn slightly.

"I want to find him, but it's even more important that I find the temple," she said. She tried to place as much urgency in her tone as possible. Perhaps it was a way to deal with her guilt at having left Cam behind.

It's not your fault.

Wasn't it, though?

With determined strides, she stepped out of the inn, her Healer's cloak billowing in the wind like a banner of resolute purpose. From the outset, she had pretended that her journey carried the weight of a singular duty: to safeguard Cam.

Yet, even before the Vanguard had charged her with keeping him well, The Tool had given her the far more significant task of finding the Scepter.

She might have failed Cam, but there was still time to save Avoni.

Chapter 32

Cam's head throbbed with pain, a relentless drumbeat that echoed through his consciousness. As he blinked, the world around him appeared hazy, obscured by an enigmatic fog that clung to his senses. The world felt as if it were bobbing about, disorienting his senses. Confused, he blinked his eyes, trying to make sense of his surroundings.

He lay on his back, staring up at the swirling red sky of the Sundered Lands, the sound of a biting wind in the air. Around him, he could hear the sound of heavy footsteps against rock. An attempt to shift caused him to let out a groan as pain seared through his side.

The pain caused him to become more alert. He was being carried on some kind of board, with tight ropes keeping him immobile. A makeshift splint fashioned from wood and cloth was tied around his left arm.

Luik? His thoughts were weak and bleary. *Are you there?*

Yes. The Elmia's voice was solemn. *For a moment, I wondered if we had died.*

I'm still not sure that we didn't, Cam thought in return. Yet even as he thought the words, the pain he felt in his body convinced him that he could not be dead just yet.

Awareness began to return to him as his brain roused itself from its stupor. *I'm being carried somewhere.*

Do you think you can look around?

I'll try.

Slowly turning his head, so as to not aggravate his injuries, Cam looked around. Surrounding him were perhaps twenty or so people. They did not quite appear to be soldiers, but they marched in a disciplined manner.

Their bodies were covered in a peculiar armor, made out of some sort of form-fitting, flexible black metal with small red streaks running through it. Each of them wore a mysterious and imposing black helmet that concealed the entire face.

Each helmet was made of two interlocking sections. The first was an outer shell, rigid and unyielding, encasing their heads. Underneath was a softer inner layer, molded snugly to their faces, eerily resembling a skull. Emerging from this inner piece were two tubes that connected to the breastplate.

Each member of the group had an identical broadsword strapped to their back.

Interesting, Luik said. *Are you familiar with this group?*

No, replied Cam. *I've never seen these people before.*

Perhaps it is time to have a dialogue with our new friends? Luik suggested.

Cam agreed.

"Where are you taking me?" For a few moments, nobody responded to him. He was just about to call out again, when a woman's muffled voice spoke up, just next to him.

"Relax. You're in bad shape. When we found you, you were close to the point of death."

"Who are you?"

The woman hesitated before responding.

"Your savior. My name is Morwenna."

"Where are you taking me?"

"Someplace we can treat your wounds. Please, try to relax. I don't want you to aggravate your injuries." Though there was a hardness in her tone, Cam detected a hint of sympathy. "I know that this must feel very disorienting," she continued. "However, what is safest for you is to not move much. We'll be there soon." She then stepped away.

The group moved with purpose across the desolate landscape, Cam bound to the makeshift board. The terrain beneath was rocky and unforgiving, every jostle sending waves of pain through his battered form.

Look around you, if you can, Luik commented. *It appears this place was once a forest.*

Shifting his eyes, Cam glanced around. Indeed, the environment appeared to have once been a thriving forest. A plethora of stumps dotted the rocky ground around him. Morwenna must have noticed Cam's glance.

"We have claimed this corrupted land. It took many years and cost many lives, but we eradicated plant life in this region, securing it for ourselves."

After an hour of relentless travel, the group approached a cavern yawning open on the side of the mountain. The cold, stale air emanating from within sent shivers down Cam's spine.

As the group approached, several people—also in the same strange black armor—exited the cave. In their hands, they wielded similar broadswords. One of these people, a large man who appeared to be the leader of the group, approached them.

"Was anyone exposed?"

"One, but not one of our own," Morwenna said. "We found him injured and close to death." The large man tilted his head slightly.

"Is there any evidence of scaletaint transformation?"

"Yes. He was in Crimson Limbo when we found him. His right hand is completely transformed, up to his elbow."

"Bringing anyone in Crimson Limbo here is forbidden!" the man shouted.

"Oh, be silent," Morwenna said in an exasperated tone. "He still has control over his mind, and he needs our help. Our numbers are small as things are, and if the Aurora Shrouds continue to weaken, we may soon become the last stand of humanity against the darkness in Avoni."

"I can only follow the orders I have been given," the man replied.

"Then consider your orders changed," the woman declared in a commanding tone. "I, Morwenna, the Sundered Sovereign, command you to stand aside and grant access to this wounded man."

Interesting, Luik said. *She appears to be in charge of this group.*

Not just any group, Cam thought in return. *She called herself the "Sundered Sovereign." This is the Cult of the Sundered Shadows.*

I am unfamiliar with this group, Luik said. *They did not exist in Avoni before the Sundering.*

I wasn't convinced they existed today, Cam admitted. *They were more of a myth. Supposedly, they learned the secret to living outside the Aurora Shrouds.*

Fascinating.

Tilting his head, Cam watched as the man slowly nodded and motioned for his guards to stand down. They all stepped to the side, creating a path. As they moved forward, the woman in charge, Morwenna, walked back over towards Cam.

"We are almost there," she said, her tone filled with sympathy and compassion. "Just a few moments longer."

The group cautiously entered the cavern's yawning mouth, the transition from the stark exterior to the subterranean depths marked by an immediate change in atmosphere. The rocky terrain outside gave way to the cool, dim ambiance of the cave. The narrow passage gradually widened, revealing a cavernous expanse veiled in shadows.

The cave's interior was a labyrinth of irregular formations, stalactites hanging like petrified fingers from the ceiling and stalagmites rising defiantly from the rocky floor. The air within carried an acrid, metallic scent, and a faint hissing sound filled the air.

Cam could feel Luik's emotions stir. Something about this place made the Elmia very uncomfortable.

After they had gone a short way down the tunnel, the armored figures removed their helmets, revealing a diverse assembly of individuals beneath. Men and women of varying ages stood side by side, their features obscured by the play of shadows and the lingering smokiness in the air.

They gently lowered Cam to the ground, untying his restraints.

"I apologize for any pain you might have suffered at our hands," Morwenna's voice rang behind Cam. "Please understand that any discomfort was not our intention."

Cam sat up and groaned, his right arm clutching at his pained ribs. Turning his head, he looked at Morwenna's face.

She was an older woman, perhaps in her sixties, although she appeared quite strong. Her hair was gray with several streaks of white. Her green eyes appeared tired, resilient, and compassionate, and the skin on her face was stretched too tightly around her skull. The right half of her face was covered in scales.

Despite the visible traces of hardship, there was a warmth in Morwenna's gaze.

As Cam shifted, wincing in pain, Morwenna's expression softened further, her eyes conveying both sympathy and a deep understanding.

"What hurt you?" she asked, her voice kind and gentle.

Cam's mind flashed to his near-death encounter, and he shuddered.

"A Reaper," he said quietly.

"It's a wonder you're alive at all," she replied.

"How did you find me?" Cam asked.

"One of our members pointed us in the right direction," Morwenna said, nodding her head at someone.

Cam turned and looked in the direction the woman had indicated. There, one of the black-armored figures had just removed his helmet and was staring at him with cold eyes.

"Soren?" Cam said, his voice a surprised whisper.

Soren glared back.

"You're an idiot, Cam. If only someone had said that you'd need some help," he said, his face still serious. "Did the others survive? We didn't see any sign of them."

Groaning, Cam rose to his feet, clutching his aching side with his transformed right arm.

"I think so. They escaped while I held it off."

Soren nodded. "I assume they went back to Perth then. I'll send some scouts to check."

He's a leader in the Cult of Sundered Shadows? Luik said, his tone amused.

Soren turned and left before Cam could say anything more.

"My my, it appears that you're quite lucky to find yourself in our care," Morwenna said. "The Sundered Shadows are Avoni's best hope right now. Against the corruption and the Reapers."

Cradling his ribs, Cam said, "I heard the Reapers came from the Jaram Mountains. Is that true?"

Morwenna stood thoughtful, contemplating Cam's question. It appeared as if she were weighing options in her mind, like she wasn't sure if she'd tell him the truth or not. However, after a few moments, the conflict left her face, resolve taking its place.

"We are not entirely sure. These creatures are new to us. However, we find the timing of their arrival suspicious, showing up as soon as the Aurora Shrouds start to weaken."

She frowned, a deep weariness entering her voice. "I have my own theories. There are rumors of a hidden temple in the mountains." Cam perked up when he heard this. "It...was a strange place. According to our doctrine, it was guarded by spirits, who were quite helpful to our people. They taught us many things about the nature of the Sundered Lands. Through their knowledge, and our own scientific pursuits, we learned the secret of living in the Sundered Lands.

"Anyway, this temple had its own type of Aurora Shroud protecting it. When we learned that Aurora Shrouds were weakening across Avoni, we sent scouts to the temple. While we did not find the protective spirits, we did find the Reapers."

Realization struck Cam and Luik at the same time.

The Reapers are the Elmias designated to guard the temple, Cam thought. Inside of him, he could feel Luik's heart break.

If they transformed, that means the temple...it is no longer an astral Nexus Point, Luik whispered. *I...I can never be free.*

"Can you take me to this temple?" Cam asked in earnest. Morwenna shook her head.

"No, it is too dangerous. The path up the mountains is treacherous, and the presence of the Reapers greatly complicates things."

"I must get to that temple. There is an artifact there that I must find. It is the key to strengthening the Aurora Shrouds and saving our people."

Morwenna frowned.

"The Sundered Shadows have survived for decades without the protection of the Aurora Shrouds. If the people of Avoni would have listened to us, they would have learned the secret. Even now, we stand ready to share our knowledge with anyone who would take the Sundered Oath."

"Morwenna, lives are at stake. Human lives. You can aid me in my search for this artifact, or you may not, but I will not let you stop me in my search."

"No!" Morwenna shouted. Her voice carried not only anger but also an underlying complexity of emotions, a curious blend of strange hurt, a touch of sadness, and something else.

Was that guilt?

Longing?

What are you hiding?

She paused for a moment, collecting her emotions.

"You cannot seek out the temple."

Cam rolled his eyes. "And you cannot keep me here. I will seek out this temple with or without you. I beg you, please give me help. If you know the way, share it with me."

Morwenna turned her back to Cam. As she did, Cam thought he saw tears streaking down the woman's face.

"You're hurt," she said in a still and quiet voice. "You're hurt badly. Please, at least stay here until you are whole again."

"No. I'm going to continue searching," Cam stated flatly.

Morwenna shook her head.

"That idea is foolishness. You almost died. You have a broken arm, broken ribs and the stab wounds in your chest will need to be tended to. You're too weak, Cam. You are to remain here."

Cam's eyes snapped wide open, and he clenched his fists instinctively.

"Why do you care so much?" he asked in a firm voice.

A look of shame and sadness flitted across Morwenna's face, a deep vulnerability replacing her facade of composure.

"Because I am your mother."

Part Four
Cycles of Failure

*W*hat is verifiable is the impact of The Treaty of the Tethering. It stands as one of the most uneven and desperate bargains in recorded history. Facing extinction, the Elmias accepted terms that stripped them of freedoms and bound them in servitude to the royal line. In doing so, they relinquished their ancestral capital, the Vorunis Citadel—one of only two remaining astral Nexus Points. The treaty further cleaved their people in two: those bound to the citadel were forbidden from entering the Elmia Temple, and those of the temple were forever barred from the citadel.

Shadow Three
Morwenna - 23 Years Ago

I t would take about a day and a half to reach Perth.

At least, that's how long it took her to reach the cave when the Sundered Shadows had come for her five years ago. Since then, the Shadows had done an excellent job culling the plant life in the area, so her path was a bit more open. She might be able to get home even faster than that.

That openness had allowed her to move more quickly, but she was thankful once she finally reached the treeline. It would be harder to be spotted from far away. The trees were covered in long thorns, some with poison visibly dripping from the ends. As she ran, branches and vines began to swing after her, chasing her with malicious intent.

Morwenna ignored them, forcing herself forward.

She'd waited years for this moment. It had taken years of planning, but Lucian appeared to trust her now. He'd left with a group of acolytes, and she knew it was time to run. She'd found a young man—a newer member of the Sundered Shadows—and had demanded he deliver a note to her husband.

Cammond, the note had read. *I've been in the Jaram Mountains, but I'm coming to you now. Be ready for me, and be ready to leave quickly. I'll see you soon.*

She had wanted to write more, but there was so little time. Once she was safe with him, she'd explain everything.

Her breath rasped as she rushed down the mountain. Her lungs ached, begging her to slow down, but she forced herself onward. Lucian wouldn't be gone for long, and he'd realize that she was missing and come after her.

She heard a dull scraping sound on her shoulder. She glanced down and cringed as she saw the poisonous thorn she'd just bumped into. If it hadn't been for her armor…

A quick flash of shame shot through her. Ever since she'd learned what the armor was, she'd hated wearing it. When escaping, she almost decided to leave it behind. However, wearing it helped deal with the corruption of the Sundered Lands. It wasn't perfect, and the armor sets lost their efficacy over time, but it kept her moving.

She burst through a thicket that was trying to wrap its branches around her waist. She felt the branches tearing as she ran through, tripping over an exposed root. She fell to the ground in a heap, rolling onto her side before springing back to her feet.

Reflex. Pure, trained reflex.

She hadn't even thought. Her body just moved. Her time over the last few years had shown her that for Lucian, staying down was worse than falling. Crying out simply meant more pain. Even now, with no eyes on her, the lesson stuck. Her body reacted before her mind caught up. She stood there, breathing hard, hands clenched at her sides as if waiting for the next blow.

Morwenna forced her legs to move forward again.

Suddenly, she heard a rushing sound, like the air itself was twisting around her. Then, Lucian burst forth from a nearby Aetherfern plant.

Her blood ran ice cold.

He glared at her, dark eyes burning with fury. His left arm—the one marked by the creeping plant tattoo—was clenched in a white-knuckled fist. In his other hand, he gripped a man by the scruff of a tattered shirt.

The figure writhed in his grip, caught in the final stages of Crimson Limbo, almost completely transformed into a scaletaint. His arms and legs had already transformed, and most of his face was already covered in scales. He thrashed in Lucian's grasp, biting at the air in a mindless fury.

She felt a sudden, aching swell of pity for the creature he had become.

And then, her breath caught as she suddenly recognized him.

Cammond!

Her heart broke as she looked at him. Her husband. The man she had dreamed of for five long years. She had often wondered how much he might have changed, but nothing could have prepared her for this. His face was nearly unrecognizable, twisted by the transformation. And his eyes...whatever clarity once lived there was fading fast. She could see it slipping away.

She still tried to reach him.

"Cammond!" she cried out. She reached back, undoing the buckles that kept her black helmet on. Maybe, if she could just get him inside the armor, he'd be safe.

"What you have done today," Lucian said, his words cold, barely restrained in his rage, "was quite foolish."

He glowered at her, continuing to hold her husband by the throat.

"I want to go home, Lucian!" Morwenna said. She'd managed to undo both clasps and she pulled the helmet off her face. The painful air stung instantly, and she fought the urge to cough.

"You swore an oath."

"I was saving my son!"

"You swore an oath!" Lucian repeated, firmer and louder. "To the Shadows of the Sundered Lands. To me!"

Morwenna shook her head, fighting the desperation and panic that was clinging to her.

"Please. Let him go. I...I want to go home."

"Home?" Lucian said, his tone mocking. "Home...to this?" He threw Cammond onto the ground. Her husband twitched violently, caught in the painful pangs of transformation. He might only have a few minutes left before becoming a scaletaint.

There was no time. She rushed toward Cammond, but Lucian moved far too quickly. He stepped forward, backhanding her across the face. She fell in a heap, groaning, as white lights danced across her eyes.

When she sat up, she saw that Lucian had one foot planted on Cammond's neck, pinning him to the ground. Morwenna blinked back tears. She knew it was over.

"How...how did you find me?"

"You think the only purpose of that armor is to protect you?" He scoffed. "I know where all my followers are at all times. Even if removed. It leaves its mark."

Morwenna allowed her eyes to drift back down to Cammond, who continued to thrash on the ground. There was a wildness in his eyes, his jaw snapping, as if trying to sink teeth into her very image.

It was happening too fast. Morwenna's mind raced. He should have only been exposed to the Sundered Lands for a few hours—maybe a day at most. How was this happening?

"Lucian!" Morwenna cried out. "Help him! Please!"

Lucian glared at her. "You doomed him with your actions today. When I found him, I knew the only true punishment I could give you would be to introduce him to...well...something Complex about me."

Morwenna lowered her head. She didn't know what Lucian meant. She didn't care what Lucian meant. Tears began to sting her eyes.

"Please..." she whispered again, her fingers scraping up dirt as they clenched into fists. "Please don't..."

Lucian shook his head. He bent over, touching her husband lightly on what little flesh remained on his face. Cammond began to convulse, scales rapidly appearing across the rest of his scalp. Seconds later, his scaletaint transformation was complete. Lucian stepped off him, and the monster rushed at Morwenna.

If I can't save you, then I will free you, my dear Cammond.

She rolled to the side and pushed herself to her feet. Her hand flew to her hip. The captain's sword was still there. She drew it in one motion and charged, driving the blade deep into the scaletaint's side. Then, she gave it a violent twist.

I'm so sorry, Cammond.

For a few moments, all she could do was breathe, the air still and silent around her. A solitary tear rolled down her cheek, carving a small path through the dirt and grime. She turned her gaze towards Lucian, her eyes alight with hatred.

"You will obey," Lucian said, his words still ripe with fury.

"No," Morwenna snarled, stepping towards him.

Lucian moved faster than her eyes could follow. In an instant, his hand struck her across the face again. She hit the ground hard, her sword clattering beside her. A scream tore from her throat as he grabbed a fistful of her hair and yanked her upright.

"You. Will. Obey," he seethed. "Or I will find that son of yours, and he can die in the same manner as his father. I wonder if you'd be so quick to kill him once he transformed?"

"Don't," she breathed out, equal parts begging and making a threat. "Don't do it."

She cried out again as he pulled her face close to his, his hand still tightly gripping her hair.

"Then you will obey."

He then released his grip on her, and she collapsed into the dirt, breath ragged. As the pain burned behind her eyes, something colder stirred beneath it.

I will be the end of you...

This was no longer about escape.

This was war.

Chapter 33

Chek sat at the edge of the Aurora Shroud, staring from safety out into the Sundered Lands. The perspective was otherworldly. Around her, the world was lush and bright, filled with thriving plants and a clear blue sky overhead. Mere feet away from her was desolation and corruptive decay, her view of it blurred slightly due to the Shroud wall.

She sat alone, her splinted left leg stretched out on the ground and her right pulled up to her chest. Before Illyria left, she'd told Felix that she needed to keep weight off that leg and rest. Apparently, she had also said that it was possible Chek would be able to walk on it again.

Possible.

If Illyria could feel the pain in her leg, she might grasp the harsh reality that Chek had already come to accept.

Her days of walking on two legs were over.

She stared out through the Aurora Shroud into the oppressive world that had claimed its latest prize. At some point, she'd tell Felix. For now, she let him hold onto the hope that his sister would return to normal. Hope was the only luxury she could afford to give him.

And where did that leave her?

Trapped. Alone. Crippled.

Waiting for the world to end.

She narrowed her eyes in hate, staring into the Sundered Lands.

I won't let you beat me.

Reaching up, she placed a light touch on the top of her head. She felt prickles where her hair was beginning to regrow. It would take years before her hair was the same length, but at least it was something.

Glancing down, she saw a single yellow flower poking up from amongst the weeds. Somehow, it had refused to let the weeds choke it out and continued growing towards the sun. Seeing it brought a defiant smile to her face.

No, wallowing in self-pity while she waited for the world to end wasn't an option. Yes, she may have sacrificed her body to the Sundered Lands, but there was much more to her than what she could do physically. The Sundered Lands hadn't dared to touch her greatest asset.

Her grit.

And it was time to start using it.

I won't let you beat me.

Grabbing her makeshift crutch, she let out a pained groan as she rose to her feet. As helpful as her determination was at moving her forward, it unfortunately couldn't take pain away. Pivoting on her good leg, she began heading back towards the center of the town. It wasn't far away, but getting there would take her a while.

The sudden sound of footsteps caused her to startle and glance over her shoulder. Behind her, four individuals—all wearing black armor with slight patterns of red running through—crossed under the Aurora Shroud. Chek cocked her head, curious.

They aren't Vanguard.

"Are you from Rath?" she called out.

The four figures halted for a moment before slowly removing their skull-like helmets. The faces underneath appeared weathered and aged, dotted by a few scales. There was a haggardness to their expressions, like they hadn't slept in days. However, as they walked, they stepped with surprising coordination and precision, as if they were trained soldiers.

Walking in front of them was a middle-aged man with black hair streaked with gray.

"No, we are not from that dying city, although we have sent our people to help them. We are members of the Sundered Shadows."

Chek opened her mouth in surprise.

They're real?

Her instincts told her to learn more.

"I'm sorry to inform you of this, but you won't find much help here. A Reaper got under the Aurora Shroud and killed almost all of the inhabitants."

Her experience in the bookstore told her that it was best to make a statement before starting to probe. Leading with a question put people on edge, and they become less cooperative.

"We are aware of the tragedy," the man said in a curt tone as they approached her, eventually drawing to a stop once they were close. "We've been sent to check on the safety of the traveling companions of a Vanguard Courier named Cam."

Chek's heart leapt.

He survived.

"You found Cam?"

"Yes. The Courier had nearly succumbed to his wounds when we found him. He's recovering with our people right now."

"You have no idea how good that is to hear. Let me go tell my brother."

"Just your brother?" the man asked, raising an eyebrow. "Was there not another companion?"

"Oh, Illyria. She..." Chek paused.

She's alone looking for Cam.

"Was she hurt?" the man asked.

Chek shook her head.

"No, but she went back out there. By herself." Chek let the words hang in the air for a moment before adding, "Can you help her?"

The man started to nod, taking a step closer to Chek and resting an armored hand on her shoulder. As he did, the thin red lines marbling his armor began to glow faintly. His eyes widened in surprise for a moment.

Keeping his arm raised, he took a few steps forward, walking past Chek. As he did, the red lines streaking through his black armor glowed brighter. His eyes hardened, but a slight smile turned up his lips. The look made Chek shiver.

With a swift movement, the man grabbed Chek by the arm. In one violent motion, he ripped the sleeve of her shirt up. Seeing nothing, he did the same to her other arm. The sudden jerk of her wrist caused her to drop her crutch. Letting out a yelp, she collapsed, hitting the ground once the man let go of her.

Turning towards his companions, the man said, "Astral resonance. Another Elmia is here. Find it."

The other three nodded, striding forward past Chek. As they did, the red streaks marbling their armor took on a similar glow.

The man reached out a hand to help Chek to her feet.

"Do you know where the Elmia is?" he asked. His tone had an air of forced, unnatural warmth to it. "The survival of my people depends on it."

Still on the ground, Chek swatted away his hand and glared.

"I don't know what you're talking about."

The man smiled, pulling back his hand. "Of course. Maybe your brother can help us then."

"Aren't you going to help Illyria?"

"I'm afraid that something much more pressing has taken my attention," he said. With that, he turned and followed his companions.

Chek sat in a heap watching him walk away. There was no way she could warn Felix they were coming, but she knew she didn't have to. Her brother was odd, often uniquely perceptive. He'd see through any facade they presented to him.

Reaching out her hand, a bruise already forming on her wrist, she grabbed her crutch. Groaning, she slowly rose to her feet and took a few weak steps following the four members of the Cult of Sundered Shadows.

"I can't use my legs, but I can use my mind," she whispered to herself repeatedly as she hobbled back towards the town.

Cam's world shattered.

"You're lying," he said through gritted teeth, anger flashing across his face. "My mother died when I was born."

Morwenna shook her head, her expression tightening with emotion.

"No, Cam. I am your mother."

"How dare you say that," he growled, his stomach twisting. "She died of infection. That's what they told me. She was sick, and the Vanguard couldn't deliver the medicine in time."

Tears welled in Morwenna's eyes.

"Cam, I was never sick. You were. Just a baby. Burning with fever. We sent for help, but...you know how slow Couriers can be." Her voice broke. "And then...the Shadows came. I don't know how they knew, but they had what we needed. They gave me the medicine that saved your life. In return, they demanded one thing."

She looked down, her hand trembling.

"A lifetime of servitude."

The two of you do share the same eyes, Luik murmured.

Cam swayed, his balance unsteady as the truth pressed down on him like a storm. His breath came hard. His chest ached. He stared at her.

"I don't understand. Why keep this from me? Why let me grow up thinking you were dead?"

Morwenna held his gaze, the truth pulling her features tight with pain.

"I tried to run. So many times. But there's a man here...he's not like us. He...he has gifts, Cam. Incredible, terrifying gifts." She paused for a moment, collecting herself before she spoke again. "He always knows where I am, Cam. Always. Every time I escaped, he found me... Hurt me. And he'd make me watch while he hurt others too."

Her voice trembled now, softer than before. "I wanted to tell you. I wanted to find you. But I couldn't let him punish you or someone else just because I tried to leave."

Cam's throat tightened.

"Did my father know? Did he ever learn the truth?"

Morwenna nodded faintly.

"I managed to sneak him a letter. Told him I was alive. He left Perth to find me. A few days later, the Shadows caught him. They turned him into a scaletaint."

Cam staggered back a step.

"They killed him?"

"They transformed him," Morwenna whispered. "And then I killed him."

Silence hung between them.

"All these years..." Cam's voice faltered.

Morwenna reached out, placing a hesitant hand on his shoulder.

"I am so sorry, my son. The pain I've caused... I carry it every day. I've spent many years biding my time and earning their trust, hoping to avenge your father."

I apologize that such a personal moment had to be shared with me, Luik said. *Although, Morwenna may be even more upset when she realizes she's not alone with you.*

Cam ignored him.

"But earlier, you called yourself the Sundered Sovereign. Everyone obeys you. Doesn't that mean you're leading them?"

Morwenna shook her head, shame clouding her face.

"No, Cam. I'm the Sovereign in name only. The one they follow is my husband. The Sundered God."

Oh my, Luik muttered. *They really are a cult.*

Chapter 34

Felix had always found it difficult to connect with people. People were just so complicated and hard to understand. They often said things that were not true to prove a different point. Chek said it was called sarcasm.

Felix called it confusing.

It's not that Felix didn't like people; he found most of them tolerable. Rather, he struggled to engage in the intricate dance of interpersonal communication. There were so many rules and steps to the dance, which nobody bothered to explain to him, and though Felix often did not understand what people were trying to say, he did understand what it meant when they visibly cringed as he spoke.

It made him so tired.

But not as tired as this, he thought, exasperated, watching Vaelin devour the bread he had just baked for him.

Getting Vaelin to relay messages from whatever Elmia he was Tethered to was akin to ripping teeth out. The wild man was unpredictable, sometimes appearing to be very willing to share what the Elmia was telling him, while at other times, he seemed very closed off. There were even times the man would randomly hide. Felix had figured out where his favorite hiding spot was, but he decided not to interrupt him.

Felix again found himself in a situation where the social rules were undefined and appeared to be ever changing.

At least he was familiar with the frustration he was feeling.

And at least Vaelin's vocabulary was growing.

At first, Felix had made quick progress with Vaelin, learning that the Elmia's name was Uriel. However, Vaelin quickly grew suspicious of Felix and had stopped talking. No amount of pressure from Felix would loosen his lips.

After a frustrating hour of trying to coax the man to speak, Felix had an idea. Vaelin liked to eat, and Felix liked to cook, so on a certain level, they made an excellent match for each other. Cooking for Vaelin had led to another spurt of messages from Uriel.

"Get to the Grove," Uriel had said. At least, according to Vaelin.

Once Vaelin realized he'd receive food for sharing messages, things turned into a vicious cycle. He'd refuse to speak again until Felix made him more food, and he began sharing less and less. Now, he had stopped speaking altogether, instead choosing to point at letters scrawled on the wall.

A new treat from Felix meant a new letter from Vaelin.

This is going to take forever.

For what it was worth, Vaelin appeared to be enjoying himself. Felix assumed that he'd been an outcast his entire life and he was savoring every moment of attention he was receiving. He gave a sly smile as he wiped breadcrumbs out of his beard.

"Okay, you ate the bread. Now, please, tell me what Uriel is trying to say," Felix said, unable to hide his annoyance.

Vaelin smirked. Reaching out his arm, he held his hand palm up. Felix groaned.

He was asking for more.

And Felix had finally had enough.

"I'm not doing this anymore, Vaelin. Either tell me what Uriel is saying or don't. I promise, I'll cook you whatever you like once you tell me."

Felix was, of course, bluffing. His natural passion for Elmias was overwhelming, and he could not rest until he knew what Uriel was trying to say.

Vaelin sat contemplatively for a moment. After a few agonizing seconds, he rose to his feet, stepping over towards the wall where Felix had scrawled various letters and characters around a small window. As Vaelin passed the window, he casually glanced out. He clearly saw something, because he started and let out a quick yelp.

Turning towards Felix, Vaelin hissed, "Cannot talk. Must hide." With that, he scurried on all fours out of the room.

"Vaelin, you can't be serious!" Felix shouted after the man. When Vaelin did not respond or return, he added, "Fine. I'll make you more chocolate. But just this once!"

Still nothing.

I need to take a break. Chek will know what to do.

A sudden creaking sound indicated that the door to the inn was opening. His sister must have returned from whatever errand she was on. Turning, Felix stepped out of the dining hall into the main chamber to greet her.

His sister was not there. Rather, there were four men in strange black armor, thin glowing red streaks running through it.

The group saw him and moved without speaking. Two grabbed at his arms, yanking his sleeves up and examining his arms. Felix jerked away.

"What in Aurora's Name was that?" he spat, pushing his glasses back up the bridge of his nose.

"Where is the Elmia?" a man said in a commanding tone. He appeared middle-aged and his black hair was speckled with gray.

Felix glowered back at him. He may not quite understand the rules of social interactions, but he did know when to play dumb.

"What's an Elmia?"

The man narrowed his eyes, a sly grin coming to his face. The expression made Felix's skin crawl, and he took a small step backward. This elicited an even wider smile from the man, who turned towards his companions.

"It's either Tethered itself to an object under the Shroud, or there's other people here. Spread out and search." Then, turning back to Felix, he sneered. "I don't know why you and your sister are trying to hide the Elmia, but it will not work out for you."

Felix started.

"My sis—"

At that moment, Chek stumbled through the open doorway, crutch under her arm and chest heaving with exhaustion. In spite of the problem with her leg, she'd clearly rushed to get to Felix.

"Chek, did they hurt you?"

"Kind of," she said, pointing to a bruise on her wrist. "They're not the friendliest bunch."

"You'll find us much more accommodating if you let us know where the Elmia is," the man said as his companions stepped out of the building. Felix raised a curious eyebrow.

"I told you, I don't know what you're talking about. And why do you need this Elmia anyway?"

"The survival of the Sundered Shadows."

Felix sighed.

First Vaelin, and now members of a cult.

This makes me so tired.

"You remarried? And you call him a god?" Cam said, his mind spinning.

"I know what you must think of me, but you have no right to judge me," Morwenna said, her tone sorrowful. "This was part of the arrangement with the Shadows. I would marry the Sundered God, and in turn, he would heal you."

"But to call him a god—"

"Cam, who do you think is the one that's kept me trapped here?" Morwenna spat, anger seeping into her words. "He may not be a god, but by Aurora's Name, he's not a normal mortal either. He's—"

"Morwenna, come on. He has you living in a cave!"

"At least he freed some of us from the Shrouds!" Morwenna snapped, her tone turning harsh. She blinked a few times, regaining her composure. In a calmer voice, she continued, "He has taught us how to survive in the Sundered Lands. If all Avoni were following him, there would be no need for Vanguard. We'd have our nation back."

Cam glared at her. "If he's a god, why doesn't he just end the corruption?"

Before she could answer, the steady crunch of footsteps drew their attention.

"I plan to," a deep voice said.

Fear flickered across Morwenna's face and Cam turned, wincing at the pain in his ribs, to see the newcomer. He stood at the top of a short staircase, silhouetted against the firelight behind him. The flickering torchlight played upon the contours of his face, revealing a man of striking presence. His hair had mostly grayed, although there were a few streaks where the black was visible.

His attire matched the charisma and intensity on his face. A black cape draped gracefully from his shoulders, billowing with each purposeful step. A sleeveless shirt clung to his muscled chest, revealing a snaking Aetherfern tattoo winding its way up his arm. The thorny tendrils of the ink seemed to pulse with a life of their own.

Eying the tattoo, Cam felt as Luik sensed a power emanating from the man. He let out a quick breath of surprise.

This man had somehow Tethered an Elmia.

Well...that explains the powers, Cam thought.

A survivor of the Vorunis Citadel? Gaalron, perhaps? Or perhaps a guardian of the Elmia Temple? Luik mused.

As the man descended the short staircase into the chamber, Morwenna instantly dropped to her knees and fell face first onto the ground, arms stretched out in front of her. She twisted her head slightly and gave Cam an urgent glance, as if she wanted him to follow her example.

Cam ignored her, choosing instead to lock eyes with the newcomer who he could only assume was Morwenna's new husband.

The Sundered God.

"I see you've met Morwenna," he said, striding into the room. His voice was deep and serious. He glanced towards the Aetherfern mark on Cam's arm, and his expression darkened. After a few moments, he turned towards Morwenna.

"To your feet, Sovereign." She did as he commanded, but kept her head lowered as she stood. The Sundered God walked over to her and gave her a kiss on the cheek.

For a fleeting moment, Morwenna flinched.

"You are the Sundered God?" Cam asked. Ignoring him, the man stroked Morwenna's hair, and the woman closed her eyes, her brow furrowed. Continuing to stroke her face and hair, he spoke.

"That is what they call me. A rather hyperbolic title, I must say. I don't mind it, but it's just...so formal, even if it's not exactly wrong. Why do people insist on such hierarchies? Please, call me Lucian."

Cam's eyes narrowed menacingly, and Lucian continued speaking.

"The Sundered Shadows walk a painful path. But the pain makes us stronger." His voice got a touch darker. "Doesn't it, Morwenna?"

She hesitated before giving a quick nod.

Find out more, Luik pushed in his mind.

"Lucian, how is it that your people survive outside of the Aurora Shrouds?"

Lucian removed his hand from Morwenna's face. As he did so, her body visibly relaxed. Turning, he eyed Cam. There was very little emotion in his expression. The man did not appear to feel threatened, happy, or fearful. Rather, he stared at Cam with curiosity.

When he spoke, his words were dry and measured.

"There are many ways to survive. The Aurora Shrouds are one such way. We follow another." He pointed to the armor that Morwenna was wearing. "That armor helps my people survive separate from the Shrouds. Unfortunately, surviving is different than thriving. But the thriving is coming."

"What's that armor made out of? And what do you have planned?" Cam asked, feeling Luik's shared interest in what Lucian was intending.

Ignoring the questions, Lucian pointed at Cam's left arm and said, "Tell me, how did you get that tattoo?"

The question stunned Cam, who stood silent, wondering how he should answer the question. Lucian must have interpreted the silence as an answer in itself, because he continued speaking.

"I don't ask to be rude. Quite honestly, I like it. It's...well...this is rather embarrassing for me. You see, it's just so similar to my own." He flung back his cloak, giving Cam a better look at the man's tattoo.

"Aetherferns are amazing plants. If I were to be honest, though, I'd say that I prefer roses. A rose is a beautiful thing, isn't it? Bright...colorful. And covered in thorns," Lucian said, a sneer coming to his face. "While I may not be able to claim the same beauty as the rose, you might find that I am covered in thorns."

From the folds of his cloak, Lucian extracted a sword. Holding it aloft, he paused for a moment, his fingers tightening around the hilt. Suddenly, the blade pulsed with an enigmatic energy, and as quickly as it had stiffened, it went as limp as a rope.

He then cracked the sword like a whip towards a group of wooden chairs and a table. Despite the sword's apparent pliability, it cut through the air with a potent force, cracking like a whip as it met its target. In a matter of moments, the table and chairs lay shattered on the cavern floor, marked by impeccably clean cuts.

Fascinating. He's found an Astral Edge, Luik said. Sensing Cam's confusion, he explained, *It's an Elmia weapon and changes forms based on the desire of the wielder.*

Lucian gave the sword a quick snap, and the blade became rigid again. He deftly placed the sword back in its sheath and continued speaking.

"And just like a thorn protects the rose, so will I protect what is mine."

He locked eyes with Cam, his expression hungry and predatory.

Uncomfortable, Cam broke the silence. "I'm grateful to you and your people for saving my life."

"You're only grateful, boy, because of when we saved you. If this had been days ago, the mark on your arm would have been your death sentence. As things stand today, however, I no longer require what your death would give me."

"And what is that?"

"Oh, please don't feign ignorance," Lucian spat, his face disgusted. "We both know that you do not journey alone."

"And is that such a crime?" Cam stammered, his heart beginning to race. "I assume you also do not travel alone. Like you said, our tattoos are very similar."

Lucian smirked.

"No, it is not a crime. Rather, what you have is a requirement of our survival. Fortunately for the both of you, the solution to my predicament is not far away, so I have no need of your companion."

"What do you plan to do?"

"It won't be long before all of Avoni walks the path of the Shadows. The days of hiding under the Aurora Shrouds are almost over. And I will lead this nation to glory as its first Divine Monarch. You may not join us now, but you will not oppose us."

Lucian turned to leave the room. As he walked away, he looked back at Morwenna.

"Bow." His voice was dark and authoritative. Morwenna nodded, quickly slipping down to her knees and lying flat on the floor, her hands outstretched. The Sundered God smirked and stepped away.

Chapter 35

Cam had endured much in his life, but his near-death encounter with the Reaper, discovering his mother was alive, and meeting the Sundered God shattered something within him. Decades of repressed fear and anxiety erupted violently to the surface.

It broke Luik's heart.

Well, it would have if he had one right now. Being Tethered was strange.

Knowing that Cam would be able to share any emotion Luik was experiencing, the Elmia did his best to repress his own feelings. The young man was struggling enough, and Luik did not want to complicate things.

In his many years of being Tethered to people, he'd become very familiar with the emotional experiences of human beings. The human soul, for all its potential and adaptability, was not infinitely pliable. Like all things in the world, there existed a point at which too much complexity broke a person, and Luik could sense that Cam was nearing this point.

He'd often described people as vessels. Pour kindness into them, and it would spill over into the lives of others. Fill them instead with pain, and that pain would eventually leak out the same way.

For Cam, a lifetime of living in the shadows of the Sundered Lands had mercilessly filled his vessel with stress, fear, and trauma.

And now, the weight inside had begun to overflow.

Cold sweat dotted Cam's brow as his breathing quickened. He lay on the cold stone floor in a private room the Cult had provided him. Luik could feel Cam's mind racing. Images flashed through his mind, haphazard and random, and made visible to Luik.

Luik saw many things.

He saw a five-year-old Cam watching his father leave the safety of the Aurora Shroud, wondering if he had done something to drive the man away.

He saw Cam's uncle whip Cam's back after he had accidentally broken a window.

He saw Cam in the aftermath of killing his first scaletaint. He was doubled over, tears in his eyes. The ground was covered in his vomit, as the grief-stricken man wondered who the human behind the monster had been.

And still the images kept coming, along with the landslide of emotions.

Luik saw and felt them all.

You poor, poor man, Luik thought.

"Luik, I…what's wrong with me?" he gasped, his chest heaving as he tried to catch his breath. "Please, I…I can't calm down."

As Luik heard Cam's ragged voice, he could sense the man accessing his astral powers, likely seeking an anchor to use Verdalink and escape.

Fortunately, Luik had many years of experience dealing with humans. Using a voice that was equal parts firm and gentle, he spoke to Cam.

Cam, I need you to breathe.

"No, I need to get out," Cam responded as he tried to get to his feet, tears beginning to form in his eyes. "I have to get out."

We will. But not like this. Take a deep breath.

This time, Cam did so.

Now hold that breath. Good. Just like that. Now, let it out. Slowly. Now, deep breath again.

For the next minute, Luik guided Cam towards controlled breathing. He kept his voice steady and tried to force a sense of calm through their bond. After a few seconds, he could feel Cam start to relax.

Good. Now, you said you want to get out? That's fine. Let's go for a walk.

Go for a walk where? Cam thought in response.

Anywhere. There's something off about this place, and I think it's time we figured out what it is.

Really? Cam thought back. *Something is off about the spot a cult decided to call home?*

Humor. That was a good sign.

Truthfully, I feel it might help you relax to move around a bit.

I'm not sure they're going to appreciate me sneaking around.

Luik expressed mock disdain, as if he were jokingly rolling his eyes.

Astral powers, remember? We're in a cave network at night. Literally everything is covered in shadows. I'm fairly certain they won't find you.

Right.

With practiced ease, Luik invoked Shadowmeld, allowing Cam's form to dissolve and blend seamlessly into the cavern floor. The transition was instantaneous, the world around him shifting to a dark, nebulous expanse as he began to swim through the shadows, gliding silently down the tunnel.

The cave itself was starkly ordinary, its simplicity almost disappointing. Rough, un-yielding stone formed its walls, the air surprisingly dry for such an environment. As they moved deeper, faintly illuminated murals came into view, their faded pigments depicting scenes of Lucian locked in combat with grotesque monstrosities.

The smell in the air was unsettling to Luik. It wasn't the musty, damp odor one would expect in such a place. No, this was different, sharper. A scent of charred metal, acrid and foreboding. It clung to the air, making every breath feel heavy.

After they'd gone deep into the caverns, they started to hear the screaming.

It began as a faint, distant wail, barely audible over the whispering shadows and the soft, echoing drip of water in the cave. But even muffled by distance, the sound was unmistakable, cutting through the silence like a jagged blade. It was a scream born of pure agony and despair, a chilling cry that seemed to reverberate through the very stone around them.

Luik and Cam both froze, the scream sending shivers down their spines.

What in Aurora's Name is that? Cam wondered to Luik.

Let's find out, Luik suggested.

It was difficult to find the source of the screaming. The cave network was a labyrinth, its twisting passages and countless chambers creating a disorienting maze, but as they moved deeper, the screams began to change. They grew louder, more distinct, cutting through the oppressive silence with renewed intensity.

Any guesses what we're going to find? Cam thought to Luik.

I have no guesses, Luik said. *I can only hope that this poor soul finds relief soon.*

Cam continued swimming through the shadows, searching out the source of the screaming. He was silent for a few minutes before he spoke.

Thank you. What happened earlier has happened to me before. I've never had someone help me.

Your fear is nothing to be ashamed of, Luik said. *In my experience, episodes like what you just experienced are the result of your body trying to keep you safe. You're not broken. At least, no more broken than the rest of us.*

Through their bond, he could feel Cam contemplating his words.

I'm sorry you're stuck with me, Cam thought.

What do you mean? For all my jokes about your smell, I quite like our bond.

I mean, you're essentially trapped inside of me. I know you'd prefer to be on your own.

Luik was taken aback by the remark. He did appreciate Cam's company, and their shared journey had been surprisingly harmonious.

Yet, if he were to speak truthfully, he yearned for the days when he could roam independently. Once, being confined to Vorunis Citadel had felt like a prison sentence. Now, by comparison, he realized that those days were when he was most free.

Would those days ever return to him?

Cam must have sensed his emotion. Through their bond, Luik could sense the empathy the man felt for him.

It's nothing against you, Luik said. *Lacking my own autonomy is a loss of personal identity. It saddens me that I cannot go wherever I want to. Or even look wherever I want to. I'm merely a passenger.*

That makes sense.

Plus, Luik added, *if I were an autonomous being, I wouldn't be forced to put up with your smell so much.*

Before Cam could retort, the sound of the screaming intensified. The bloodcurdling noise was just around the corner. Jumping from the shadows, Cam rounded the bend, knowing that his curiosity and fear were evident to Luik through their bond.

Then, they saw it.

Both of them felt like throwing up.

They were in a vast, round chamber filled with enormous pots and bowls, each bearing a strange black liquid. Several large anvils and hammers were scattered in one corner, alongside a blacksmith's apron. A roaring fire sat in the center of the room, its heat palpable from every direction.

Above the fire hung a large metal bowl, just out of reach of the flames. Chained by hands and feet inside the bowl was a strange creature that resembled a man. This being appeared to be made of black metal streaked with red. Lying on his back and screaming in agony, his metal flesh seemed to be melting, pooling in the bowl to which he was chained.

Barbarians, Luik whispered, rage and horror filling him. *Monsters. Wretches. This...this is...this is evil.*

Through their bond, it was evident that Cam wasn't sure what he was looking at. Luik, however, knew exactly what lay before him.

The Cult of Sundered Shadows had somehow captured an Elmia.

And they were melting him.

Chapter 36

Cam's horror lasted only a moment before he rushed to the dying Elmia. He didn't know exactly what to do, but his body moved with the urgency born from years of survival in the Sundered Lands. He strode forward, ready to cut the Elmia free.

He realized that Luik must have sensed his intent, because just as he reached the Elmia, a pulse of cold moved through his arm, and a thin blade took shape in his hand. With a clean stroke, the blade sliced through the metal restraints.

The Elmia whimpered in pain, his eyes appearing glassy and distant. There wasn't much of him left. His legs and arms had completely melted away. A portion of his back was gone as well.

That's how they survive. That's how they're making the armor, Luik said in Cam's mind. *They're wearing the corpses of melted Elmias.*

Ignoring the temporary wave of exhaustion and speaking out loud for the benefit of the dying Elmia, Cam said, "Luik, can I Tether him and you at the same time?"

No. We need to get him to someone else.

Cam stared at the poor Elmia, his heart heavy with a mix of sorrow and rage. Through their bond, he could feel Luik's emotions like a tidal wave, washing over him with an intensity that nearly brought him to his knees. The deep horror and sadness were almost unbearable.

The once graceful and ethereal form of the Elmia was now a twisted mass of molten black and scarlet. The creature gagged as it tried to suck in a breath of air.

How could anyone do this to another living creature? Luik wondered.

Sometimes, humans don't need the Sundered Lands to turn them into monsters, Cam thought back.

The Elmia whimpered, turning his bald head to look at Cam and giving him a better look at him. His face, still twisted in pain, appeared to be quite young, although Cam knew that this did not necessarily mean the Elmia was young by human standards. His black metallic flesh contained slight streaks of red, like veins of ore running through rock.

"My name is Cam. I'm going to get you out of here." As Cam spoke, he grabbed an apron hanging nearby and wrapped it around the Elmia before lifting him into the air. He gave a slight wince as his injured ribs flared with pain.

"No," the Elmia whispered, his voice hoarse from screaming. "No, it's too late for me. You must save the others."

"There are other Elmias here?"

The Elmia gave a weak shake of his head.

"There are others here, but I don't mean just them. You must save everyone."

Cam laid the Elmia back on the cold stone floor, gently cradling his head in his left hand.

"What is your name?"

"Veln."

Anyone you know? Cam quickly thought to Luik.

No, we've never met.

"Veln, I need you to speak plainly with me. What has happened to you, and who do I need to save?"

Veln moaned slightly, closing his eyes. Cam gave him a quick shake.

"Veln!"

The Elmia's eyes snapped open, and for a moment, he became calm and coherent.

"The Sundered God. He seeks the Scepter of Alderia. He's planning on using it to destroy all the Aurora Shrouds. All that he needed was an Elmia to Tether with him and knowledge of its location."

"Why would that Elmia help him?" Cam asked, his voice hoarse.

"Because," the Elmia croaked, "they both want the same thing. The destruction of the Aurora Shrouds."

He Tethered Gaalron, Cam and Luik thought at the same time.

"Does he know the location of the Scepter?" Cam asked, urgency in his voice.

"By this point, it is likely. I'm sure one of my brethren has broken and told him."

"Why hasn't he gone to get it yet?" Cam asked.

"Because I had to negotiate terms of ruling with my Elmia. He was being quite stubborn. Thankfully, your appearance today gave him the motivation he needed to expedite a deal."

Cam spun, his hand instinctively reaching for his hip daggers, which were not there. In front of him, Lucian, the self-proclaimed Sundered God, strode into the room with an air of dark authority. In his hand, the Astral Edge shimmered ominously, its edge seeming to drink in the light around it.

Illyria continued her climb up the rocky path in the Jaram Mountains. She had long since passed the spot where they had been attacked by the Reaper, and still there was no sign of Cam. All she could hope was that he'd somehow escaped and that no pain had come to him on her account.

Her breath came heavy and labored. The air of the Sundered Lands no longer bothered her lungs, but the near constant journey up the steep, rocky incline was taking its own toll. Scratches and calluses were beginning to dot her hands, and she'd bruised her arm after tripping on a loose stone.

In spite of the warning she'd received about carrying The Tool through the Sundered Lands, no Reapers bore down on her. This surprised her. It had been right about everything else.

Was it possible that the instructions could be wrong?

She gritted her teeth, shaking her head. It was too late to start thinking that way. The words from The Tool had guided her this far. She wasn't about to change her plan now.

But what even is my plan? she wondered. All she knew was that she needed to get the Scepter of Alderia, but what next? Was she even capable of using it?

In reality, she knew that she was completely out of her depth. She had been out of her depth since she first left Kevilton with Cam. She was just a Healer from a small farming community, unacquainted with ancient artifacts, temples, and mythical creatures. It was a wonder that she even made it this far.

It is a wonder. But I DID make it this far. That counts for something, she thought, trying to silence the gnawing doubts. It had taken weeks, painful journeys through the Sundered Lands, her conscience eating her alive and possibly the death of a friend.

She would have to trust that she'd know what to do if she made it farther.

As she climbed up the rocky terrain, a shadow shifted next to her, causing her to jump, her bare hand tightening on The Tool. It seemed to sense her sudden anxiety and formed itself into that long blade with the gentle curve. In spite of herself, she snickered at the sight.

"It seems like this is what you want to be. But I'm fine now. Go back to being a staff."

Just as the blade reformed into a staff, she saw the shadows shift again and a few disturbed rocks rolled down the hill.

Something's out there.

She stepped closer to investigate and almost screamed as a scaletaint leapt at her from behind a rock. The sudden movement caused her to fall flat on her back. She let out a pained grunt at the impact.

Get up, more are coming.

She rolled to her feet. Her hands were still gloved, so she had to yell out her command to The Tool.

"Sword!"

The Tool obeyed her command, transforming itself back. The scaletaint hesitated for a moment, likely confused by the sudden transformation of the staff. Behind it were three other scaletaints, hissing loudly at her.

Illyria smirked, pointing the tip of the sword at the creatures in a defiant challenge. With a snarl, they jumped towards her.

Lucian's cold eyes fixed on Cam, a cruel smile playing on his lips.

"You admire my work, I see," he said, his voice dripping with mockery.

Cam's fury bubbled up in him.

"This is your work?" he spat, motioning to Veln. "This is an abomination."

"I prefer the term 'evolution.' After all, it is their fault that we humans find ourselves in this plight."

"I'm not letting you hurt anyone else," Cam said, his eyes darkening. Lucian simply smiled at him.

"I must admit, I expected some sort of confrontation from you. Just not one so soon." He stroked his chin with a gentle hand. "If I may be transparent, I'm disappointed. You're not exactly...at your best right now."

Cam let out a growl, slowly rising and meeting Lucian's eyes. He tried to conceal the pain of his wounds with a mask of determination.

"I think you'll find that I'm more than capable."

Cam, a physical confrontation is not wise. You're hurt and unarmed, and he has full access to the astral powers. He may have even discovered his Complex.

Cam grit his teeth.

I know that! I'm not trying to beat him. I just need to get to the Scepter first.

We don't know the location of the temple.

We don't. But I have a feeling that Veln does.

Cam felt Luik nod with approval and understanding.

I'll see if I can find us a way to escape, Luik said. He then tapped into his astral powers and began to seek out an anchor to use Verdalink.

"Must we fight?" Lucian said. "Can't you see that giving people a way to live outside of the Aurora Shrouds is a good thing?"

"Not if it's like this," Cam said, motioning to Veln who whimpered quietly behind him. Lucian glanced at the Elmia and a brief look of empathy crossed his face.

"Quite right. This one's suffered enough." With a flick of his wrist, his Astral Edge turned into a whip, arcing around Cam and slashing against Veln's chest. Veln let out a quick cry before his body relaxed, black smoke billowing out from the new wound on his chest.

Cam cried out in shock.

Luik, is he dead?

No. As long as you can see smoke coming out of him, he's still alive.

Snarling, and still seeking out an astral anchor, Cam charged at Lucian.

Let's try to Time Shift his weapon, Luik yelled in his mind. Cam obeyed, tapping the blade still stuck in Veln, pausing its momentum through time.

This brought a smirk to Lucian's face. Stepping back, he glanced down at Cam's feet. The next instant, Cam lurched as he became completely immovable.

No, not immovable. Lucian has Time Shifted my boots, Cam thought. His forward momentum caused him to fall flat in front of Lucian, the fall only broken by his hands.

"Earlier you didn't want to call me a god, but now you're bowing before me. I knew you'd figure things out."

Cam struggled, trying to right himself, but his boots were completely stuck. Lucian clicked his tongue in condescension.

"Which Elmia are you Tethered with? Clearly he wasn't a warrior. Didn't he tell you that it's foolish to be the first one to use Time Shift in a fight? Without the Scepter, you can only shift one item at a time, and you may need to use it to cancel out someone else's Time Shift. Such as in the situation you currently find yourself."

Cam grunted as he struggled to his feet, and Luik stopped Time Shifting Lucian's Astral Edge, instead focusing on reversing the Time Shift on his boots. A moment later, Cam was charging forward towards Lucian.

Only this time, Cam went far too quickly, his feet flying out from under him. He groaned as he struggled to maintain his balance.

Lucian stopped Time Shifting your boots. You're moving too fast now, Luik chided.

You think?

Lucian chuckled as Cam fell on his back.

"For all your strength, boy, you have no idea how to use the gifts provided by your Tethering. No more than a child knows how to use a spear. You're just going to hurt yourself."

Have you found an anchor yet? Cam's mind screamed.

Stop distracting me, I'm working on it!

Cam cautiously rose to his feet. It was difficult enough fighting while injured. Feeling Luik mentally searching for an astral anchor added a completely new level of confusion.

But the longer Luik searched, the more likely he'd be to find one. They just had to keep Lucian busy a little longer.

"I may know a thing or two," he said, leaping towards Lucian. The man must have not expected Cam to move so quickly, because he didn't react quickly enough. Cam tackled him, landing on top of him. His injured ribs and shoulders groaned, but he ignored the pain.

With a grimace, he brought his fist down, aiming for Lucian's jaw. The man's eyes flashed, and with a swift movement, he Time Shifted Cam's fist, freezing it in mid-air just inches from his face.

"Predictable," Lucian sneered. He twisted his body, throwing Cam off him. Cam landed with a pained grunt, sliding across the stone floor.

Luik's voice echoed in his mind, calm and steady.

I'm going to Shadowmeld you in two seconds.

Cam nodded, faintly aware of Lucian rushing towards him. Just as the man reached him, Cam melded into the shadows, becoming a part of the darkness around him. Lucian stood, scanning the cave, his expression a mix of amusement and annoyance.

"My oh my. Wherever could you have run off to?" he mocked.

Cam repositioned, moving silently through the shadows, circling around Lucian. When he was directly behind him, he struck.

Leaping from the shadows, he wrapped his arms around Lucian, who let out a quick gasp as his arms were pinned to his sides.

Unfortunately for Cam, Lucian was still holding the Astral Edge. As Cam squeezed his quarry, the blade lengthened, twisting and snaking up towards his face. He shifted at the last moment, moving his head out of the path of the sword. It plunged into his shoulder instead.

Cam let out a howl of pain, letting go of Lucian and slumping for a moment, his scaly right arm clutching at the wound in his shoulder. He fell backwards, landing next to Veln, who moaned slightly as the black smoke escaping his body began to slow down.

I found an anchor! Luik exclaimed. *It's far away, but we are not in the position to be selective.*

Agreed!

Turning, Cam scooped up Veln in his arms.

"That one won't be much use to you," Lucian said. "We've already used most of his essence to build our armor."

A smirk coming to his face, Cam winked at Lucian before Luik activated Verdalink. The world spun around him in a crazed kaleidoscope, shifting from the dark walls of the cave back to the stony expanse of the Sundered Lands.

When the world snapped back into focus, Cam stumbled, barely able to keep his footing. His vision swam, and he fought the urge to vomit. The disorientation was unlike anything he had ever experienced. He took a deep breath, trying to steady himself, and looked around.

The air was thick with the stench of decay. Cam's head pounded as he tried to make sense of his surroundings. The ground beneath his feet was littered with the corpses of scaletaints, their twisted, corrupted forms lying in unnatural poses. Fear gripped him as he instinctively reached for his weapon, his eyes darting around for any sign of movement.

This brought a new wave of dizziness upon him. He fell to the ground and darkness crept along the edges of his vision.

You jumped too far. You'll likely fall unconscious, Luik explained.

"Cam?" a woman's voice sounded behind him.

Twisting his head, he saw Illyria. Her robes were stained with the blood of the scaletaints, and in her hand was a long sword with a gentle curve. It was emanating astral energy.

Is that an Astral Edge? Luik said in wonder.

Cam tried again to rise, but collapsed, darkness overtaking his vision.

Chapter 37

F elix had found life frustrating when Perth only had one other resident. With five newcomers—including Chek—things had become even more taxing for him.

Who knew the short time with just him and Vaelin would be something he'd miss?

It didn't bother him that Chek had returned; she had always felt like an extension of himself. She was one of the few people that he truly felt comfortable around.

But she was different now. Something in the Sundered Lands had changed her. She seemed sadder and a bit slower, as if she were carrying a weight around on her shoulders.

Felix wanted to do something to help her, but he wasn't sure how.

Also, there was the problem of the disappearing Vaelin.

The thought of Vaelin brought to mind the four other newcomers to Perth, and Felix grimaced. Now, those were some people he could do without. They were rude and rough.

Worse, one of them was staying near the inn's kitchen, robbing Felix of one of his deep joys in life. He found himself longing to cook again.

Without anything to distract him, Felix's mind kept wandering back to the problems at hand. He tried to ignore them, but the thoughts kept returning.

Finally, he let out a deep sigh and decided that it was time to solve his Vaelin problem. The problem was that the members of the Cult were suspicious. He'd played dumb this far, but they'd realize something was off if he started searching Perth too.

Chek would know what to do.

He found her sitting under a willow tree, not far from the edge of the Aurora Shroud. Ever since she'd returned from the Sundered Lands, she seemed to enjoy the solitude. As

Felix walked up to her, he noticed that she was rubbing her left leg. She gave a slight wince as she did so.

"What's wrong with your leg?" Felix asked. Chek startled slightly before turning around with a glare.

"Absolutely nothing. And don't scare me like that. You know I don't like that."

Felix shrugged. "Sorry, didn't mean to. I thought you could hear me." Her face fell slightly as he approached, and he gave her an empathetic smile. A lifetime with Chek had taught him when she needed comfort with words and when she needed comfort with his presence.

He sat down next to her, pulling his legs close to his chest. For several minutes, neither of them spoke, the only sound the quiet rustling of the leaves in the trees.

Finally, Chek spoke.

"I don't think I'm ever going to walk right again."

Felix's eyes shot open, his head jerking towards his sister.

"No, don't say that. Illyria said you'd recover!"

Chek shook her head.

"Illyria doesn't know what this feels like. My leg...it's like it's completely gone, Felix. It's useless. And it hurts so much."

"You can't know for certain—"

"I am certain!" Chek yelled. She flushed a moment later, looking at her feet again. "All I've ever wanted to do was help people deal with the Sundered Lands. But my body just can't handle it at all. It's why they never let me be a Courier."

"I thought that was because you're a woman?"

"There are female Vanguard Couriers, Felix," Chek said with an eye roll. "I know there aren't many, but they're there."

Felix shrugged.

"You think that only Couriers can help people?"

"Obviously not," Chek said, shaking her head. "But...I just don't know what to do anymore."

As she spoke, her voice quieted to a whisper.

"What do you mean?" Felix asked, his voice showing authentic curiosity. His sister shrugged.

"Just what I said." She motioned with her hands towards the distance. "Cam and Illyria are out there. Doing something. But I can't be there, and I don't know what to do here."

Felix nodded. He wasn't sure what to say, so instead, he chose to stay quiet. Moments later, his sister continued speaking.

"And now the Sundered Shadows...the Cult of Sundered Shadows"—Felix smiled as she finally included the word "cult" in the name—"shows up here, looking for Vaelin. And I don't know the first thing about Elmias, or how to help him. I keep telling myself that I can use my brain, but I don't know where to start."

"I don't think you need to know where to start." She glanced up and looked at him, her dark eyes curious. "I mean, Cam and Illyria clearly have no idea what they're doing. They're just randomly exploring the Sundered Lands, trying to find a temple. They don't even know what to do once they find it."

"They'll figure it out."

"Either that or Mr. Grumpy Muscles will finally have something to be grumpy about, besides his body odor."

The corner of Chek's lip curved for a moment, before she looked back at the ground again.

"He doesn't smell that bad."

"I'll bottle it up and buy you some perfume, then. Maybe you can befriend a group of barnyard animals."

This elicited a chuckle from Chek. Felix gave a sheepish grin, scratching the back of his neck.

"We need to find Vaelin," Chek said, her voice serious again. "The Elmia he is Tethered to wanted to tell you something."

"I know, but the Cult might get suspicious if they see me looking around."

Chek's eyes lit up for a moment. "How long do you think it would take you to find him?"

Felix shrugged.

"Not long. I'm pretty sure I know where he is. He's got to be in one of those holes he keeps digging. Could be in the well, too. He's gone to that spot a few times."

Chek's face shifted to astonishment.

"You think you know where he is? Why didn't you say something earlier?"

"I'm not sure how to find him without leading the others to him."

Chek let out a deep, almost conniving smile.

"Oh, baby brother..." He cringed at this, as he always hated being reminded that she was born first. "That's the easy part."

A few hours later, the twins stepped back into the town proper, Chek leaning on her crutch as she walked. The emptiness of the small town square was bizarre. Having lived her entire life in the cramped city of Rath, she struggled to wrap her mind around this level of personal space.

Felix's constant complaining at least provided a bit of the noise that she had grown accustomed to.

"I'm not sure I can do this," Felix whispered to her. Her glare silenced him.

They waited in the square, pretending to talk. After a few moments, a creaking door sounded, and one of the members of the Cult of Sundered Shadows exited. He was still wearing the mysterious black-and-red armor. He saw the twins and gave a dismissive look, stepping over towards the next building.

"You still haven't told me what an Elmia is!" Felix shouted.

The man rolled his eyes and walked away from them.

"I might be willing to help, but I wouldn't even know what to look for," Felix shouted again. Chek tried to hide a cringe at the wooden tone of her brother's voice. "But there's something else I can do to help." The man stopped and turned his attention to them. Felix paused, nervously looking towards Chek.

"Please, don't make me do this," he mouthed. She gave him a stern expression in response. Defeated, Felix shouted, "You must be hungry. I'm going to cook something for you." The words were awkward coming out of his mouth, but it brought a smile to Chek's face. She'd known about Felix's so-called "secret" obsession for years but hadn't said anything out of respect for her brother's strange pride. He'd looked so ashamed when she suggested this.

He ignored Felix, turning towards the next building. Felix took this as his cue, scampering back towards the inn. Leaning on her crutch, Chek stepped over towards the man.

"What exactly are you looking for?"

The man let out an exasperated sigh. "Trying to find out who or what this Elmia is Tethered to."

Good. This one was willing to talk to her. As she continued towards him, she exaggerated her limp slightly.

"Who or what?" she asked, feigning curiosity. The man nodded.

"They can Tether to any living thing. If it's under the Aurora Shroud, it would have to be Tethered in order to survive. If it's in the Sundered Lands, it would eventually get transformed."

"So, it could be Tethered to any living thing? Even plants or animals?"

"Yes. Although, if it's a plant, they're trapped. They can't just leave on their own."

Chek scratched her head, pretending to be lost in thought. A moment later, she said, "Would that change the appearance of the plant?"

"Usually they give off a bit of a glow. Why? Have you seen anything like that?"

Chek gave a small shrug of her shoulders.

"Maybe. Once you find this thing, you're all leaving, right?"

"If you've seen something, you need to tell me." His voice was mostly even, but there was an edge of excitement and desperation hidden in his tone. Chek had to hold back a smirk. He was exactly where she wanted him.

"I'm not sure I have seen anything. I'm not from here. I really just want you to help my friends. I'm worried about them, traveling through the Sundered Lands all alone."

"Look, I can't promise anything, but the only reason we're still here is because of this Elmia. Once we find him, we'll probably leave."

Chek nodded and said, "Okay. It's possible that I've seen something."

Chapter 38

When awareness returned to Cam, the shifts in light hinted that he'd been unconscious for quite a while. The sky was a deeper and darker shade of red, black clouds billowing through it.

He shook his head and pressed against the ground to lift himself, wincing as he prepared to feel the pain in his broken ribs and arm. His jaw opened in a moment of shock.

That pain was gone.

Surprised, and slightly perplexed, he extended his hand and cautiously traced the contours of his left arm. Still nothing.

What is going on? he thought to himself, although he knew Luik would hear him.

I used Verdalink and jumped way too far. It knocked both of us unconscious.

Cam rubbed the back of his head.

I figured that much. That's not what I meant. I meant...why do I feel great?

You've finally learned to appreciate me, perhaps?

Or maybe the fact that things were quiet for a minute.

I'm not quite sure I deserve that, Luik said. His voice sounded as if he were hurt, but Cam could feel his amusement.

Cam rose to his feet, still expecting the pain from his once-broken bones to flare within him. He turned to his left and froze, a smile forming on his face.

A few feet away was Illyria, an impressive array of vials lying haphazardly on the ground in front of her. Her sleeved cloak billowed softly in an almost playful manner.

Hearing him stir, she glanced at him. Although her mask obscured her face, Cam could tell from her eyes that she was smiling.

"Courier, you should know better than to scare a lady like that. It's not polite. And to think that you did it twice!"

Cam frowned, scratching at his face.

"Twice?"

Illyria nodded emphatically.

"Yes, twice. The first was when you appeared out of nowhere. The second was when you passed out in front of me moments later. Very rude." As she spoke, she began to put the many vials and containers back into her small pack.

"I apologize," Cam said. "Next time I have to make an emergency escape, I'll warn you." The memories of his escape quickly came back to his mind. "Where's Veln?" he asked, a sudden intensity in his voice. "The wounded Elmia. Where is he?"

"He's going to be fine," she replied. Her voice was calm, almost nonchalant. "We can talk about him in a minute." The next moment, he was almost knocked backwards as she gave him a deep embrace.

"When we couldn't find you, I thought you had died," she whispered, her face buried in his chest. "What happened? Did you kill that thing?"

He was still concerned about Veln, but her calm certainty, paired with the way she clung to him, was enough to quiet his fears for now. Wrapping his arms around her, Cam gave a gentle squeeze.

"I'm not sure. It at least had had enough of me."

She pulled her face back from his chest, using one hand to dab at her red eyes.

"From how you looked when I first saw you, it looks like you'd had enough of it as well."

"I'd rather not run into it again," Cam said flatly as Illyria embraced him again. Both remained silent, eyes closed, captured in the serenity of the moment. After a few seconds, she pulled back, her eyes playful.

"I'm...guessing you still haven't had a bath?"

Ouch, Luik said. Cam rolled his eyes.

"Outside of falling unconscious out here, I haven't even slept. By the way, were you fighting scaletaints?"

Her eyes shifted down, as if she were embarrassed, but there was a faint glimmer of pride in her expression.

"I'm impressed," Cam said. "Where did you even get that sword?"

"I was trying to tell you about it when the Reaper attacked," Illyria said. "And...to be honest, there's a lot I haven't told you. I don't know where to start."

Ask her again about the Astral Edge.

"Luik wants to know more about your sword. He calls it an 'Astral Edge.' What can you tell me about it?"

She nodded. "So that's what it's called. I've just been calling it 'The Tool.' I found it in the Sundered Lands near Kevilton. I was wandering far off the Safe Paths and found an old armory. When I touched the sword, it spoke to me."

"It spoke to you?"

"Yes. It said that all Avoni was in danger."

The swords aren't supposed to speak. Something is different about this one, Luik said.

"I was given instructions. It said that I had to find the Elmia Temple," Illyria continued. "I didn't even know what an Elmia was, or where to find a temple."

"Why didn't you tell me sooner?" Cam said, shaking his head.

"Would you have believed me if I said that a sword had started talking to me? The best case is that everyone would have assumed my mind was somehow transformed by the Sundered Lands. And the worst case? I mean, you saw the riots that happened in Rath when they thought you were contagious. What would happen if they knew the Shrouds were weakening?"

"You may be right. But I think I deserved to know."

"Why?" she said, a hint of irritation in her voice. "Why do you deserve to know? Because we were traveling together? Surely you're not so entitled as that."

"I could have helped you."

"And it was my choice to ask for that help or not," she said emphatically. "This knowledge was a burden that I wanted to spare others from. That includes you." She paused for a moment before adding, "And I'll have you know that this has been the hardest thing I've ever done."

For a moment, neither of them spoke. After an uncomfortable few seconds, Cam said, "I'm sorry. Bearing that by yourself...it sounds lonely."

She gave a slight shrug.

"I wouldn't say that. Anyway, you know now. So, I guess you're burdened with the knowledge too." She gave a deep sigh before her voice returned to a playful tone. "And you almost sacrificed yourself fighting a monster, so I guess you've had your share of hard things." She gave him a wink.

"Yeah, I did almost die, didn't I?" he said, stretching his arm again. "But I'm not even hurt anymore. Did you give me something while I was out?"

"Well, you were completely unconscious, and I am a Healer."

"I just..." He touched his healed ribs again and shook his head. "My arms and ribs were broken. Why aren't they anymore?"

Illyria's eyes twinkled, and Cam knew that she was smirking behind her mask.

"There are many things you do not know about healing. Maybe next time, you'll pay more attention."

He chuckled. "Whatever you did, thank you." He stretched his arms again in amazement. "I think this is the best I've felt in years."

She bowed in exaggerated fashion, waving her gloved hands as she did so. "I am always at your service, my lord."

Cam smiled, holding out his reptilian arm. "I guess there's nothing you can do about this?"

"Hmmm...I'd say it'd be wiser to start by fixing your stench."

She beat me by one second, Luik complained.

You're getting slow, my friend.

Cam rolled his shoulders, still shocked at the lack of pain, and said, "How long was I unconscious?"

Illyria tilted her head back as she considered.

"A while. A few hours at least. You had us worried."

"Us?" Cam asked, surprised.

"Yeah. After you left, I figured I'd come find you," a voice said behind him.

Cam spun and snarled.

Soren.

"You!" Cam hissed, leaping towards Soren. The man was still wearing his black armor, made from the melted flesh of an Elmia. Cam angrily gripped the sides of the armor and threw Soren to the ground.

Soren grunted as he landed. As he started to pull himself into a sitting position, he said, "What was that for? I saved your life."

Cam stepped over Soren, shoving the man back down.

"Did you know?" he hissed, pointing a reptilian finger in Soren's face. "Did you know what they were doing to the Elmias?"

The shame on Soren's face was all the confirmation that Cam needed.

"Sor? What is he talking about?" Illyria said.

Not taking his eyes away from Soren, Cam said, "Tell her, Soren. Tell her what the Cult is doing to the Elmias. Tell her where you got that armor from."

"Get off of me," Soren snarled. He pushed against Cam, but the larger man didn't budge. A quick look of surprise and intimidation crossed Soren's face. For a moment, he seemed genuinely frightened. Then, he finally relaxed.

"I only recently found out. Most of the Shadows don't know. And when I saw what they were doing, I managed to escape. I only went back because I thought they could help us."

"And you didn't tell anyone? You just left all those Elmias there to die?"

"Like you left Silva?" Soren shouted. "You failed her, Cam!"

Cam flinched, pained at the sound of her name. He rose to his feet, stepping away from Soren, who was still on his back.

"Stop with the fake righteousness, Cam. We both know it's not you. The real you is a scared weakling."

Cam turned away. Now it was his turn to feel ashamed. Illyria looked on, an expression of concern dancing across her eyes.

It had been a long time since Cam had heard Silva's name. The emotions returned to him, threatening to swallow him like a wave. Cam's heart began to race, and his breathing began to rush.

Just like it had happened on that day.

Relax. There are bigger things going on, Luik said in his mind.

Cam flexed his fingers. He breathed deeply a few times before turning back to Soren.

"Why are you here, Soren?"

Soren glared at him.

"Really? You're gonna try to fillet me but won't listen when it's about you?"

"I asked you a question," Cam growled.

Soren paused, a look of conflict crossing his face. For a moment, Cam wondered if the man was about to get up and leave. A second later, his expression softened.

"I came because you need my help." As he spoke, he slowly rose to his feet. "After you escaped, The Sundered God was furious. He's on his way to the Elmia Temple right now."

Cam nodded his head.

"We need to get there before he does."

Soren held out his arms in an exaggerated shrug. "Sure. Any clue how to get there?"

"Veln." He turned towards Illyria. "You said he was fine. Where is he?"

"He...he is going to be fine," Illyria replied, speaking in a slow and hesitant tone, "but...it's actually hard to explain what's happening with him."

"I don't know what you mean. Where is he?"

Illyria shrugged, motioning behind her. "It'll be easier to show you."

Cam stepped over towards where she gestured. He froze in shock. In front of him was a scaletaint, only it wasn't like any scaletaint Cam had ever seen. It was calm, quiet. It almost appeared to be smiling.

"Hello, Cam," it croaked, causing Cam to start. He'd never heard a scaletaint speak before. Its voice was dry and gravelly, like it had gone far too long without water.

"Veln?"

"I Tethered the first thing I could," Veln admitted. "When you used Verdalink to get here, there was a group of scaletaints. One hadn't died just yet."

"How...how are..." Cam struggled to find the words.

"How am I autonomous? How can I control this body?" Veln asked. Cam nodded. "I'm not entirely sure, though I have a theory. This one's soul is so ragged. It has...well, for lack of a better way of wording, it has holes in it. I believe my essence fills in these holes, in some way."

Cam staggered back, his mind spinning.

Luik, did you know this was possible?

No, Luik admitted. *This is uncharted territory.*

"I'm afraid that my torture at the hands of Lucian has left me with a few holes of my own," Veln said. "I no longer have access to my astral abilities, and I can feel my life force leaking away as I speak. I'm afraid that I do not have much more time among the living."

Cam frowned.

"The Scepter of Alderia. The one who tortured you...he wants to find it and use it to destroy the Aurora Shrouds."

Veln nodded. It was strange to see such human behaviors coming from a scaletaint.

"And you need me to guide you to the Elmia Temple, where it resides, yes?"

"Yes. We have to get there before he does."

The scaletaint did not speak. His eyes darted around, as if in deep conflict, and a low hiss escaped his throat.

"You do know where the temple is, right?"

"I do," Veln admitted. "But you should know that sharing the location of the temple with you is no small thing. My brothers and sisters were sworn to protect it and keep its location a secret. Until recently, it was the final astral Nexus Point on the continent."

"Until recently? What happened?" Cam asked. Through their bond, he could sense Luik's sudden jolt of fear and sadness.

"Betrayed," Veln said. "By the Elmia who Tethered with the Sundered God. Lucian's hidden ability...his Complex is inverting physical and astral energies. They drained the temple of its Astral energy in order to create his Astral Edge. It's also how he managed to imprison me and my brethren. Now, we are lost. My brothers and sisters are transformed by these lands, captured by the Shadows or vanished."

"This man, who did all this to you. He's about to do something much worse. If he gets the Scepter of Alderia—"

"Right now, his Complex allows him to damage the Aurora Shrouds," Veln said. "But it's slow work. With the Scepter, he could channel enough power to shatter every Shroud at once...letting the Sundered Lands consume all of Avoni in a single day."

"He's not trying to harm anyone," Soren interjected. "He's convinced that this will free our people from the Sundered Lands."

"He is WRONG," Veln snarled. The intensity of his voice caused them to freeze momentarily.

"Then tell us where the temple is," Cam implored.

Veln nodded.

"Follow me. Fortunately for you, it is not far. Not even a day's journey from here."

Chapter 39

Veln led them up and down twisted rocky paths towards the Elmia Temple. As they walked, the air grew colder, the eerie silence of the Sundered Lands pressing in on them. The path was lined with gnarled trees casting long, distorted shadows in the dim light. Veln moved ahead with quiet determination, his transformed body navigating the treacherous terrain with an unnatural grace.

As they walked, Cam found himself profoundly grateful for Veln's guidance. The pathways were dangerous, and there were many twists and turns that were not evident to the untrained eye. He could have wandered for months without finding the way.

Through their bond, Cam could sense a sort of nervousness in Luik. It struck him as odd.

Why would he be feeling anxious?

Cam didn't have to wonder for long.

Cam, we need to talk, Luik's voice echoed in Cam's mind.

His steps faltered for a moment, surprised at the sudden interjection.

What is it, Luik?

I want to talk about Silva, Luik said. His voice was gentle, but it stunned Cam like an open palm to the face.

What if I don't want to talk about her?

We are linked at the soul, Cam. I know you need this.

Cam shook his head.

I can't. I just...I just can't.

Through their bond, Cam could sense Luik shaking his head. It was subtle, but he was getting better at picking up on finer elements of what the Elmia was doing.

You're worried it will change our relationship. I can assure you that it will not. As the being Tethered to you, I only want to offer my aid. And through decades of working with humans and being able to feel your emotions, I know that what you need is someone to talk to.

Cam sighed. He took a moment to gather his thoughts before responding.

Silva was a Junior Courier, he began, his eyes fixed on the path ahead. *She was training under Soren. The three of us were on a food delivery mission. It was supposed to be a routine run, something we'd done countless times before.*

What happened? Luik prompted gently, his tone filled with genuine concern.

For some reason, Silva's body wasn't handling the Sundered Lands well. Cam's palms became sweaty as the memory surfaced. *It was strange because she had never had problems before. She started showing signs of the transformation much earlier than expected. We knew that we only had a few hours to get her under an Aurora Shroud. That's when scaletaints attacked.*

Cam paused, feeling his cheeks get warm. His breathing began to quicken, his hands clenching and unclenching. *They attacked so suddenly. My horse was killed in the chaos. After we fought them off, I... I couldn't move, Luik. My fear just...it paralyzed me. I couldn't do anything.*

Like what happened to you in the cave earlier?

Yes. Exactly like that.

Cam swallowed hard, the memory of that day washing over him like a tidal wave. *I am ashamed. My...episode delayed us. Not by much, but by enough. By the time we got moving again, it was too late. We couldn't move fast enough, and Silva...she was about to transform. Soren killed her, and she became an Eternal Echo. Forever trapped in the moment of her death.*

Through their bond, Cam could feel Luik's emotions shift.

Cam, I'm so sorry. That's awful.

People tell me not to blame myself, but I haven't found that helpful.

Of course you haven't. It isn't true.

Luik's words brought Cam to an abrupt halt. They were a blade, slicing through him with unsettling precision, though not with the intention to injure. As if wielded by a surgeon, the blade was sharp and exacting, designed to reveal and mend rather than wound.

Yes, there was pain in those words, but there was also a liberation, a freedom born from the act of confronting and owning one's mistake.

Pretending you didn't have a role to play in her death won't help you heal.

So what do I do? Cam thought, his stomach turning inside of him.

Accept what happened. What you're feeling—the guilt and the fear—harness those emotions. Turn them into your weapons.

Cam gritted his teeth.

I don't see how that would make me free of it.

It's not about that, Luik corrected. *It's about allowing the experience to make you better.*

I want to believe that that's possible. I just don't know if it is, admitted Cam. *I'll probably fail at that too.*

You might, Luik conceded. *But you owe it to yourself and Silva to do something. Plus, you're not alone. We are, quite literally, joined at the soul.*

In spite of how he felt, Cam managed a faint smile.

Thank you, Luik. I don't know what I'd do without you.

Your smell would be worse, but your sense of humor would be better. Overall, that might end up being a net positive.

The smile faded, the pain from their discussion settling back in. Still, he appreciated the comment. They continued the journey largely in silence.

After a few hours, Veln spoke.

"We've arrived."

Cam turned his attention to the structure before him. At first, he couldn't see it. All before him were decaying trees and a rocky cliff. Upon closer inspection, though, his jaw dropped.

The Elmia Temple was enormous, yet cunningly hidden. Rising subtly from the desolate terrain, it blended into the cliff face behind it. Pillars supporting its roof looked like trees, and the surrounding rock blended in with the stone of the temple. Despite the temple's enormity, the entrance was a small opening, just large enough for a person to walk through.

Again, Cam found himself grateful for Veln's guidance.

They stepped towards the temple, and something caught Cam's eye. It was as if something in the entrance reflected the waning light. Cam squinted, his hands beginning to ball into tight fists.

Standing in the doorway was a black-armored figure.

The Cult of Sundered Shadows had arrived first.

Cam, you're going to need to run! Luik shouted in Cam's mind, but Cam had already started moving. He sprinted towards the mouth of the temple, preparing to grapple the armored figure standing in the opening.

Hearing his approach, the guard turned, quickly reaching for the broadsword at its back, but paused upon seeing him.

That pause was the only opening that Cam needed.

He slammed into the figure, his ears vaguely registering a curse as they collided with the ground. With a growl, Cam ripped the helmet off the guard and froze.

"Morwenna?" Cam asked, temporarily stunned.

"Cam?"

He stepped off the woman and rose to his feet, extending his normal hand to help her up.

"Are there any others here?" he asked. She glanced behind him and motioned with her head towards his companions who had just joined him.

"I came with my husband. Other than that, the only ones here are you and your companions. Only the Sundered God and Sovereign are allowed to know the location of the temple."

"Lucian's already inside?"

Morwenna nodded.

"We arrived a few minutes ago. I'm supposed to warn him once you arrive. Obviously, I'm not going to do that."

Cam paused. Could he trust this woman?

"She's telling the truth," Soren said. "Even if she wasn't, we don't have the luxury of doubt."

"Then we go now," Cam said decisively. "Veln, lead the way."

Veln stepped past them, and Morwenna jumped. Up until this point, her view of him had been blocked by Soren. As he came into view, Morwenna's hand reached for her sword.

"I know this one," Veln said, his lizard-like head staring daggers at her, tongue extending for a moment. "I begged her for help. She refused."

Morwenna's jaw dropped in shock.

"That...scaletaint can talk?" she stammered, eyes wide.

"It's not a scaletaint. That's Veln, one of the Elmias tortured by Lucian and your Cult," Cam said in a flat tone. Morwenna's face fell.

"I begged him to set you free," she said, her voice a hoarse whisper. "I begged him. But I was his prisoner too."

Veln hissed.

"I didn't see you chained up and being melted alive."

"There were days where your fate would've been my preference."

"Stop," Cam said. "Veln, this isn't helpful. Take us to the Scepter." Veln glared at Morwenna, and then at Cam. For a moment, Cam wondered if Veln was going to abandon them. However, after a few seconds, he said, "Follow me."

As they walked through the abandoned remains of the Elmia Temple, the walls and floor illuminated only by a flickering torch Soren carried, Cam could feel Luik's emotions stirring. On one level, the Elmia was giddy with excitement at the opportunity to visit the ancient temple. On a different level, he was heartbroken at what had become of the place, and beneath that heartbreak was a seed of rage.

You okay? Cam thought to Luik.

This temple was the final astral Nexus Point in existence. The final place where an Elmia could manifest autonomously, without fear of transforming into a Reaper. Gaalron and the Sundered God have condemned my kind to an eternity of Tethering.

I'm sorry, my friend.

Luik didn't respond, and Cam didn't feel it would be helpful to speak more to him. Even without their bond, Cam knew that what the Elmia wanted was the space to grieve alone.

Unfortunately for Luik, that space was still shared with Cam.

They continued down the labyrinthian tunnels. The stone walls were cold. Soon, the path bent downwards at a steep angle, plunging into the ground.

"It's going to get much darker soon," Veln croaked. "Stick close to me."

Illyria stepped over towards Cam. Her face was still covered, but her eyes had a bright spark.

"When you left Kevilton with me, did you have any idea we'd end up walking through an ancient, deserted temple, following the lead of a scaletaint?"

"There are so many things I didn't even know were possible," he replied. She nodded, a look of unspoken understanding in her eyes.

After a few steps, Illyria said, "It's frightening. How little we knew...how little we know about this world."

Cam nodded, his heart beginning to race. He had always known that his world was a harsh one, but there had been a certain simplicity to that harshness. It was like learning to swim in deep water. At first, there is a sense of fear about the unknown depths below. However, when a person learns of the specific dangers lurking under the surface, their anxieties grow dramatically.

Illyria interrupted Cam's introspection.

"It just makes me wonder... Could we be wrong?"

He raised a curious eyebrow.

"Wrong?"

"About the Aurora Shrouds. About...everything. There's so much we don't know. What if Gaalron is right? That destroying the Aurora Shrouds actually ends the Sundered Lands?"

Cam shook his head.

"That doesn't make any sense. The Shrouds have protected us. Why would getting rid of them fix anything?"

She pointed at the tattoo on his arm.

"Aren't you proof that it's possible? An Elmia Tethered you, and you're not transforming. And Luik is surviving too."

"What's your point?"

"That the two of you are living evidence that we might not need the Aurora Shrouds."

He frowned.

"The Tethering process is completely different."

"How? How is it different?"

"Luik and I..." Cam paused for a moment, struggling to come up with an answer. Illyria took advantage of his hesitation and kept speaking.

"Pretend that only parts of you were Tethered to Luik, rather than all of you. What do you think would happen?"

Cam paused for a moment, considering.

Did you hear that, Luik? Any thoughts?

As a scholar, I find the concept intriguing. It is unfortunate that we have no way to test this.

Turning back to Illyria, Cam said, "We're not sure."

She nodded enthusiastically.

"Well, if the human body reacts the same way Avoni does, then you'd have parts of you that are corrupted and other parts of you that are not. What if the Aurora Shrouds are like that? Allowing parts of the land to corrupt, while others remained unchanged."

Cam held up his reptilian arm.

"Illyria, part of me is corrupted."

"No, your arm looked like that before you found Luik. He stopped it from getting worse."

"I don't think my Tethering is enough evidence to say that Gaalron is justified in trying to destroy the Aurora Shrouds."

"No, of course not," she agreed. "But don't you think that it presents an interesting area of study?"

"Sure," Cam said with a shrug. "But I'll leave that to smarter people than me."

"Quiet," Veln hissed in front of them. "Unless you'd like to announce your presence to the Sundered God."

"Is he close?" Morwenna whispered. Veln shrugged. It was an odd gesture to see a scaletaint do.

"Who knows. This place is a maze. Gaalron was never stationed here, so neither of them would know the right way through the temple. However, if surprise is still on our side, I'd prefer we not lose it."

"How much farther do we have to go?" Soren asked, his voice sounding dry. "This place is bigger than I ever imagined." Veln gave him a glare.

"You wear armor made from my melted flesh and have the gall to speak?"

Soren visibly cringed and lowered his eyes.

The group continued on for the next few minutes in silence, continuing to go down further into the depths of the earth. As they walked, the temperature continued to drop. The light from Veln's torch could only extend so far, illuminating very little.

As they walked, Morwenna moved closer to Cam. Illyria inched away, giving them a semblance of privacy.

"It's good to see you again, son."

"I'm...glad you're still doing well," Cam said, unsure what to say back to her.

She glanced at him, her eyes filled with a mix of sadness and pride.

"You've grown strong, Cam. Stronger than I ever imagined."

He shrugged. "I'm not sure I'd say that."

"You may not see it, but I do."

"It's a brutal world that we live in. Any strength I have came from that," he said.

"I suppose so," she replied, her eyes sad. Moments later, she said, "When you find the Sundered God...what are you going to do?"

"Right now, I'm just focused on protecting the Aurora Shrouds. That said, Lucian needs to be brought to justice for what he's done."

"But who would he even answer to? All of his crimes were committed in the Sundered Lands."

Cam gritted his teeth.

"I am Master of the Sundered Lands, and I will execute justice on behalf of the Elmias."

Morwenna's eyes widened.

"You're going to kill him, aren't you?"

"Even if we forget what he did to the Elmias, I have to stop him."

Morwenna nodded, a look of sadness crossing her face.

"Then, as your mother, I must ask you something. When this is all over, will you lead the Shadows?"

Cam was so stunned by the question that he actually stopped walking for a moment.

"Lead you all? You're a cult, following the teachings of a terrible man."

"He is terrible," Morwenna agreed, "but most of us had no idea what he was doing to the Elmias. Those of us who did know might as well have been prisoners."

Cam pointed at Soren.

"He doesn't seem like a prisoner to me."

"Soren is a good man," Morwenna interjected, her tone becoming harsher. "A good man who escaped when he found out. He is one of the lucky ones. Some of us have not been so lucky."

"Well, he sure came crawling back as soon as he could."

"He thought that you were way out of your depth and would need help, and he was right! Ask yourself this: were it not for the actions of Soren, would you have made it this far, or would you have died in the wilderness?"

Cam didn't answer, but his silence was all that Morwenna needed.

"The Shadows will need a leader. Someone who can show us a better path. Someone who can lead us to atone for the wrong that we have done. So, Cam, I ask you again. Will you lead the Shadows when all of this is over? Will you show us a better way?"

Cam huffed.

"Why not ask Soren?"

Morwenna scoffed. "You just claimed the title 'Master of the Sundered Lands.' Soren may be a good man, but he's no leader. Plus, you're Tethered to an Elmia.'"

It was a strange request, yet for some reason, he felt an inexplicable urge to say yes. He knew he should decline, as his life as a Vanguard Courier would be waiting for him once all this was over. However, something deep within him urged him to agree. It was a strange battle of wills inside of him.

He found himself unable to give a firm answer.

"Maybe. I'll think about it," he said, and Morwenna smiled.

"Please do. Until then, I want to give you something, my son." Reaching down to her hip, she grabbed the sheath of a sword. She undid the buckle and handed the sword to him. "This is a commander's sword," she explained. "Crafted for the leaders of our people. I will offer it to you now."

"Thank you. I don't really use swords, though. Most Couriers prefer daggers." This made Morwenna laugh, earning her a glare from Veln.

"Really? Daggers? Cam, look at you. You're built like a mountain. What you really need is an ax or a hammer."

Cam shook his head. "Swords...I don't know. It just seems more like something a soldier would use."

"Soldiers, yes. Or a leader," she said, once again offering the sword.

Cam took it from Morwenna, feeling its weight and balance in his hand. It was an impressive weapon, clearly crafted with care and precision. The hilt was wrapped in dark leather, providing a firm and comfortable grip. Intricate patterns were etched into the metal of the guard.

"Thank you," he said, strapping the sword to his back.

Her response was interrupted by Veln.

"We've reached The Chamber."

The tunnel opened into a vast room bathed in a soft blue light. Enormous stone pillars reached upward, supporting an intricately adorned roof. The air around them was cold.

In the center of the room was an elevated platform bearing a stone table.

Luik, what do you think this room was used for? Cam thought.

I do not know, Luik admitted. *This temple was shrouded in secrecy. Even I, an Elmia serving the king, was forbidden to know what happened in this place.*

They all entered the room, and Cam stepped over to investigate the stone table. Atop the table, bathed in the muted light filtering through the colossal stone pillars, rested two short chains with manacles at their ends.

The group stood for a moment, staring at the table in silence.

"Well that's horrifying," Illyria said, causing Cam and Morwenna to jump slightly. She offered an apologetic smile for startling them. "Sorry. I just hate to imagine what might have happened here."

"Let's keep moving," Morwenna said. "We still haven't seen any sign of the Sundered God or the Scepter."

"Are there other artifacts here?" Illyria asked, her tone curious. "Is this temple a treasure trove for the Elmias?" Both women looked to Cam for an answer.

This temple likely holds many artifacts, Luik suggested.

Cam began repeating the words to them, exactly as Luik had said. However, in the middle of his sentence, a new voice interrupted him.

"It appears I've been betrayed by my own wife."

The Sundered God stepped out from behind a stone pillar, his black armor glistening in the soft blue light. He pointed his Astral Edge at them.

"And Captain Soren as well."

"I said I wouldn't let you hurt anyone else," Cam growled. "It's time for you to pay for your atrocities." Reaching to his back, he pulled out his sword.

"My atrocities? Tell me, young Courier, which atrocity of mine is greater: teaching people to survive in the Sundered Lands, or destroying the Sundered Lands entirely, giving our people their nation back?"

Morwenna stepped forward.

"Anointed One, this isn't the way."

Before Lucian could reply, a new voice sounded above them.

"A feast of souls!"

They all looked up in unison.

Above, in the shadowy expanse, something emerged, slowly descending one of the massive stone pillars with an unsettling grace. It moved like a nightmarish spider, its gooey red-and-black skin pulsing like a grotesque heartbeat.

The Reaper, larger than the one Cam had fought, unfolded itself like a malevolent spawn of Hell.

"A feast!" it screeched again, racing down the pillar towards them.

Chapter 40

For just a moment, terror possessed Cam, as he remembered the pain he endured after his last encounter with a Reaper. In his mind, he could feel its fingers squeezing him and cutting him, leaving him to die alone in the Sundered Lands.

Oh no. It's happening again. I'm freezing.

Remember what I told you. Harness your fear. Turn it into a weapon.

Right.

Know you will fail. Act anyway.

Cam had just enough time to take a deep breath. In his peripheral vision, he could see the terrified expressions of his companions.

It ignited a fire inside of him.

He roared, stepping between them and the Reaper.

As the Reaper came closer, Cam appeared to freeze, as if gripped by fear. Then his expression transformed.

Determined was the wrong word to describe the shift in countenance. His expression changed to one of confident rage.

It was almost terrifying.

Illyria reached to her side, pulling out The Tool. She pulled off her gloves, smiling as the weapon shifted into the familiar shape of a sword. She wasn't sure of the best way to help. She was, after all, a healer and decidedly not a warrior.

"Quickly," Veln hissed, his serpentine tongue sticking out in the air. "To the Scepter."

She nodded, turning to follow Veln. A sudden crack followed as Lucian, with a flick of his wrist, turned his sword into a whip. It cracked as it snapped across the chamber, wrapping around Veln's scaletaint body. With a yank, the blade bit into him. He let out a weak cry before collapsing to the ground, blood pooling beneath him.

As much as she wanted to help him, Illyria knew he was past hope and would die in a few moments.

Get to the Scepter.

She ran in the direction that Veln had been heading, sparing a glance in Cam's direction. A glance that turned into an awe-stricken stare.

He was incredible.

Cam moved like a shadow, fluid and elusive, every motion calculated to perfection. As the Reaper lunged at him, Cam's body twisted and flowed, evading the attacks with supernatural grace. He ducked under one swipe, rolled away from another, and leapt over a third, his movements a blur of speed and agility. His eyes bounced between the Reaper and Lucian, every muscle in his body coiled like a spring, ready to explode into action.

Ever since she'd met him, Illyria knew something was different about Cam. Unlike other Vanguard Couriers, whose bodies bore the marks and scars of countless battles, Cam's skin remained mostly unscathed. This suggested two possibilities: either he possessed an uncanny ability to evade conflict, or he was exceptionally skilled at ending fights quickly.

Facing off against a Reaper and Lucian, it was evident to Illyria that it was the latter.

This was a man who had trained for years to be a Vanguard Ranger.

As Cam rolled to the side, Lucian tried to run his sword through him. Cam batted the blade to the side and came up with his own ferocious strike. In a fluid step, he unleashed a barrage of powerful swings that leveraged his sheer strength and size. Each blow, a blend of rage and control, landed with the force of a sledgehammer, driving Lucian back step by step.

Lucian appeared startled by the onslaught, uncertainty crossing his face. He reached up a hand, freezing Cam's blade in the air. Without hesitation, Cam threw a heavy punch that knocked Lucian to the floor, freeing his blade, which he then swung at the Reaper where it bit into its leg.

Soren grabbed Illyria by the hand, snapping her out of her trance.

"Scepter!" he shouted.

She nodded, rushing ahead with him.

It was a strange mirror of the last time Cam encountered a Reaper.

She could only hope that this would end differently.

Stepping forward, she raced towards the far end of the room. There, she saw a stone door. She tugged on the handle, but the door wouldn't budge.

"Help me, Soren."

Soren grabbed the handle, and together they pulled. Groaning with effort, the two managed to open the door just a crack.

Peeking through, Illyria saw a golden scepter.

She'd found it.

Aurora's Name, she had finally found it.

Cam stood amidst the chaos, heart pounding, every sense heightened and afraid.

And he allowed that fear to focus him, turning him into a weapon.

The Reaper's monstrous form loomed, claws slicing through the air. Cam moved on instinct, slipping past a swipe and rolling clear, never letting the beast corner him.

Lucian's laughter echoed from somewhere in the shadows. His Astral Edge morphed into a whip, lashing toward Cam with a crack that split the air. Cam leapt aside, only for the Reaper to lunge from behind, forcing him to dive again. A flicker of movement, and Lucian was suddenly there, driving him to the ground, his fingers losing grip on his sword.

Cam scrambled for the weapon, but Lucian reappeared and ripped it from his hands. Their eyes locked for a heartbeat before Lucian smirked and surged forward with both blades.

Cam's gaze locked on the sword. If Luik could Time Shift it, even for a heartbeat, he might gain the upper hand. Luik must have sensed the thought, because the blade froze mid-swing—then, just as quickly, the Shift transferred to Lucian's Astral Edge. The sudden change broke his momentum, and Lucian stumbled, both swords clattering to the floor.

We're getting better at this, Luik cheered.

In one motion, Cam dove forward, picking up his sword.

For a brief moment, all three combatants paused, their breaths heavy in the stifling air. Cam's eyes darted between the Reaper and Lucian, assessing their next moves. In the distance, he was faintly aware of Morwenna hiding behind one of the room's many pillars.

Cam took a deep breath, allowing himself to feel his fear.

Allowing himself to harness it.

Excellent, Luik commended.

Lucian stabbed forward, blade flashing. Cam jumped back with a growl. He was about to swing when he saw the Reaper turn toward Illyria and Soren. They were struggling with a door, backs to the monster, unaware of the danger closing in.

There would be no warning.

Reaching inside himself, he willed the creature to stop. To relent. To relax.

And miraculously, the creature did just that. It hesitated, as if having second thoughts.

What in Aurora's Name?

Cam barely had enough time to leap out of the way of Lucian's whip-sword. He'd extended the blade to an enormous length, trying to use distance to his advantage. As he ducked to the side, Cam's concentration broke, and the Reaper let out a joyous scream, charging at Illyria and Soren.

Luik!

The Elmia accessed Verdalink, using Illyria's own sword as an anchor.

The world spun around him in a dizzying kaleidoscope of colors and shapes. He leapt from the Astral Edge, swinging his sword as he did so. The blade bit deeply into the Reaper's already injured leg. It let out a scream, falling to the ground.

Cam turned towards Illyria, whose cloak was stained with the Reaper's blood.

"You okay?" he asked, breathing heavily.

"That's going to scare me every time," Illyria replied.

"Get to the Scepter. I'll keep them occupied."

"I'm trying, but—"

A sudden shout cut off her response.

"Cam!"

The Reaper had found Morwenna. The woman stood before it, holding her broadsword in both hands. It leapt forward, biting into her shoulder. She screamed as it landed on top of her.

"Morwenna!" Cam yelled desperately, rushing to reach her. Luik Time Shifted him, causing him to move with supernatural speed. He sped over towards the creature, the world moving in a blur as he did so. With a cry, he slammed his sword into the side of the beast, followed by his shoulder.

The Reaper was flung backwards off Morwenna. It rolled a few times before leaping to its feet. It hissed at Cam, then charged at him with the same unnatural speed that Cam himself had just demonstrated. Of course, to Cam's eyes, it was now moving at a normal pace.

Stop Time Shifting me, Cam thought.

What? I don't under—

Cam felt Luik's emotions shift when he realized what Cam was thinking.

As the monster ran towards him, Luik stopped the power, instead Shifting the broadsword still stuck in the Reaper's chest. Since the Reaper was using Time Shift on itself, it was no longer able to block the attack, and the sword froze in time. The Reaper howled as the sword ripped free of its back, covered in gore.

Grabbing the sword, Cam turned to face the Reaper. It was growling, a gaping hole in its chest.

What does it take to kill one of these things? Cam thought in desperation.

The Reaper screeched at him before charging.

And Cam charged back, ducking under a swipe from Lucian.

Just before they reached each other, Luik used Shadowmeld to hide on the floor. The shadows were plentiful, and there were many places to hide.

The Reaper soared through the empty air where Cam had been mere moments before. Just as the creature passed him, Cam leapt back out of the shadows, slashing again at the creature's leg. He managed to slice the back of its leg, leaving a deep gash.

In a heartbeat, the Reaper launched itself airborne with an eerie agility, its monstrous form ascending the towering pillars like a spider. As it scaled the stone heights, it vanished into the shadows above.

Cam glanced around, but didn't have enough time to look. With the Reaper out of the way, Lucian had reengaged, leaping towards Cam with a startling ferocity.

Before he could reach his opponent, pain flared in Cam's shoulder as the Reaper reappeared, its long, dagger-like teeth sinking into him. It lifted him off the ground, shaking him violently before dropping him onto the ground.

Grunting in pain, he grabbed the Reaper's injured leg. Summoning every ounce of strength he had, he twisted and pulled.

There was a quick ripping and popping sound before the leg tore free. The Reaper flopped to the ground, but quickly raised itself, using its arms and remaining leg as a tripod. Even losing one of its limbs barely slowed the monster down, as it moved with an unnatural grace, skittering across the floor.

Again, he reached inside himself, willing the monster to stop.

And just like before, it did just that. It turned towards Cam, its expression almost serene.

With a primal scream, Cam swung his sword, a swing enhanced by the power of his Time Shift.

He cut the Reaper cleanly in half. Flopping to the ground in a revolting manner, it opened its mouth in a silent cry. It twitched violently a few times before lying still.

All stood still for a moment, stunned, the only sound echoing in the chamber being Cam's heavy breathing. All eyes were locked on the Reaper, its black-and-red blood pooling beneath it.

Then, heads turned to Cam, expressions of awe on their faces.

Cam stood tall, the Reaper's twisted body sprawled at his feet. He planted one boot firmly on the creature's chest, his tattered cloak billowing slightly behind him like the wings of a dark angel. Cam locked eyes with Lucian, unintimidated and spirit unwavering. Gripping with his reptilian hand, he held his sword up in defiance and challenge.

An expression of doubt crossed Lucian's face. He glanced back towards the tunnel, as if considering running away. Then, he shook his head, as if the motion would dispel any uncertainties he had. Chuckling, he charged at Cam.

Now that his attention was not divided between the Reaper and Cam, Lucian showed the true power of a Tethered warrior. He moved with inhuman speed, ducking, dodging, and slashing faster than Cam could process.

Each strike drove Cam further back, his defenses crumbling under the relentless assault. Lucian's mastery of Shadowmeld was terrifyingly brilliant. He would vanish in front of Cam's desperate attacks, only to reemerge seconds later from a different spot, launching another barrage.

To an onlooker, it appeared as though a wraith were attacking Cam. Lucian's figure flickered in and out of existence, evading Cam's strikes and countering with lethal precision. Cam's breath came in ragged gasps, his arms heavy with exhaustion. He struggled to predict where Lucian would materialize next, his mind racing to keep up with the impossibly fast onslaught.

It wasn't long before Cam was knocked to his back. Lucian wasted no time in cracking his whip-sword, wrapping it around Cam's ankle. The blade cut through the leather boot into his flesh, and Cam let out a cry of pain.

Lucian's smile widened as he gradually pulled Cam towards him, the sword biting into the limb. Every inch of resistance only fueled Lucian's amusement, evident in the cruel glint of his eyes.

"You should have listened to me, boy. You're far out of your depth."

Cam's hand brushed a loose stone. He wrapped his fingers around it and hurled it towards Lucian, who easily ducked out of the way.

Lucian, obviously reveling in the moment, pulled the whip-sword back, readying for a final, fatal strike.

The strike never came. Just as he prepared to bring his blade down on Cam, a broadsword exploded through his chest. He gasped, his stunned eyes looking down at the blade. Morwenna appeared from behind him.

"You won't separate me from my son again," she hissed.

Lucian coughed blood and slumped to the floor. Morwenna sank to her knees, tears streaming from her eyes, her chest heaving.

"It's over," she whispered.

Cam gingerly reached down and touched his ankle. It burned, but the wound was not deep. He would be able to recover quickly.

He glanced over at Morwenna, still crying beside the body of the man who had been her second husband.

"You gonna be okay?" he asked.

She gave an embarrassed nod, wiping her eyes as she did so.

The Scepter, Luik reminded him.

Cam turned and froze.

Illyria stood at the front of the room, holding a massive golden scepter. It was as long as a man was tall, coming to a sharp, hooked point at the end. Her other hand gripped her Astral Edge.

He squinted at her. She had a strange expression on her face.

"Give me the Scepter," Cam said, his voice calm, yet commanding.

She silently shook her head.

Cam cocked his head.

That is the Scepter of Alderia, right? he silently asked Luik.

Yes. That's it.

What in Aurora's Name was going on?

"Illyria, let's go. We can fix the Aurora Shrouds now."

She shook her head again.

"Cam, no. I mean, maybe later. But we have to study this. Test this. See if we can bring about the end of the Sundered Lands."

"We can talk about that later. Let's repair the Shrouds first," he said.

Her expression darkened as she edged away from them, towards the tunnel that led out of the temple.

"I'm sorry. I have to do this."

"What are you talking about?" Cam said, throwing up his arms in frustration.

"We have to destroy the Aurora Shrouds to see if it gets rid of the Sundered Lands," she said. She'd banished all signs of playfulness in her tone. Instead, she simply sounded calm and confident.

No.

From the room behind her, Soren dove for the Scepter. She hadn't seen him coming, evidenced by the shocked expression on her face when he wrapped his fingers around the handle and tried to pry it away from her. A second later, his body stiffened, and he stepped back, Illyria's Astral Edge in his gut.

"No!" she said, pulling the sword back. "No, I didn't mean to. It... I didn't mean to." Soren slumped to the ground, a bloody hand covering the wound in his abdomen.

The blade, having sensed her desire to protect the Scepter, had elongated, running itself through Soren and possibly delivering a fatal wound.

Illyria stepped over his body, placing a hand on his chest. As she did so, she instinctively pulled back the long sleeves of her shirt.

Only then did Cam see it.

A tattoo of an Aetherfern plant, starting at her fingertips and snaking up her arm.

His eyes widened in surprise.

"The voice you said you heard...that was never from the sword, was it?" he asked, his voice almost a whisper. She glanced his way and gave a weak nod.

Cam glanced at her Astral Edge, now lying on the ground beside her.

"An Elmia Tethered itself to that sword, and then it Tethered you."

She ignored him, instead examining Soren's sound.

"I'm so sorry, Sor," she said. "I'm doing what I can. But there's only so much healing I have in a day."

Cam's mind raced as the puzzle pieces clicked into place. Illyria's hidden ability—her Complex—was healing.

He glanced over at the body of Lucian, and new questions formed in Cam's mind.

How had that man known how to find the temple and navigate it so quickly? Gaalron supposedly didn't know its location or layout.

It only made sense if he had somehow Tethered an Elmia stationed at the temple.

He was never the one Tethered to Gaalron... He wasn't sure if it was Luik or himself who thought the words.

He turned his eyes back towards Illyria.

"The Elmia you're Tethered to... It's Gaalron, isn't it?" Cam said flatly.

She met his eyes. Moments went by where neither of them moved. Neither dared to breathe. In that moment, all Cam could do was stare into her eyes and hope he was wrong.

And then she nodded.

Without a second thought, Cam charged for the Scepter.

"No!" she cried, leaping to her feet and pointing the Scepter at him. Pain stopped him in his tracks and he collapsed to the ground. It felt as if his own soul were ripping in half. Then, with a sudden snapping feeling, the pain ended and a strange ball of light streaked towards the Scepter.

Luik, what was that? Cam thought.

No response came. Shocked, Cam realized he could no longer feel Luik's emotions and thoughts. Even in his confusion, he understood what had just happened.

Somehow, the Scepter had broken their Tethering.

His body, no longer protected by Luik, then reacted to the air of the Sundered Lands, a violent coughing fit seizing him. The fit was especially painful, and he found himself gagging, collapsing to the ground.

"I'm sorry," Illyria said. "Truly, I am. But I can't have this disrupted. We only have one chance."

And with that, she raised the Scepter into the air. It gave off a bright flash of light, illuminating the ancient stone walls of the temple. Cam's heart pounded as he watched, dread creeping into his veins.

The Scepter of Alderia, a symbol of hope and restoration, was now being wielded to a different end. Illyria's intentions became painfully clear. She was using the Scepter to destroy the Aurora Shrouds, the very barriers that protected the last bastions of humanity from the Sundered Lands.

"I'll see you on the other side," she said. "There's not much I could do for Soren. Please, help him."

And with that, the Tethered pair accessed Verdalink, disappearing before Cam's eyes, and taking the hopes of all Avoni with them.

Chapter 41

Chek led the four members of the Cult of Sundered Shadows away from Perth, her crutch tapping rhythmically on the uneven ground. Twilight enveloped her surroundings in shadows, casting long, ominous silhouettes across their path. The four cult members followed her, their heavy footsteps and wary glances creating an air of tension.

Her leg ached with every step, but she used that pain to her advantage. She kept her pace deliberately slow, using the limp as an excuse to buy Felix more time. Every few minutes, she'd purposely trip. Each time, she'd give a groan before standing back up and dusting herself off.

The snail's pace was clearly agitating the people following her.

"Where exactly did you say you found this Elmia?" the leader of the group asked, his tone edged with impatience.

Chek turned her head slightly, offering him a strained smile.

"It's not far now. I've been taking it slow because of my leg."

The leader's eyes narrowed, but he didn't press further. Instead, he motioned for the group to keep moving, his gaze flicking to Chek with a mix of curiosity and irritation.

She gave an innocent shrug, wincing as she adjusted her weight.

"Also, I never said I found the Elmia. I just might have seen something."

The leader's eyes remained fixed on her, though he said nothing. He seemed to be weighing her words carefully, as if trying to discern any deception. The rest of the cult members kept their focus on the surroundings, their senses heightened for any sign of the Elmia.

She knew that she only had one shot at this. Once they realized what she was doing, there would be no fooling them again.

Assuming they even let her live.

Please, Felix. Don't screw this up.

Felix was annoyed that Chek had discovered his cooking hobby, but it shouldn't have surprised him. She was quite perceptive, and they were, after all, twins.

Although cooking was his excuse to go back into the inn, Felix had no plans of making any meals.

The inn's kitchen had a door that led into a back alley in Perth. Felix navigated through the quiet, darkened streets with a mix of urgency and focus. His mind buzzed with the pressing need to find Vaelin's secret spot. Though he had never visited, he was fairly certain he knew where it was.

He walked down the narrow alley between the two buildings, gently letting his fingers glide along the rough stone of the walls. After taking a few steps, he began to see the subtle clues, like an old, disused well partially covered by overgrown vines and a series of carefully concealed traps meant to deter intruders. Felix approached the spot with a practiced ease, his movements precise and deliberate, as he carefully lifted the camouflaged cover.

The space beneath was a tight fit. As he descended into the darkness, he relied on the faint light filtering through the cracks above to guide him. The subterranean chamber was cool and damp, filled with the musty smell of old earth.

A sudden, familiar hiss sounded to his left, causing Felix to roll his eyes.

"Don't think I don't know about your hiding spot. I figured it out really quickly," Felix said. A man emerged from the corner, his face suspicious.

Vaelin.

He was filthy, his dark hair matted and clothing torn. He pointed at himself with a long, crooked finger.

"Safe?"

Felix shook his head.

"No, you're not." Vaelin's face was alarmed, and he made a motion as if to run away. Felix threw up his arms. "I mean, you're safe right now. But you're not safe here. The Cult of Sundered Shadows is here, and they're looking for you."

Vaelin nodded, pointing to the Aetherfern tattoo on his arm.

"She says to be afraid."

"Then, I'd believe her. We need to find a better spot for you. You're going to have to go into the Sundered Lands."

Vaelin gave a slow nod. His expression was sad.

"Is goodbye," he whispered, moving to step past Felix.

"Wait!" Felix said, grabbing Vaelin by the arm. "The Elmia you're Tethered to... Uriel, right? She had something she wanted to say to me. Something about a grove. What is it?"

"No," Vaelin said, his tone almost sad. "Can't say. Too many words."

"Please." Felix reached into his bag. He pulled out a muffin, handing it to Vaelin. The man, clearly hungry, ate it quickly. As he wiped the crumbs from his beard, Felix said, "I can't pretend to know what it's like to walk in your shoes, but I can imagine it's been a tough road." His words made Vaelin pause, his curiosity piqued. Felix pressed on, his tone growing more earnest.

"People treat me differently too. Sometimes, I'm too much for them—too exuberant, too intense. Other times, I'm too quiet, too withdrawn. It's like I never quite fit. So I get it. I get why being alone feels safer." Felix glanced around the small chamber, sensing the solitude that had become Vaelin's refuge. "I see why you like it down here."

Vaelin huffed, shrugging his shoulders, then pointed to Felix's bag.

"More?"

Felix nodded, pulling out another muffin and handing it to him.

"Vaelin, right now, we're counting on you. The Elmia you're Tethered to knows something, and for some reason, it wants to tell me what it knows. I know it's hard, but we need your help. This is our only shot." He looked pleadingly into Vaelin's eyes. "Please. Can you try? Then, we'll do what we can to get you out of here."

Vaelin looked taken aback. His crazed eyes appeared almost calm as he considered Felix's plea. Then, he shook his head.

"Can't. Too many words."

Felix's face fell, defeated.

"Please, Vaelin. I need—"

Vaelin held up a hand, stopping Felix. He shook his head again and said, "Better idea."

Reaching out, he grabbed Felix's wrist. A strange energy appeared to come buzzing out from his arm into Felix. It wasn't painful, but Felix's instinct was to jerk back. He tried, but Vaelin's grip was too tight.

He was about to shout for Vaelin to stop when he saw his arm.

The Aetherfern tattoo had moved from Vaelin's arm to his.

"Did...did you...?" Felix stammered.

Hello, Felix, a feminine voice said in his mind. *I need your help.*

Chapter 42

The fear hit Cam like a wave. This time, it didn't threaten to drown him; it simply swallowed him up whole.

He willed himself to move forward, but his feet betrayed him, breaking into a sprint. When he tried to stop, his legs gave out, sending him sprawling to the ground. Dizzy and disoriented, he rubbed his brow as the world spun around him.

Another violent coughing fit seized him. It reminded him of the first time he'd ever ventured into the Sundered Lands. The hacking, the gagging. The struggle to breathe.

Breathe.

He couldn't breathe.

In between coughs, he was gasping for air, but he didn't feel like the air was doing anything. He felt himself getting dizzy.

I'm going to die out here, he thought to himself.

Himself. Just himself.

He was reminded that Luik was no longer with him.

Falling to his knees, he placed a hand over his heart, desperately trying to slow his breathing.

Morwenna was at his side seconds later.

"What happened? Did she do something to you?" she asked, crouching next to him and cupping his face in her hands.

He couldn't speak, so he nodded and held up his left arm. The tattoo of the Aetherfern was gone.

Morwenna frowned, her face worried.

"Lucian once told me the Scepter was capable of inverting astral and physical energies. She must have somehow cut your Tethering."

Cam gritted his teeth. The coughing fit was finally beginning to subside, but each breath still came in ragged gasps. The weight of his failure settled heavily on his chest, cutting deep like a knife between the ribs, leaving him hollow and aching.

Know that you will fail. Act anyway, Luik's voice echoed in Cam's mind. Cam knew that the Elmia was not directly speaking to him, but the words still stirred something in him.

Accept what happened. What you're feeling—the guilt and the fear—harness those emotions. Turn them into your weapons.

Cam closed his eyes, letting the memories wash over him, the faces of those he'd lost, the cries of those he couldn't save. Each one was a dagger to his heart, sharp and unforgiving.

But instead of recoiling from the pain, he leaned into it, feeling the emotions pulse through him. The guilt was there, gnawing at him like a relentless beast. The fear, too, a cold shiver running down his spine. Beneath it all, something else stirred.

Resolve.

Legs trembling, Cam rose to his feet.

Breathe. Just breathe. Cam recalled Luik's instructions when his panic had overtaken him. He did his best to follow them now, taking a deep breath in, holding it, and then slowly letting it out.

It worked. The tightness in his chest began to loosen, and he found himself breathing more regularly again.

"We have to help Soren," Cam croaked, his voice hoarse from coughing. He stepped forward towards the man, who was still lying slumped at the front of the chamber.

He didn't appear to be in great shape. The man's chest rose and fell weakly, his eyes staring off into the distance. Whatever healing Illyria had offered him had been minimal.

She must have a very limited supply of astral healing and used up most of it on me, he thought, sinking down next to Soren. The Courier frowned when he saw him.

"I don't think this looks good for me," Soren whispered. He coughed up some blood.

"You're going to be fine," Cam said, not believing his own words. "We just need to bandage you up and get you back to Perth."

Soren gave a weak shake of his head.

"A dead man knows when he's dead. Don't spend any energy on me."

Cam ignored him, reaching into his pouch and pulling out a bandage. Soren grabbed his hand.

"I'm too far gone. She got me good." Then, looking down at Cam's arm, he added, "Looks like she got you good too."

"I guess that makes us both fools."

Soren gave a weak nod.

"Cam, did she ever tell you about our conversation in Rath?"

Cam shook his head, so Soren continued.

"I told her I was considering leaving the Couriers and asked her what she'd think of me moving to Kevilton."

"Kevilton?"

"Yeah. To be...closer to her. I thought there was something between us." He made a grunt that might have been an attempt at a laugh. "In hindsight, it's obvious she just wanted a Courier to help her through the Sundered Lands."

"Me too. I had no idea she was Tethered," Cam said.

"Once I found out about you and Luik, I started to get suspicious that something was going on. She just seemed to be handling the Sundered Lands so well."

"Well, I had no idea. I feel like such a fool."

"Either a fool or someone who has never felt betrayal before," Soren said, a little too directly. Cam paused for a moment. There was a rawness in his tone, something deeper that Cam recognized instantly.

Instead of pushing it away, Cam leaned into it.

"I'm so sorry about Silva," he whispered, her name catching in his throat. He'd never said those words out loud, and even mentioning her name stirred up all of his old emotions. "I...that was my fault."

"Your fault?"

Cam nodded.

"Yeah. I froze. We never got to the Aurora Shroud in time." He hung his head, pointing at his chest with this reptilian hand. "My fault. And seeing you here...I've failed all over again."

Soren's eyes softened, a rare flicker of empathy crossing his usually serious face. He tightened his grip on Cam's hand.

"Silva... She knew the risks. So did I. The Sundered Lands have claimed more lives than we can count, and we've all lost people we care about. It's broken all of us in different ways."

"I think it broke me a long time before I became a Courier," Cam admitted.

"It broke us all," he repeated, his voice getting weaker. "You never understood that. But...being broken doesn't mean you're purposeless. The trick is to find the strength to keep going, even after you're broken. I just wish you could have found that strength before it came to this...before it all ended."

Cam swallowed hard, his breath beginning to quicken again.

Know you will fail. Act anyway.

"It's not over. There's still a Vanguard Courier who can stop this," Cam said.

Soren's eyes flickered with the faintest hint of a smile, one that didn't reach his lips but was there in the depth of his gaze.

"You...always were stubborn," he whispered, the effort of speaking taking more out of him than before.

"No. I've always been afraid," Cam replied.

"And you're not now?"

"I'm terrified. But that's exactly why Gaalron should be worried."

"Why's that?"

"Because my fear isn't a weakness," Cam said, a determined fire coming into his eyes. "It's my greatest weapon."

Soren nodded.

"Then...don't waste it. Get...get back out there."

The weight of those words settled in Cam's heart as he watched Soren's eyes close. A part of his brain screamed at him to leave and find Illyria, but he refused to let Soren die alone. He waited patiently, watching the rise and fall of the man's chest slowly fade, his body succumbing to his wounds.

After a few minutes, Soren's body began to glow as he became an Eternal Echo, forever trapped in that moment.

"I'll end this, brother," Cam whispered. "Don't worry. I'll end this. And then you can rest."

He then stood and turned and began walking towards the tunnel they'd used to find the chamber. Morwenna stood to the side, giving him a curious expression.

"What are you planning?" she asked.

Reaching down, Cam picked up his sword, its weight feeling like an extension of his own will. His tattered cloak billowed softly behind him, a banner of defiance and rage.

He stepped forward, feeling more like a force of nature than a man. For most, the Sundered Lands was a landscape of ruin and despair, but in Cam's mind, it was his domain.

In a powerful voice of retribution, he declared, "I am still Master of the Sundered Lands. Gaalron and Illyria need reminding of that."

Chapter 43

The heavy stone doors of the Elmia Temple groaned as they swung open, revealing the desolate landscape beyond. Cam led the way, his eyes narrowing as he took in the sight.

The sky above was an ominous shade of red, streaked with black misty clouds that rolled across the heavens like a gathering storm. Flashes of lightning crackled within them, illuminating the wasteland below in harsh, jagged bursts of light. The air was thick with the scent of ash and decay, the ground trembling slightly beneath their feet.

He'd spent many days in the Sundered Lands, but something felt different this time. In his bones, he knew the truth.

"She did it," he said, his voice hoarse. "She destroyed the Aurora Shrouds. The Sundered Lands are spreading."

Morwenna coughed as she stepped up beside him, scales rapidly appearing on her face and hands. The corruption appeared to be working much faster than normal, and the woman who had spent years in the Sundered Lands was seeing it catch up to her.

"Where...do you think...she went?" Morwenna said, stumbling as she followed Cam. Her voice was weak and guttural.

"Not far. There aren't many objects she could have used as an anchor." He turned his head, surveying the world around him. "It's a wasteland out here."

Suddenly, Morwenna fell to the ground, clutching her chest as a sharp gasp escaped her lips. Cam whirled around, his heart leaping into his throat as he saw her body convulsing.

"Morwenna!" he shouted, rushing to her side.

But as he reached out to help her, he recoiled in shock. Her skin was shifting, scales rippling across her arms and legs, her eyes glowing with an eerie, reptilian light. The transformation was quick and brutal. Morwenna's human form dissolved as the curse of the Sundered Lands took hold.

"No...not you too," Cam whispered.

Morwenna looked up at him, her expression filled with pain and fear as her body twisted and contorted, her form becoming that of a scaletaint.

"Fight it, Morwenna," Cam urged, his voice desperate.

For a moment, her glowing eyes met his, and he could see the struggle within her, the battle between the woman she was and the monster she was becoming.

Then, she shook her head.

"No." Moving quickly, her face still twisted in pain, she reached back and began undoing her protective armor. "Thank you...for...this time," she said through gritted teeth. Her back contorted, and she convulsed. Her fingers elongated into claws, her mouth into a reptilian snout.

A guttural growl escaped Morwenna as the last vestiges of her humanity were swallowed by the curse. She slumped forward, panting, her breath ragged and uneven. Then, her head snapped up, snarling as she saw Cam.

Cam moved quickly, driving his sword through the scaletaint that had once been his mother. He forced himself to look away, focused on the task at hand. Illyria was out there, somewhere, and she held the key to stopping this nightmare.

Stepping away, he began searching for her. Fortunately, he didn't have to look long before he spotted her distant figure. Even from this distance, he could see the Scepter of Alderia clutched in her hand.

As he drew closer, he could see Illyria more clearly. She stood frozen, staring at the Scepter, her face twisted in shock and grief.

"No..." she murmured, more to herself than to Cam. Her voice was low, almost lost in the wind. "This wasn't supposed to happen. I..."

Hearing Cam's approach, she turned to look at him. He could see the fear and desperation etched into her features, but her reaction was muted, almost numb.

"I thought I could fix it," she said, her voice barely a whisper.

Cam's expression hardened.

"You lied to me, Illyria. You've been hiding the truth all along. And now look where it's led us." He swept his arms around him. "Forget the Sundered Lands. You've turned Avoni into a Sundered Nation."

Illyria's shoulders slumped, and she seemed to crumble under the weight of her guilt.

"I didn't know it would come to this," she said, her voice tinged with despair. After speaking, she was seized by a violent coughing fit.

"The air you brought to everyone bothering you? Or are you faking that too?" Cam bit out. Illyria shook her head.

"Gaalron left. It's...it's just me now," she said, pulling back the sleeve of her shirt, revealing her bare arm devoid of any tattoo. "He said he'd rather die out here than spend the rest of his life Tethered."

Cam shook his head in disdain.

"Illyria, what were you thinking? Why did you listen to him?"

Her eyes stared blankly at the horizon. When she spoke, her voice seemed hollow.

"When I found him, he told me that the Shrouds were going to start failing. I didn't believe him. Actually, I thought I was going crazy. But it wasn't long before everything he predicted started coming true." She gave a deep sigh, tilting her head up to stare at the red sky overhead. "There's a part of me that still thinks he may be right. That in a few minutes, the air will stop hurting and the sky will turn blue again. And then I go home." The last words were choked out.

In spite of himself, Cam felt a sudden pang of empathy. Taking a deep sigh, he sat down next to her. For a few minutes, neither one of them spoke. Instead, they stared out at the world of death and decay around them.

In the silence, Cam turned his gaze toward Illyria, locking eyes with her. For a moment, the world around them seemed to fall away as Cam saw something that struck him to his core: the same fear that gnawed at his soul, the same self-loathing that had shadowed his every step. It was as if he were looking into a mirror, seeing his own struggles reflected back at him in her haunted gaze.

He wanted to hold on to anger, but upon seeing a reflection of his own pain in her face, all he could feel was pity.

"All of this might have come by your hand," he said, sweeping his hand to indicate the Sundered Lands around them, "but you were manipulated by Gaalron. It's wrong that he should leave you to suffer alone."

She blinked back tears.

"I deserve much worse than to die alone out here."

"There's got to be something we can do," Cam said, his voice strong. "You still have the Scepter."

She shook her head.

"It won't work for me anymore. Not without an Elmia Tether."

"Can I see it?" Cam grunted, rising to his feet with a scowl.

He reached out and took the Scepter from her gloved hand. Illyria barely reacted, her eyes following his movement. He opened his mouth to speak to her, then froze as a strange buzzing took over his arm. He glanced down at the Scepter. Its light was beginning to dim.

A familiar voice sounded in his mind.

I take back everything I said about you marrying that woman. She is my new least favorite human being, and it's not even close.

Luik.

Cam turned away from Illyria. He stumbled forward before falling to his knees, mouth agape. For a moment, he was too shocked to feel anything else.

And then, the emotions hit him.

They violently crashed into him like a tidal wave, overwhelming and disorienting as they tangled with Luik's feelings. Gratitude clashed with loss, hope with defeat, creating a chaotic swirl that left them both reeling.

Luik's voice broke the silence.

You really have a talent for getting us into impossible situations, don't you?

As Luik spoke, the Aetherfern tattoo began snaking its way up Cam's arm. He heard Illyria gasp behind him at the change. Grinning, Cam squeezed his fingers around the Scepter of Alderia.

Not impossible. Look what I have. He looked down at the Scepter for Luik.

Hmmmm, Luik mused in Cam's mind. *That should help.*

How does it work? What do I need to do?

Inside him, Cam felt Luik's emotions shift. For a brief moment, it was as if a beacon of hope flickered in the darkness, casting a warm, reassuring light. But just as quickly, that light was snuffed out, collapsing like a house of cards in a gust of wind, leaving only the cold emptiness of despair in its wake.

Luik? What's wrong?

The Scepter's drained, Luik said, a bitter edge in his voice. *It has very little power left.*

Drained? What do you mean?

Through their bond, Cam could feel Luik shaking his head in disappointment.

Illyria used most of its remaining energy to destroy the Aurora Shrouds. It needs to rebuild its supply before it can do something so great again.

And how long would that take? Cam asked, fearing the answer.

Decades.

For a moment, they stood together in the heavy silence of their defeat, like two warriors at the edge of a battlefield littered with broken dreams. The weight of failure pressed down on them, as if the very air had turned to stone, crushing their spirits and leaving them rooted to the spot, unable to move or speak.

Finally, Luik broke the silence.

I must admit something. I have no idea what we do now. Would that we could have another opportunity to repeat events. Perhaps we could have been better prepared.

An opportunity to repeat events.

An idea struck Cam. He glanced down at the Scepter. Trying to keep himself from hoping, he spoke to Luik.

What all did you say the Scepter can do?

Invert astral and physical energies. Our engineers designed it to create astral Nexus Points where necessary.

Invert energies, yes. But you also said that its wielder has their powers expanded, right? Including Time Shift?

Cam felt Luik nodding, his emotions curious at what Cam was thinking.

That's correct. I once saw Gaalron Time Shift multiple objects at the same time. That feat should be impossible. Why? What do you have in mind?

Despite his best efforts, hope was beginning to creep into the edges of Cam's thoughts.

Can you Time Shift us, reversing the flow of time to send us back?

A quick pang of disappointment shot through Luik, and Cam knew what his answer was going to be.

No, I doubt that would work. Time would continue moving forward for the rest of the world. It's not as simple as shifting yourself backwards through time. You'd need to shift every object in the universe. Even with the Scepter, I doubt that is possible. Even if it were, the cost would be tremendous. You could age decades in a single moment.

Cam nodded thoughtfully.

Maybe we don't need to Time Shift us. Just a very specific part of me.

Luik's curiosity piqued.

Just a part of you? What do you mean, Cam?

My memories. Can you Time Shift my memories back to a younger version of myself?

For a few minutes, Luik did not answer. He appeared conflicted, torn between curiosity and caution. Finally, he said, *It might be possible. However, there's no telling what the cost would be. It could kill you, or perhaps cause severe aging to your younger self. We have no way of knowing that this will succeed.*

Cam smiled, shaking his head.

It likely won't. But an annoying friend once told me this: Know you will fail. Act anyway.

Through their bond, Cam could feel Luik beaming.

I'm pleased to know that someone finally decided to listen to me.

Whirling around, Cam turned to Illyria, who was staring at him with a bewildered expression on her face.

"We're going to Time Shift my memories. Try to do this again."

She raised an incredulous eyebrow.

"Is that even possible?"

"Does it matter? I have to try. What do I need to do differently to get you to not destroy the Aurora Shrouds?"

"I'm not sure. I was very convinced that I was doing what was right. I don't know if you could change my mind."

"Think, Illyria. Who knows how many chances we'll get. What do I need to do differently?"

She tilted her head back thoughtfully. After some contemplation, she said, "You need to get Gaalron to break the Tether. Do that, and I can't use the Scepter."

Cam frowned. "But then Gaalron will just use it."

She nodded enthusiastically.

"Yes, but he'll be battling the Sundered Lands, too. That weakened version of him will be easier to stop." Her expression lightened a shade as she spoke.

"How do I get him to break the Tether?"

"Gaalron needs to lose confidence in my ability to handle the situation," Illyria said, her tone growing more excited. "He hates being Tethered and was regularly threatening to break the Tethering if I didn't do what he said. We never really figured out how to work together." She tapped on the side of her head. "Two brains, both fighting for control. Never could get synchronized. If you can make him think I'll fail, he'll be exposed."

I think that's as good a plan as we'll come up with, Luik muttered.

Gripping the Scepter tighter, Cam gritted his teeth, when Luik suddenly interjected.

Cam, before you do this... I want you to know something. You've been more than just a friend, more than just a partner in this madness. You've been a brother, the one who made all of this bearable. Whatever happens next, thank you for allowing me the honor of being Tethered to you.

Thank you, Luik, Cam said. *Thank you for everything.*

I'm not sure how far back you can go, Luik said. *But I'll send you back as far as I can.*

With that, Luik accessed Time Shift and, enhanced by the remaining power in the Scepter, commanded Cam's memories to travel backwards through time.

Chapter 44

Cam's mind reeled as the world around him twisted and warped. The Scepter of Alderia's dim light pulsed rhythmically in his grasp. He focused intently, trying to hone his thoughts and memories, feeling the surge of power coursing through him. Each beat of the Scepter seemed to sync with his racing heartbeat.

The swirling void of time began to stretch and elongate. Cam could almost see the threads of reality weaving and unraveling before him, like a tapestry being rewoven by unseen hands. He concentrated on the fragments of his past.

A sudden, sharp pain erupted in his head, and Cam gritted his teeth, fighting through the onslaught. His memories surged and collided within him, a storm of experiences, emotions, and regrets. His vision blurred as the edges of his consciousness frayed, struggling to hold on to the present while reaching back into the past.

Cam stumbled, his knees buckling under the strain of the Time Shift. The ground beneath him felt like shifting sand, and he could barely maintain his footing as the world around him continued to distort.

"Hold on," he muttered to himself, eyes clenched shut. "Hold on..."

The pain intensified, and a blinding flash of light enveloped him. For a brief, disorienting moment, everything ceased to exist—the Sundered Lands, the decay, even the Scepter's dim light. Time itself seemed to freeze, holding its breath as if awaiting the outcome of Cam's desperate gamble.

And then, he opened his eyes.

He was back inside the Elmia Temple.

He glanced around, dizzy.

Luik, are you still there?

What was that? Luik screamed. *Did we somehow Time Shift your memories? Oh my goodness, this hurts my head.*

Turning his attention to the front of the chamber, Cam turned and saw Illyria kneeling over the body of Soren.

"No!" she said, pulling her sword back. "No, I didn't mean to. It...I didn't mean to."

I don't understand what's going on, complained Luik.

I'll try to explain later, Cam said, dashing forward.

Illyria then turned her head to see Cam running for her. She must have somehow sensed his intent, because she leapt back, pointing the Scepter at him.

Again, Cam felt a strange ripping sensation as Illyria snapped his Tethering with Luik. Just like before, the sudden exposure to the Sundered Lands was overwhelming to his body, causing him to fall to his knees in a coughing fit.

"I'm sorry," Illyria said. "Truly, I am. But I can't have this disrupted. We only have one chance. Please help Soren."

And just as before, she used Verdalink to vanish from view.

Cam let out a groan, rising to his feet. He took a deep breath, steeling himself against the pain and exhaustion that threatened to overwhelm him. He needed to find a way to break through, to stop Illyria's catastrophic plan. With steely resolve, he braced himself and moved forward.

Well that didn't work. Time to try again.

Hours later, he found Illyria in the same spot in the Sundered Lands. Taking the Scepter from her, he tried for a second time.

And then for a third.

And a fourth.

And a fifth.

Nothing worked.

His second attempt had been another direct assault. Cam charged at Illyria with all his remaining strength, his every muscle straining as he lunged to seize the Scepter by force, but Illyria's defenses were formidable.

With a flick of her wrist, she sent a powerful shockwave crashing into him, knocking him off balance and sending him sprawling to the ground, again breaking the Tethering to Luik.

His third attempt focused on a different approach. This time, he and Luik tried Shadowmelding, as he attempted to slip through the shadows and surprise her from behind. He moved silently, but as he reached out for the Scepter, Illyria's eyes flicked to him with uncanny precision. She countered his attack with a burst of blinding light before using Verdalink to whisk herself away.

Cam's fourth attempt was fueled by desperation. He screamed at Illyria, his voice raw and desperate.

"Stop this! You don't understand what you're doing! This will destroy everything!"

But his pleas fell on deaf ears. Illyria's face remained impassive, her grip on the Scepter tightening before snapping his Tethering with Luik.

Each time Luik Time Shifted Cam's memories, Cam felt a relentless toll on his body, as if the very fabric of time was extracting a price from him. With each attempt, he grew older and more fatigued, the weight of his repeated efforts aging him and deepening his exhaustion.

But he didn't stop.

He couldn't stop.

Know you will fail. Act anyway. Harness your fear and use it as a weapon, he kept reminding himself.

Before long, Cam had lost count of the number of times he'd gone back. Each attempt seemed equally fruitless, no matter what strategy he employed. The Scepter of Alderia made Illyria an insurmountable force, her power seeming to repel his every effort with chilling efficiency.

So...why aren't you taking the Scepter from her? She's right there, Luik said on Cam's next attempt.

I'm just trying to think this through. Trying to come up with a better plan, Cam said, glancing around the room. His gaze fell upon the corpse of the Reaper lying sprawled on the floor. The sight sparked an idea.

Luik, do you remember when we fought the Reaper? How it reacted to my mental commands?

Yes. What are you thinking?

Could that be my Complex?

Perhaps we can find out.

Focusing, Cam accessed Luik's powers and willed help to come his way. The effort was taxing and fraught with resistance, but after several strained moments, a small figure emerged into the chamber: a Necrothorn Beetle, its carapace gleaming dully in the dim light.

Interesting. Just how many of these things can I influence at a single time?

And so, he tried a different tactic. Each time he Time Shifted his memories, he focused on influencing more of the transformed creatures around him. After a few attempts, he managed to summon three Necrothorn Beetles.

The next attempt he summoned five.

After that, he summoned twelve, plus a scaletaint.

Over the course of several attempts, Cam discovered that, while he could not directly control the creatures, he could influence them, guiding their actions. It was similar to how one might influence the flow of water without being able to manipulate every drop.

Each time he sent his memories back, Cam tapped further into this power, becoming more adept at this subtle manipulation.

Each time, he got just a bit closer.

Each time, he failed.

Chapter 45

Chek's breath came in sharp, controlled bursts as she leaned heavily on her cane, the weight of her injury pulling at her with each step. The dense forest surrounding the outskirts of Perth was eerily silent, the kind of quiet that only heightened her senses, making every rustle of leaves, every snap of a twig, seem amplified.

She couldn't afford a single mistake.

The four members of the Sundered Shadows trailed behind her, unaware that they were walking into a carefully laid trap. Chek smirked to herself in grim satisfaction. Her leg may have slowed her physically, but her mind was as sharp as ever, and she intended to prove it.

She led them deeper into the forest. The ground here was uneven, littered with fallen branches and thick with underbrush.

As they stepped into the clearing, Chek moved with deliberate slowness, making sure they were all within the perimeter. The cultists exchanged glances, their suspicion growing as the seconds ticked by. They had expected to find something waiting for them, but there was nothing here but the trees.

Trees, and the woman they had underestimated.

"Where is it?" one of the members huffed.

Chek turned to face them, a faint smile tugging at her lips.

"Right here," she said, her voice calm, almost pleasant. With a swift, practiced motion, she shifted her weight and slammed the butt of her cane into the ground.

Suddenly, the ground beneath the four members collapsed, plunging them into a deep pit. Chek and Felix had spent hours preparing this trap after finding one of the holes

Vaelin had dug. Using the existing hole as a foundation, they worked tireless hours to shape and expand it, transforming it into the perfect concealed snare.

The second part of the trap didn't go so smoothly, though.

The underbrush around the pit began to smolder, thin tendrils of smoke curling upward instead of the roaring flames Chek had envisioned. She gritted her teeth in frustration. The fire hadn't caught as planned. Instead of creating a blazing inferno to corral and disorient the cultists, all they had were weak embers and thick, choking smoke. It wasn't ideal, but the smoke still served its purpose, clouding their vision and slowing their movements as they scrambled in the pit.

The cultists' fury erupted as they realized the extent of her deception. They cursed her name, their voices thick with rage and desperation. One screamed in frustration.

"Oh, you're dead now, cripple!"

Chek didn't flinch. She knew better than to engage with them now. The trap was holding, but it wouldn't last forever. She had to move, and quickly.

Turning away from the pit, she started back toward Perth, her pace brisk despite the pain that shot through her leg with every step. She gritted her teeth, pushing past the throbbing ache. Felix needed more time, and she had bought him as much as she could.

She could only hope that she'd bought him enough.

The walk back to Perth felt like an eternity. Each step sent sharp pangs through Chek's leg, the dull throb of pain now a constant companion. She forced herself onward, leaning heavily on her cane, sweat slicking her brow. The forest path stretched on, winding through the trees, and she could almost hear the clock ticking down.

They'd be chasing her soon.

By the time she reached the outskirts of Perth, the sky was beginning to darken, the sun sinking low on the horizon. She staggered through the narrow alleys, her breath ragged, until she reached the small inn where Felix was supposed to be waiting.

"Felix!" she called out, her voice strained. She looked around, heart pounding. "Felix!"

A few agonizing moments passed before the inn's door creaked open, and Felix stumbled out. His usually sharp features were slack, his eyes wide with confusion. He seemed dazed, as if he had just woken from a nightmare and hadn't yet shaken off the terror.

"Felix!" Chek called again, relief flooding through her as she limped toward him. "Did you find Vaelin?"

Felix blinked, his gaze unfocused.

"Yes," he muttered, the word barely audible.

Something wasn't right. Chek could see it in the way he moved, the way he looked at her without really seeing her. She reached out, gripping his arm.

"What happened? Talk to me."

He opened his mouth, but no words came. Instead, he glanced down at his arm, his hand trembling as he rolled up his sleeve. Chek followed his gaze, her breath catching in her throat when she saw it: a tattoo, vivid and unmistakable, snaking up his forearm. The intricate pattern of an Aetherfern, its delicate leaves etched in dark ink, winding its way toward his wrist.

"What?" Chek gasped.

"Uriel," Felix whispered, finally meeting her eyes. "Her name is Uriel. She says she was the queen of the Elmias."

Chek's heart skipped a beat. The implications hit her like a blow.

"She...she told me about a grove," Felix continued, his voice distant, as if he was struggling to comprehend it himself. "A grove of Aetherfern plants, just a few miles away. They hold the souls of many Elmias. She showed me..."

He trailed off, pulling a crumpled map from his pocket and handing it to Chek. She took it, her mind racing.

"It's not far from here. Maybe a day or two into the Sundered Lands," Felix explained, pointing to a spot on the map. "She said that it was a contingency plan for the Elmias living at the temple in the mountains. A spot for them to go to, if the temple ever fell."

"Are they safe?" Chek said, scratching her head where her hair was beginning to regrow.

"No, they're not," Felix said, violently shaking his head. "For starters, she says that the Cult is using the Grove as a way to farm Elmias. They must be running out, which explains their desperation to find Uriel. Also, Uriel says that that much astral energy in one place is beginning to attract the Reapers."

"So, what do we do?"

"We've got to get them someone to Tether to."

Find the Grove. Get the Elmias someone to Tether to. Right.

"Felix, I can't go there. I..." she began, struggling to get the words out. "My body just can't handle it. I could die before we get there."

Felix gave a quick nod.

"I know. Either I go alone, or you have to Tether to Uriel."

The sound of footsteps brought a sudden chill to Chek's heart.

The cultists had arrived.

They emerged from the shadows of the alley, their faces twisted with fury. Some bore the marks of their fall into the pit. One even had a strong limp.

Their leader spotted the tattoo on Felix's arm and sneered.

"So, the Elmia Tethered itself to you," he hissed, shoving Chek aside as he advanced on Felix. Chek stumbled, her cane slipping from her grasp as she fell to the ground, pain shooting through her leg.

Felix tried to back away, but they were on him in an instant. They grabbed him, their hands rough and unyielding, yanking him toward the center of the street. The man leaned in close, his voice low and menacing.

"And to think you could have helped us from the beginning. Spared yourself lots of pain."

Felix struggled, but there was no escape. He twisted in their grip, his eyes locking onto Chek's for one final moment.

In that moment, the chaos around them seemed to fade into the background, the noise and confusion falling away. His expression was pleading.

Chek felt her heart wrench, an ache that reverberated through her entire being. She wanted to reach out, but she couldn't move, held fast by the gravity of his gaze.

"Hurry! Go!" he mouthed, his expression filled with a mix of resolve and urgency.

Chek's heart twisted in her chest. She wanted to scream, to rush to his aid, but she knew what he was telling her.

Then, the cultists ran a sword through his back.

For a moment, time shattered. Chek couldn't breathe. Her vision blurred as tears welled up in her eyes. A scream clawed its way up her throat, but she swallowed it down. She allowed herself one moment to memorize every detail of his face. Then, she stumbled as she rose to her feet, grabbed the map, and hobbled away as quickly as she could manage.

"I'm so sorry, Felix," she whispered, though she knew he couldn't hear her.

It has to be me. Find the Grove.

She moved as quickly as her injury would allow, her breath coming in ragged gasps as she pushed through the narrow streets of Perth. The pain in her leg was a constant, gnawing presence, but she forced herself to keep going, clutching the map tightly in her hand.

After what felt like hours, the outskirts of Perth gave way to the open wilderness, and she pressed on, following the path indicated on the map. The landscape grew wilder and more rugged, the ground uneven beneath her feet. She stumbled more than once, catching herself on her cane and gritting her teeth against the pain.

She had covered several miles when she finally reached the edge of the Aurora Shroud. Just as she reached it, she slowed to a stop, heart pounding in her chest and doubt clawing at her mind.

It has to be me. Find the Grove.

With a deep breath, Chek tightened her grip on her cane and stepped forward, crossing the boundary of the Aurora Shroud into the Sundered Lands.

Cam stood alone in the desolate expanse of the Sundered Lands, the barren landscape stretching out endlessly around him. The ground beneath his feet was cracked and lifeless. A cold wind whipped through the air, biting at his skin and tugging at his worn cloak. He barely felt it, though, his mind focused on the task ahead and the toll it had already taken on him.

Okay. One more time, he told himself.

He'd told himself that several times already.

He had lost track of how many times he'd done this. The memories blurred together, a chaotic jumble of moments, victories turned to failures, hopes dashed over and over again. Worse, each return made the past harder to hold onto. His memories of what worked and what didn't were growing thin and slippery, like trying to recall a dream after waking. The more he reached backward, the more uncertain the path ahead became.

He wasn't sure how many years he had aged himself, but the wrinkles forming on his hands told him it was too many.

Cam opened his eyes and looked down at the Scepter. The dark surface seemed to pulse with a life of its own, as if it was aware of his thoughts, aware of the decision he was about to make.

There was no other decision he could make.

Again.

Chapter 46

The moment Chek crossed the threshold of the Aurora Shroud, an overwhelming wave of pain crashed over her. It was as if the air itself turned hostile, each breath she took searing her lungs with sharp, invisible spikes. Her leg, already a source of constant agony, began to throb with an intensity she hadn't thought possible. She gasped, instinctively doubling over, but there was no relief to be found.

She had no choice. There was no turning back. She gritted her teeth, tightened her grip on her cane, and forced herself to move.

Each step was agony. The pain in her leg grew worse with every passing hour, the throbbing now a dull roar that echoed through her entire body. It took everything she had to keep putting one foot in front of the other. The terrain was treacherous, the ground uneven and littered with sharp rocks that threatened to trip her at every turn.

But she couldn't afford to slow down. She couldn't afford to stop.

In the stillness, the grief of losing her brother finally caught up to her. Somewhere in the chaos of her mind, she could still see his face as he died. It was like being torn in two, hurting her deeper than anything else this world had ever thrown at her.

It wasn't just her body that was broken. Her mind kept looping back to Felix. His final breath. The way his body crumpled. The moment the light in his eyes vanished like a snuffed flame.

Shoving the thoughts aside, she kept moving. She could grieve once she made it through this hell.

Night fell quickly in the Sundered Lands, but Chek didn't rest. She pressed on through the darkness, her body screaming and her mind frayed by exhaustion and fear. Her breath came in ragged gasps, each inhalation a fresh wave of pain, but she wouldn't stop.

By the time the sun began to rise, casting a pale, sickly light over the wasteland, Chek was barely holding on. Every muscle in her body ached, her vision blurred from fatigue and the constant, unrelenting pain. She staggered onward, her cane digging into the ground with each painful step.

Not far into the next day, her body finally gave out. She was just stepping over a sharp rock when her right leg suddenly buckled. Chek gasped, her cane slipping from her grasp as she fell forward, hitting the ground hard. The impact knocked the wind out of her, her face pressed into the dry, cracked earth of the Sundered Lands.

For a moment, she remained motionless, too exhausted and in too much pain to move. As she lay there, the reality of her situation began to sink in. She was alone, in the heart of a land that seemed intent on breaking her, and she was out of time, out of strength.

Chek's vision blurred with tears of frustration and fear.

It has to be me.

A spark of determination flared in her chest. Her fingers clawed at the ground, sinking into the dirt. Crying out with the effort, she pulled herself across the ground. Every movement was agony. Every nerve in her body screamed for her to relent, but she refused to give in.

Screaming, she dug her fingers into the dry, cracked earth, feeling the rough texture bite into her skin. She pulled herself forward, dragging her body inch by inch.

One of her fingernails broke as she scrabbled at the ground, but she barely noticed. Her entire world had shrunk to the simple, desperate act of moving forward.

She didn't know how long she crawled like this. Time had lost all meaning, each second stretching into an eternity of pain and effort. Her vision swam, her strength waning with every pull of her arms, but she kept moving.

She almost didn't hear the warning sound.

Chek paused, listening, and heard it again—a scuttling, like the rapid movement of tiny legs across the cracked earth. Her heart skipped a beat, dread seizing her as she turned her head to look back.

Her blood ran cold at the sight.

Necrothorn Beetles.

Dozens of them.

The terrifying bugs raced towards her, their carapaces glinting in the eerie red light of the Sundered Lands and mandibles clicking together as they advanced.

Panic surged through her, adrenaline giving her a brief surge of strength. She clawed at the ground with renewed desperation, dragging herself forward as quickly as her battered body would allow. The pain in her legs was nothing compared to the terror now gripping her.

Just then, one of the beetles lunged forward, its sharp mandibles snapping dangerously close to her hand. Chek let out a strangled cry and swung her arm back, smacking the creature away with the heel of her hand. The impact sent it skidding across the ground, but it quickly righted itself, joining the others in their relentless pursuit.

Chek pushed herself harder, clawing at the earth with everything she had left. Her hands were raw, her arms shaking with the effort, but she couldn't stop.

Another beetle got too close, and she had to stop again, swatting at it with the last of her strength. The movement cost her precious seconds, and she knew she couldn't keep this up much longer.

She had to keep moving, had to reach the Grove before the beetles caught her. With a sob of desperation, Chek forced herself forward once more, her hands scrabbling at the earth, dragging her body across the cold, unforgiving ground.

Chek's frantic crawl forward was interrupted as the ground beneath her suddenly dropped away. She didn't have time to react, didn't even see the steep hill ahead until it was too late. With a startled gasp, she tipped over the edge and began to tumble down the rocky slope.

The world spun violently as she careened downward, her body battered by the unforgiving terrain. Sharp rocks tore at her skin, slicing into her face, arms, and hands as she rolled uncontrollably. She could feel the sting of fresh wounds, the warm trickle of blood mixing with the dirt and sweat on her skin, but there was nothing she could do to stop the fall.

The Necrothorn Beetles, the pain, the terror—all of it became a blur as she was tossed like a ragdoll down the hill.

Finally, she crashed to the bottom with a heavy thud. The impact knocked the wind out of her, and she lay there, gasping for breath. For a moment, she couldn't move, couldn't think. Everything was a haze of agony and exhaustion. Her vision swam, and the world around her felt distant, as if she were viewing it through a thick fog.

Slowly, she blinked, trying to clear her sight. The rough ground beneath her was cold, the jagged stones pressing into her battered body, but as her eyes focused, she became aware of a soft, radiant light surrounding her. It was different from the harsh light of the Sundered Lands.

A warm, ethereal glow that seemed to pulse with life.

Chek forced herself to sit up, wincing as the movement sent sharp pains shooting through her limbs. She looked around, her breath catching in her throat as she took in her surroundings. Towering above her were several massive Aetherfern plants, their leaves shimmering with an otherworldly luminescence. The glow emanating from them cast the entire area in a soft, golden light, illuminating the small clearing at the base of the hill.

She had made it.

Chek, still trembling from the pain and the harrowing journey, forced herself to focus. Glancing behind her, it appeared the beetles had chosen to give up their chase and were not following her down the cliff.

With her body aching and her hands raw from the climb, she slowly crawled over to the nearest Aetherfern plant. Its leaves shimmered in the soft light, their gentle glow inviting her closer. She hesitated for a moment, the memory of what she had witnessed replaying in her mind. Then, with a surge of determination, she reached out and plucked one of the delicate leaves.

As soon as her fingers closed around the leaf, a rush of energy flowed through her, spreading from her hand and coursing through her entire body.

Chek gasped in surprise, her eyes widening as she felt the change within her. She looked down at her arm, where a strange tingling sensation had begun. Before her eyes, an Aetherfern tattoo appeared, winding its way up her forearm in intricate, glowing patterns.

"Thank you," she said. Her words came out more as a hoarse whisper because of the rawness in her throat.

Wow, you're thanking me? I feel like I should be thanking you! I was stuck in that plant for AGES, a feminine voice sounded in her mind.

"Uriel sent me," she explained, stammering to find the right words.

Wait, you got to talk to the queen? Color me impressed.

"You're all in trouble. You all need to go."

Go? Go where? This was supposed to be the safe spot.

"It's not anymore. The Cult of Sundered Shadows is using this place to farm Elmias."

I'm...not sure what any of that means. But, I'll take your word for it. Okay, so this isn't safe. Any idea where we should go next?

Chek thought for a moment.

"My friend...his name is Cam...is trying to reach the Elmia Temple to stop Gaalron from destroying the Aurora Shrouds. We need your help."

Wait, Gaalron is alive? And he's trying to destroy the Aurora Shrouds? Ugh. That egomaniac won't stop till he wrecks everything.

There was a pause, a moment of silence as the presence within her seemed to consider her words. Then, gently, the Elmia spoke again, her voice filled with calm resolve.

I need to unTether from you, but I need your permission first.

Chek nodded, though she realized a moment later that the Elmia could sense her agreement without the gesture.

"Yes."

As soon as she agreed, the energy within her shifted, and she felt a slight pull, as if something was being drawn out of her. A soft, glowing light began to form in front of her, gradually taking shape until it coalesced into the figure of an Elmia woman.

Her skin was a rich, dark green, streaked with veins of lighter green marbling that gave her a striking, almost otherworldly appearance. The light played off her metallic flesh, casting subtle reflections that danced across the clearing. She looked at Chek with a gentle, empathetic expression.

The Elmia opened her mouth to speak, but was quickly seized by a violent coughing fit, her face twisting in pain. After a few seconds, she managed to stop hacking.

"Sorry, this place is the worst," she said, her voice somehow both hoarse and ethereal. "My name is Ink."

"Ink," Chek repeated.

"Yes. Ink." The Elmia sucked in a deep breath. "And you are...on the ground for some reason? What, did you break your leg?"

"I...it's hard to explain. What do I need to do?" Chek asked.

"Pluck the next leaf. Tether the next Elmia. Then, cut it loose. That simple."

Chek frowned.

"You can't just unTether yourself?"

"Oh Lady on the Ground—sorry, I don't know your name—you must not know much about us. Once Tethered, we need permission to unTether. Now, what are you waiting for? Aren't we in trouble or something?"

Chek nodded, still processing the surreal encounter, but there was no time to lose. She pushed herself up, the pain in her body now bearable, and moved to the next Aetherfern plant. With determination, she began plucking the leaves, one by one, speaking to each Elmia that was released.

Each Elmia, upon hearing her plea, agreed without hesitation. They manifested briefly before vanishing into thin air, their forms dissolving like mist as they set off to answer the call.

Finally, as the last Elmia vanished, Chek found herself standing once more before Ink. The Elmia regarded her with a mixture of gratitude and something softer.

Understanding.

"Seems like you could really use some help. Would you allow me to Tether again?" Ink asked, her voice carrying a note of empathy.

"Yes."

Ink smiled, a warm, gentle expression that softened her features. She reached out, her hand hovering just above Chek's arm. The connection reformed almost instantly, a familiar rush of energy flooding back into Chek's body as the Aetherfern tattoo glowed brightly on her skin once more.

The air around them seemed to hum with renewed vitality, and Chek felt the lingering pain in her body recede further. The fatigue that had weighed her down lightened, replaced by a sense of resolve and purpose.

So, what's your name? I'd keep calling you "Lady on the Ground," but it's too wordy.

"Chek. My name is Chek."

Chek. I like it. Much less wordy. Tell me, Chek, are you familiar with Verdalink?

Chapter 47

C am's eyes opened slowly, and he let out a sigh of exhaustion. Each breath felt labored, the weight of countless repetitions pressing down on him. Blinking away the remnants of disorientation, he took in the stone chamber once more. The cold stone walls, the dim flickering of ancient torches.

It was all too familiar. He felt like he had spent years in this room.

How many times had he been here? How many times had he sent his memories back, each attempt blending into the last?

And how much longer could he continue to do this?

He felt weaker, with every movement accompanied by a sharp pang or pop. He glanced down at his hands, which were beginning to gnarl, wincing as he tightened his grip on the sword.

Again, he thought, gritting his teeth and trying to summon as much determination as he could.

Illyria appeared as she always did, attempting to help Soren, even as her blade had just pierced him.

Cam wasted no time. Drawing on Luik's powers, he summoned the creatures of the Sundered Lands.

As always, the Necrothorn Beetles appeared first, emerging from the cracks and crevices in the walls. Initially, they came in a slow trickle, but soon it was as if a dam had burst. In moments, hundreds of beetles surged forward, their mandibles clicking as they charged toward Illyria.

She let out a sharp shriek of surprise and horror, her eyes widening as the swarm charged toward her. Without hesitation, she leapt back, instinctively raising the Scepter high. It emitted a brilliant flash of light, and in an instant, every beetle froze in place, trapped in a Time Shift.

Taking advantage of the momentary stillness, Cam melded into the shadows, disappearing from sight.

Then came the sound of footsteps. It was faint at first, but as the seconds went by, it grew louder and louder, until it became like the roar of a rushing river. Illyria glanced around nervously, her hands tightening on the Scepter.

The air was filled with a deafening buzz as a massive swarm of scaletaints from a nearby hive burst into the room. The creatures flooded the chamber, startling Illyria. She quickly recovered, her eyes narrowing.

"What is going on?" she cried out, confused. She gripped the Scepter in one hand, her Astral Edge in the other. Then, the scaletaints were on her. The room was a blur of motion as she fended them off, her sword slicing through the air with deadly precision. Each strike was swift and calculated, the blade's ethereal glow matching the brilliance of the Scepter.

Despite being outnumbered, Illyria fought with an almost supernatural skill. The power of the Scepter coursed through her, amplifying her strength and speed. She moved like a force of nature, seamlessly transitioning between offense and defense, her blade and Scepter working in perfect harmony. Even as the scaletaints pressed their attack, she held her ground, an indomitable figure amidst the chaos.

Cam burst from the shadows, his hand reaching for the Scepter. Illyria gasped, momentarily paralyzed by the sight of his face.

"Cam?" she said, her voice confused.

"It doesn't work." His voice cracked, knowing she wouldn't believe him. "Destroying the Shrouds doesn't work."

Illyria's expression darkened as she aimed the Scepter at him, ready to sever his connection with Luik. But Luik Time Shifted the Scepter, buying himself just enough time to dive out of harm's way. Illyria screamed in frustration as the group of scaletaints closed in on her. Her focus shattered, releasing the beetles from their Time Shift. They, too, swarmed toward her.

Here they come, Cam thought.

Here who comes? Luik responded.

You'll see.

From somewhere in the darkness above them, a Reaper appeared, letting out an otherworldly wail. Its grotesque body, covered in a strange black-red goo, seemed to have a life of its own. Tumorous growths writhed and squirmed beneath the surface.

It was joined by another Reaper.

Then another.

Then three more.

They saw Illyria and shrieked for joy, charging at her.

Stunned, Cam stood up and stared for a moment.

Six? Last time I was only able to call two.

You brought those things here? Luik's voice was screaming. *I don't know if I should be proud or panic.*

Well, we're in new territory now. I've never been able to summon this many.

Chaos erupted in the chamber. Morwenna screamed and scrambled to the far side of the room while Illyria spun, wielding the Scepter's power to hold her ground.

In his most recent attempt, Illyria had barely managed to fend off two Reapers, but against six, she stood no chance, especially with the relentless swarm of scaletaints and Necrothorn Beetles closing in on her from all sides.

She let out a desperate scream. Seconds later, a strange man seemed to leap from her arm. His metallic flesh was pitch black with dark blue lines streaking through it.

That's Gaalron, Luik said in amazement. *Were you able to get him to unTether before?*

No, admitted Cam. *This is new.*

No longer Tethered to an Elmia, Illyria collapsed to the ground, seized by a coughing fit. One of the scaletaints leapt forward, its teeth clamping down on her shoulder. She let out a quick scream as Cam directed the monsters away from her and towards Gaalron.

Cam raced forward, picked her up, and carried her to the far side of the room where Morwenna was hiding.

She whimpered slightly as he carried her, clutching at his arm. As he set her down, she said, "Cam? What is going on?" Her face was stunned. Cam glanced back over his shoulder towards Gaalron. The Elmia, now powered by the Scepter, was fighting the many creatures of the Sundered Lands. He looked too distracted to access Verdalink.

Cam turned his attention back to Illyria.

"It doesn't work," he said in a grinding tone. "It doesn't work!" he then shouted, bashing his reptilian hand into the wall. "You destroyed everything."

"I don't...I don't understand," Illyria said, dazed. "Cam, what happened to your face?"

But Cam was finished with Illyria.

It was time to face Gaalron.

He joined the swarm of monsters attacking the Elmia.

Gaalron stood at the center of the chamber, his grip firm on the Scepter of Alderia. Its ancient power surged through him, crackling with a vibrant blue energy illuminating the chamber. The six Reapers encircled him like vultures ready to feast. A sea of scaletaints and Necrothorn Beetles skittered and swarmed around him. With a roar that echoed across the stones, Gaalron leapt forward, swinging the scepter.

The Elmia moved with an uncanny power and precision, dashing back the scaletaints and beetles with ease. His speed was inhuman, almost a blur.

It's the staff, Luik said. *It's amplifying his powers. Cam, you have to get the staff away from him.*

Got it.

Cam descended upon Gaalron with a vicious snarl. His eyes burned in anger as he swung at Gaalron with a feral ferocity. The Elmia slapped the blade away, like it were nothing more than an annoying bug.

Cam swung again, but in a single fluid motion, Gaalron sidestepped Cam's charge, bringing the Scepter down in a swift arc. The force of the blow sent Cam sprawling, his weapon clattering to the ground.

"Do not think that I do not realize what you've done, boy," Gaalron growled, ducking back as a Reaper swiped at him. "I see the effects of the Time Shift on your face."

"Your plan doesn't work!" Cam shouted, leaping to his feet. Gaalron twisted around him, stabbing the Scepter into a nearby Reaper's chest. The creature let out a shriek before falling to the ground motionless.

As Cam leapt to his feet, the air itself seemed to shudder as time began to warp and distort. He and the Reapers, caught in the blast, froze mid-attack. Their movements slowed, then halted entirely, as Gaalron Time Shifted all of them at the same time.

"You've been consumed," Gaalron said, his face a mask of rage. "But not even the darkest forces can extinguish the light within. My people will be free." The Elmia turned towards Cam, preparing to deliver a lethal blow.

A sudden force slammed into Gaalron's side, sending him stumbling backward. Before he could regain his footing, another invisible blow struck him, this time from behind. The second hit was even more powerful, driving him to his knees.

That wasn't one of the Reapers, Cam thought.

The world around them shuddered as the Time Shift began to unravel. The frozen Reapers twitched, their limbs jerking as if waking from a long slumber. The energy that had held them in stasis dissipated, and in an instant, they were freed.

Cam's eyes snapped open, and with a fierce snarl, he sprang to his feet as flashes of light revealed strange metallic creatures materializing around him, all converging on Gaalron.

By Aurora's Name...it's the Elmias, Luik said, his voice amazed.

As Chek appeared in the room, using what Ink had called an "astral Anchor," her head spun. She took a step forward on her bad leg, falling to the ground in a heap.

Sorry! I should have warned you! Verdalink can make you very dizzy, Ink said in her mind.

"It's not that. It's my leg...I thought it might have healed," Chek said, reaching out and gingerly touching her knee. "My other leg seems just fine."

The Sundered Lands must have damaged your leg beyond repair. Are you able to stand?

Chek tried and stumbled back down again. She tried again successfully, using the rough stone wall to help support her weight.

I'm wondering if I shouldn't have brought you here. With only one working leg, you may be in more danger.

"I'm where I need to be. There are other ways I can help," Chek corrected, glancing over towards where the fighting was taking place. She let out a quick yelp of fear. "Reapers! And so many scaletaints. What is going on?"

How would I know? I just got here?

The Grove Elmias darted towards a large figure that Chek assumed was Gaalron. They moved with unnatural speed as they clawed and slashed at him, desperate to wrest the Scepter of Alderia from his grasp. Gaalron fought back with fierce determination, swinging the Scepter in wide arcs. One of the Elmias got too close and was blasted back, his chest caving in on itself.

But for every one he destroyed, another two seemed to emerge, relentless in their assault.

Chek stood still, trying to take everything in. Her vision began to narrow, sharpening her perception far beyond what she felt should be possible, as she filtered out everything but the patterns in Gaalron's movements.

So, why are we just standing here? Ink asked. Chek could sense the Elmia's impatience.

"I'm... I'm learning," Chek said, staring intently at Gaalron.

Suddenly, something seemed to click in her head. She found herself calculating torque, velocity, and his angles of rotation. Her mind raced ahead with frightening precision, projecting trajectories before Gaalron even moved.

Zero point six seconds between full-body swings. Wide arcs. Right-handed dominant. Maximum reach is just under two point three meters.

Chek didn't know how she was doing it, only that she could.

She had never been in a real fight, but she'd seen people practice her entire life. Gaalron was a terrifying figure. He was strong and deadly, and empowered by the Scepter, he was capable of holding his own against hundreds of opponents.

But her analytical mind had noticed flaws in his form.

Slight overextension every time he swings to the left, she realized. *Creates an opening for zero point one four seconds.*

The Elmia was angry, and as opponents swarmed around him, his strikes were vicious, but increasingly unfocused. His attack pattern was also fairly predictable, with long, powerful strikes being focused on large groups of enemies, followed by quick slashes and jabs at any individuals he might have missed.

Interesting, Chek thought.

What? What's interesting? Ink responded, startling Chek. *Sorry*, she said, her voice bashful. *You'll get used to it.*

No, you're fine, Chek said, giving her head a slight shake. *I just have an idea.*

Ooh, that sounds awesome. Let's hear it! Ink said enthusiastically. *Or...I guess I'll hear it. Unless you say it out loud. Then you can hear it too. But then Gaalron might also hear. Better to just think it and let me hear it.*

Can we Shadowmeld? Chek asked.

Amid the chaos, Cam seized the opportunity to regroup. He called out to the scaletaints and Reapers, and the monstrous creatures answered his command, surging forward.

Together with the Elmias, their combined forces numbers were slowly wearing him down. Cam, his eyes burning with determination, pushed harder, leading the charge as they closed in on Gaalron, intent on seizing the Scepter.

Cam and Luik used Shadowmeld to silently creep up on Gaalron, slipping through the darkness like a wraith. When he was close enough, he sprang from the shadows, aiming for a decisive strike. But Gaalron, anticipating the attack, caught Cam's sword mid-swing and, with a crushing grip, shattered the blade in his bare hand.

"What gives you the right to try to stop me from freeing my people?" Gaalron spat.

Dropping his broken sword, Cam leaped forward with renewed vigor. Luik, sensing his intent, Time Shifted the Scepter, so that Gaalron temporarily couldn't swing it.

Unfortunately, Cam was unable to take advantage, as Gaalron's metallic fist slammed into his face. Cam's vision flashed with light as he fell onto his back. The blow was so hard that it appeared to even impact Luik, whose concentration broke as he released the Time Shift on the Scepter. With a roar, Gaalron made another wide, sweeping swing, battering back the Elmias and scaletaints that were closing in.

A sudden blur of movement surprised Cam. A feminine figure leapt from the shadows just after Gaalron had completed his swing, grabbing Cam's broken sword and stabbing forward at Gaalron. The attack was haphazard, but it bit into Gaalron's shoulder.

It was Chek.

Gaalron looked stunned for a moment before giving Chek a shove that sent her flying back. Her head smacked a stone pillar, and she collapsed to the ground in a heap. He began to turn, but he was just a hair too slow for Cam, who was already back on his feet leaping towards him.

Cam buried his reptilian claw in Gaalron's chest. With his free hand, he ripped the Scepter out of his grasp, tossing it out of reach. Gaalron's eyes widened in shock and disbelief as the claws sank in. He fell onto his back, Cam atop him, the claw still embedded in his chest.

"You asked me what gives me the right to stop you. Well, I'll tell you." He pressed his claw further into Gaalron's chest, hearing the Elmia let out a gasp as he did so. "I am Master of the Sundered Lands."

Gaalron's eyes, wide with shock and pain, seemed to plead for understanding as the life drained from him.

Climbing to his feet, Cam stood over Gaalron, his chest heaving with the weight of exhaustion. His hands trembled slightly as he pulled them away from the fallen Elmia, and the cold reality of his victory settled in.

Without Gaalron present, the summoned creatures began to attack the Elmias.

"Leave!" Cam snarled, his voice commanding and threatening. Once again under his influence, the monsters began to disperse.

Cam's gaze drifted to Illyria, who was now slumped against the wall, her face pale and her breaths shallow. Morwenna, emerging from her hiding place, rushed to Illyria's side, checking her wounds.

Breathing heavily, Cam took a moment to collect himself. The weight of countless failures and countless repetitions had finally borne fruit.

We did it. Luik, we actually did it.

No. Not yet.

Cam cocked his head in surprise.

Not yet? What are you talking about?

Through their bond, Cam felt the shift in Luik's emotions like a cold wave washing over him. The Elmia wasn't just sad. He was despondent, as if a shadow had fallen over his soul.

Luik? What's wrong?

The Scepter, Luik said, his voice quiet and serious. *You have to use it.*

Use it? I don't understand.

It has the power to invert energies. If you invert the energies, you'll destroy the Sundered Lands and restore Avoni.

Cam's eyes opened wide. Luik was right. Reaching down, Cam gripped the Scepter in his reptilian hand. Its power coursed through him.

Then, he paused.

Luik...I don't know if I can do this. There are no remaining astral Nexus Points. You and the rest of the Elmias will always have to be Tethered.

I know.

Cam swallowed hard.

You'll never be free.

I said I know. Luik's voice was steady, but laced with sorrow.

Bewildered, Cam shook his head, glancing around the chamber.

The Elmias have had our chance, Luik said, his voice calm. Almost reassuring. *Gaalron already destroyed our world. But you get the chance to save yours.*

Gazing at the Scepter, Cam felt a mixture of dread and hope.

And he shook his head.

I can't do it. Not without seeing you face to face.

Cam could sense Luik's surprise.

Face to face?

Yes.

Right now?

Right now.

A shimmer of light began to coalesce in the center of the chamber, growing in intensity until it formed a figure. Luik materialized from the brilliance, his appearance a mesmerizing blend of metallic hues, light blue and purple swirled together in a harmonious dance.

"Cam," Luik said out loud. Cam's breath caught in his throat, hearing the Elmia with his ears rather than in his mind for the first time.

Luik smiled. It was an odd expression, with one corner of his lip turned up slightly higher than the other. "I never thought I'd feel the ground beneath my feet again. I'd say that the feeling is pleasant, but it's even easier to smell you now." He waved a hand in distaste in front of his face, as if trying to ward away bugs. It made Cam chuckle.

"Cam, please tell me that you're still planning on destroying the Sundered Lands."

"I am. But I needed to make a promise to you first." Cam lifted both hands and placed them on the Elmia's shoulders. "I will find a way to restore you and your people."

Luik smiled.

"Most likely, you will not be able to keep that promise."

Cam shook his head.

"No. It is a promise that I intend to keep. When we first met, you told me that all of Avoni was once habitable for the Elmias, but over time, the astral energy went away." Cam gave Luik's shoulders a quick squeeze. "Luik...something caused that. And if we can figure out what happened, we can figure out a way to restore the Elmias."

Luik gave his wry smile again. Then, he reached up, his hands gripping Cam's. A moment later, he vanished, an Aetherfern tattoo appearing on Cam's left arm.

Restore your people first, Luik's voice echoed in his mind.

Chapter 48

Weeks later, Illyria sat huddled in the dim, cold cell of Rath, her back against the rough stone wall. The cell's sparse furnishings, a narrow bed with a threadbare blanket and a small, barred window high above, did little to offer comfort.

From outside the prison walls, a cacophony of laughter and music filtered through the iron bars, punctuated by the occasional roar of music.

At least everyone else gets to be happy.

In the weeks since Cam had used the power in the Scepter of Alderia to destroy the Sundered Lands, people had continued to celebrate. It had taken them some convincing to leave their settlements at first, but once people realized that they were safe, very few people remained within the city walls.

Of course, Illyria wasn't able to celebrate with them.

She sat back in her cell, resting her head on the wall behind her. She wondered where it all went wrong. Had she been right in trusting Gaalron? What should she have done differently?

The door to the building creaked slowly, and she sat up a bit straighter, brushing her hair from her face.

A figure stood silhouetted in the doorway. He was a broad-shouldered, well-built man. He looked at her with tired eyes, his hands behind his back.

"They said I'd find you here," he said, his voice dry as rocks in the sun.

"Not like I'm going anywhere else," she said with a shrug.

He stepped forward through the door, allowing the light to illuminate his face. Illyria gasped.

Cam stood before her, but he was no longer the man she remembered. His once-youthful face was now marked by the passage of time, etched with deep lines and wrinkles. His hair, once a vibrant chestnut, had turned a ghostly white.

"Cam? What...what happened?"

He shook his head.

"The price of Avoni's salvation, I'm afraid."

"Last time I saw you...I thought it was a trick of the light. I don't understand."

Cam took a few steps forward, his expression turning dark.

"But I think you do understand. Astral abilities always come at a cost to the host human. And for Time Shift, the price is that you age faster." He swept his arms, indicating his body. "And in my case, much, much faster."

Illyria lowered her head, remembering Gaalron explaining that to her so many months ago.

"Why are you here?" she said, her voice weak as she stared at the cold floor.

"I came here to tell you that, for all the harm you caused, I understand why you did what you did."

Illyria looked up, surprised.

"What?"

"I understand. And on one hand, I admire you for it. You wanted what was best, for Elmias and humans. Were I in your situation, I might have done the same thing."

His intentions were kind, but kindness was a cold comfort to her.

"That doesn't help me now," she said with a dismissive shrug. "But I'm where I belong. I accept this."

Cam's face softened, but he didn't say anything. Instead, he just looked at her with sad eyes.

"How did you do it?" Illyria asked him. He gave her a curious expression.

"Do what?"

"Destroy the Sundered Lands."

He shrugged. "The power of the Scepter. It inverts energies."

Illyria shook her head. "No, I understand that. How did you stomach dooming the Elmias?" She stared at him with inquisitive eyes.

"They found other people to Tether—"

"They're trapped," Illyria bit out. "Trapped forever. If they ever leave their Tether now, they'll die."

Cam hesitated before answering.

"It was the hardest decision I've ever made. I was only able to make it because I made a promise first."

"A promise?"

Cam nodded, turning to leave the building. Illyria quickly rose to her feet, grabbing the bars that made up her prison. "What was the promise?"

The mountain of a man paused in the doorway, silhouetted against the sunlight outside.

"That I'd free them."

The door slammed shut behind him.

For the rest of the day, Illyria sat alone in the cold, dim cell, the silence pressing down on her like a weight she could no longer bear. The passage of time was marked only by the shifting shadows on the walls, as the light from the high, barred window moved slowly across the stone floor. She had thought the solitude would bring her peace, a moment to gather her thoughts, but instead, it magnified the turmoil within her.

Her mind replayed the events that had led her there, each memory sharper and more painful than the last. She and Gaalron had been so certain, so convinced that their actions were justified. They had believed they were doing the right thing, that their cause was noble.

But now, in the stillness of her confinement, the truth gnawed at her.

They had been wrong.

Terribly wrong.

How could she have been so reckless?

She buried her face in her hands, feeling the sting of tears she could no longer hold back. She had failed, not just herself, but everyone who had trusted her. The shame was almost too much to bear.

The door creaked open again, and she hurriedly turned her face. A man's voice rang out.

"Tears, eh? Is it the guilt or do you just not like your accommodations?"

Illyria sniffed, wiping her eyes and lowering them to the ground.

The man let out a quick snort. "So it's the guilt then."

Looking up, Illyria got a good look at the speaker. It was Lorian, leader and general of Rath.

Not feeling up for talking, she gave a quick shrug. Lorian nodded, stepping over to the cell.

"They tell me you thought that you were doing good. That you wanted to help as many people as you could. And then you almost doomed us all."

"Why are you saying this?" Illyria said, allowing her frustration to show. "You think I've thought about anything else since it happened?"

Lorian gave the wicked smile of a predator on the hunt, but he spoke in a kind voice.

"Seeing you now...hearing your voice...I believe you."

She stood up and turned her back to him, looking out the small window in her cell.

"And I'd like to give you the opportunity to redeem yourself."

Illyria huffed. "Not much I can do about that."

"I disagree," Lorian replied. "I'd say there are a great many things you can do."

Illyria turned to face him. Her confusion must have been written all over her face, because Lorian let out a quick chuckle. She glared at him for that, and he raised his hands apologetically.

"I'm sorry. I just...it's been a long day. Been a long year, if I'm being honest with you." His face darkened. "And I don't think it's going to be any easier for us moving forward."

"What do you mean?" she asked.

"The days of the Sundered Lands were brutal, yes, but they were also simple. We all had one goal: survive." He let out a long sigh. "That simplicity was beautiful. Things are about to get a lot more...complicated."

"Complicated?"

He nodded.

"Complicated. For almost two centuries, our nation has been run through independent cities and towns, but now, we are reforming as a people. Building a new government. We need a king again."

She glanced down towards the rapier at his side. It was beautifully designed, but appeared mostly ceremonial. She raised an eyebrow.

"And I suppose you're seeking the throne?"

He gave an embarrassed shrug, like a child caught stealing sweets.

"With command of the largest formalized military in the nation, I'd argue that it's mine if I want it." He brushed his hands through the air, as if he were sweeping away the topic.

"Regardless of who is on the throne, there are many concerns. We'll have to worry about protecting our settlements from each other. Organizing our people together to form one nation. And, we'll have to protect our borders against enemy nations." He shook his head for a moment before continuing. "We don't even know what the global political stage is like. We're disorganized and will have a new king on the throne. It's like we're asking to be invaded."

Illyria nodded. Ironically, "complicated" was an overly simplistic term to describe their situation.

"And, there's the situation with the Elmias," Lorian added. "There are many unaccounted for. A kingdom can't have random citizens with...godlike powers running around."

"Why are you telling me this?" Illyria asked.

"Because you have experience with the Elmias," Lorian whispered. "You know how they work and you're highly motivated to serve your people."

She tilted her head in confusion.

"I don't get it."

"Sometimes, you need something more than what an army can provide. You need something faster and blunter. You need a war hammer." He looked her directly in her eyes. "I want you to Tether an Elmia and be that war hammer."

"War hammer?" She scoffed. Lorian nodded, holding up two fingers.

"I want you to think about what kind of life you want to lead from here on out. Option one, you can spend it in here, wallowing in guilt, or option two, you can use that guilt to fuel something greater. You can choose to rot in this cell, or you can fight to make things right."

She stared at him, her mind racing. The thought of Tethering an Elmia again sent a chill down her spine, but beneath that fear, something stirred. The desire to atone, to find a purpose beyond her mistakes, began to grow.

Lorian took a step back, his eyes never leaving hers. "I'm not asking you to decide now. Just think about it."

Without another word, he turned and walked out, the heavy door creaking shut behind him. The sound echoed through the empty chamber, but it didn't feel as oppressive as before.

For the first time in weeks, a playful smile crept up Illyria's face.

Epilogue

Cam stood alone at the edge of the cliff. The wind whispered softly through the grass, carrying with it the scent of the silent lake below him. The sun bathed the landscape in a warm, golden light, making the blue of the sky above seem impossibly vast and clear. It was a sight so different from the blood-red skies of the Sundered Lands that it felt almost unreal, like a dream he had finally awakened into.

His reflection in a nearby pool of water startled him for a moment. He wasn't used to seeing the face of an old man, with hair silvered by time and heavy wrinkles around his eyes.

I'd say the look is an improvement, Luik said in his mind, bringing a smile to Cam's face. Moments later, the smile faded.

This is where Silva died, Cam thought to Luik. *This is where it all happened.*

With the banishment of the Sundered Lands, all of the Eternal Echoes were finally able to find peace, vanishing from the landscape. Knowing that Silva's soul was finally able to move on was a small comfort to Cam.

He felt a deep and abiding sorrow in his bones. In spite of what the world had just gained, this place reminded Cam of what it had also lost. He knelt down, feeling the grains of dry dirt under his fingers.

"I'm sorry," he whispered, closing his eyes.

When he finally opened them, he tilted his head back to gaze at the sky, its endless blue expanse unmarred by the crimson that had once signaled danger and death.

"I wish you could see this," he said. "I think you'd really like it."

"Felix would like it too," Chek said, somewhere behind him.

Joints protesting, Cam rose to his feet, turning to look at Chek. Somehow, her brother had managed to Tether an Elmia before being attacked by the Sundered Shadows. When Chek and Cam had returned to Perth, his body was nowhere to be found.

The whereabouts of the Elmia he had Tethered were also unknown.

"I'm sure," Cam said, his voice serious.

Chek smiled.

"Though, the passing of the Sundered Lands would excite him only slightly more than getting the chance to Tether an Elmia."

Cam allowed himself a quiet chuckle, stepping away from the site of Silva's death. The two of them stood in silence for a moment, letting the weight of their memories settle between them, as the wind quietly rustled the grass.

With one last look at the sky, Cam nodded, a sense of quiet resolution settling over him. "We should head back," he said softly. "There's still work to be done. Are you and Ink sure you want to help?"

She nodded.

"That's all I ever wanted to do. There's no need for the Vanguard anymore, so I guess this is what's next. I'm just not sure where to start."

Cam's gaze grew distant, fixed on the far-off Jaram Mountains.

"We start by leading the only other people who have interacted with the Elmias over the last century. They were also the last ones to interact with Felix. We have to find out what they know," Cam said, strapping the sword Morwenna had given him to his back.

The blade was still broken, but that didn't bother Cam.

Like Soren had said, broken didn't mean purposeless.

Following his eyes, Chek's expression darkened.

"They'll pay for what they've done," Cam added. "But we also need what they know. Will you help me?"

She gave an exaggerated shrug. "If you'll take someone who can barely walk."

"I wouldn't have it any other way." Cam said, a deep smile lining his wrinkled face.

Plus, she can do the thinking for you. I'm not sure it's your best trait, Luik chimed in.

Ignoring Luik, Cam walked slowly away from the cliff's edge with Chek. As they walked, Cam glanced one final time behind him. The sun, beginning its slow descent, was just beginning to cast long shadows across the land.

I can only hope those shadows aren't an omen.

Together, they stepped into the lengthening shadows, moving towards the Jaram Mountains in the distance. As the sun began to dip below the horizon, the sky turned into a vibrant shade of red. Cam glanced up, his eyes catching the vivid hues.

"How beautiful," he murmured.

Symphony of Scars

Enjoy an exclusive preview of the first portion of Symphony of Scars

Overture
The Chorus of the New Year

S ilence.

Marek existed in a world of complete and utter silence.

Such was the existence he had endured since being cast among the Scorned. Marek's jaw tightened, his teeth grinding as the memory surfaced. A day etched into his soul like a wound that refused to heal. The Canticle of Silence, with all the cold precision of a butcher, had taken his ears and tongue, stripping him of his voice, his hearing, and his humanity.

They had called it justice. A punishment for his crimes.

His eyes narrowed, his vision tinging with red.

His crimes.

The words reverberated in his mind, a bitter echo that never seemed to fade. His hands curled into trembling fists, the rough calluses pressing against his palms. Rage simmered beneath the surface, harder to contain on some days than others. It burned not only for what had been done to him but for the hypocrisy of it all. In the name of justice, an injustice so profound had been inflicted on him.

And the shame of the injustice was too deep to bear.

A forceful tap of a finger interrupted his thoughts. Turning, he saw a Kellanite soldier standing in front of him. Judging by the yellow coloring on his otherwise blue jacket, the man was a low-ranking officer, possibly fresh out of the academy.

The officer gave a look of sick pleasure before spitting in Marek's face.

Marek had just barely closed his eyes in time, feeling the thick warm liquid rolling down his eyelids towards his mouth. He gently lifted his hand, wiping the spit from his face before opening his eyes again.

The officer grinned sadistically at him before raising his hands and beginning to sign.

"Looks like my boss is having trouble holding his liquor. Threw up all over the place. Clean it up, Scorned."

Marek nodded before signing back.

"Yes sir. I'll have it cleaned in moments."

"See that you do, Scorned." The officer signed before spitting at him again. Once the officer turned his back, Marek signed in the air.

"My name isn't Scorned. It's Marek." With no one looking, he allowed himself to glower at the empty air, underscoring the emotion he wanted communicated through those words.

Not that the visible emotion would change anything. Ever since the High Choir had chosen to take his hearing and voice, he, like anyone else who had been given the punishment, had only been referred to by one name.

Scorned.

Grabbing a nearby cleaning rag, Marek left the confines of the back room and stepped through the open door into the central chamber where the men were engaging in their annual Officer's Celebration. They smiled as they chatted with each other, their faces and movements cordial. In the corner, a quartet of musicians played a song on their instruments. Judging by their faces and the way they bobbed their head, the song must have been fairly upbeat.

Marek paused, biting his lower lip, wondering what the instruments sounded like. Were they tuned properly? Was the music soft-allowing for conversation-or was it loud and celebratory?

Something wet forcefully struck into the side of his head. Turning, Marek saw a different officer glowering at him. The man then opened his mouth and began speaking, his face twisted in frustration.

Marek cringed, partially in embarrassment and partially in frustration.

Many people assumed that, just because he was Scorned, he could read lips. The truth was that very few Scorned ever got very good at it, and even those who did often struggled to decipher what people were trying to say. There were simply too many words in the Kellanite language that used similar facial movements in order to say.

He raised his hands in deference.

"I'm so sorry. I only know sign."

"Stupid Scorned." The officer signed back, spitting on him again, before turning and walking away.

Apparently, the man didn't know the sign to say whatever it was that he was trying to say. Some people knew enough to communicate with the Scorned, but most never bothered to learn. Marek stifled a glare, stepping through the crowded room of officers, ready to clean up the mess he'd been promised.

Later that evening, after the officers had gone to bed and the room had been cleaned, Marek sat by himself in his hovel. The dirt walls of the tiny room were only lit by a flickering candle that Marek had placed on the ground. In his hands was his entire world.

At least, the entire world that he could call his. His one possession.

The Hymnal of Aurora.

As was his practice every night, he opened the large book and read by the light of the candle. When he was younger-before he had become one of the Scorned-the book had been a source of hope and inspiration for him. It had been his moral north star, as he strove to live a life in accordance with the commands of the Sibling gods, Aurora and the Almighty Creator.

Now, it only brought him pain.

Pain with every promise he read and struggled to believe. Pain at the hollowness of the words. Pain that the Sibling Gods he had worshipped, trusted, and served so faithfully had abandoned him.

And yet, tonight, like all nights, he read it, and then he prayed.

Only this night, his prayer was different.

"Unknown God," his trembling hands signed, each motion deliberate, almost desperate. "You who designed the laws of the universe, who gave us the gift of music, I believe in You. I believe You are good. But, I must confess something to You. I am struggling. Truly struggling."

His fingers hesitated midair, his shoulders shaking as the weight of his words bore down on him. What he was doing was sacreligious. He could be put to death for this. However, the raw ache in his chest burst free, and tears began to spill, tracing silent paths down his face.

"Why does it feel like You've turned away from me?" He signed, his gestures faltering, as though his hands carried the same exhaustion his spirit did. "I gave everything for You. My voice. My music. My life. All I've ever wanted was to serve You, to feel the harmony of Your creation in my soul. And now... now I have nothing. No voice. No song. No hope."

The silence pressed in around him, oppressive and unrelenting, and his hands stilled. He could feel the absence of sound like a wound, a vast, yawning emptiness that swallowed every whispered thought and every unspoken plea. It was too much, and his body sagged under the weight of it.

With a sharp, shuddering inhale, Marek raised his hands again, forcing his signs through the tremble of his fingers. "Please, Lord, heal me. Restore my hearing. Restore my voice. Return to me the gift I thought was from You. Please, Creator, let me sing again. Let me hear music again."

He bent forward, his forehead pressing into the rough ground, his hands resting limply in his lap. His tears dampened the dirt beneath him, but still, the words poured forth, now fierce, now pleading, as if his very soul depended on them.

"I'll give You everything I have. I will trust You, though the world turn against me. Why have You abandoned me? Am I no longer worthy of love? Am I no longer Your creation? Tell me why. Tell me what I have done. Why am I so forsaken?"

His fingers curled into fists, then opened again, trembling as they continued.

"If You hear me—if You are even there—please, help me. Send me a savior. I can't do this on my own. I don't know how to carry this weight any longer. Show me You haven't forgotten me. Show me there is still a reason for all of this."

The tears came harder now, blurring his vision, but his hands moved with a fierce determination.

"Please. Send me a savior."

And like all nights, Marek was given the same answer.

Silence.

Movement One: A Rising Melody

The First of the Sacred Decrees Concerning the Scorned, as Spoken in the Canticle of Silence

The Scorned shall bear their shame upon their bodies. Their ears shall be taken, that they may no longer hear the songs of the righteous. Their tongues shall be cut, that they may no longer profane the air with corrupted sound. Thus they are marked with judgment and scorn everlasting. They are made low, and they shall remain low, bound in flesh to the punishment they deserve.

Six Months Before the Chorus of the New Year

Passage One: Lia Arlyn

M orning Mom! Couldn't sleep, so I'm up early. I know. It's crazy, but I guess miracles do happen. Anyway, I stepped out quickly to get some fresh air. Be back soon.

Songbird

Lia Arlyn smiled into the mirror, her reflection capturing a moment of triumph as she finally managed to tame the untamed cascade of pink and black hair that had become her signature. The vivid streaks cascaded in soft waves, framing her heart-shaped face with a blend of rebellion and elegance. Her pale skin seemed to glow faintly in the morning light filtering through her window, her sharp cheekbones accentuating the defiant tilt of her chin.

She reached a hand up, slender fingers wrapping around a last defiant lock of hair, tucking it behind her ear.

"This," she said in a triumphant tone to her reflection in the mirror, "will do."

Grinning, she ran a hand through her dual colored hair. Over the last few decades, advancements in symphonics had made it possible for unique hair colors-such as blue or green-to become a hereditary trait. In Lia's case, hers was a vibrant pink.

The pink in Lia's hair was a gift from a man she'd never met. He was a stranger who had raped her mother, leaving her pregnant with Lia, before disappearing. There'd been no sign of him since that day, his only mark on Lia being the vibrant strands of hair on her head.

Though the pink came from her father, she had no idea where the black came from, or why she'd always had dual-colored hair. Her mother's hair was a bright, fiery red, and none of her relatives had exhibited black hair. It remained a mystery, but Lia didn't mind.

The unique look was bold, raw and unapologetically imperfect.

It was her.

As the morning light began to peek through the window, she stretched her arms overhead, trying to relieve the tension in her shoulders. It was her 21st birthday. The day she'd been waiting for, preparing for, for as long as she could remember. Her fingers flexed instinctively, itching to find the smooth, familiar weight of her flute.

A simple smile crept onto her face again. Yes, she was anxious, but she wasn't going to let the nerves rule her. She was going to enjoy this day.

After all, one only got a single Assessment Day in their life.

With the weight of anticipation weighing heavy on her chest, Lia left a quick note for her mother, telling her where she was going. Then, she tiptoed-so as to not wake her sleeping mother- through the small inn room towards the door. She opened it, cringing as it creaked, before stepping into the quiet streets of Rimachon, the capital of the Holy Republic of Kellanis.

The gentle light of dawn bathed the city in a golden glow. Rimachon's stone buildings rose majestically around her, their graceful arches and spires casting elegant shadows that danced along the cobblestone streets. Vibrant greenery cascaded from window boxes, draping over balconies like a patchwork of living tapestries, adding splashes of color to the stone.

Despite the early hour, the city was already alive with activity. Merchants bustled about, flinging open shutters and arranging their wares with practiced efficiency. Errand boys darted through the streets with purposeful strides, their quick footsteps echoing against the cobblestones as they raced to complete their morning tasks. Street performers began to gather in quiet corners, tuning their instruments and rehearsing their routines for the day's performances.

A Scorned woman walked past her, and she felt bile rise in her stomach. Lia averted her gaze, unwilling to look too long at the woman's mutilated form—ears cut away and tongue removed. The Scorned were the lowest of the low, condemned to a life of silence and servitude, unable to hear or create music. Their punishment was considered a fate worse than death. She could only imagine the horrible crimes they might have committed. Murder? Or worse, harming a child?

Her mother had always taught her to show compassion for the Scorned, pitying the broken lives they led. Lia respected that about her mother. Yet, as the Scorned woman passed, Lia couldn't stop herself from curling her lip in quiet disdain. These people had committed crimes so vile, so harmful to society, that the Republic deemed them unworthy of the very thing that defined their humanity: the ability to hear and create music.

She shuddered at the thought.

To distract herself as she walked, she hummed a quick prayer to the Sibling Gods, Aurora and the Creator. Through her quiet song, she prayed for their wisdom and strength in the upcoming Assessment, and that she'd make her mother proud.

As she hummed her prayer, Lia found herself grinning at the early rhythm of the city. The aroma of freshly baked bread drifted from nearby bakeries, filling her senses with warmth and comfort. The sweet strains of birdsong floated through the air, mingling with the distant hum of conversation. It was almost enough to distract her from the looming event that waited for her later in the day.

Almost.

"Young lady, would you like a flower?" a voice called out, breaking through her thoughts.

Lia stopped humming and turned toward the voice. Her gaze fell upon a woman standing nearby. Tall and robust, the woman exuded an air of quiet authority, her plump figure draped in flowing robes that resembled those worn by the Low Choir.

She nodded, stepping forward.

"What's your name, young one?" the woman asked, smiling brightly as Lia approached.

"I'm Lia," she responded, her voice soft and steady. "And you?"

"You may call me Veer," the woman replied with a wink. She reached into her bag, fishing around for something as she continued speaking. "I'm assuming you're a traveler?"

Lia nodded. "Yes, I'm here to take The Assessment."

At this, Veer's eyes lit up with recognition. "Ah, Assessment Day. A momentous occasion indeed. I wish you the best of luck, dear. I'm a Symphonic myself, you know." She paused for a moment, her smile growing. "Though, I suspect you already guessed that."

Lia smiled back. While many Symphonics served in the Kellanite military or medical fields, some used their abilities in more mundane ways, such as street performances.

Veer pulled her hand from her bag with a dramatic flourish, holding something tiny between her thumb and forefinger. She extended her hand toward Lia, revealing a tiny, delicate seed. It was so small that Lia had to squint to see it properly.

"Would you like a flower?" Veer repeated, a twinkle in her eye. Lia nodded in response, intrigued.

Veer slipped a ring onto her finger and then held the seed in the palm of her hand, bringing it close to her lips. She paused for a moment, as if gathering energy from the world around her. And then, with a deep breath, she began to sing.

Her voice, pure and crystalline, cut through the noise of the bustling city like a beacon of light. Lia felt a calm wash over her. The tension that had gripped her moments before seemed to dissolve, replaced by a deep sense of peace and wonder. She watched in awe as the tiny seed in Veer's hand began to glow, responding to the magic woven into the music.

The transformation was subtle at first, but as the song swelled, the seed began to change in earnest. It softened, its shell cracking open to reveal tender green shoots. They unfurled, stretching upwards, seeking the warmth of the sun. In moments, Veer held a vibrant golden flower, impossibly perfect, cradled in her palm.

With a knowing smile, Veer held the flower out to Lia, who accepted it with wonder in her eyes. She slipped a coin into the woman's hand in thanks, as was the custom in Kellanite society. Veer accepted it with a gracious nod.

"Thank you, young Lia," Veer said softly. "May this flower bring you luck on your Assessment Day. You only get one, after all."

With that, Veer turned her attention back to the passersby, offering flowers to those who stopped, her voice calling out amidst the growing hustle of the city.

Yellow flower in hand, Lia made her way back to the inn. As she walked inside, she saw her mother, with the help of the innkeeper, had already begun packing for the journey home. They didn't have the money to stay in Rimachon beyond today, so after The Assessment, they would begin the long ride back.

The innkeeper looked up as she approached, a playful grin tugging at the corners of his mouth. "Thought you could sneak away from packing duty, eh? Don't worry, there's plenty more to be done."

Lia laughed softly and walked up to her mother, holding out the yellow flower. "This is for you," she said with a smile. "I got it from a Symphonic performer this morning."

Her mother's eyes softened as she took the flower, a smile spreading across her face. "It's beautiful, Songbird. Thank you."

Lia grinned back at her mother, the only family she'd ever known. If her mother had ever felt shame over the circumstances of Lia's conception, she had never once let it surface. In twenty-one years of raising her, she had shown nothing but unwavering love and adoration for the daughter she cherished, calling her affectionately, "My Songbird."

"And where's my flower?" The innkeeper chimed in, his tone mock-serious. "What, you think just because I run an inn, I have no appreciation for things that smell nice?"

Lia chuckled, shaking her head. "If I pass The Assessment, I'll grow you an entire rose bush."

He raised an eyebrow, feigning skepticism. "You promise? Because if you don't, I'll have to steal the flower your mother's got, and I don't think she'd appreciate that."

They shared a laugh as Lia moved to help finish packing. Her mother joked and teased, trying to ease the tension of the day ahead, but beneath her playful tone, Lia could sense an undercurrent mixed with pride and concern.

Once the last of their things were secured, and after a quick meal, they set off through the streets of Rimachon, heading toward the Office of Symphonics Testing. The walk carried them deeper into the city, and as they ventured closer to its heart, Rimachon's full beauty and dedication to music revealed itself in all its intricate glory.

The air itself seemed to hum with melody, vibrating with an energy that could only exist in a place like this. Musicians were everywhere. A violinist played just outside the bakery, his bow moving with expert precision, coaxing soft, mournful notes from his instrument as a small crowd gathered to listen. A trio of flutists stood in front of a stone fountain, weaving together a lilting, joyful tune that seemed to float above the gentle rush of the water.

The people who walked by didn't hurry past. In Rimachon, music was more than just a background sound. It was the city's pulse, the heartbeat that guided its every movement.

As they walked, Lia noticed the small details that made the city so unique. The stone pillars that rose above the streets were intricately carved, designed not just for beauty but for sound. Holes and slits were cut into their surfaces, placed with meticulous care, allowing the wind to whistle through them, creating beautiful melodies. As the breeze shifted, so did the notes, transforming the very architecture of the city into a living, breathing orchestra.

The city itself was one giant instrument.

As wagons rumbled down the cobblestone streets, Lia could hear the faint sound of a song rising from the wheels striking the ground. It wasn't random. Certain sections of the road had been built with raised stones or hidden mechanisms, creating notes as the wheels rolled over them. It was as if the city itself had composed a symphony for its inhabitants, every movement in harmony with its design.

"In Rimachon, even the roads sing," her mother said. "The city is always alive with music. It's what makes this place so special, Songbird."

Lia nodded, her fingers nervously tightening around the handle of her flute case.

Before long, they arrived at the Office of Symphonics. The building stood at the center of the city, its dark stone walls rising high above the streets. The architecture was less ornate than the rest of Rimachon, but it carried an imposing air of authority.

Lia took a deep breath as they approached the entrance. She was ready. She had spent years honing her craft, preparing for this moment. Her hands felt steady on the flute case, her heart calm but filled with purpose.

"Songbird?" Her mother asked, pausing her in her approach. Lia turned, looking back at her mother's contemplative face.

"Forget something?"

"No. Just something I need to say." She bit her lip before continuing. "Whether you pass the Assessment or not, know that you're going to accomplish incredible things."

This brought a smile to Lia's face. Walking back to her mother, she put an arm around her shoulder and squeezed her close.

"I'll let you in on a secret. But only because I love you." Lia said with a wink. "It's never mattered to me what I accomplish. I just want a peaceful life filled with music and people I love."

"Then, I guess there's no pressure on you then."

"I guess not!"

With that, Lia stepped through the doors of the Office of Symphonics, leaving the sounds of the city behind as the quiet, expectant air of the building enveloped her.

A Note to the Reader

I've dreamed of writing fantasy books my whole life. My first attempt came when I was just nine years old. At fifteen, I even completed a full-length novel. While I was proud of finishing it, even teenage me knew it was terrible. It was cheesy, full of plot holes, and painfully written. I scrapped it and was too afraid to try again for years.

When I was twenty, I gave it another shot. I dreamed up a world filled with corruption, where only a few scattered communities survived under mysterious shrouds, and a messenger had to join forces with a spiritual figure to save the nation. I outlined the full story, filled notebooks with lore and background, and started writing.

Once again, I failed.

"I'm just not good at this," I told my wife. "I think I'm meant to read books, not write them."

Years later, during a move, my wife found those old notebooks. I told her to throw them away. They were painful proof, in my mind, that I had failed. Instead, she quietly hid them, hoping I'd return to them someday. She was right.

Over the next decade, I grew as a professional. I learned to present statistics and data in compelling ways by telling stories. I honed my writing through my career and sports blogs, and even worked as a writing tutor while pursuing my MBA. Without realizing it, I was building the skills I needed to finally write *Shadows of the Sundered Lands*.

As I approached my thirtieth birthday, I looked back at my twenties. They were years filled with struggle, unhealthy choices, doubt in my faith, and crushing pressure to never fail. Older me had learned some hard lessons, and so I returned to my story, writing with that younger version of myself in mind.

At first, I was embarrassed. I wrote in complete secrecy, even from my wife. My previous failures at writing a novel made me afraid that I'd look cringey.

My first draft was awful. My second was better, but still not good enough. By the fourth draft, I felt like I had something, so I finally shared it with others. Feedback from friends led to a fifth draft, feedback from strangers to a sixth.

Then came querying. Over and over, the rejections poured in. Most were generic, but one agent told me my book was good but would never sell without an existing audience or platform. I was ready to give up when I stumbled across Svetling Press's debut novelist contest. Honestly, I almost didn't submit, as the thought of another rejection was just too painful. However, after a lot of thought, I decided to shoot my shot one last time.

And I'm proud to say *Shadows of the Sundered Lands* won.

This is, in many ways, a book about failure. Younger me thought failure meant the end. Older me learned that failure, if you let it teach you, can be the beginning.

Don't be afraid to fail. Develop a growth mindset. Let every failure be a stepping stone, not a gravestone.

As Luik says, "Know you will fail. Act anyway."

Thank you for reading *Shadows of the Sundered Lands*. If you've made it this far, I'd be deeply grateful if you left an honest review online. It helps more than you know.

You're the best.

Until next time,

Corbin Rook

Acknowledgments

First and foremost, my deepest thanks go to Jesus Christ, the true Author of every story and every work of art. You have always been with me. May this book bring honor to You.

To Sima and Kaden at Svetling Press: thank you for believing in me and selecting me as the winner of your debut novelist contest. It's been an incredible honor to work with you both. Your encouragement, professionalism, and genuine kindness have made this journey unforgettable. I'm grateful not only for the opportunity you gave me.

To my beta readers, Tim, Eugene, Jake, Hannah, and Emily. This book could not have taken shape without your time, insight, and honesty. You pushed me to see what the story could become and helped me raise it higher than I ever could have alone.

To my editor, Rachel. You are a gift. I always thought my grammar was impeccable, but you proved me wrong in the best way possible. Thank you for sharpening every page and making sure my words carried the weight they were meant to.

Thank you to Robin Sullivan for meeting with me and give me your perspective on writing, book marketing and how to be successful in this space. You and your husband are legends, and I'm so grateful for you so graciously giving me your time.

To my parents, thank you for opening the doors of imagination by putting *The Chronicles of Narnia* and *The Lord of the Rings* into my hands when I was young. Those stories lit a spark that has never gone out.

And finally, to my wife, Emily. This book exists because of you. From the very beginning, when I asked if I should even try, you told me to go for it. When I gave up and told you to throw away my worldbuilding notes and outlines, you quietly kept them safe.

Your encouragement, patience, and faith in me carried this story through every doubt and setback. This book is as much yours as it is mine.

About the author

Corbin Rook writes clean, dark fantasy with hope at the heartbeat. His stories plunge readers into dangerous worlds where ordinary people face extraordinary trials and remind us why it's worth fighting for the light, even in the darkest places.

Winner of the Svetling Press Debut Novel Contest, Corbin is launching his fantasy world with Shadows of the Sundered Lands.

Corbin is a husband and father who loves endurance sports (especially obstacle course racing), a good game of chess, and an excellent cup of coffee.